Ranger

TIMOTHY ASHBY

CONTENTS

RANGER

Prologue

Colony of Grenada
West Indies
November 1795

"They be jumbies," said the black soldier in a faded red coat, voice tremulous from supernatural dread.

"Spirits," another Ranger agreed, eying the shadowy figures flitting through the dark jungle around them.

"Shut yer gobs!" snapped the white sergeant, his hoarseness betraying equal fear of the unknown.

"They're men!" Chart shouted. "Brigands. Stand to!"

Red tongues flamed from the muzzles of three score muskets surrounding the twenty British soldiers in the hut. Lead balls perforated the rotted bamboo walls, killing or wounding a third of the Rangers. The top of the sergeant's head exploded, splattering his brains on the sixteen-year-old ensign, the platoon's commander and the only other white man. The boy shrieked and huddled sobbing in a corner with hands over his eyes as a pair of barefoot privates tumbled beside him, one dead and the other screaming as blood pumped from the remnant of his severed arm. A man whose jaw had been shot away writhed on the dirt floor, gurgling "Ah, ah, ah".

Chart had less than a minute to act, the time it would take for the enemy to reload their muskets after the volley. The Brigands – the British term for the insurgents - were not as skilled in reloading as the Black Rangers, whom he had relentlessly drilled to get off three aimed shots a minute. He heard the scraping of ramrods and shouted orders in French. The enemy shunned close quarter fighting and wouldn't assault the hut, preferring to riddle it until its occupants were killed or surrendered.

He realised that the frightened Rangers were looking to him, the strange soldier who spoke like the white officers but was a fellow slave, to lead them.

"Give up now or you all die!" a voice outside yelled in heavily accented English.

Surrender was not an option. Chart knew that he would die anyway if captured by the Brigands, and his death would be all too imaginably gruesome.

"Fix bayonets!" he ordered.

Chapter 1

Colony of Grenada
June 1774

The freshly dug grave waited beneath the Royal Poinciana tree, its heaped red soil seemingly reflecting the tree's flame-coloured blossoms. Arthur Charteris stood by the pit, gazing unseeingly across the cane fields to the ocean where the dark curtain of an approaching storm gathered strength on the horizon.

He was a tall man dressed in the nearest attire he had to a mourning suit: black broadcloth coat and weskit stained by mildew, breeches fastened over silk stockings, silver-buckled shoes buffed to a shine by his manservant, Cuffie. Hatless, he eschewed a wig, wearing his own hair clubbed. The elderly Papist priest, a holdover from French rule of the island a decade earlier, waited with him, leaning against the flame tree's bole in his tattered alb yellowed with age. Arthur had smelled rum on the cleric's breath when he arrived a short time earlier and hoped he could remain coherent enough to conduct the service. An Anglican priest would have been preferable, but the last one on the island was sick a'bed with the yellow jack.

Not that it would have mattered to Weju, who had clung to her Garifuna ways until her death.

He saw the procession winding down the hill from the laundry behind the Great House where the black women had washed the body and kept vigil throughout the night, chanting and wailing. Numbed by grief, his mind churned with memories of their all too brief time together.

***

Arthur had found Weju by chance three years earlier. He rarely rode the dozen miles across the island to St. George's, believing the capitol town to be pestilential. But he had heard that a ship had arrived from London and he was hungry for news from home and the comforts of new books and a few foodstuffs that may have been commonplace in England but were luxuries in this speck of land in the Caribbean.

Riding his bay gelding, which had miraculously survived a rough Atlantic crossing and two years in a climate that had proved fatal to his other horses, Arthur set out in the morning's relative coolness. He was followed by Cuffie driving a donkey cart to carry back imported wines and cheeses if they were to be found, as well as books by Voltaire, Hume and Rousseau that Arthur had ordered from Henry Hewitt of Old Brompton Road, Kensington.

Arthur left his factor's office with a bundle of weeks-old newspapers and a packet of letters and crossed the market square, pushing through a boisterous throng of polyglot humanity of every hue from Congo jet to spectral paleness. A huckster's voice roared from a platform in the middle of the square, and Arthur recalled that today was Tuesday, when slaves were sold along with fresh fish, produce and cast-off clothes.

He was not inclined to buy slaves; he owned 92 negroes on his La Sagesse estate and was accused by fellow planters of being too soft on them, chiding him that sugar production could be doubled if he used harsher methods. He had to admit they were right, but as a man who prided himself on being a disciple of the Enlightenment he abhorred deliberate cruelty. When slaves needed to be punished for thievery or running away, he had his overseer or drivers – the latter responsible for enforcing discipline and work routines among their fellow slaves - scourge them, but never to the point of incapacitation or death like other planters did. And incorrigible ones were sold rather than hung or burned at the stake as was common punishment on other plantations.

Arthur admired John Locke, the great philosopher of the previous century. He agreed with Locke's assertion that "every man had a property in his own person, this nobody has any right to but himself". Yet he had no problem reconciling his enlightened philosophy with the institution of slavery, seeing himself as a *pater familias* to his "people" as he preferred to call them, believing they were like children needing the guidance, and occasional discipline, of a wise master.

A sudden chorus of hoots and catcalls drew his attention back to the scaffold, where a naked young woman was exhibited. Arthur was immediately struck by her beauty and poise. He guessed her age at no more than fifteen. Russet-skinned, with long black hair cascading over her shoulders down a straight back to her buttocks, her large black eyes stared regally over the crowd, ignoring the ribald comments of the planters, soldiers and drunken sailors encircling her.

"Now 'ere's a ripe 'un,' proclaimed the auctioneer, sweating red face leering beneath an oversized tricorne. "Daughter of Chatoyer himself, chief of the Black Caribs, taken by Portugee raiders just last week in St. Vincents. Twenty quid to start?"

"I'll give yer a half crown if the wench can suck me off," yelled a soldier.

"Now, now gentlemen," the auctioneer chided, "cross me heart she's a virgin."

The bidding began, quickly becoming a contest between two planters of Arthur's acquaintance, Welsh brothers with a reputation for sadistic treatment of their slaves. At fifty pounds, Arthur overheard one brother say to the other: "Tell you what, Owain, if you'll split the price with me, we can share her. Break her in good and proper".

The other brother nodded and signalled to the auctioneer with a hand slice across his throat that he was out.

"Goin' then to Mr. Daffyd Griffuth for—".

"Seventy-five!" shouted Arthur.

The Welshmen turned to look at him, shaking their heads.

"Seventy-five quid will buy ye a pair of trained French mustee wenches," Owain said. "Yer a fool, Charteris, so ye can have her."

Even as he paid the auctioneer's assistant, Arthur tried to understand what compelled him to buy the girl. It wasn't lust – he had his choice of the two-score slave women on the plantation though he rarely indulged there. Something that he struggled to define drew him to her. Perhaps, he thought wryly as he returned to La Sagesse with the girl – now clothed in a cotton shift and sitting in the donkey cart on a copy of

Rousseau's *Discourse on Inequality* - he saw in her the archetypal Noble Savage.

And so Weju entered the life of Arthur Charteris.

To the surprise of everyone on the estate, and especially the house slaves who thrived on gossip, Arthur did not take Weju as his concubine for well over a year. This disconcerted the servants, many of whom were themselves mixed race and proudly considered themselves at the apex of the plantation's slave hierarchy. The girl didn't seem to have a formal role, seeming more like Arthur's pet than a servant. She chose to sleep on a coconut fibre mattress on the floor of a Great House bedchamber and ate the same yams, plantains and salt fish as the house staff. Unlike the other slaves, Weju was privileged with total freedom to do as she pleased each day, which they resented.

Arthur assiduously taught her to speak English and she was soon able to tell him about her life. She was indeed the daughter of the great Black Carib chief Chatoyer by one of his five wives. The Black Caribs - who Weju insisted should be called Garifuna - were a tribe descended from indigenous Caribs who had mixed with the African survivors of a Spanish slave ship that had been wrecked on the island of St. Vincent in the last century. Her father ruled half of the island and had defeated British campaigns to conquer his tribe. Weju and two siblings had been captured by slavers in a raid on their village. Her brother had drowned himself rather than submit to enslavement by leaping off the slave ship in his heavy manacles. A sister had been flogged to death after nearly scratching out the Portuguese captain's eyes.

"And you," Arthur asked tentatively, "Do you want to return to your people?"

"My spirit will return," she replied slowly, "but I was always meant to be here. It was foretold by the *sano* of my *sano* – my grandmother."

Weju began to spend time in the "hot house" – a hut serving as an infirmary where half a dozen slaves were usually to be found. She told Arthur that her grandmother had been a Fulani medicine woman and seer who had taught her which herbs and potions to use in curing sickness. Weju soon gained the respect of the other slaves for her healing powers, restoring the health of a pair of fieldhands who were on the edge of death, and making an Aloe Vera salve to ease the agony of a young woman who was badly burned in the cane boiling house.

Word spread to neighbouring plantations of the seemingly miraculous cures of the young woman rumoured to be an Obeah priestess. The enslaved and freemen alike flocked to La Sagesse. One planter who had half of his workers ill with Yaws as planting season neared, offered Arthur £150 in gold for Weju.

"She can't be sold," he replied huffily, "because she's free".

The other planter was baffled because he knew that the girl had been purchased at the slave auction. He shrugged, assuming that Charteris had legally manumitted her.

Arthur always intended to do so, but never quite got around to it. So the bill of sale for "One zambo wench a.o. 15 name Weeju sold at St George's town, Grenada, 19th November 1771 received £75" was forgotten amidst a substantial sheaf of purchase documents for slaves, livestock and other chattels in Arthur's disorganised estate office.

One night, amidst a tempest which brought torrential rain and wind that shrieked through the Great House jalousies like the tortured souls of jumbies, Weju came to Arthur's chamber naked as the day he bought her and joined him in the big mahogany bed. Gossip was a pastime enjoyed by all, and within hours the entire estate knew that Weju was now the master's woman. This brought a sense of stability to the estate workers, who had been discomfited by Weju's uncertain status.

Arthur knew that enslaved women often sought sexual liaisons with white masters for better living conditions and monetary awards, as well as higher status within the plantation social structure. But Weju took no liberties, made no demands, and had no interest in serving as chatelaine in the Great House. She seemed happy, often heard singing in the Garifuna tongue. Arthur believed that she genuinely loved him, and he adored her in return.

As her ability to communicate improved, she asked about Arthur's life, usually in bed whilst both were spent by lovemaking. *"Was his father a great chief like hers?" "No,"* he would answer, concealing his amusement as he pictured his arrogant father, the third baronet, *"just a little chief." "Had he always lived at La Sagesse?" "No, he was born on the other side of the great dark sea in a cold country called England." "Then why was he here?"* Arthur did his best to explain that his father had won the Grenada plantation in a game of whist at White's Club and he had sailed to Grenada to manage the estate at the old baronet's suggestion, happy to escape his overbearing presence. The look of bafflement in her eyes caused him to change the subject by drawing her close and making passionate love for the third time that night.

"Never lose your innocence, my little savage" he whispered as she drifted to sleep in his arms, "for 'tis a sacred thing."

He lay awake for hours, scrolling through his life like unrolling an ancient Roman book. Weju's childlike questions raised memories of the twenty-nine restless years he had spent on earth so far. The baronet had always seemed disappointed that his eldest son and heir was uninterested in the gaming, hunting and wenching expected of a man of his class. Nearing sixty, Arthur's father was still notorious in London clubs and country houses for his rakehell lifestyle, whilst his younger brother was one of the macaronies who were fastidious to the point of never wearing the same twenty guinea suit for a week and refused to directly speak to coachmen, servants and other lower orders, yet had contests to see who could roger the meanest harlot in a Chick Lane brothel, French pox be damned.

Arthur earned a scholarly reputation at Westminster School, followed by three years as a fellow commoner at Peterhouse, Cambridge. He undertook the pro forma Grand Tour with a group of other young aristocrats shepherded by a spurious Florentine count, but unlike his colleagues was more interested in collecting artworks and books than carousing. He began keeping a diary, recording his thoughts and observations, often with terse entries such as "7 May 1762. Rome. Christ's Vicar banquets whilst beggars die of starvation outside St. Peter's."

Returning to England he was rudderless, only vaguely interested in the running of the family's 2,000-acre

Leicestershire estate. He pursued a series of half-hearted courtships of neighbours' simpering daughters, and sowed a few wild oats with country matrons whose husbands were the baronet's huntin', fishin', shootin' and wenchin' cronies.

It was his father's idea to send Arthur out to the Caribbean after winning the Grenada sugar plantation. Considering the high mortality rate among white people in the West Indies, Arthur had wondered if the old baronet had hoped he would also succumb to disease so his younger brother William could succeed to the title and the estate.

Arthur had been searching for something indefinable since childhood. Looking tenderly at Weju, he drew a deep breath and smiled as he realised that he had found contentment at last.

One evening she was not in her usual place on the long gallery cooled by sea breezes on the eastern side of the house. Arthur found her sitting on the grass beneath the giant poinciana on a knoll above the cane fields, hugging her knees. When she looked up at him he saw that her face was wet with tears.

"What is wrong, Weju?"

"I see …" she struggled for the English word, as she swept her arm towards the gossamer clouds drifting across the cerulean sky, "… over there".

It was many months later when he realised that she was trying to say "future".

The following week she told Arthur that she was going to have a baby.

***

The child came too early for the Scottish doctor to be summoned from St. George's. He was birthed by an elderly woman, nearly blind from ocular syphilis, assisted by her frightened granddaughter who hadn't washed her hands after slopping out the pigsty. Arthur paced outside their bedroom door until Weju's screams ended and a baby's robust cries began. He took his son, still slippery with bloody fluid, into his arms and gazed rapturously at the tawny-skinned infant with his own blue eyes. He kissed the moist cap of soft black curls and handed him to Weju to suckle.

"We'll name him, Alex. Alexander Meynell Charteris."

"Ch-Chart …." she said feebly.

"Yes, Chart".

The next day Weju was feverish. The doctor came, examined her and took Arthur aside.

"'tis the childbed fever, I'm afraid. Not much I can do."

He hurried away after collecting 10 shillings for his trouble. Treating slaves was beneath his fine Edinburgh medical education. *Next time send for the veterinary surgeon*, he grumbled to himself as he rode away from the plantation.

The fever steadily consumed her. By the fourth day her skin was scalding. Arthur slept on a pallet in the bedchamber, wincing at her whimpers, silently cursing his helplessness. He listened to the intermittent cries of the infant in a room across the corridor, praying that it would not succumb to the fever. After Weju's breast milk stopped flowing Arthur found a Fulani woman named Phibbah usually employed in the cane fields whose baby had died shortly after birth. He heard her cooing to Chart as he suckled during the night.

During the day Arthur sat by the bedside wiping Weju's face with a damp cloth as a succession of wide-eyed children swung plaited palm fans in a vain attempt to stir the air in the stifling chamber. Like the enlightened philosophers he admired he was sceptical about organised religion, but now he prayed fervently.

On the sixth day she rallied for a few hours after an Obeah man from Westerhall Estate brought her a potion of fever grass and mimosa in a calabash. She asked for her son. While the infant gripped her left thumb in his tiny fist, she used her right hand to touch his eyes, nose, ears and mouth, the crown of his head and his genitals, whilst whispering in Garifuna. Arthur realised it was a blessing.

Weju raised her head and looked at him, black eyes blazing with intensity.

"He will have much pain and sorrow, but he will survive and be a great warrior like his grandfather. Promise me you will raise him as your true son and place no others above him."

Arthur nodded.

"I promise," he said huskily.

The light receded from her eyes. Arthur took the baby,

squalling in fury to be separated from its mother.

That night, in the darkest hour between midnight and dawn when jumbies slink from silk cotton trees and stalk the living, Weju died.

***

The funeral procession drew near, the black people singing African dirges as they swayed rhythmically, those in the vanguard beating drums, shaking rattles and blowing on conch shells. A simple mahogany coffin was borne on the shoulders of four men whom Weju had cured. Dozens of slaves from other plantations mingled with the La Sagesse workers, watched warily by Munro, the grizzled Scottish overseer, and his drivers.

The storm struck as the coffin was lowered into the grave, rustling the pages of the breviary held by the priest as he recited the Latin burial ritual. Weju had steadfastly refused to be baptised, trusting to her peoples' gods, but Arthur knew a Christian ceremony was expected by his slaves, who mixed the religion of their enslavers with African beliefs.

He dribbled a handful of muddy soil onto the coffin and stood erect as the grave was filled, rain mingling with the tears flowing down his face. The poinciana's long scabbard-like seed pods rattled in the branches above him and scarlet flowers dislodged by the storm carpeted the raw mound.

That night tears smudged the ink of his diary entry: "24 June 1774. Weju gone. Heart shattered."

***

Some part of Arthur's spirit seemed to have departed with Weju's. Introverted by nature, he withdrew further, taking little interest in management of the plantation or great events beyond Grenada's placid beaches and jungle-girt mountains such as the rebellion of the American colonies thousands of miles north. He sought solace in his library, which he routinely re-stocked from London.

A year after Weju's passing the donkey cart delivered a fine marble headstone inscribed simply with her name, death date, and *Mon Coeur est á Toi*. Several months later a ship arrived with a wrought iron bench which he placed beneath the poinciana. On most evenings he would sit there with a bottle of white rum and a crystal glass, telling her about their son. He believed that he felt her presence when the moon was full, convinced that he could smell the palm oil she had used on her glossy black hair.

Arthur's one passion was the child. He doted on Chart as the living connection to Weju. The boy thrived. Despite his religious scepticism, Arthur was mindful of the prevalent infant mortality and had the baby christened by the old Papist priest, considering that the last Anglican parson had succumbed to Yellow Fever.

Phibbah continued as Chart's nurse after he was weaned, and she was envied by the field hands for escaping the cane fields into what was considered a life of relative ease in the Great House. She expected to be called to her Master's bed when his mourning was ended, but he was disinterested. At first, she felt somewhat rejected, especially as Munro the overseer had tried forcing himself on her several times and she preferred the Master as lover and protector. But she shrugged it off. It was common knowledge that white people were strange, and the Master was one of the oddest.

She spoiled the boy, feeding him tamarind balls, cassava pone and other sweets. She taught him Fulani songs such as *Kaa Fo* – a sad cradle tune - and folk stories about Anansi the spider, Mami Wata, her husband Papa Bois, and the tiny Bacco that lived up in the rafters of the great house and could only be seen if he was a good boy and ate all of his callaloo soup. By the age of three Chart was speaking to Phibbah and the house servants in the island patois, a mixture of African dialects, English and French. Chart called her *Mami*, except when in his father's presence who insisted that she was *Nanny*.

His father spent several hours with him each day in the bedroom that was now a nursery, holding the boy on his lap while seated in a massive armchair that he had ordered from Mr. Chippendale's workshop on St. Martin's Lane. He captivated Chart with picture books of animals and plants, gently teaching him the alphabet and his numbers. He also took pains to converse with the child in the diction that he had absorbed at Cambridge. By his fourth year Chart could switch effortlessly between patois and the King's English.

In early July 1779, Arthur received an oilcloth packet that had been dispatched from Bristol seven weeks earlier. It contained a letter from Mr. Bryan Cave, the Charteris family solicitor in Leicester, informing him that his father had died in March and he was now the 4th Baronet and legatee of Knossington Hall and various other properties and chattels, including a townhouse in London, a dozen horses, a pack of hounds, a carriage, a brace of silver-mounted fowling pieces built by 'P. Gandon at the Cross Guns, Coventry St.', and "the La Sagesse estate Grenada with its negroes to the value of £7,729 4s 8d current money".

The lawyer enclosed a letter from Arthur's mother, Dorothea, now the dowager Lady Charteris, begging him to come home to 'take his rightful place' and bring his son with him. In Arthur's rare letters to his mother, he had told her about Chart with ambiguous terms about his ancestry.

After reading the letters, he heard childish laughter on the lawn outside his office. Arthur saw Chart happily playing with slave children who were still too young to be put to work. He watched the five-year-old, skin the colour of fine muscovado sugar highlighted by miniature white linen breeches and smock, curly black hair cascading to his shoulders like his Garifuna relatives. *Already a handsome lad,* he mused. *What kind of life do I want for him? What would his future be here?* The boy had a quick mind which deserved the type of civilised nurturing that could only be found in Europe.

During the remainder of the day he spent hours under the poinciana communing with Weju, but no answer could be discerned in the gentle breeze or the high-pitched twitter of the bright little tanagers fluttering amidst the branches. That night she came to him in a dream, radiant as the Caribbean sun at midday.

'Go,' she said, then merged with the light as he reached for her.

The next month was a flurry of activity. Passage to England was booked and decisions were taken about what to take. Daunted by the paper shambles in his office, Arthur considered leaving it all, but knew that to do so would mean the records would be destroyed by rats, insects and damp. He told Cuffie to pack all the documents in chests to accompany the other luggage. Arthur's biggest regret was leaving the bulk of his library, but he took enough books for a two-months voyage and accepted the fact that he was now rich enough to replace the volumes left behind. He was confident that the plantation had been left in capable hands under the care of Munro, the overseer, and that its income of upwards of £1,800 per annum from sugar, rum and cocoa would continue to flow into the Charteris family account at Mr. Hoare's bank.

On the morning of their departure, Arthur took Chart to the grave beneath the poinciana. He tenderly traced the inscription on the headstone. To his surprise, the child copied him, then turned in concern at his father's quiet sobs and hugged his leg.

"I hope you can remember this place," Arthur told him hoarsely.

The brig *Fair Nancy* weighed anchor on the evening tide and left St. George's Harbour, carrying Arthur, his son, and Cuffie and Phibbah. As the jib and topsails filled and the ship glided under the guns of Fort George, Arthur held his son up to see over the bulwark at what he assumed would be his last view of the island of his birth.

Chapter 2

The square-rigged ship was a playing ground for the five-year-old boy. Chart gleefully explored every part of the *Fair Nancy* from quarterdeck to fo'c's'le, following the bosun like a puppy deep into the hold, chortling as he swung in the crewmen's tightly packed hammocks. He was largely unsupervised except by the rough sailors, who tolerated him at first and then treated him affectionately. One sailor sewed a miniature pair of petticoat breeches, a shirt and a pea coat for the child, and another presented him with a shrunken Monmouth knit cap like the crewmen wore.

They laughed when repeatedly disengaging him from climbing the ratlines, regaled him with stories of pirates and sea monsters, and gave him a carved toy sword and pistol which he brandished on deck hoping that buccaneers would appear on the horizon. Chart clapped palms to ears and shrieked with excitement when the nine-pounder guns were run out and fired for practice. The captain watched him with an amused smile while keeping a weather eye out for French warships and Yankee privateers.

Arthur took the air three times a day, nodding at his son's happy chatter, left hand grasping the boy's tiny one, right clutching shrouds and bulwarks to keep his feet on the heaving deck. The remainder of the time he devoured books in his cabin and shared suppers with the captain, mates, and the black clad widow of a major in the 45th Regiment who had perished from the Yellow Jack in Barbados along with nearly half of his battalion.

Phibbah rarely stirred from her pallet in the dank cubby-hole cabin shared with Chart, alternating between sea-sickness and terror as the ship rolled and plunged in heavy seas. The voyage revived the horror she had experienced on a slave ship a dozen years earlier during the voyage from a dungeon at Cape Coast Castle on the African Gold Coast to Grenada. Her nightmares were so vivid that she slept fitfully, waking up shaking with panic that she was still aboard the slaver. Phibbah was too incapacitated to care for Chart. She developed a fear – which

Arthur would have thought irrational – that her master would punish her for not tending to his son, and would cast her overboard. She lived on lukewarm gruel and grog, and refused to take the physic brought to her by the captain's steward who served as a makeshift ship's doctor, having the notion that it was poison.

Cuffie slept in the passageway outside Arthur's cabin, alert for the summons of his bell to empty the chamber pot or fetch coffee from the galley. On the rare occasions when he ventured on deck, he fearfully scuttled on hands and knees, laughed at by the crew, including a handful of free black sailors, who mocked him as "Crab".

***

They were all on deck as the *Fair Nancy* rounded Cuckold's Point, the child wrinkling his nose at the fetid whiff from the Thames-side gibbet hung with the bodies of river pirates and thieves in rusty chains. Chart was as awestruck as Phibbah and Cuffie as they maneuvered into the Pool of London through a forest of masts sprouting from East Indiamen, colliers, warships and a fleet of smaller craft. Hundreds of barges and wherries encircled the ships, rowed by brawny tattooed watermen. Arthur remembered a poet's description of London's port as "a very wood of trees disbranched to make glades and let in light, so shaded it is with masts and sails."

A wherry set them ashore. Arthur alighted with Chart in his arms, the boy's head swivelling constantly as they edged through a throng of shouting, swearing, gesticulating stevedores, whores, sailors and cutpurses. Phibbah and Cuffie followed, shivering beneath cut down old sails as flimsy protection from the cold drizzle, overwhelmed by the sights, sounds and smells. Arthur's agent met them outside the gate on Red Maid Lane, doffing his tricorne and bowing deeply. He had a hackney coach waiting. The coachman held open the door while Chart was boosted inside followed by his father. The driver curtly ordered Phibbah and Cuffie to take their places on the open rumble seats, standing by muttering impatiently and tapping his whip handle on his palm as Cuffie helped the black woman to climb aboard.

***

The prior baronet bought the townhouse at 7 Chesterfield Street because of its proximity to White's, the gentlemen's club. When one is legless at 3:00 am after hours at the gaming table and three bottles of claret it was convenient to be carried across the street to one's own bed by a pair of porters. The old man was in a red fury after White's moved to St. James's in 1778, a factor which may have contributed to his demise a few months later.

Arthur – now Sir Arthur – discovered that his father had succumbed from an apoplectic fit at the townhouse while rogering a teenage doxie. After the baronet expired, the girl stole four guineas and a gold watch from the dead man's pocket. She was caught, incarcerated at Bridewell, and hung at Tyburn Tree along with a dozen others who were convicted of capital crimes such as being in the company of gypsies and stealing food.

The house was short-staffed, with only the elderly housekeeper and a maid in residence since the old baronet's death. Arthur told the housekeeper not to bother about hiring more servants as he would only be there a short while. He ordered her to look after Phibbah and Cuffie and find them clothing more suitable for the climate. The housekeeper found some of the former owner's cast-off suits and worn shoes which had gone out of fashion a decade earlier for Cuffie, and a couple of gowns left behind by some of the "actresses" who used to entertain the old man upstairs. Phibbah wrinkled her nose at the smell of cheap perfume which still permeated her new clothes. They were each given a room in the garret where with only a thin blanket each they shivered through the first few nights until Phibbah sought Cuffie's pallet. Warmed by lovemaking and each other's bodies, they shared memories of Grenada, good ones outweighing the bad.

Arthur's first order of business was to attire himself and Chart in a manner befitting their status. The family tailor, Mr. Weston, arrived with his assistant in the forenoon of the day after their arrival, diligently measuring father and fidgeting son for identical suits. He advised having a dark green coat with gold binding, dark brown with the same, a plain blue, and for half dress a *Bon de Paris* with gold frogs in the latest French fashion, all which he said were of the highest ton. "My goodness," the tailor said, "you'll both be proper Bond Street loungers, so you will!"

Chart explored the town house as exuberantly as he had the ship, charging up and down the stairs and hiding from Phibbah. Each morning during his first week in London, he would press his nose against a cold window pane in the drawing room, summoned by the cries of little chimney sweeps making rounds with their masters, and the milk woman with her pails slung from a yoke across her shoulders uttering a queer yodelling call. In the evenings he would watch as the lamplighters emerged from the gloom to trim and light the oil street lamps, burdened with a formidable pair of scissors, a flambeau of pitched rope and a rickety ladder.

Arthur hired sedan chairs at a shilling per hour and perched the boy on his lap to show him the sights of London. Chart's favourite was the Tower Menagerie, where his father helped him to count ten lions, a panther, a pair of tigers and four leopards. He was fascinated by a large monkey, wide-striped like a tiger, which guzzled from a mazer of ale provided by the sly keeper for a thruppence. They would stroll hand-in-hand through St James's Park and Green Park, stopping at stalls where milkmaids would squeeze warm frothing milk from cows' udders into a pewter mug for the child to guzzle. Afterward, Chart would beg for one of the goldfinches in cages hung from trees along Birdcage Walk, then gaze in fascination at the scarlet-coated guardsmen on Horse Guards Parade Ground, where young shoeblacks, the 'Blackguards', waited to clean the boots of soldiers for a copper.

***

They took a stage coach from London to Leicester, departing under an incessant rain. Chart begged his father to let Phibbah ride inside with them, and Arthur would have agreed but both the coachman and the other two passengers, a pinch-faced parson and his bonneted wife, were having none of it. So Phibbah was hoisted up to the curved roof to join Cuffie and five other miserable people clutching small wooden handles as the *Leicester Flying Coach* rumbled away from the Two Necked Swan on Lad Lane. The clerical couple spent much of the time between reading religious tracts glaring at the chattering dark-complexioned child and complaining about the outrageous cost of the trip at two guineas for the pair of them.

Exhausted from the three-day journey, Arthur took a room at a coaching inn on the outskirts of Leicester and sent a note to his mother via an ostler to apprise her of their arrival. Phibbah and Cuffie, increasingly bewildered and frightened, were grateful for their bowls of mutton stew and makeshift beds in the hayloft above the stable.

The next day the family coach arrived, gleaming with a fresh coat of varnish and the gilt mantling of the Charteris arms emblazoned on the door. The coachman told Arthur that he had ordered a farm wagon to collect the two servants and luggage. Harness bells jingling, they drove down lanes and across gently rolling countryside, past green pastures dotted with sheep and through neat villages of thatched brick and stone cottages watched over by sturdy medieval churches, all unchanged from Arthur's life before his self-exile to the West Indies. On tropical nights in Grenada when heat and humidity made sleep impossible, he had longed for chill Leicestershire mornings, riding his hunter across fields where mist lingered in the hollows and jackdaws cawed from copses. With his father gone, he was glad to be back. The island and the plantation were fading into bittersweet memories, and sometimes he struggled to visualise Weju's face until he looked at her child, who now turned widespread, incongruously blue eyes and a large grin on him as he excitedly bounced on the leather seat.

As the coach turned into the mile-long avenue leading to Knossington Hall, the coachman blew blasts from his trumpet to announce their arrival. Sir Arthur craned his head out the window, savouring the vista of the brick Jacobean house built by an ancestor a century and a half earlier. The four matched grey horses came to a perfect halt in front of the main entrance and the butler, Barnicle, and a pair of footmen appeared, resplendent in silver embroidered green livery and powdered wigs. Barnicle and the footmen bowed in unison as the new baronet greeted them before turning to lift Chart to the ground. He didn't catch the servants' quizzical looks as he took the boy by the hand and led him up the stairs.

Lady Charteris awaited them in the marble floored entry hall. Dorothea, daughter of a successful Newcastle coal merchant who had brought a substantial dowry into the marriage with Arthur's wastrel father, was a no-nonsense type who saw little point in turning out the full complement of fifteen house servants, four gardeners, and assorted grooms and stable boys to greet her son. Properly restraining her immense joy at his safe return, she let him peck both of her cheeks. Arthur stepped back and gestured to Chart.

"Mama, may I present my son."

On cue, as taught by his father, the child doffed his hat, made a leg and in a high-pitched voice said "Pleased to meet you, grandmama."

The only sign of Dorothea's mental agitation was a twitching eyelid.

****

"So, the lad's a bastard then?"

Lady Charteris and Sir Arthur had supper after Phibbah put Chart to bed in the nursery. Little urging was needed for the child, as the toys assembled for Arthur and his younger brother William had been undisturbed in the room for a quarter of a century, waiting for the next generation. Chart had immediately climbed on the rocking horse before being prised loose by Phibbah.

"He's my son," Sir Arthur answered defensively.

The unanswered question was the only confirmation needed. Dorothea couldn't conceal her relief.

"Well, never mind that he's a blackamoor, he's still family. We'll see to it that he's properly educated and get him an apprenticeship with the East India Company. He'll fit right in out there, looking like a little Hindoo. Plenty of other half-castes working as clerks, so I hear. And we'll find you a girl who can give you a good legitimate brood, an heir and a few spares, eh. Shukburgh Ashby over at Quenby has a couple of likely daughters, and there's the Hesilriges at Noseley. I'll make a list!"

Sir Arthur gave her a tepid smile, unwilling to admit that he had no intention of marrying, and no interest in having more children.

She gave him news of his younger brother, who had followed in the dissolute footsteps of their father. Seven years earlier, William had married the heavily pregnant daughter of a Shadwell tavern keeper whom he had seduced. The girl's father confronted William at his Whitechapel lodgings, giving him the choice of having his foppish head blown off by the blunderbuss he brandished or taking her in legal matrimony with a dowry of £250. Valuing his head and collection of wigs to cover it, William had chosen the latter option, and their son, Pemberton, escaped bastardy by a fortnight.

"Poor little hunchback, Pemb." Dorothea shook her head sorrowfully. "And the mother is such a gin sot that she can barely rise from her bed to use the slops jar. I doubt if he's seen his daddy more than once in the past few years. Fortunately, your father left the lad £100 a year for his education. He was packed off to board at Crouch End Academy in Hornsey when he turned six last year and we put him down for Westminster after he was born. Mind you, there's no telling who his real father was. You know what they say about innkeeper's daughters!"

She sighed.

"As for William ... your father was more than generous to him in his will, five hundred a year! But he burns through that with his gambling faster than a stoat down a burrow and came to me cap in hand weeks after the will was read. Just to keep him away from here, I've had Mr. Cave give him an extra £50 per quarter.

"So you see," she said, ringing the handbell for Barnicle, "It's up to you now so I don't only have a dwarf and a black as grandsons!"

***

Despite her early inclination to tolerate Chart as an unwelcome family appendage, the boy soon won Dorothea's heart. Arthur was relieved to let his mother assume the child's upbringing as efficiently as she ran the estate.

Phibbah lasted a week as nursemaid until Lady Charteris was

shocked to overhear her chattering with Chart in West Indian patois. Muttering that she "would have none of that jungle gibberish" in her house, she promptly ordered Phibbah to the scullery and engaged a nanny who was highly recommended by Lady Harborough. Pleased to discover that Chart knew his numbers and letters, she advertised for a tutor in the *Leicester Journal*. When to her horror she discovered that the boy had been christened by a Roman Catholic priest, she quickly arranged for him to be baptised in the village church by the vicar of Knossington. When the register was inscribed and Sir Arthur was asked the name of the mother, he thought for a minute before stating "Weju de St. Vincent."

Having loved the boy since birth like her own child, Phibbah was devastated at being separated from him. She blamed herself, believing that she had been replaced because she had been too ill to tend to Chart during the transatlantic voyage. She hated the endless toil in the scullery as much as the bland fare of bread, mutton and cheese. She missed the fresh fruits, vegetables and fish of her island life, longing for her comparatively easy work in the La Sagesse great house and thinking that even the earlier backbreaking labour in the cane fields was preferable to her current drudgery amidst strange white servants, who she had assumed were slaves like herself until she saw the butler pay their paltry wages.

Dorothea Charteris took charge of Arthur's life as well. On Barnicle's recommendation, she promoted a promising young footman to serve as the new baronet's valet. Cuffie was sent to the home farm on the farthest reaches of the estate, where he was ill-treated by the farmworkers, made to sleep in a shed next to a pigsty, and fed offal and turnips. Phibbah had twice tried to visit him, but gave up after being nearly raped by a pair of farmhands. Cuffie tried to defend her but was beaten senseless for his efforts.

It was one thing to endure enslavement among one's own kind, but Cuffie had been relegated to a totally alien environment. Malnourished, without contact with Phibbah and subjected to constant verbal and physical abuse, he grew deeply depressed. He decided to run one night, but became disorientated and returned at first light after getting soaked in a cold autumn downpour. He took to his straw pallet shivering with an ague that rapidly turned into pneumonia. By the time Arthur got word, Cuffie had died. As he wasn't a Christian, the farmhands buried him in the same waste ground where they disposed of livestock found dead in the fields. There was no funeral, but Sir Arthur rode across the fields and said a prayer over the grave, sad that another link with Grenada and his life with Weju had been severed.

He visited Phibbah in the scullery to give her the news and left her weeping, which added to his sadness and sense of guilt. The next week he read an article in the *Gentleman's Magazine* titled "The Case of Our Fellow-Creatures, the Oppressed Africans', written by one Granville Sharp, Esquire. The author extolled The Sierra Leone Resettlement Scheme, a charity established to resettle black people living in England to their presumed homelands in Africa. The magazine provided Sharp's address and Sir Arthur corresponded with him.

On Christmas Eve 1779, Arthur summoned Phibbah to his library where he sat behind a walnut desk. She stood in front of him clutching her hands, head down, fearful that she would be sold and sent away to an even worse situation. Her shoulders were hunched, thin arms crossed across the bosom of her patched kersey gown. The brown face under the mobcap that had once glowed now had an unhealthy greyish tinge.

He looked closely at her, realising that this was the first time he had actually seen a black person as a fellow human being.

Except Weju, of course. But he was more her slave than she was his.

"Phibbah," Sir Arthur said gently, "would you like to go back to Africa?"

She looked at him warily.

"Phibbah?"

"Yes, master." She nodded slowly, red-rimmed eyes now raised to meet his, unable to conceal her hopefulness.

Arthur beamed.

"Well, I have a wonderful Christmas gift for you! Next month a ship will sail to Africa with a number of other negroes. I have arranged for you to be on it. You are going home, Phibbah!"

It never occurred to Arthur that Phibbah's homeland deep in the highlands of Guinea was more than 400 miles from Sierra Leone. What mattered was that his lingering guilt was assuaged and enlightened beneficence substantiated. Phibbah – who had been captured by an enemy tribe at the age of ten before being sold on the coast - had no understanding of geography; she had known Coromantees, Mandingoes and other enslaved people in Grenada, but thought of Africa as a bigger island where she had been free.

Now he handed her a document adorned with red wax seals and scarlet ribbons. She took it uncomprehendingly.

"You are free, Phibbah. Always keep this with you. Now you may go."

Granville Sharp had arranged for Phibbah to travel to the new Sierra Leone colony on the condition that she was legally manumitted, which Arthur readily agreed to. Mr. Cave, the lawyer, took possession of the La Sagesse estate documents hauled across the Atlantic and had his clerk organise and catalogue them chronologically. He created a file for 137 bills of sale for the plantation's slaves dating to before Arthur's possession of the property. Among them he found a document recording that "one Fulani wench, Phibbah, age 11 or thereabout" had been bought for £24 8s 12d. In precise copperplate writing, Mr. Cave drafted Phibbah's manumission paper for Sir Arthur's elegant signature.

Near the top of the file, ignored by the clerk and his employer, was the proof of Weju's enslavement.

Lady Dorothea strictly forbade any contact with Chart, so Phibbah was not given an opportunity to say goodbye to him. At first, the child had missed her when she was assigned to the scullery, but little boys are easily distracted and the prim young woman chosen as his new nanny was diligent about keeping him occupied with games, reading and walks in the estate's extensive grounds. Sometimes in the middle of night he awoke frightened and called out to Phibbah in patois, but the comforting memories soon faded.

***

In the company of 43 other freed slaves, Phibbah sailed from Portsmouth on a decommissioned East Indiaman. The accommodation and food were basic but no different from that provided to white immigrants. As the weather changed from thick and hazy to bright, clear sunshine the passengers became festive. The black people danced on deck as crewmen played *The Bay of Biscay* and *Married to a Mermaid* on fiddle and fife.

Off Tenerife their ship was run down and taken a prize by an American privateer out of Savannah. The white crewmen were put ashore, but the passengers were shackled below and taken to Georgia where 31 survivors were sold in Wright Square.

Phibbah wasn't among them. She died in her chains and was unceremoniously tossed overboard.

***

Chart was given a Welsh Cob for his sixth birthday, and by his ninth he was such a skilled horseman that he graduated to a sweet natured Arab gelding standing at a smidgeon over 14 hands. The following Christmas he received a double-barrelled flintlock fowling piece built specially for his immature size by Durs Egg, gun maker, of Princes Street, London. He excelled at sporting pursuits as well as reading, writing, Latin, French and maths set by his tutor, who also taught him manners, social graces, and proper decorum with servants. At Arthur's insistence, the curriculum included works by Enlightenment writers, most of which were incomprehensible to the child. Chart invariably completed his lessons by midday so he could spend the afternoons riding, shooting and exploring the countryside.

In the early years of Chart's life at Knossington his grandmother had been embarrassed to acknowledge his existence to her cronies in the county. Although Arthur was generally not assertive, he stood firm on the point that his son was to be treated as a full member of the family. He would take Chart with him on rides to Melton Mowbray, Oakham and village fairs. While there was general curiosity about the swarthy little gentleman with luminescent blue eyes, they encountered no overt hostility. Dark-skinned people were a rarity in rural Leicestershire and speculation about his origins ranged from Musselman, Portugee or Jew. When word spread that he was Sir Arthur Charteris' son from "the Indies", gossips whispered that he was the orphaned son of a maharaja adopted by the Baronet. As Chart grew older, though, it became obvious that his aquiline profile, stature and eyes strongly resembled Arthur.

Lady Dorothea's austere demeanour masked a kind heart. Privately, she called Chart her "Little Midnight Shade" – a term of endearment for her - while bemoaning his illegitimacy and mixed race. "'tis such a pity," she told Arthur, "that he's not white and a bastard, as he would be a perfect son and heir otherwise." As the years passed, she continued to chide Arthur about his bachelorhood. Not one for balls, which she considered an unwarranted extravagance, she hosted a series of dinners and music evenings to which she invited every remotely eligible woman from sixteen to thirty. To please her, Arthur paid some of them gentlemanly court but quickly distanced himself when the ladies – or more often their parents – broached marriage.

In the autumn of 1784, five years after his return, she confronted him in his library where he was reading Immanuel Kant's recently translated essay *What Is Enlightenment?* She turned the key in the door lock to avoid intrusion by servants or Chart and stood over him with crossed arms and a fierce scowl.

"If I didn't know better I'd say you were a molly," she snapped. "And some people hereabouts must think you fancy men. But I know better; you're still mooning over that black wench who was Chart's mam. It's time you got over her and did your duty."

"I'm only forty," he answered mildly. "Plenty of time for it:"

Trying to control a palsy in her hands that grew worse when agitated, Dorothea pulled up a claw-footed chair and sat on its edge.

"As you know all too well," she answered, thinking of her undisclosed ailments and her late husband's welcome passing, "life is fickle. I have spoken with Mr. Cave. He said that the title can only be passed on to a legitimate male heir. The courts ruled that it was illegal for the ultimate ownership of land to be longer than two generations and an extra twenty-one years. The estate is entailed, but unfortunately neither your father nor your grandfather bothered to make what he called a new settlement to extend the entail. After which the heir could mortgage, sell or give away the property."

Her withered lips tightened to a thin line.

"Thank God I've managed to discharge the debts your father ran up against the estate, largely because of the income from the Grenada plantation. But if you should die without a *legitimate* son or daughter, William will inherit and all the wealth that our family have built up over generations would be squandered within months. You *must* have Cave draft a new settlement to protect the estate even if you don't have a legitimate heir, which now seems very unlikely to me!"

Arthur met her gaze with blue eyes that showed unusual steeliness.

"Mother, I have also consulted with Mr. Cave and all has been arranged. But we needn't think about that now."

***

Chart became popular with the village boys. On summer afternoons he would tether his horse on the edge of the village green and join the youngsters watching the older youths and men play cricket. As the squire's son, at first he was treated warily but was soon accepted without comments about his ethnicity. In the autumn he played Foot-Ball with them, and the entire village was grateful for the leather balls his father had ordered from a harness maker in Oakham. He was large for his age and became respected for defending smaller boys from bullies with mild fisticuffs and wrestling.

Chart began inviting his friends to the estate to play soldiers in the grounds, organising them into units with sticks as muskets and leading the brave redcoats against the traitorous Yankee Doodles or Johnny Crapaud. After their battles, Dorothea tolerated them in the kitchen, where they guzzled sweet cider and Bosworth jumbles, but refused to let the villagers into other parts of the house. "The grocer's lad and smith's son must learn their place, it's just not done to let them become too familiar."

She tried to nudge him into friendship with boys of his age who were more socially acceptable, such as the Vicar of

Barleythorpe's twin boys and another baronet's consumptive son who was so exhausted from coughing that he couldn't climb the staircase to see Chart's enviable collection of lead soldiers. But her grandson found them boring, preferring the rough and tumble company of the village boys.

Arthur visited London twice a year, to browse bookshops, savour the Royal Academy exhibitions and engage in intellectual conversations at the Turk's Head coffee house on the Strand. He always took Chart with him to expose him to the world beyond rural Leicestershire, regaling him with stories of his Grand Tour during the long journeys south in the family coach. Bookshops and modern artists such as Reynolds and Gainsborough were of limited interest to the boy, but to Arthur's surprise Chart was mesmerised by the works of Haydn and Mozart performed at Gallini's on Hanover Square.

Arthur gleaned the *Morning Chronicle and London Advertiser* for more prosaic amusements. They would spend a day at Bartholomew Fair seeing the mechanical puppets, waxworks, exotic animals such as Toby the Sapient Pig, oiled Lascar wrestlers, Mrs. Bark the Giantess, mermaids and musical extravaganzas. In September 1784 they joined a crowd of 200,000 at Finsbury Square to watch Signor Lunardi ascend into the heavens in a hydrogen balloon accompanied by a dog, a cat and a pigeon.

On All Hallow's Eve of 1787 they were dining on chops at Simpson's Tavern when a man in a powdered wig who Arthur recognised as a former Westminster classmate noticed them across the dining room. After dabbing his lips, he rose from his table and approached them.

"I say, Charteris, frightfully sorry about your brother."

Arthur frowned.

"My brother?"

"Erm, sorry if I'm the first one to break it to you, old man. He was killed in an *affaire d'honneur* this morning 'neath the Wimbledon windmill. Never a good thing to duel when one is short-sighted, especially after a night at Mrs. Harrison's Bagnio at Charing Cross."

Chapter 3

"He's got no one now that both his mother and father are gone," said Arthur. "You're always talking about Christian charity; certainly, it would be the Christian thing to invite your other grandson for Christmas."

"Who's to say the imp *is* my grandson," Lady Charteris snapped. "I've heard that he looks nothing like William. At least there's no doubt about who *your* bastard's sire is, apart from the tint of his skin! And you've already been more than charitable, covering his school fees plus an allowance!"

Arthur cleared his throat, controlling his impatience with his mother who had become more irascible since being confined to a wheeled chair several months earlier.

"Chart will be going up to Westminster in the new year. It's time he met his cousin to help smooth his path there if for no other reason."

"Hrrmph!" the old woman answered, but Arthur got his way.

***

Chart first met Pemberton Charteris four days before the Christmas of 1787. He had been keenly anticipating his cousin's arrival. Arthur had told him about Pemb's rather sad life, saying that he hoped the boys would become good friends as they would be together at Westminster School.

He heard the coachman's horn and raced to an upstairs window overlooking the drive, straining his eyes across the snow-sheathed park until the estate's calash appeared through the flurries. Barnicle the butler went out to meet the carriage as it arrived and placed a mounting block under the door. A slight, cloaked figure, face hidden by an outsized tricorne, emerged unsteadily. Chart raced down the staircase to stand with Arthur in the entry hall.

Pemb shrugged off his cloak, letting it fall to the floor along with his hat, which were quickly scooped up by a footman. His whey face was round and pimpled, brown eyes resentful, ginger hair tightly clubbed. Arthur stepped forward to welcome him with a handshake, noting that while one of the boy's shoulders was higher than the other, Pemb was not the hunchback tattled by Lady Dorothea. With pity, he saw that the young man's coat and waistcoat were shabby, the pleated white stock at his neck yellowish and his stockings raddled.

Chart stepped forward as his father presented him. At thirteen years, Chart was already taller than fifteen-year-old Pemb, who scowled as he limply took his hand before quickly dropping it. Arthur explained that his grandmama was "indisposed" but would greet him later. *Heaven knows*, he thought wearily, *she may be "indisposed" throughout the poor lad's visit if she decides to be obstinate.*

Dorothea relented, and had the footmen carry her in her mahogany chair down to the drawing room, where she silently surveyed her other grandson through a lorgnette. Almost immediately she rang a silver bell and asked Arthur to wheel her into the dining room, with the boys following.

Supper was an uncomfortable affair. Pemb had little to say, grunting in answer to questions while slurping his soup with a spoon in one hand and a bread roll in the other, prompting Lady Charteris to acidly ask if etiquette was taught at Westminster. Between courses he gazed enviously around the dining room, seemingly appraising the massive silver candelabra and the family portraits hanging by gilt chains from picture rail moulding.

Pemb spent most of the following days wandering the Hall as if inventorying its contents. Once, Chart caught him in his dressing room fingering his finely embroidered blue velvet suit tailored for the Christmas festivities. He brushed past Chart muttering under his breath something that sounded like "too good for black jackanapes." Later, Chart found his cherished lead soldiers, arrayed in battalions on a long table in the old nursery, scattered on the floor, some crushed as if stomped. Saddened and puzzled, he asked the chamber maids if they had an explanation, but they demurred without meeting his eyes.

Next day, Arthur entered his library to find Pemb leafing through one of his diaries taken from the row of calf-bound volumes with the years stamped on the spines in gold leaf. With his back to him, Pemb didn't notice his uncle until Arthur snapped, "What are you doing here, young man?"

Pemb dropped the book and spun to face him, blinking rapidly.

"Looking for a book, Uncle," he stammered. "Something to while away the time."

"Next time you must ask me. Now please begone."

After the door closed behind Pemb, Arthur picked up the diary from the floor. It was dated 1774, the year of Weju's death and Chart's birth. He replaced it and gazed thoughtfully out the window at the snow falling outside. That evening, he was perturbed when the butler took him aside and told him that Master Pemberton had asked him for the key to the gun room, which he had refused.

The weather cleared on Christmas Eve, prompting Arthur to suggest that the two boys go riding with him. A set of Chart's outgrown riding kit was found for Pemb, which he accepted sullenly. He followed his uncle and Chart to the stables, standing apart as the grooms led out Arthur's bay hunter, Chart's Arab and a rather spirited young grey. Noticing that Pemb appeared worried, Arthur surmised that he had limited experience as a horseman and quietly instructed the groom to bring out an older Connemara gelding instead. In truth, Pemb had almost no riding experience. As he awkwardly climbed into the saddle he seethed with anger, believing that his uncle was trying to humiliate him.

Arthur led them in a gentle canter through the park and across the fields beyond, the horses' hooves throwing up clods of snow. Chart was puzzled by the sedate pace, and his father did not want to embarrass Pemb by explaining. Chart lived in a world where everyone - even the village boys – learned to ride when they could barely walk and he would have found it hard to understand Pemb's predicament. With an open stretch of long pasture opening ahead, he whooped and spurred his horse into a gallop. Pemb's gelding perked up its ears and followed despite Arthur's cries of alarm. Chart's Arab knew all the jumps and sailed over the first fence. Pemb, screaming with rage and fear, hauled back on the reins, cruelly sawing the bit. Confused, the

horse refused the jump, halting suddenly and flinging its rider
heels over head to land in a snowdrift on the other side. When
Arthur reached him, he was shocked to hear Pemb hurling
curses at the "fucking dirty blackamoor" blithely riding far
ahead.

As Arthur dismounted and helped the shaking, red-faced boy
to his feet, he silently chided himself for not heeding his mother.

They returned to find Knossington Hall decorated with a
profusion of greenery - bay, laurel, ivy and holly leaves. That
evening, Christmas candles of prodigious size illuminated the
Yule Log as it was hauled into the great hearth beneath a
massive armorial sculpture displaying the Charteris arms with
numerous quarterings. The entire household, including bibulous
red-cheeked servants, feasted to a late hour upon Yule-dough,
Yule-cakes, and bowls of frumity, with copious music and
singing. Pemb stayed in his bedroom after asking that a tray of
pork pie and a hot toddy be left outside his door.

The next morning, he reluctantly joined the family for
Christmas service at St. Peter's. The men walked while Lady
Dorothea, bundled in an ancient bearskin, was carried in a sedan
chair by a quartet of hungover grooms and footmen. Afterward,
the gentlemen repaired into the hall to breakfast on brawn,
mustard and malmsey. Christmas dinner was sumptuous. The
pièce de résistance was the traditional peacock pie, the cock
cooked whole with the head projecting through the crust,
beautifully decorated, the bill gilded, the tail extended in
coloured grandeur.

On the old feast day of St. Stephen, they embarked in the
coach on the traditional round of visits to relatives, friends and
neighbours that would last until Twelfth Night. Lady Dorothea's
chair was lashed to the boot and she seemed to have shed 20
years from the anticipation of socialising and exchanging
gossip. Pemb begged off, claiming he was unwell and wished
to stay behind.

Revels and dancing followed supper at nearby Cold Overton
Hall, resurrecting happy memories of Arthur's gambols as a
youth. He shook his head fondly, thinking that Sellinger's
Round and Tom Tiler would have been sneered at as dances fit

only for country bumpkins by the glittering aristocrats in London. Shrieking with laughter, Chart and other youngsters amused themselves playing Hoodman Blind, Hot-Cockles, Shoe the Mare and other games.

They returned to Knossington long after midnight, satiated with claret, punch and good cheer. Inside the marble foyer Barnicle, the butler, and Mrs. Titchmarsh, the housekeeper waited with anxious looks on their faces. Mrs. Titchmarsh was wringing her hands. They waited until the coachman and groom set down Dorothea in her chair and left.

"You needn't have waited up," said Dorothea.

"We must speak with you urgently, m'Lady and Sir Arthur," Barnicle told them.

Arthur was instantly sober.

"What is it?"

"If we could go into the library, Sir." He looked pointedly at Chart. "I'm afraid it's something not fit for Master Chart's ears."

"Of you go, Chart, goodnight," Arthur said before leading the adults towards the library in the east wing of the hall, Barnicle pushing Dorothea's chair.

Chart pretended to move up the staircase, pausing to listen for the sound of the chair's wheels squeaking and library door shutting. He removed his gold-buckled shoes and moved stealthily through the darkened passage. As he grew closer to the library, he heard the rumbling of Barnicle's voice, followed by sharp exclamations from his father and grandmother. He placed his ear at the keyhole.

"Poor wee Molly," said Mrs. Titchmarsh. "Fortunately, another chambermaid was passing outside his door and heard her cries for help. She pounded on the door and then ran to find me and Mr. Barnicle."

"Aye, she was crying most piteously when we got there, and Master Pemb was swearing the vilest oaths! I called out to open the door and threatened to break it down. All the staff were now awake, and your valet, Evans, had the common sense to hasten back downstairs and bring Mrs. Titchmarsh's set of keys."

"When we got inside we saw Molly on the floor," the housekeeper continued. "Her clothing was half torn off and she was bleeding from her, uh, nether parts, and her head where he had hit her. Master Pemb was like a madman, swinging a poker and screaming. We managed to get her out of there and took her to my room. We cleaned her up and I think she'll be alright, but we should send for the doctor in the morning. She hasn't stopped crying!"

"And what of Pemb?" Arthur's voice demanded, hoarse with fury.

"Locked him in the room," replied Barnicle, "though he has a key. We could hear him cursing and smashing things in there. Evans and a footman are up there now, standing guard outside his door."

"Bring me my riding crop!" Arthur roared. "I'll teach that monster a lesson he'll never forget then chuck him out in the snow to find his own damned way back to London!"

"No!" Dorothea said. "I would like to see him hung, drawn and quartered, but we must avoid a scandal that would set all the county's ears a'buzzin' for months. No, we keep this in the family. He'll leave at first light. Barnicle, order the coachman to be ready."

Hearing the chair creaking as it turned towards the door, Chart hurried back to the staircase, retrieved his shoes and dashed upstairs. Before entering his bedroom, he glanced down the corridor to where two figures kept watch outside Pemb's chamber. He didn't really understand what he had overhead, but it was clear that his cousin had committed some grave crime.

He slept until the forenoon next day. When he went down to breakfast his father and grandmother halted their whispered conversation.

"Pemb's gone," Arthur stated with no further explanation.

"Never speak his name in this house again!" Dorothea rasped, face pale and hands more palsied than Chart had seen them before.

***

Pemb's rape of the chambermaid marked the beginning of Lady Dorothea's rapid decline. She took to her bed, shunning the remainder of the seasonal festivities, which Chart enthusiastically participated in. Arthur reluctantly accompanied him at his mother's urging, knowing that she was still hopeful that he would meet a suitable woman who could quickly bring an heir into the world.

After Twelfth Night, Dorothea grew despondent at the realisation that Arthur was unlikely to produce a legitimate heir and that the despised Pemb seemed destined to succeed to the title and estate. As she lay in bed, nightcap covering sparse white hair, chilled to the bone despite the coal fire in the grate and regularly replenished warming pans, she thought about her regrets and sorrows, comparing them to rare times of fleeting happiness. Although her austere character would not allow her to express it, she loved Arthur deeply despite her disappointment and bafflement at his contrariness which she blamed on too much reading, especially about that foolish subject he called Enlightenment.

With the approach of Easter and Chart's impending departure for school in London her depression grew. She knew in her failing old heart that she would miss him terribly. She had grown inordinately fond of the boy. He would indeed have been the perfect grandson and heir if it were not for his birth on the wrong side of the blanket … and his colour.

What of the lad's future? Arthur was maddeningly lackadaisical about his son's path in life, seemingly unconcerned about the huge social barriers that would confront him because of his illegitimacy and mixed race. Arthur wanted Chart to matriculate at his old Cambridge college, Peterhouse, and become an academic, but Dorothea knew the young man had no interest in furthering his education beyond public school and had his heart set on being a soldier.

Over the past two years, Dorothea had discretely written to trusted friends and relatives, including her cousin William Bensley, a director of "John Company"- the Honourable East India Company. She had discovered that coloured men, however well-educated and gentlemanly, could never hope to become British Army or Royal Navy officers regardless of how much their families were willing to pay for commissions. Bensley advised her that he knew of several mixed-race gentlemen of West Indian origin who, after lengthy petitioning and certain "fees" being paid, had been accepted as cadets in the service of John Company's army.

As long as they're not too black in appearance, he had warned.

She called Arthur to her bedside on several occasions, speaking with him at length, soliciting his promise to read her collection of letters regarding Chart, and relating her post-mortem wishes. Arthur cheerily assured her that she would soon be on the mend, but Dorothea knew better.

On Yew Sunday Dorothea awoke from a troubled sleep with a raging soreness in her throat. The doctor came that afternoon, diagnosed a quinsy, and opened a vein to bleed four ounces into a pewter bowl. He came each day during Holy Week to bleed her and attempt remedies including gargling with a mixture of molasses, vinegar and butter, swabbing her throat with a salve and a preparation of dried beetles, and inhaling a steam of vinegar and hot water. By good Friday morning she was so weak that she could barely open her eyes.

Lady Dorothea bade her personal maid to arrange candles on every flat surface of her room, then summoned Arthur and Chart to sit either side of her bed. She fought hard to maintain lucidity. Arthur asked if she wanted the parson but she whispered that the time had passed for both the doctor and the priest. Arthur read from the Book of Psalms, which seemed to bring her some comfort.

As darkness fell outside, the replenished candles began a strange guttering. She extended her arms, and her son and grandson each took one of her trembling hands, the bones birdlike in fragility. She turned her face slightly towards Chart and smiled.

"My boy," she said, then with great effort swung her head to Arthur.

"Take good care of him."

Chapter 4

Through his tears, Arthur had clipped locks of his mother's hair before her body was washed by the servants, shrouded and lifted into the walnut coffin for the wake. He sent the hair in an envelope to a silversmith in Melton to be made into memento mori for him and Chart. He regretted not taking a swatch of Weju's lustrous black hair, thinking that a relic would stave off the dissolving of her features from his memory.

They were still in mourning dress as the family coach carried them to London. With his mother gone, and Chart to be at school, Arthur could not bear to remain at Knossington. He engaged a land steward to manage the farms, collect rents and continue the efficient running of the estate as he had promised his mother. The Hall was left in the capable hands of the butler and housekeeper. Arthur's valet and the cook rode with them to augment the staff at the Chesterfield Street house.

During the journey south, Arthur tried to prepare Chart for his matriculation at Westminster. The boy was excited about starting school, only half-listening to his father's experiences there and his attempt to explain the bewildering range of rules, the fagging, and the expected abuse. Arthur's decision to move to London was largely due to his desire to protect Chart from what he knew would be more than the usual maltreatment due to his mixed ethnicity. The young man's life in Leicestershire had been largely free of racist animosity, partly because of his father's status as an aristocrat and large landowner, but also because people who came to know Chart not only accepted him but liked him for his engaging personality.

While a comparatively large number of Black, Indian and mixed-race persons lived in London, Arthur knew that prejudice was rife and that this would especially be the case at a public school such as Westminster where English homogeneity was so pervasive that even Scots and Irish were considered outsiders. A contemporary of his at the school had been a coloured Jamaican youth named Robert Dalzell, who endured an extraordinary amount of cruel treatment but managed to survive, unlike an effeminate boy who drowned himself in the Thames.

Arthur was deeply apprehensive about Pemb's presence at the school, and wished that he had chosen Eton or Harrow rather than his alma mater. Pemb was a King's Scholar – a boarder – whereas Chart would live at home on Chesterfield Street as a Town Boy, or day student. Arthur fretted that there was no proper way to prepare his son; he hoped that he had the fortitude to rise above what was to come.

On the morning of his first day of school, Chart refused to be driven in the new-fangled French-style cabriolet or allow his father to accompany him. Clad in a dark green suit and simple cocked hat without braid, he left Chesterfield Street at seven-thirty, savouring the sense of freedom as he avoided horse droppings on Piccadilly, strolled down St. James's Street and across the Mall into the Park, where vagabonds lay asleep under cherry and apple trees, their figures dusted with pink and white blossoms.

He was introduced to the bewildering community of Westminster School upon entering Great Dean's Yard, which he soon learned was always called the Green. A student in a trencher and open gown rushed up and screamed at him to remove his hat. As Chart stood stupefied, the boy muttered "Not done, Blackie," knocked the hat off and stormed away to confront another newcomer. Chart retrieved his tricorne and proceeded towards the grimy stone entrance, crudely incised with student's names and dates. Boys in gowns and street clothes dashed about the Green or stood in clusters but Pemb did not appear to be among them.

He joined a bunch of chattering, equally perplexed-looking new boys, who fell silent as they noticed his exotic appearance. One spat on the ground and another remarked "What's a blackamoor doing here?" They were all distracted by a commotion at the archway between Great and Little Dean's Yard where a large crowd of shouting students parted like a shoal of herring as a dour man in a gown wearing an enormous white periwig emerged followed by versions of him with progressively smaller wigs. "'tis the Headmaster, Dr Vincent," a boy whispered, forgetting about Chart as the dour presence approached. "My brother says he's plaguely severe!"

The Headmaster and lesser masters made their stately progress into the school room, followed by a horde of jostling boys who assumed a semblance of order once inside the cavernous hall, the walls of which were adorned with generations of graffiti. Chart was elbowed in the ribs a few times but thought it was impersonal as he noticed other new boys pummelled as well.

As Chart entered, he saw a tall young man with neatly clubbed red hair kneeling on a small square in the centre of the room, his first glimpse of Lord Hugh Drummond. Lord Hugh read Latin prayers from an ancient breviary as the masters knelt in a line of precedence behind him. When he finished, the Headmaster was helped to his feet by the Undermaster and sat in an elaborately carved chair at the top of the room. After affixing a pair of spectacles to his beaky nose, he consulted a scroll and began calling out the names of new boys, each of whom warily approached and stood in the centre of the hall while he examined them, asking questions in Greek and Latin. The students stumbled through parsing and translations. Following whispered consultation with the Undermaster, each boy was assigned to a different form based on his proficiency.

"Charteris Minor," the Headmaster called.

A buzz swept through the assembled youths as Chart squared his shoulders and marched up the hall ignoring sibilant jibes. He bowed to the Headmaster, who watched him with narrowed eyes over a deep frown. His examination was twice as long as the boys who preceded him, including translating passages from Aristotle's *Elenchi* and construing theme, verses and Virgil. For the first time, Chart saw the wisdom of his father's insistence that he familiarise himself with Mr. Busby's Westminster Grammars.

Dr. Vincent seemed disappointed when Chart answered each question unhesitatingly. "Upper Fourth," he said dismissively, and called the next name.

The master in charge of Chart's form, Mr. Wingfield,

beckoned him to join his group of boys. When the assembly ended and the Headmaster exited to the bows of students and masters, Wingfield called a boy whom he assigned as Chart's "Substance", while Chart was to be his "Shadow". It was explained that for the space of a week the Substance was responsible for the proper conduct of his Shadow to indoctrinate the new boy in the school hours, books to be obtained, lessons to be learnt, and to instruct him generally in all of Westminster's ceremonial rules and etiquette, both inside the schoolroom and out.

Chart's substance motioned to follow him out to the Green where he introduced himself as Fortescue Minor and explained that he could be punished if he was found to have neglected his duty in any way and would be held responsible for whatever offence was committed by Chart as if he were the culprit. He explained that Chart's first serious transgression had been wearing a hat into the Green, as all Town boys below the Sixth, and the two junior Elections of King's Scholars, were obliged to go bareheaded between breakfast and school, and between dinner and school.

Chart nodded solemnly, inwardly groaning at the absurdity.

Fortescue studied him for a few moments before blurting out.

"If ye don't mind me asking, what are ye, a Portugee?"

Chart fought a rising temper, on the point of snapping that he was an Englishman like the Substance, before realising that the boy meant no disrespect.

"Er, yes. Quite. Royal family on my mother's side."

Fortescue nodded and seemed on the point of bowing, but held out his hand instead. Chart was ashamed and tried to understand why he had lied.

That evening, as he walked the mile and a half to his father's townhouse, he was lost in thought, barely avoiding being ridden down by a troop of dragoons whilst crossing Birdcage Walk. Although he had not experienced overt hostility during the remainder of his first day at Westminster, he had been increasingly aware by the looks given him, the subdued conversations and shunning by many boys, that he was different. An alien. In Leicestershire he had never thought of himself as other than a young English gentleman even when he saw his light brown face in the looking glass.

Over the years of his young life, his father had told him about his mother, Weju, of her kindness and healing powers, as well as her quiet pride and strength. With tears in his eyes, Arthur described her resting place under the Royal Poinciana tree. He related stories Weju had told of her father – Chart's grandfather – Chatoyer, the great Black Carib chief, who had fought the British to a standstill on the island of St. Vincent and forced them to sign a peace treaty in 1773. Arthur had left him in no doubt that he considered Chatoyer a hero – the epitome of the noble savage – in contrast to his own father, whom he had despised.

That evening Chart shared a simple meal of cold tongue with his father. He described the events of his first day, then, with uncharacteristic tears flooding his eyes, he told of his lie to Fortescue after the series of small slurs which had combined to weigh on his soul.

Arthur struggled to contain his own emotions.

"I'm afraid that it was all to be expected. The world can be a cruel place regardless of whether one is rich or poor, black or white. I have strived to prepare you, but fear that I have failed."

He drew a deep breath.

"I realise that you are a warrior, like Chatoyer, and not a man of letters as I would have wished. You have a warrior's brave heart and you *can* endure. There will be times in your life when you feel you cannot go on, but you *must* always find the strength to triumph."

Arthur asked if he had encountered Pemb. Chart shook his head.

"You will, and you must be prepared for his torments. I have been deemed to be his guardian because I pay his school fees, and the headmaster sends me reports that Pemb spends more time loitering in Tothill Fields and St. James's Park with a pack of fellow miscreants than he does in the classroom. But the school is his only home, and he returns for meals and to sleep in the dormitory."

Chart had been forewarned to expect regular floggings for the most obscure infractions, and that even sons of the highest-ranking noblemen could not escape beatings. Town boys like Chart were also forced to serve as fags – personal servants – to a particular student in a higher form. In Arthur's time as a Westminster student, senior boys were considered weaklings if they were not cruel to their fags, and some of them had revelled in sadism that continued into later life. One of his classmates became a plantation owner in Jamaica and was killed by his slaves after torturing more than a dozen of them to death. Another Old Boy had committed unspeakable atrocities against American civilians while serving as a British officer during the recent Revolution.

Despite his father's warning, Chart was unprepared for the ordeal that began the following day.

Like a flock of slovenly crows, Pemb stood just inside the Green with a handful of other boys in black gowns and mortarboards. They quickly surrounded him, blocking his way.

"Coloureds ain't allowed in here," Pemb hissed. "Servants' entrance is round the back in the alley."

Chart clenched his jaw and tried to force his way through. Pemb immediately swung his fist, which landed on Chart's shoulder. Another boy tripped him and he tumbled to the stone courtyard, grabbing Pemb's gown so that he fell with him. In soaring rage Chart punched his cousin with both fists while the other boys kicked at him, rarely connecting as the two rolled on the ground.

"Enough you little buggers!"

A tall red-headed youth pushed into the fray, thrusting aside the kickers to reach down and haul Chart and Pemb upright by their ears. Chart recognised him as Lord Hugh Drummond who had led the morning prayers the previous day. Fortescue had told him that Drummond was Captain of the School and head monitor, responsible for making sure that all rules were enforced.

"Be off with you!" he roared at Pemb and his cronies. "That'll be six of the best for fighting on school grounds!"

As the others hurried away, he rounded on Chart.

"Name."

Chart told him. The older boy nodded.

"Heard about you. That cousin of yours is a wicked little sod." His fierce scowl softened. "Not a bad right hook there, but could be improved. Look, old man, sorry but you'll have to take your punishment like the others. I saw what they did, but rules are rules."

***

When you've never experienced corporal punishment, a first beating comes as a shock. Unlike most other boys of his age and era, Chart's father had refrained from disciplining him by hand or rod, and had forbidden his tutors to touch the boy in any way. That afternoon following dinner, the punishment ritual was convened. Floggings were administered before the whole school. Two lines of sullen students formed in the school room - Upper School boys at the right-hand side of the Headmaster's table, those from the Under School by the Undermaster at his chair.

In explaining what to expect, Fortescue said they were fortunate that the other masters had no punitive powers, except the unofficial ones of pulling hair or boxing ears. He suggested that if one pleaded "first fault" he could be let off today, but Chart brushed this aside and prepared to take the flogging while inwardly seething at the injustice. His only consolation was seeing Pemb's black eye when he turned in the Upper Line to glower at him.

When Chart reached the head of the line, the Headmaster solemnly accepted a Westminster Rod from the Undermaster. The Rod was a tight bundle of thin branches with a handle formed of the thicker parts of the twigs from which the fine ends sprouted forth besprinkled with buds. Chart held out his hands, palms down. The Headmaster looked at him malevolently, drew back his arm and slashed down, raising a welt on both hands.

By the sixth stroke Chart was biting his lip to keep from crying out. He stumbled back to his form and leaned against the wall. "Never mind," Fortescue whispered, "We all get flogged. Just the first of many, so best get used to 'em." Chart watched as Pemb and his friends approached the Headmaster. Even in the School Room's dim light, he saw that each of the boys was given only three, relatively mild, whacks with the rod, half the number dealt to him.

More humiliation came after lessons ended at five of the clock that afternoon. One of the junior monitors introduced him to a porcine youth named Hanley who Chart was to serve as a fag. Over the following days the senior made him run up and down the stone stairs to the kitchen to make hot rounds of toast and bring them to the common room. Other tasks were added such as fetching ham, eggs, potted meats and buns from Sutcliffe the grocer and Shotton the confectioner on Thieving Lane. One of the non-academic lessons Chart learned was that he did not have to buy Hanley's tuck using his half Guinea per week allowance. For several weeks he found this tolerable, especially as he saw that other junior Town Boys were subjected to similar servitude. Pemb and his gang avoided contact with him, except for occasional taunts and what they thought were monkey imitations. Fortunately, they spent little time at school.

Then things changed.

Fortescue, who was Chart's only crony because he still believed him to be Portuguese royalty, reported that Hanley had a bet going with Pemb and his gang to see how far Chart could be humiliated before he was "broken". Hanley ordered him to empty and clean his chamber pot, fly-ridden and overflowing with an accumulation of ordure. Chart refused and walked out of the room before the Senior could react. Next day, he was commanded to clean and polish Hanley's horse dung-encrusted boots. Again, Chart shook his head, but this time the older youth blocked his exit and cuffed him on the head until his ears rang while hissing "think you're too good to do slave's work, don't you!"

Hanley reported that Chart refused to fag for him, and for the following week he found himself in the Under line inching towards the Headmaster's flogging. At home, he did not mention the incidents to his father, although Arthur knew his son's heart was hurting more than his lacerated hands. Chart refused to discuss the cause of his unhappiness, and Arthur could not allow himself to probe into another's emotions without permission. Stoicism had been the foundation of their breeding for generations, and Chart had been equally indoctrinated.

His fagging duties returned to what was acceptable within the Westminster culture. Hanley curtly ordered him to carry these out whilst otherwise ignoring him. To escape from the school between classes, Chart took up rowing on the Thames. He pushed himself to the limit, often going as far as Putney or the pool of London. In the process, he built up the muscles in his arms and shoulders whilst burning off pent up wrath. On other days he roamed the wharves along both banks of the Thames, gazing longingly at the hundreds of ships moored in the river or alongside the quays, wondering which exotic ports they were bound for.

The early summer of 1788 was unusually hot and humid. Tempers frayed and fights on the Green were common. Westminster boys patrolled the Green, assaulting coalies, bakers, dustmen, sweeps and any other trespassers of the lower orders who dared to take a short cut across it. Soldiers were excepted because the previous year a jockey-sized hussar had put two Scholars who attacked him in the infirmary for a month.

Two days after Chart's fourteenth birthday and a week before the school's summer break, Hanley ordered him to go to the old bear garden in Tothill Fields to meet a man who owed him three guineas for a wager he had won. Chart was annoyed, having hoped to indulge in rowing during the fine long evening, but the command seemed reasonable enough. His hands were still scabbed after previously defying Hanley, and he didn't want to give him an excuse for another beating.

He left Palace Yard winding past the familiar sight of cinder women scavenging for coal and bones on the Tothill laystalls. Gaggles of ragged children watched him with dull eyes from their perches atop hillocks of dung collected from streets and houses. The bloated corpse of an infant lay half covered at the foot of a manure mound,its feet worried by skeletal dogs.

The bear garden was enclosed by a rotting wooden wall that had fallen in places. The gate was ajar and Chart could smell the mingled reek of decaying flesh and the communal privy inside.

"In 'ere," a muffled voice croaked. "Gotcher money 'ere."

In later years Chart would have trusted his instinct warning that danger lurked, but when one is barely fourteen and has lived a relatively sheltered life, naivete ruled. He stepped inside to see a hooded figure standing by a pile of benches. He sensed movement on his left and right, but before he could turn something slammed into the back of his head and he tumbled to the ground like a poleaxed ox.

Chapter 5

Racked with an excruciating headache amidst a reddish fog, Chart heard the voices.

"You've killed him, you bugger. Now there'll be hell to pay!"

"Nah," Pemb replied. "He's just out. This'll revive him."

Chart felt liquid splash into his face and smelled the ammoniac reek of urine, followed by laughter as he tried to move. His eyelids fluttered

"Bind his arms," Pemb ordered.

Chart felt his arms pinioned and bound tightly at the wrists. His legs were seized and he was dragged across the filthy ground to the public latrine which was nothing more than a malodorous ditch topped by a line of flimsy boards cut with holes. He managed to open his eyes despite the scarlet pain and kicked futilely at the boys who had dragged him. He recognised them as Pemb's gang, one of whom brandished a cudgel.

"Enjoy your refreshment, darky?" Pemb sneered. "Massa not so high and mighty now, eh?"

He bent to pick up Chart's silver-buckled shoes that had fallen from his kicking feet, glancing at them enviously before tossing them in the privy.

"Let's get to it before someone comes." He took an ivory handled razor from his pocket and snapped it open.

Galvanised by fear that his throat was about to be cut, Chart thrashed and snarled like the generations of bears that had been tormented by dogs on the site. He called for help but on Tothill Fields people knew to keep themselves to themselves.

"Hold his fucking head!" Pemb screeched. When Chart bit the fingers of the two boys trying to subdue him, Pemb kicked him until he had to be pulled away by his cronies.

"'struth," one said, "Now you've truly murdered him!"

***

Chart woke with a start, hands flying to his throat as if expecting it to be laid open like a second mouth. The sudden movement caused a massive wave of pain to cascade over him, from the soles of his feet to his head, which seemed to be covered. He tentatively raised his hand to discover that his cranium was shrouded in bandages.

"He's awake, sir," a voice said, and he opened heavy eyes to see his father's anxious face peering down at him, eyes awash with relief.

The doctor arrived half an hour later, examined him, and pronounced himself satisfied. "No reason to bleed or clyster him," he told Arthur. "Just a few cracked ribs and a great knot on his head, nothing broken. He's a strong lad and will mend quickly if he keeps out of trouble."

The doctor dosed him with laudanum and Chart slipped back into slumber. When he awoke again his father was sitting by the bed and the candles were lit.

"How … how long?" Chart rasped.

Arthur explained that he had been unconscious since he was found the previous evening by a cinder woman slumped in the jakes pit on Tothill Fields. Fortunately, there were only a few inches of shit and piss in the ditch, and he had been lying on his back with his face raised.

"Who did this, son?"

Chart told him everything he could remember.

"I-I thought they were going to cut my throat."

"They carved off your hair with the razor. That's why your head is bandaged. They cut you in the process."

Chart had never seen his father angry. Now Arthur's fury shocked him.

"Those scum left you for dead!" He stood up, trembling, and went out.

When he returned his wrath was even greater.

"Rousted that sorry excuse for a Headmaster out of bed! Flat out denied that Pemb and his scum had anything to do with the attack. Insists it must have been Gypsies or Irish thugs. Suggested that you may be advised to seek education elsewhere after the summer break!"

Two days later Chart had an unexpected visitor while his father was out.

"Lord Hugh Drummond," the butler announced.

Carrying one of the newly fashionable bicorne hats under his arm, Drummond strode into the room. Chart was embarrassed to be seen in bed and in his battered and bandaged state. Both young men eyed each other warily. Chart's heart was thumping, expecting Hugh, as Captain of the School, to formally tell him not to return.

"I know what happened," he said gruffly, and Chart saw that he was vexed. "The whole school knows because those villains are boasting about it. Inexcusably bad form all around.

"I spoke to the Headmaster but he refuses to send them down. One's father sits on the Privy Council and another's is an admiral. I suggested that at least Pemb should be expelled as a lesson to the others, but he's having none of it."

Chart sighed.

"Well, I suppose you're here to tell me that I'm not to return then, as the Headmaster suggested."

Hugh shook his head.

"Quite the contrary. You have every right to return, and you *must*. See here, Charteris, you can't let them get the better of you."

He stepped forward and laid an engraved calling card on the ormolu nightstand.

"I understand that you'll be off to the country soon. When you return, please let me know. I have an idea for a way to smooth your path at school."

***

Three weeks at Knossington worked wonders for the healing of Chart's body, if not his spirit. At the end of his first week in Leicestershire he forced himself to get on his horse, even though his aching body and healing ribs couldn't take more than a trot. By the time he and his father had to return to London, he could manage a good gallop without having to grit his teeth.

His lacerated scalp had healed, but the once luxuriant curly hair sprouted in patches. On their first day back in London Arthur took him to a peruke maker on Dover Street who fashioned a wig that was a remarkable semblance of his own hair. That evening he found Lord Hugh's card still on his nightstand. He recalled Drummond's rare expression of sympathy if not friendship, and on a whim dashed off a note informing him that he was back in London. A footman accepted the letter on a silver salver and took it to the address on the card.

On the night before his return to school Chart was sleepless from apprehension. When he entered the Green, Pemb and two of the other youths who assaulted him followed from the entrance to mock him.

"Got scalped by a red Injun, Blacky?"

"Yer kind ain't welcome here, guess yer too fuckin' stupid to learn that."

Other boys shook their heads sorrowfully as he passed. Even Fortescue shunned him. He made it through the day without a beating and was grateful that verbal abuse was forbidden in the classroom. At the end of lessons, he hurried away, not caring whether he was still expected to fag.

Chart had just entered Green Park when he heard a cry behind him. He spun nervously, expecting another attack, but saw Hugh Drummond hurrying towards him.

"Well, Charteris," he said, "You're looking better than last time we met. Do you mind if I walk with you?"

Their conversation was mainly one-sided, Drummond chatting about current events such as Parliament debating legislation to end the slave trade and King George seen wandering naked through Windsor Great Park. Chart grunted warily, not trusting anyone associated with Westminster. Hugh said that even though he was a King's Scholar, boarding at school, his family had a house nearby on Berkeley Square.

When they reached the corner of Chesterfield and Curzon Streets, Drummond surprised Chart by holding out his hand. After a moment's hesitation, Chart shook it. Drummond smiled.

"I say, old man, there's someone I'd like you to meet. Can you be at the Horse and Dolphin tomorrow around six? It's just off Leicester Square."

***

It was a working man's public house, and the fashionably dressed youth with the dark skin met some raised eyebrows when he stepped inside. The barman seemed to be expecting him and gestured towards a side door.

"Out back."

Chart was prepared for anything, wearing a small sword which he felt adept with after endless hours with a fencing master during his younger days.

The pub, which Chart learned was known as The Prad and Swimmer to its clientele, had once been a coaching inn, but now the courtyard held a makeshift ring of ropes tied to moveable wooden stanchions. Several men and boys sat on straw bales pushed under the eaves of the old stables.

"You won't need that," Hugh said, gesturing towards Chart's sword as he rose from a bale.

Chart's attention was focused on the man following him. At nearly five feet, ten inches, Chart was unusually big for his age, combining his father's height with his Garifuna grandfather's brawn, but the black man accompanying Hugh was a good four inches taller. He was elegantly dressed in an embroidered canary yellow coat and waistcoat over silk breeches the colour of robins' eggs. A white bag wig emphasised his grinning dark brown face.

"Mr. Charteris," said Hugh formally, "May I present my friend Bill Richmond, the celebrated pugilist. He's kindly consented to give you some pointers in the fine art of bare knuckles fighting."

***

Later that evening, after Richmond's first lesson in upright, semicrouch and full crouch stances, Hugh sat with Chart in a corner of the tavern and told him the black boxer's extraordinary story. Richmond was born a slave on Staten Island in the colony of New York. After the Americans rebelled against King George III, Lord Hugh's uncle, Earl Percy, commanded the royal forces in New York. Percy witnessed Richmond - then aged fourteen, the same age as Chart currently – fighting a trio of drunken Hessians who had insulted him. Percy was so impressed by the youth's pluck and prowess that he arranged fights with other British soldiers for entertainment. The Earl purchased Richmond's freedom and took him back to England with him, letting him live in his home, Alnwick Castle, paying for tutoring, and arranging an apprenticeship with a cabinet maker in York. After Percy succeeded to the Dukedom of Northumberland in 1786, Richmond and his family moved to London. The Duke lent him money to buy the pub, although Richmond now spent most of his time giving young gentlemen boxing lessons.

Over the next two months, Chart spent two or three evenings a week being trained by Bill Richmond. The pugilist's mild demeanour was deceptive; twice he saw him break up pub brawls like a whirlwind, knocking half a dozen drunks out with a few well-aimed punches and chucking them effortlessly into the street. He was patient with Chart, gently correcting his mistakes and praising his ability to learn quickly. Occasionally Hugh would arrive to observe the lessons, and stay to watch sparring between other young rakes, which sometimes ended with blackened eyes and bleeding noses. On alternate evenings, Chart returned to rowing, which Richmond encouraged to build up his strength and stamina.

One evening in early October, Hugh walked with him back to Mayfair, brusquely dismissing beggars, keeping cutpurses at bay with hands on the hilts of their swords and bantering with trollops who propositioned from dark alleys.

"Bill thinks you're ready, and I agree," he told Chart.

"Ready?"

He explained what he had in mind.

***

By the standards of a school that valued manly fist fights, the combat was epic, the source of legends for generations of Westminster boys. While duelling with pistols or swords was not allowed in the school precinct, bare knuckles fighting was not only tolerated but encouraged as a means of settling disputes.

In his role as Captain of the School and Chief Monitor, Lord Hugh approached Pemb and his four henchmen whilst they were idling on the Green between classes. He had waited until they were surrounded by a throng of other boys, whose jabbering hushed as he purposefully pushed through them. He drew himself up like a guardsman on parade, towering over Pemb.

"Charteris Minor challenges all five of you to fisticuffs. Monday week, half past five of the clock, on the Green."

***

On the appointed day, over a hundred students gathered around a chalk dust square on the Green, with several masters lurking on the fringes. A number of townsfolk watched from farther away, ladies and gentlemen mingling with milkmaids and off duty soldiers. The day was dry and warm for October, the sky overcast.

Accompanied by Hugh, Chart arrived coatless in a flowing white silk shirt and buff waistcoat matching his breeches. He was clad in soft leather pumps. His hair had regrown, but not enough to be tied in a queue. It framed his face like a curly black mane, which Hugh told him was "à la Titus" and becoming "wickedly fashionable".

Ten minutes passed while Hugh impatiently checked the time on his gold hunter. The crowd stirred as Pemb and three of his chums swaggered through it amidst a few cheers and a larger number of heckles about "the hunchback". Everyone at the school knew what had befallen Chart; while many of the students considered him an inferior due to his mixed race, unworthy of attending Westminster, the attack by Pemb and his fellows was beyond the pale. Everyone seemed to be betting, with odds heavily against Chart.

They halted just outside the chalk ring, standing shoulder-to-shoulder, sneering at Chart. In answer to Hugh's question about the whereabouts of their fifth confrère, Pemb said he was afflicted with the trots, raising hoots from the spectators.

"Well, he must be scared shitless," one wag called to the hilarity of other students.

One of Pemb's gang members had suggested that they draw lots to decide the order of fighting, but as their leader Pemb had chosen the array with himself last. He wasn't a fool, and was wary of his taller and stockier cousin. He had figured that his cronies could toy with Chart, successively wearing him down to the point where he could finish him off.

"Broughton's Rules," Hugh announced. "If one chap is knocked down, he has until the end of a count of thirty to get up or he loses. No biting, scratching, strangling, grasping or punching below the waist, and no kicking if one's opponent is on the ground. There are four of you and one of Charteris Minor, so he'll take you on one at a time."

He stepped back as the first youth sauntered arrogantly into the ring and raised his fists.

"Time for another haircut, Blackamoor?"

Both Richmond and Hugh had ceaselessly counselled Chart against letting wrath diffuse his fighting concentration, warning that his opponents would try to distract him with taunts. He took deep breaths to slow his pounding heart.

Richmond was a swarmer and had taught Chart the same technique of closing inside an opponent and overwhelming him with powerful, lightning-fast blows. Chart danced forward and hammered the boy in flurries of hooks and uppercuts that laid him flat on his back in less than a minute. There was a collective rumble of appreciation from the spectators, which rose to actual cheers as the next two gang members were dispatched as quickly, leaving one with a bloody nose and the other vomiting after a double punch to the solar plexus.

"Bloody hell," Hugh exclaimed from the side-lines, "three down in less than five minutes!"

Chart was barely winded although his knuckles were badly abrased despite following Richmond's advice to soak them in brine for an hour each day. With deep satisfaction, he saw fear in Pemb's eyes. His blemished face seemed paler than usual and his twisted spine more pronounced. Chart forced his lips into a wolfish smile that belied his nervousness.

Pemb hung back, reaching into his waistcoat pocket before raising clenched hands and stepping across the line. He sensed that his cousin's rage verged on incandescence and thought to provoke him into losing control.

"Filthy black bastard. Father's a sodomite and mother was a slave whore."

He stood his ground and let Chart advance on him as had done in the previous three fights. When they were two paces apart, Pemb flung the contents of his right hand into Chart's face.

The pepper blinded him. He automatically raised his hands to his eyes and Pemb moved in to deliver a double punch to his exposed abdomen.

"Foul!" cried Hugh, and as the crowd realised the trick it erupted in a chorus of boos and shouts of "For shame!"

Ignoring them, Pemb batted away Chart's protective hands from his face and slammed an uppercut into his jaw. He stepped back and grinned as Chart shook his head muzzily.

"Maybe you'll finally learn your place now, Black Boy."

Chart's self-control burst its banks like a raging torrent, releasing his pent-up outrage from the vicious attacks and humiliation. He wanted to kill. Despite his blurred vision and streaming eyes, he charged Pemb's hazy figure with an atavistic cry inherited from his Garifuna ancestors. He used every ounce of his strength to propel a straight punch to his cousin's face, accompanied by a left jab. Pemb staggered as Chart pounded an overcut onto the crown of his head accompanied by a left hook to the jaw. He collapsed like a stringless Punch and Judy puppet. Consumed with fury, Chart drew back his right foot for a kick but Hugh grabbed his shoulders and restrained him.

"Enough. He's finished in more ways than one."

Chapter 6

Pemb left Westminster the following day, sent down for the unforgivable sin of bad sportsmanship rather than habitual truancy and sadism. The Headmaster's decision was expedited by a letter from Sir Arthur Charteris, Bt, written two months earlier informing him that after the current term he would no longer pay his nephew's school fees and had ceased his guardianship.

Pemb's cronies were spared and they ceased tormenting Chart, who was now tolerated due to his pugilistic skills if not really accepted by his classmates. He was approached by some of the wealthier boys about exhibition fights, possibly in tandem with his friend Bill Richmond, but Chart was appalled by the suggestion. He had become a skilled cricketeer in Leicestershire, sometimes playing with Knossington youths against other village teams, but his request to join the school team was rebuffed. He had better luck with the Boat Club, the members of which valued his strong back and powerful stroke without concern about his ethnicity.

Hugh was studiously neutral towards Chart at school, but met up with him at the Prad and Swimmer a few times a month to watch Bill Richmond referee sparring matches and sit with the pugilist and some of his pupils afterwards over a pint of ale. Chart declined to continue his boxing training, but relished the all too brief times of camaraderie when he could let his guard down and feel that he was amongst friends. He was saddened when Hugh told him that he was leaving school at the end of Michaelmas term to join the Duke of Northumberland's old regiment the 5th Foot, his father having bought him a lieutenant's commission as a seventeenth birthday gift.

Chart envied him, trying to overcome bitterness that a career in the regular Army was closed to him because of his racial background. Over too many farewell flagons at Richmond's pub, Hugh told him that rumour had it Pemb was working for his tavern keeper grandfather on Cutthroat Lane in Shadwell fencing stolen goods using his posh accent and public school affectations to sell them to shops in Mayfair and St. James's.

**

At the beginning of the London Season in November 1789 Arthur began holding weekly evening gatherings, which he described using the French term *soirées* in his engraved invitations to demonstrate his sophistication to the artists, writers, politicians and those he considered enlightened members of the aristocracy. These varied from musical evenings with performances by the gifted young female pianist Theresa Jansen and violin concertos by Mr. Janiewicz, a refugee from France, to heated discussions about politics, especially the Revolution across the Channel. Arthur insisted that Chart attend the evenings to broaden his awareness of the world beyond Britain and meet people whom he hoped would have a positive influence. Knowing of his son's interests, he invited explorers and soldiers, including Captain Portlock, who had recently returned from circumnavigating the globe, and a series of John Company officers, resplendent in silver-frogged scarlet coats. As Arthur hoped, Chart gravitated towards the latter, who initially treated him with frigidity but thawed when relating tales of their adventures in Bengal and Madras.

Arthur was inspired by the French Revolution to become a radical thinker, although his aristocratic sensibilities were offended when he invited the militant pamphleteer Thomas Paine to attend a soiree and speak on the Declaration of the Rights of Man which had been decreed by French Revolutionaries the previous year. Paine, arriving late and inebriated, launched a verbal attack on his host and other attendees who owned plantations in the West Indies.

"Hypocrites!" he thundered, voice slurred. "How dare you fancy yourselves righteous from the comfort of your gilded drawing rooms when you keep multitudes of negroes in bondage with no rights, labouring from dawn to dusk in the most hellish conditions! Shame, oh shame! If you truly believed in the Rights of Man, you would free your slaves!"

The elegantly coiffed and attired ladies and gentlemen were stunned, not so much by Paine's accusations – which some agreed with – but by such outrageous behaviour in polite society. All eyes turned to Sir Arthur.

"S-sir," he stammered, "Your particular friend Thomas Jefferson wrote that to give liberty, or rather, to abandon persons whose habits have been formed in slavery is like abandoning children. I'm sure that we could all agree that giving them freedom would be casting them out to become public nuisances like the poor waifs on the streets of London, to die of starvation and be preyed upon by evil men. My own negroes on my Grenada plantation are better treated than the lower orders in this country!"

"Bah! Tom Jefferson is as much a hypocrite as ye all are! Despite proclaiming that all men are created equal, he claims that blacks are inferior to whites in the endowments both of body and mind. And, he has a gaggle of mulatto children with a slave woman, all of whom remain legally enslaved!"

As all eyes turned uncomfortably to Chart, Paine downed his glass of port and swept out of the room.

Arthur had more success in his quest to be recognised as a member of the intellectual set by advocating equality for women, which for him created fewer moral qualms than the abolition of slavery. London had a remarkable number of well-educated upper and middle-class women who espoused unorthodox views on religion, political and social equality, and – daringly – sexuality. Among his regular guests was Augusta, Dowager Countess of Rochester.

Age 36, Augusta was the widow of the 7th Earl who had been nearly forty years her senior. Her son, the 8th Earl (who actually had been sired by one of her many lovers, the putative father being homosexual) was safely packed off to Eton to allow her to indulge in the various liberties available to highborn ladies in London. One of her closest friends was the unorthodox writer Mary Wollstonecraft, who occasionally joined her at Arthur's Chesterfield Street circle. Sir Arthur was platonically smitten with Wollstonecraft, avidly reading her books and treatises and hanging on every word when she offered her opinions. Both agreed with Locke's creed that men and women should be treated as rational beings, and that a new social order founded on reason was the best hope for mankind. Augusta, who had a harder edge, considered them dreamers, whereas she believed that deeds mattered more than words and lived her life accordingly.

The moment that the Countess set eyes on Chart she decided to seduce him. She thought he was a remarkably handsome young man. He had his father's refined aquiline features, and the sapphire blue eyes seemed even brighter in a face which had been darkened deeper by his rowing on the Thames. She approached him as he stood rather awkwardly by the fireplace to elicit his views on the sensational news about the mutiny on HMS Bounty and his choice of literature. Chart was reticent, trying to keep his eyes from straying to Augusta's low décolletage while mumbling that he had little time for reading aside from Mair's *Introduction to Latin Syntax*. When he finally admitted to having an interest in exotic lands, she told him that she had just the book for him about Mr. Bruce's *Travels to Discover the Source of the Nile*. However, she said in a teasing low voice, he would have to come round to her house to collect it.

On a winter's day when the cobbles were sheened with ice and the new newspaper called *The Times* reported that over a hundred beggars had frozen to death so far that week, a wax-sealed letter addressed to Chart was delivered to Chesterfield Street. After he returned from school, he opened it, breathing in the perfume remembered from his encounter with Lady Augusta a few days earlier. In truth, like most boys of his age, he had fantasised about her, imagining the lush body beneath her gown whilst indulging in what the school chaplain called the sin of Onan.

He left school early the next afternoon and took a hackney to the address on Portman Square written in the letter. The butler took his hat, cloak and sword, before leading him up a wide marble staircase to a small drawing room, warmed by a log fire and set with a silver tea service. The butler bowed out, leaving him alone.

Lady Augusta floated in from the adjoining chamber wearing a diaphanous wrapper that caused Chart's pulse to race. She left tho door open and bade him sit at the delicate marquetry tea table.

The Countess considered seduction an art form, and she was as accomplished in its practice as she was on the spinet. She poured tea, offered a slice of quince tart, and toyed with him, appreciating his steadily increasing breathing as his fevered eyes roved her body. When she judged that he was at the peak of excitement, and not wishing the pistol to be discharged too early, she rose, took him by the hand and led him into her bedchamber.

They became friends as well as lovers, and Augusta took it upon herself to teach him that there was such a thing as the life of the mind as well as the body. She encouraged him to drop his stoic mask and reveal his heart. He confessed that he was "frightfully bored" with school and was keen to leave England, hoping to be appointed to a John Company cadetship later that year.

After gentle urging, usually following rounds of lovemaking with a teenage passion and stamina that she marvelled at, he unburdened the deep bitterness at his mixed ethnicity, how he sometimes hated his father and mother for cursing him with "blackness" for life. He desperately wanted to fit in to English society, but had come to realise that he would always be an outsider. She held him as he wept, kissing away his tears.

Unlike Chart's father, who chided him for missing school, Augusta agreed that years of Latin and Greek were a waste of time, and encouraged him to stay away as long as he did not lose his place. Nonetheless, she told him, time away from Westminster should still be spent in learning rather than idleness.

Her house became his refuge, where he would repair afternoons when he wasn't rowing or wandering through London. The Countess loaned him books from her fine library, expecting him to read and discuss them with her. She also took him to plays and concerts, usually with groups that included Sir Arthur.

In the early spring of 1790, she gave him a copy of *The Interesting Narrative of the Life of Olaudah Equiano*, the autobiography of a freed African slave. The book made him uncomfortable and he began to resent Augusta's enthusiastic questioning about his thoughts on it. She disregarded his complaints, rather haughtily telling him that he, especially, needed to have his eyes opened to the horrors of the slave trade.

Shortly before the end of the Season she took him to a shabby Quaker Meeting House to hear Equiano address the Society for the Abolition of the Slave Trade. The hall was packed with an eclectic blend of humanity, including mixed-race gentlemen dressed in the latest fashion, dour Quakers in plain grey, black men and women in threadbare clothes, and a host of gentry with religious fervour in their eyes. Discretely holding a silver-gilt pomander to her nose to ward off body odours, Lady Augusta led Chart to a circle of chattering people surrounding a middle-aged black man elegantly attired in a red coat. Conversation ceased as the Countess edged through the throng to be greeted by the black man's warm smile.

"Mr. Equiano," she announced, "this is the young gentleman I told you about, Alexander Charteris."

Rather than the customary bow, Equiano extended his arm and gripped Chart's hand firmly.

"Welcome," he said, "You must be pleased to be back amongst your own kind."

He seemed startled as Chart bristled, removed his hand, bowed and turned on his heel. Augusta shot him an angry look before regaining her composure and resuming her conversation. As Chart stood stiffly at the back of the hall with his emotions churning, an elderly white man with angular features and a receding hairline approached him.

"Granville Sharp. I corresponded with your father some years ago but we never met."

Chart accepted his proffered hand, wishing he could avoid further conversation.

"Such a tragedy about poor Phibbah," Sharp told him, face twisted as if in pain.

"Phibbah?" Chart hadn't thought about his *Mami* for years, but mention of her name revived dormant memories of a loving woman and bright tropical sunshine.

"Your father didn't tell you? I wrote to him about it, but I'm sure Sir Arthur is a very busy man."

He briefly related Phibbah's fate. Chart didn't know how to respond, so said nothing, leaving Sharp perturbed by what he thought was callousness. With a curt nod, Sharp returned to the eager congregation as someone announced that Mr. Equiano was about to speak.

Chart ignored Lady Augusta's gestures to join her near the speaker's podium. He listened to the first part of Equiano's lecture about his childhood in the Kingdom of Benin, enslavement in the Caribbean and Virginia, and service in the Royal Navy. He spoke in a clear voice with a sing-song West Indian accent that dredged more memories from the recesses of Chart's mind. His chest tightened. Grabbing his hat and cloak, he hurried outside to lean against the brick wall and draw deep breaths. The Countess found him there an hour later.

"You embarrassed me!" she hissed. "How dare you behave so rudely"

"Why did you bring me here?"

"Why? I am trying to help you accept who you are, which you confided that you struggle with. These are *your* people, not because of your racial background but because they accept you as a person without prejudice. They can be your friends whereas others will always turn their backs on you!"

"They are *not* my people!"

He walked quickly away so that Augusta could not see his stifled sobs.

The Countess was angry for several days, then reminded herself that Chart was only fifteen years old and was torn between two worlds - one in which he could never really belong, and the other in which he did not want to belong. She sent notes as a peace offering, but he did not reply. The books he borrowed were returned by one of his father's footmen, with Equino's *Interesting Narrative of the Life* on top.

***

Chart formally ended his unhappy sojourn at Westminster School at the end of Lent term 1790, although in reality he had barely been a presence there for months. Arthur had devoted considerable time and effort, albeit reluctantly, to carry out his mother's wishes to secure a cadetship for Chart in the East India Company Army. Dorothea's kinsman Sir William Bensley was still a director, and after the conveyance of a few gratuities such as a small coffer of gold Louis d'or coins, an emerald and diamond necklace, and a racehorse reputed to be the son of the famous thoroughbred, Eclipse, an examination appointment was scheduled for Chart at East India House on Leadenhall Street. Arthur surmised that the timing of his son's candidacy was auspicious as the East India Company was again at war with the Kingdom of Mysore in southern India, and fresh officers were needed to replace those few who died in combat and the many more who succumbed to disease.

In keeping with the John Company's conservative tradition, he arrived wearing a powdered wig, a modest dark blue broadcloth suit and white kid gloves to conceal the dark skin of his hands. His nervous father had engaged a fey little man from the Theatre Royal, Drury Lane, to powder his face to make it appear lighter.

Chart was made to wait in the vestibule outside the Directors Court Room. When summoned, he executed a perfect bow in front of Bensley and two other Directors who were the beneficiaries of Sir Arthur's consideration. They asked some perfunctory questions about his school (happily, one was a Westminster Old Boy), and whether he could ride, shoot and wield a sword. They seemed more interested in his physical appearance. After the brief questioning, Chart overheard one say "Not as black as I'd thought he'd be," answered by Bensley muttering, "Exactly. He'll do. Are we in agreement?" Bewigged heads nodded, Chart bowed again, executed an about turn that would have done credit to a Guards officer, and marched out, barely concealing his glee.

He promptly went to Anthony Marcelis, the military tailor on Suffolk Street, Charing Cross, to be measured for uniforms. He spent the rest of the day visiting Thurkle & Sons, cutlers, to choose a fine cut and thrust sword of Solingen steel, then spent two pleasant hours in Mr. Cuff's shop on St. James's Street where he chose a brace of silver-mounted pistols. Cuff, who was also an optician, also sold him a pair of tinted spectacles which he claimed were all the rage for British officers serving under the Indian sun.

Chapter 7

Arthur planned a grand jollification at Knossington Hall to celebrate Chart's 16th birthday and his departure for India in the autumn. He had no patience for frivolity and no idea how to organise balls, formal dinners and the other festivities expected for the son of a wealthy baronet. He wrote to several aristocratic lady friends including Lady Augusta, asking if they could come to help. All declined except for Georgiana, Duchess of Devonshire, who loved planning parties and eagerly seized any opportunity to escape from her husband.

Sir Arthur was deeply melancholy about Chart's military service in India. He had a persistent premonition that he would never see his son again, knowing of the fearsome mortality rate from disease among Europeans – even those of mixed race – as well as the perils of the long sea voyage around the Cape of Good Hope and the added risk of death and maiming for soldiers. He could not confide his fears to Chart, who was happier than he had been for years at the prospect of a life of adventure with the John Company. The young man's spirits had also brightened upon leaving London, which Chart associated with bigotry and disappointment. Although Chart had been an accepted member of the rural Leicestershire community since childhood, Arthur knew that his son would never be considered as a true equal by the gentry or a potential spouse for their daughters.

**

The Honourable Arabella Sherrard was the second youngest of eleven children born to an impoverished Rutlandshire viscount who had little beyond his pedigree, a haunted medieval manor house, paltry rents from his remaining acres and mountainous debts. Her elder brothers had gone into the Army with scant chance of promotion beyond subalterns because their father was unable to buy field grade commissions. The young officers prayed for war with France so they could fill the boots of more senior officers.

The viscount could not afford even a pittance of a dowry, so most of his eight daughters were doomed to spinsterhood – thornbacks, in the vulgar term for old maids used by the lower classes. Arabella's eldest sister had considered herself fortunate to wed the son of a textile mill owner, and another was envied when asked for her hand by the elderly vicar of Heckington. But the marriage well seemed to have run dry for Arabella and her remaining sisters, who spent most days doing needlepoint and reading by the light of tallow candles and nights listening to ghostly footsteps traipsing the hallways.

If she had been beautiful, like her father's kinswoman the Duchess of Devonshire, she may have had better luck finding a husband despite her penury. The burgeoning mercantile class in London, Bristol and Manchester were keen to move up in social status by marrying sons and daughters into the aristocracy. But there was a glut of upper-class girls on the market, some of whom had dowries, and Arabella would never be described as beautiful, or pretty for that matter. For those who knew her well, her plainness was overcome by vivaciousness and quick wit. Needlepoint and novels such as Ann Radcliffe's *Sicilian Romance* bored her to tears.

In her case, being a member of the nobility was a curse. Approaching her 16th birthday, Arabella had resigned herself to either being a doddering old auntie to the children of whomever inherited the estate (if any of her brothers survived to sire another generation) or becoming a companion to a lady of equal aristocratic status.

Arabella's passion was riding. Fortunately for her, even the poorest nobleman *had* to have horses, and while the viscount's stable wasn't of the best quality, he hunted regularly with the Belvoir. Women were not allowed to hunt, but this was of no concern to Arabella who had her pick of the stable and took better care of the half dozen horses than the sole remaining groom, a toothless septuagenarian. She detested riding side-saddle, preferring to sit astride wearing her brothers' old breeches. If her mother were alive she would have been scandalised, but the poor woman, exhausted by decades of child-bearing, had died of typhoid fever five years earlier. Her father couldn't have cared less about how she spent her time; she sometimes wondered if he could even remember her name and those of her siblings except for the boys.

She and her sisters were rarely invited to balls, so the invitation from the Duchess of Devonshire on behalf of Sir Arthur Charteris caused a flurry of excitement followed by anguished cries of "what can we *possibly* wear?" They scoured the attics and cupboards for ball gowns that hadn't been nibbled by mice or ruined by leaks. Fortunately, a tinker had sold them a dog-eared copy of *Magasin des Modes Nouvelles, Francaises et Anglaises* for December 1789 and the girls were able to use their sewing skills to remake dresses from decades earlier into ballgowns which they hoped would be *á la mode*.

The viscount's coach had succumbed to age and rot, and the sisters could not bear the humiliation of taking the manor's last functioning vehicle – a farm wagon – to the ball. The Duchess kindly sent her personal calash to carry the girls the short distance to Knossington on the early afternoon of the ball, where they were ensconced with their portmanteau of gowns in one of the Hall's sixteen bedrooms.

Knossington did not have a formal ballroom and the event was held in the Great Hall which had never been intended to accommodate over two hundred guests plus a string quartet and servants. By the time Arabella and her sisters descended from their room nervously fluttering their fans, the ballroom was a stifling miasma stoked by the hot June night, a plethora of lighted candles, and the cloying scent of perfumes worn to mask the majority of people who thought bathing more than once a month was excessive. Arabella took one look at the press of bodies at the doorway and escaped to the terrace outside where half a dozen swooning ladies were draped over chairs.

Silk gown swishing on the flagstones, she walked to the balustrade overlooking the park. In the semi-darkness she failed at first to notice a tall figure in what appeared to be a uniform. She hesitated. Seeming to sense her presence, the figure turned.

"Oh, I-I beg your pardon," she stammered. "I did not see you there in the darkness."

"I blend in," a young man's voice answered with what

sounded like a touch of irony.

An awkward silence followed. Well brought up ladies weren't supposed to speak to men unless they had been formally introduced. She was on the point of curtseying and moving away when he said "Did you enjoy the dancing."

Oh tosh, she thought, *what difference does it make?*

"I prefer not to be baked alive inside. And … to be honest, I'm not really one for dancing." This was not quite true; Arabella loved dancing, especially the country dancing still popular in Leicestershire among all classes, but she had never been asked to dance by a man at the few balls she had attended.

Her companion chuckled.

"My feelings too. Although I did manage to partner the Duchess in a gavotte for the opening dance without tripping over my feet."

She remembered the invitation from the Duchess of Devonshire, and realised who she was talking to.

"Oh, you're …."

"Chart." He took two steps back and made an elegant leg, allowing her to see his face for the first time in the light cast from the windows. "*Le célébrant d'anniversaire.*"

***

They spoke past dawn, with occasional interludes for Chart to fetch glasses of punch and collations from the buffet. The music and dancing had ended hours before but a few hardy souls wandered the grounds, bottles in hand, until collapsing to snore on the grass. They giggled as hungover couples furtively emerged from the bushes, attempting to smooth rumpled clothing.

Aside from her brothers, who generally ignored her, Arabella had never had an intimate conversation with a man of her own generation, or *any* man for that matter. As the rising sun fully revealed Chart, her pulse quickened. In his high-collared scarlet coat with royal blue facings, she thought him immeasurably handsome. His luminous sapphire eyes caught the rising sun, and his brown face with its regal nose and full lips reminded her of engravings of Roman emperors or Indian nawabs.

But as the day brightened she felt pangs of trepidation, fearing that once he saw her plainness his seeming interest would quickly wane.

Chart was captivated by her. He had learned to suppress his desperate loneliness, the omnipresent sense of being an outcast. Even at the opening of his birthday celebration the previous evening, he knew that behind the smiles and toasts the guests were seeing him as an inferior being, a blackamoor bastard elevated beyond his natural station in life by a father who lacked good sense. Looking at Arabella, he didn't see her as a plain teenage girl in a somewhat shabby ballgown but as a person who shared his interests in riding and thirst for adventure. Beyond that, he found her physically attractive and was equally apprehensive that she would reject him once his complexion became obvious.

She reluctantly said that she must retire to her room to catch some rest. Chart escorted her to the foot of the staircase and watched her climb. When she looked at him over her shoulder from the landing, his heart leaped.

That afternoon he was waiting by the calash as Arabella and her sisters emerged from the Hall to make the journey home. He bowed to each simpering sister as they climbed into the carriage. Arabella was last, and he took her hand and kissed it while pressing a note into her palm, much to the other girls' amusement.

***

Two days later he appeared in the forecourt of the crumbling manor house at the hour stipulated in his note. Arabella led her favourite chestnut mare around from the stable block. She was amused when his eyes widened in surprise upon seeing her attired in buckskin breeches and a scarlet light dragoons coat that an uncle had worn in the American war. She swung into the saddle and grinned as she saluted him under her small cocked hat.

They rode together most days, and she missed him when thunderstorms interrupted their assignations. The Knossington cook packed what the French called a *pique-nique* which Chart carried in panniers slung across his gelding's withers. They explored deep into Lincolnshire and Northamptonshire, counties where they would not be recognised, unlike Leicestershire and Rutland. Their favourite place became a chapel in a deserted village depopulated by the local lord 200 years earlier. It was there that they kissed for the first time, and where a week later they made love on a quilt that Chart carried rolled behind his saddle in anticipation of their coupling. Afterwards, Arabella lay in his arms and cried because she knew her happiness would soon end.

They had spoken honestly about the hopelessness of their romance. Arabella's family, like other aristocrats, may have tolerated a brief dalliance with a mixed-race man, especially as she was considered unmarriageable and therefore of no value for dynastic purposes. But a deeper alliance would create a scandal that would tarnish the family name as badly as running off with a costermonger or gypsy.

And Chart had always been honest with her about his determination to go to India.

She tried her best to hide her broken heart when they parted a week before Chart's departure for London in mid-September. As young lovers do, they promised to write, but both knew even at their tender ages that time and vast distances would render that impractical.

After several sleepless nights and no appetite for days, Arabella wrote a letter to Chart that laid bare her love. Swearing the elderly groom to secrecy, she ordered him to take the letter to Knossington, paying him two silver sixpences for his trouble. Unfortunately, the groom stopped off en route to drink away the sixpenny bits, arriving at Knossington the day after Chart's departure. Mrs. Titchmarsh, the housekeeper, placed the message in an escritoire in Chart's bedroom to await what she hoped would be his return.

***

Arthur went with Chart to Portsmouth. On a fine late summer's evening the day before Chart was to board the *Ponsborne*, East Indiaman, they sat in the Dolphin tavern's garden sharing a bottle of madeira and a fish pie. Something compelled Chart to look closely at his father, more so than he had ever done in the sixteen years of life he had shared with the man. He noticed the greying hair and the lines in the face that was so like his own. Arthur noticed his gaze, and the identical blue eyes, now bright with tears. Chart's heart squeezed as if in a giant's fist. Both men yearned to embrace the other but were restrained by the mores of time and place.

Chapter 8

Seringapatam, Kingdom of Mysore
India
February 1792

By late afternoon the Sultan's Redoubt was a charnel house
after repulsing four attacks by Mysorean forces. The bodies of
dead British regulars and John Company sepoys had been piled
against a gun carriage to block the little fortification's entrance,
but the bloating corpses had been pulverised by enemy cannon
fire. Now Indian and English flesh, blood, shit and shattered
bones were commingled in a stinking melange. The wounded
had been dragged to decreasing shade as the sun rose higher.

Cries for water diminished as men died. There was no water
for the injured or the dwindling number of defenders, and only
a few rounds of ammunition left for the latter. The men's
muskets were fouled with burnt powder. Some resorted to the
time-tested method of urinating down the weapons' barrels to
clean them, but even bladders had run dry.

Lieutenant Charteris of the First Bengal Native Infantry
Regiment took off his lacquered straw hat and used it to fan a
dying havildar whose legs under the short trunks worn by
sepoys had been shattered by a round shot. Chart looked around
the redoubt, counting less than fifty men out of the original two
hundred who were still able to heft a musket. He realised that
he was his company's sole surviving European officer.

"Abandoned!" a British private ranted. "Old Cornwallis
forgot us!"

"Silence man!" his platoon commander barked. "We'll be
relieved soon."

"Fuck you, Rupert!"

The young subaltern leaped up, brandishing his sword. "Put
that man on report for--." He was flung backward by a shot from
an enemy jezail that tore through his chest.

The insubordinate infantryman spat towards the dead man and

laughed.

The enemy cannonade stopped, which Chart knew meant that another attack from Tipu Sultan's army was imminent. He looked around for his unit's subadar, the senior native non-commissioned officer. "Man the ramparts," he ordered, and the bearded soldier in a braided red coat repeated the order in Bengali. Eleven exhausted sepoys rose and followed the NCO to the wall. Chart picked up a .76 calibre musket and a leather pouch containing four waxed paper cartridges and joined his men, shoulder-to-shoulder with the British soldiers. Their fear was palpable as they watched a horde of the enemy congregate in the distance.

Chart took out one of the cartridges and used his teeth to rip off the end. He held the heavy lead ball in his mouth, tasting the salty gunpowder, as he flipped open the musket's pan, sprinkled a dab of powder and snapped it shut. With an eye on the wave of advancing enemy troops, he poured the rest of the gunpowder down the barrel followed by the cartridge paper, spat the ball into the muzzle, then pulled out the ramrod from its brass ferules under the barrel and rammed the charge down tight.

All done in less than twenty seconds, he thought with incongruous pride despite awareness that he could die within the next few minutes.

"Cavalry?" a British regular officer said in a puzzled tone.

"Blimey," a sergeant answered. "Must be a couple thousand of 'em."

The horsemen advanced at a canter. Trumpets halted them in a cloud of dust just outside musket range. Several hundred turbaned men dismounted, drew their talwars, and charged waving the swords overhead.

"Steady!" the senior surviving British officer called. "Wait for my order!"

The British India pattern muskets had a target point range of 100 yards, and the officer perfectly timed his order to fire. The besieged troops broke the charge with two volleys, then exhausted their ammunition pouring fire into the Mysorean soldiers as they retreated in disorder, leaving scores of dead and wounded on the field.

"That's it then," the insubordinate private said, upending his empty cartridge pouch. "Another charge by the buggers and we're well and truly fucked."

But the dead subaltern's prediction proved correct. After night fell, the redoubt was relieved by the Commander-in-Chief, Lord Cornwallis, leading six battalions with bandsmen in the vanguard playing the Grenadiers' March.

***

Chart was stumbling from fatigue as he led his men to the vast British encampment in the Cauvery Valley two miles outside the walls of Tipu Sultan's city of Seringapatam. They commandeered a bullock cart to carry the eight wounded; its load was lightened after three of the men died en route, their bodies carried off the road rather than dumped in ditches with numerous other casualties.

Upon reaching their lines, he ordered the sepoys to take the wounded to the hospital area before finding his way to the bell tent he had shared with another officer before the man's death from cholera. After drinking from a large waterskin suspended from a pole, he collapsed onto his folding charpoy bed and closed his eyes while his khidmatgar - servant - pulled off his boots and bathed his feet. Chart was just drifting into sleep when someone called to him from the tent opening.

"Charteris sahib."

The regimental clerk, an Anglo-Indian with blue eyes like his own, stepped inside, saluted and handed him an oilcloth packet with several wax seals. It was addressed to Chart in care of his regiment. He was intrigued that underneath was written "By Express Command of the Directors of the Honourable East India Company."

"It came with the Governor-General's dispatches from Calcutta," the clerk said, unable to conceal his curiosity. "So quickly! Only six days by the post riders!"

Dismissing the man, Chart used a penknife to break the seals. Inside were two letters and a bank draft for 200 guineas drawn on C. Hoare and Company. He opened the top letter, noting it was from B. Cave, Esq., and read "Dear Sir, it is with the greatest regret that I must inform you …."

And Chart's world turned upside down.

***

Chart lay on his charpoy for two days after receiving the letters, unable to move except to sip tea brought by the khidmatgar. The First Bengal's Scottish adjutant stopped by when he failed to show for parade, but left him alone assuming that the teenage subaltern was experiencing the nervous and mental shock that many others – including himself – had confronted after days of heavy combat. He did not know that Chart was in the depths of profound grief at news of his father's death.

At first, Chart could not comprehend that the man who had been at the centre of his existence was gone. The words of the family lawyer's letter were etched on his mind, so he could visualise them with his swollen eyes closed. His father had died over six months earlier, not long after Chart had stepped ashore at Calcutta. Mr. Cave reported that Sir Arthur had "met his end after being set upon by footpads while taking the air in Hyde Park." The lawyer wrote that the will had not been formally read but that a "most disturbing" challenge to it was made shortly after the late baronet's interment at Knossington. As the primary beneficiary, it was imperative that Chart return to England at his earliest convenience. For that reason, the enclosed letter from Sir William Bensley, East India Company director, should be presented to his commanding officer to secure his furlough and used as *laissez-passer* for passage by the most expeditious means. The bank draft would cover his expenses.

In the disordered depths of his grief, Chart considered ignoring the lawyer's summons and turning his back on England forever. He was forging a career in India, however difficult and dangerous the military service and the fragility of life generally. The sepoys under his command seemed to respect him. They gave nicknames to their officers; one of the British officers in his regiment was the "Prince" sahib, another was known as the "Camel" because he had a long neck, while a captain was called "Damn" sahib because he always preceded orders with the expletive. The men called Chart "Pathan" sahib, likening him to the northern frontier warriors because of his blue eyes, hawklike profile, and fierce fighting ability. Through the attrition of combat and disease, Chart had quickly won promotion to lieutenant.

While he had no close friends among officers in the First Bengal and other regiments, he knew that he had earned their respect as well. Many were outcasts or misfits like himself, and he had met a few other mixed-race West Indians trying to escape racism in England and the Caribbean sugar islands. Those officers who treated the native soldiers under their command with contempt seemed to have a higher mortality rate than ones who were liked by the sepoys, with mysterious deaths and disappearances commonplace.

Through the pain of his splintered heart he asked himself what his father would want him to do. He recalled Arthur's premonitory statement that although there would be times in his life when he felt he could not go on, he believed that his son would always find the strength to triumph over adversity. Mr. Cave had stated that Chart was the primary beneficiary of Sir Arthur's will - he could not selfishly ignore his father's last wishes, especially as he was being asked to return to resolve whatever problem was affecting his testament.

On the morning of the third day he ordered his orderly to fetch hot water. After bathing and shaving, he donned his least patched and stained uniform and sought out the regiment's adjutant. The major didn't quibble after reading the letter from Sir William Bensley. While the John Company army was under the nominal command of Lord Cornwallis, the Governor-General of India, they were not soldiers of the Crown like the British regulars who fought alongside them. They were under the supreme authority of the East India Company and the order of a civilian director was subject to unquestioning obedience.

After consulting with Cornwallis' staff, who were engaged in tightening the siege of Tipu Sultan's capitol, it was decided that Chart would carry dispatches to London. Rather than undertake a long and perilous journey to Calcutta, Chart was directed to go to the nearest large west coast port, Mangalore, where it was likely he would find a ship bound for England.

Mangalore was 156 miles from Seringapatam, a three- or

four-day journey by horseback under good conditions. The Mysorean light horse were a constant threat, ranging at will throughout the countryside, attacking British supply lines and cutting down stragglers. A squadron of the Nizam of Hyderabad's irregular cavalry was detailed to escort Chart. They were shadowed by Tipu's horsemen but avoided a fight and made good time to Mangalore where Chart presented his letter to the chief John Company official at the fort overlooking the harbour. The Yorkshireman, who had floury trails of sweat running down a florid face from his powdered wig, said Chart was in luck as the Company's fast packet *Swallow*, out of Bombay, had put in for repairs and would shortly sail for home.

The three-masted ship was less than 100 feet in length and Chart's airless cabin would have been scorned as a kennel by any decent foxhound. Until the *Swallow* rounded the Cape he spent most of the voyage on his narrow hanging cot, shunning meals with the officers and few other passengers, only venturing onto deck long after midnight during the middle watch. After months of grieving, he resolved to shake off his melancholia, having reached the point of being disgusted with his weakness. By the time the ship reached St. Helena to collect mail he was outwardly sociable, although he found that the quantity of wine consumed at the captain's table failed to relieve the grief crushing his soul.

On 2 June 1792, after a voyage of twenty-one weeks, the *Swallow* dropped anchor in The Downs and Chart was rowed ashore to the town of Deal with his cylindrical campaign portmanteau and Lord Cornwallis's dispatches. Following a restless night in a waterfront inn, he set off at dawn on a post horse, determined to reach London within two days. The weather was fair, he encountered no highwaymen along the old Roman road named Watling Street, and managed to get to Rochester by nightfall, exchanging horses there. The next afternoon, he rode across London Bridge to East India house and delivered the dispatches.

By the time he reached Chesterfield Street he was bone weary. He left the horse with a stable boy in the mews, tipping him tuppence to return it to the nearest inn. Carrying his portmanteau, he trudged to the front door of his father's townhouse, emotions churning. He tried the door, but finding it locked pulled the bell. When it was opened by his father's valet, Evans, the man's face went white and he stepped back as if he seen a ghost.

"M-Master … Master Chart." Evans looked nervously over his shoulder.

Chart forced a smile as he greeted him, before saying "Take my kit to my room, Evans. Is Cook here? Ask her to make up a tray for me, I'm famished and parched. I'll have it in the drawing room."

Evans was frozen in indecision.

"Something wrong, man?"

The valet cleared his throat twice.

"P-Please wait here, Sir."

Tired, hungry and troubled to be back in his father's London home, Chart lost his temper.

"I'll damn well not wait here! Now do as I've ordered. I'll be in the drawing room."

Thoroughly disgruntled, he strode into the room off the entrance foyer. He looked at his haggard face in the Rococo gilt mirror over the chimneypiece, wryly thinking that it looked far older than a man who was not yet eighteen years of age.

He fumed with impatience as a skeleton clock ticked off the minutes. He heard the front door open and a whispered conversation in the foyer, but ignored it, angry that the staff seemed to have deteriorated so badly since his father's passing. He pulled the heavy silk sash to summon the servants, hearing the bell tinkle in the recesses of the house. He was on the verge of marching downstairs and sacking them all after a thorough dressing down, when he heard the front door open followed by the scrape of hobnailed boots on marble floor tiles.

The drawing room door flew open and three men trooped in. The leader was middle-aged with a pot belly and several days growth of beard. The other two were younger but equally disreputable looking. Each carried an oak truncheon. None had the courtesy of removing their cocked hats.

"What the bloody hell is the meaning of this!"

The leader pointed to an engraved tin gorget dangling from his neck conferring some sort of official status.

"You go by the name Alexander Charteris?" the man growled.

"How dare you address me like that! Leave this house immediately or I will call for the watch!"

All three intruders laughed.

"We *are* the watch," a younger man sneered, "and *he's* the sheriff."

The sheriff nodded, slapping his truncheon into the palm of his hand.

"No need to answer my question. You fit the description, me bucko."

He turned to his accomplices.

"Bracelets, lads."

The pair of watchmen advanced on Chart, one dangling manacles. His right hand automatically reached for his sword, but he had left it with his portmanteau. Shaking with rage, he went into a fighter's crouch, but the men threatened him with their cudgels, pulled his arms behind his back and snapped the fetters on his wrists. The sheriff stepped in front of him and displayed a document with a large red wax seal.

"By order of the Westminster magistrate, you are hereby placed under arrest."

"On what grounds!" Chart bellowed. "Why am I being arrested?"

The sheriff smirked.

"You are charged with the theft of property of Sir Pemberton Charteris, baronet."

"What property? What are you talking about?"

"*You*, me jackanapes. *You* are the property of the right honourable gentleman. You are his slave and have committed theft by taking yourself beyond the seas."

Chapter 9

Hell was not the fiery subterranean lake portrayed by the Knossington vicar and Westminster's chaplain; it was the Poultry Compter prison.

It was probably a good thing that Chart had been incarcerated in the ancient prison amidst its demonic population. In a solitary cell he would have sunk into the black hole of despair, whereas in the Poultry's cavernous communal gaol he was too busy fighting for survival to dwell on his terrible misfortune. He had been dragged inside the barred gate by his captors, fetters removed, and thrust into the dimly illuminated chamber, where he was immediately surrounded by a horde of grotesque figures crying "garnish, garnish" while plucking at his uniform, wrenching off silver gilt buttons and an epaulet.

"Ye must pay 'em two shillings," the fat sheriff called from the entrance, "or they'll have yer clothes and leave ye naked as Adam. And another shilling for me if ye want food and drink."

Chart lashed out with his fists, clearing a space to allow a moment to fish a handful of coins from his pocket. He threw a few coppers and silver pieces across the cavernous space and the ragged prisoners streamed after them, snarling and fighting each other like a pack of ravenous Bengali jackals. He turned back to the doorway and handed the sheriff a shilling, grateful for the money belt which still held nearly half the funds drawn before departing Mangalore.

He found a corner from which he could more easily defend himself and observe the other prisoners. The scattered straw reeking of urine, faeces, vomit and blood probably hadn't been changed in decades. He kicked it aside, removed his coat, turned it inside out, and sat on it. The mixture of scents of mundungus tobacco, the overflowing latrine and long unwashed bodies was far worse than a Southwark ditch or a tallow-chandler's melting-room.

As his eyes accustomed to the gloom, he was able to observe his fellow prisoners. There were over a hundred, primarily men but a dozen or so women, two of whom were on their backs servicing men. Many looked as if they were long-term residents, with long beards and claw-like fingernails, swaddled in rags, with heads covered with thrum-caps or the tops of old stockings. Bearded Jews in long black gowns and skullcaps prayed in an area that had been swept of filth; a handful of black men and women huddled together for mutual protection, chanting psalms. Chart subsequently learned that the Poultry was the preferred prison for Hebrews, negroes, homosexuals and other undesirables.

Along the wall near the entrance flies swarmed and buzzed over a pair of bodies stripped of clothing, so blackened and swollen with putrefaction that their ethnicity was undetectable. Corpses were only removed once a week, by which time a dozen usually awaited the death wagon that took them to the potters field in Camberwell.

As daylight faded the sheriff appeared at the gate and called to Chart. The man passed a jug of weak ale and a half loaf of hard bread through the bars.

"I'll pay you well to let me out of here," Chart hissed.

"Oh, in that case it will be two shillings for yer vittles' tomorrow. And I was paid well enough to put ye in here, bucko, so here ye'll stay until the magistrate returns ye to yer master or ye perish like most others in here."

Chart turned back towards his corner in time to see a skeletal wretch bending to steal his coat. He flew across the room carrying his meal, taking his fury out on the prisoner with a mighty kick in the gut that doubled him up and left him gasping on the floor like a landed fish. He barely restrained himself from a final kick to the head that would have killed the tatterdemalion thief.

I won't fall to their level, he told himself. *I won't become a brute!*

As night fell the prison was in nearly complete darkness, relieved only by an exterior streetlight that shone through the barred door and windows. The cacophony of howls, screams, babbling, grunts and weeping rendered sleep impossible, and he quickly learned that surviving the night depended on staying awake.

He heard a slithering as silhouettes loomed in the darkness. A knife glinted.

"We knows ye got cash, so 'and it over," said a harsh voice.

Chart sprang up, using his right arm to smash the ceramic jug at the darker blob where the voice came from while grabbing with his left where he hoped the arm that held the knife was. His instincts were right. As the knifeman screamed, Chart gripped the man's wrist and twisted it around to plunge the blade up under his sternum. Several others rushed him, but Chart was strong and they were weak from malnutrition. He swung the groaning knifeman like a shield while ripping out the knife from his body. Thrusting the dying man into his accomplices, he slashed at them, swearing with every oath learned from deepwater sailors as they melted back into the darkness.

Chart kept the knife, eyes squinting at vague shapes roaming the room, nerves frayed to the breaking point. He ached for sleep but forced himself to stay awake, one part of his mind alert for more attacks, the other trying to make sense of what had befallen him.

Pemb. Now *Sir* Pemberton since the death of Chart's father. Obviously, Pemb was behind this. But what had the sheriff meant by proclaiming that he was his slave, his property, and guilty of theft for having taken himself beyond the seas? It was madness, another diabolical trick by his cousin.

For which Pemb would pay.

In the morning a trail of drying blood led to the corpse of the man who had tried to rob him, already stripped of its pathetic rags, soon to join those rotting by the entrance. Chart waved the knife and glared at the eyes watching him like a flock of vultures.

The sheriff appeared late morning. Chart donned his coat and met him.

"That'll be two shillings for yer breakfast, and a shilling extra for the broken jug'. He eyed the cadaver lying a few yards inside, then glanced knowingly at Chart. "Tsk, tsk, what *will* these scoundrels get up to? Well, makes me job and the magistrate's easier. Less fruit for Tyburn Tree."

"Wait," Chart said as the man turned away. "I'll give you another shilling for some writing paper and a pencil."

The sheriff raised a speculative eyebrow.

"A half crown."

"I want it today."

Two sheets of grubby paper torn from a copybook and a stub of a graphite pencil were delivered mid-afternoon. When the sheriff returned in the evening with what he termed supper, Chart handed him a folded paper with a name and address written on it, displaying two guineas in the palm of his hand.

"Can you read?" he snapped.

The sheriff started to retort, then shook his head truculently. Like most members of the working class, he found himself reacting subserviently to a clipped public school accent, even if the speaker was what he considered a "blackamoor".

"Do you know Portman Square?" The man nodded. "Then you'll take this to number twenty-five. Now repeat where you will take it."

The sheriff did so, licking his lips at King George's golden profile.

"Here's a guinea for you now, and the other when you return with a message from the person this is addressed to."

As darkness fell the drunken gatekeeper who lived in a room over the entrance appeared with a bottle in his hand and called to the female prisoners. They congregated by the gate, pushing and shoving to gain his attention before he chose one of them. He unlocked the gate and let her out. "'ere now," one of the disappointed trulls yelled, "Ye can 'ave me for a tuppence!"

"Next time, me love," the gatekeeper slurred.

A passing watchman had just called ten o'clock when the sheriff reappeared.

"Where's me guinea?" he asked as Chart hurried to the gate.

"Did you bring a reply?"

"Butler or whatever he was told me his mistress wasn´t home. Gave him yer letter but he looked at it like it were a dog turd!" The man guffawed, exuding gin fumes. "Now where's me money?"

Disappointment hit Chart like one of Bill Richmond's fists.

He swallowed.

"I said you get the other with a reply."

The sheriff's smile revealed a mouth of broken, blackened teeth. He grabbed Chart by the throat, choking him as he dragged his face into the aperture of the bars. His other hand snaked into the uniform's coat pocket from which he had seen coins withdrawn. Clutching a handful, he shoved Chart back so violently that he landed on his buttocks.

"Not so high and mighty now, darkie!" He spat towards the putrefying corpses. "I wager that ye'll be sleeping with 'em before the dawn."

Fatigue was Chart's enemy. He fought it by walking back and forth, shaking his limbs and his muzzy head. Retreating to his corner, he pricked his arms with the knife when he nearly succumbed to sleep, aware that predators were watching from the darkness, ready to pounce. His traumatised mind began playing tricks on him. He nodded off momentarily, hearing his father lecturing that it was unthinkable for a gentleman to give in to despair or weakness. You *must* fight on, said Sir Arthur's spectre. Chart jerked awake as something scuttled across the floor next to him, but it was only a rat as big as a tom cat. At night they feasted on the corpses.

He planned to charge the gate when the keeper returned his whore to the prison. He thought it likely that he would be able to escape, and possibly evade the hue and cry for a time. If cornered he would fight, and die if necessary, rather than be returned to the Poultry where death seemed inevitable, whether slow or fast.

But the harlot failed to show.

Chart was at his lowest ebb when a pair of torches illuminated the entrance and voices loudly rousted the gatekeeper from his slumber. When the man appeared, there was rumbling conversation, a clink of coins, and the scrape of the large iron key being turned in the rusty lock. The gatekeeper preceded two tall cloaked figures and pointed towards Chart. He pushed himself to his feet and reached for his knife, but his reflexes were slow and the two intruders each grabbed a bicep and frogmarched him out the door, passing the gatekeeper who was bowing and saying "thankee gentlemen" while jingling the contents of a cloth bag.

He struggled in their vice-like grips as they approached a chaise drawn by a black horse visible through the pre-dawn twilight. The door was opened and he was pushed into the coach's interior that was redolent with a well-remembered perfume.

"Heavens," a husky feminine voice drawled, "You do stink. Overdue for a bath, methinks."

***

Lady Augusta gazed fondly at the young man sprawled fast asleep in the copper bathtub in front of the fireplace. There were barely perceptible lines on his face, weathered and darkened by the Indian sun to the colour of seasoned mahogany, while the skin of his limbs and torso where they had been protected by his uniform were

honey-golden. He had grown since she last saw him nearly two years earlier. She guessed that he topped six feet in height even though not yet eighteen years old. He had the lean hard muscle of a soldier who knew how to wield sword and musket. He wore his hair cropped short as most young men did these days, although his had been uncut long enough to show its natural ringlets. Now looking at him as the early morning sun lightened the room, she felt a curious mixture of lust commingled with maternal feelings.

Steady on, old girl, she chided herself, *there are more important, and immediate, things to consider.*

***

Chart slept twelve hours in the luxurious guest room, awakening with adrenaline surging and fists clenched as he imagined being in the Poultry Compter and having fallen asleep. It took several minutes before he remembered the events of the past few days, wondering how much had been a nightmare.

He realised that his experience had been all too real.

He rose, used the commode, and saw a piece of crested notepaper propped up on a side table next to a decanter of water and a plate of bread rolls, ham and cheese.

Come down when ready. Sorry – had to burn your uniform but tailor came round and ran up new suit for you in wardrobe. A.

He was unsurprised that the cutaway green coat and breeches were a perfect fit, as was the silk shirt and linen. His boots had been salvaged and buffed to a military gloss.

Remembering his churlish behaviour the last time he had seen her, he felt sheepish as he entered the drawing room to find the Countess alone at her spinet plucking a concerto by the late Mr. Mozart.

"Augusta, how can I thank …."

"Hush!" She rose in a swish of skirts and kissed him on his cheek before taking his hand and leading him to a gilt settee. She explained that she had returned from the theatre the previous night to find his crude note. Mobilising her two brawniest footmen, she had recalled her coach and hurried to the prison.

"That little gatekeeper would have released everyone for ten pounds, but he was given an extra five to keep his mouth shut as long as possible, which wasn't long as it turned out. Word on the street is that the sheriffs are looking for you and your cousin Pemb is behind this."

Taking a deep breath, Chart told her about the sheriff's claim that he was Pemb's slave and had been arrested for the theft of himself.

"Is that even possible?" he asked.

She sighed.

"I'm afraid so, based on what terrible things I've read in the Society for the Abolition of the Slave Trade pamphlets. But you're safe here for now, and I'll ask my solicitor, Mr. Lawson, to come round this evening. But why did you come back to London, my dear?"

Chart explained about the letter from his family lawyer, informing him of his father's death and that there was a problem with the will.

"Then we need to get this Mr. Cave down from Leicester without delay. You're safe here for now. My footmen served with the Grenadiers during the American war, and we've got a

86

decent little arsenal in the wine cellar. I'm sure they'd relish a battle with the sheriff and his thugs."

Chapter 10

Bryan Cave, the Charteris family solicitor, came from Leicester a week later. He declined a room at the Countess's house, preferring an inn. He arrived at the meeting in Augusta's library clutching a large leather portfolio. Cave was icily polite to Chart, seeming to avoid meeting his eyes. Lady Augusta's lawyer, Mr. Lawson, was already present.

"So, let us begin," Cave said fussily as he began taking papers from his satchel. "I'm afraid that--."

"Wait," snapped the Countess. "We are waiting for someone else."

Cave fidgeted, scratching his shaven pate under the grey bag wig. Minutes later, the door opened and a somewhat stooped man entered the room. He was vaguely familiar to Chart, but he could not remember his name. The man bowed to Lady Augusta and Lawson, then extended his hand to Cave.

"And you are, Sir?" the solicitor asked after a limp shake.

"Granville Sharp."

Chart was mortified as he remembered his rebuff of Sharp at the abolitionists meeting, but the elderly man seemed unfazed. He shook Chart's hand warmly, kindly grey eyes twinkling.

"Good to see you again, sir. I understand you've had some adventures since last we met."

The five of them sat around a large library table, Chart sandwiched between Lady Augusta and her lawyer, with Cave across from them and Sharp slightly apart at the end of the table. Cave laid out sheafs of papers and cleared his throat loudly.

"As I wrote to …. the person sitting across from me after Sir Arthur's tragic demise at the hands of persons unknown, he was the named principal beneficiary of his father's will. Aside from various small bequests to other relatives and servants, he left the bulk of his estate, both real and personal, in England and on the island of Grenada, to Alexander Meynell Charteris, whom he acknowledged as his natural son. Sir Arthur also left the sum of one shilling to his nephew Pemberton Charteris, now Sir

88

Pemberton, with the proviso that he had no further claim on his estate, with the baronetcy to be inherited by him separately per the original letters patent by King Charles the First."

"So, I take it that the estate was not entailed?" asked Lawson.

"That is correct. Sir Arthur was at great pains to ensure that the hereditary fee tail of the property was broken, and that he could leave it to whomever he wished."

"Even if the beneficiary was illegitimate?"

"Er, yes. Anyone, regardless of birth."

"So, what is the problem?" pursued Lawson, face earnest beneath his wig as if he were questioning a defendant in the Common Pleas rather than a man he considered a lowly provincial lawyer. "You wrote to Mr. Charteris here that the will had not been formally read because a 'most disturbing' challenge to it had been made."

Cave mopped his perspiring face with a large handkerchief and nervously shuffled his papers before answering.

"Under the ancient principle of *partus sequitur ventrem*, children born to enslaved mothers were considered enslaved people; the enslaved status of a child followed that of the mother. Sir Pemberton claims he has evidence that Alexander Meynell Charteris, the alleged beneficiary, is the son of an enslaved mother owned by the estate, that said slave was never manumitted, and that Alexander Meynell Charteris was therefore born a slave and similarly never legally freed. Therefore, Alexander Meynell Charteris remains a slave and is a chattel of the estate. The current baronet contends that slaves have no rights of property, even of themselves, and he has therefore brought suit in Chancery Court to challenge the will of Sir Arthur Charteris as invalid."

***

Struggling to mask her agitation, Lady Augusta fluttered her silk fan as Cave was ushered out by the butler.

"He barely acknowledged Chart's existence!" she exclaimed as the door closed.

"Can't really blame the little man," Lawson said. "He represents the Charteris estate, not Chart personally, and he obviously thinks Pemb has the stronger case."

"By what right did Pemb have me arrested and occupy my father's houses if the will has not been ruled on?" Chart demanded, face contorted in rage.

"None, actually," Lawson replied. "Conceivably, an action could be brought against him for false imprisonment and trespass but it would go nowhere pending the outcome of the decision on the validity of the will. Pemb has undoubtedly inherited the title, and the powers-that-be can be relied on to take the side of a wealthy baronet against a, er ...."

"Against a half-caste bastard," Sharp spat, speaking for the first time.

The lawyer grimaced.

"Sir Pemberton will have bribed the sheriff and the watch to arrest you, sir. That was an illegal act, but he could do so again if you venture out without an armed escort. And I daresay that if you had perished in the Poultry he would have avoided the need for litigation to establish his inheritance to the estate."

"What evidence does Pemb have?" asked Lady Augusta.

"Apparently, Mr. Cave has not been made privy to the evidence. I have no doubt that it will be presented by barristers who are much more skilled at Chancery matters than Mr. Cave."

Lawson noticed Chart's puzzled expression.

"The Court of Chancery has jurisdiction over all matters of equity such as disputed estates," he explained.

Granville Sharp leaned forward, grey eyes now hard as polished steel.

"There are much bigger issues at stake here," he growled. "We will take this to the King's Bench, the highest court in the land, if necessary."

***

"Certainly we should seek a motion for removal to the King's Bench before this proceeds," whispered Granville Sharp.

"Not yet," said Francis Hargrave, the attorney engaged by Lady Augusta to represent Chart in the Chancery Court. "We must wait until we hear their evidence."

Like Sharp, Hargrave and his fellow barristers were evangelistic Christians who advocated for abolition with equal religious fervour. Despite Lady Augusta's offer to pay for their legal services, they had refused, stating that they were anti-slavery crusaders on behalf of the Lord. While the Countess was equally passionate about ending the African slave trade, she was far less sanctimonious. Sharp's comment about "bigger issues at stake" had made her wonder if establishing Chart's freedom was part of a grander plan. But she kept her suspicions to herself.

Now Chart sat with the Countess in the Chancery Court's gallery, surrounded by the two stalwart footmen who had rescued him from prison. Believing that Chart's personal appearance should impress the court, Augusta had insisted that he wear a new John Company uniform she had ordered tailored for him. They listened to sonorous opening remarks by Pemb's London barrister, Sir Godfrey Pennyman, followed by Hargrave arguing that the testamentary wishes of a titled English gentleman were sacrosanct. One of the three peruked judges on the bench seemed to be napping.

Pennyman rose again and began introducing his evidence.

"My Lords, may I call your attention to the first exhibit, being a bill of sale for one female slave named Weeju, purchased in St. George's Town, Colony of Grenada, on the nineteenth day of November in the year of our Lord 1771 by the late lamented Sir Arthur Charteris."

Out of the corner of her eye, Lady Augusta saw Chart grow rigid, his face turning greyish as more evidence was introduced.

"Do you need to take some air outside?"

He shook his head, eyes misting.

Pennyman introduced several of the calf-bound diaries that Chart remembered so well from his father's Knossington library. His hands began trembling when the lawyer read entries from June 1774 describing his birth and his mother's lingering death.

"Now?" breathed Granville Sharp, and Hargrave nodded, rising to his feet.

"My Lords, if I may crave the indulgence of the court?"

The lead judge acknowledged him, while the slumbering one opened bleary eyes.

"The matter before this court today concerns the validity of the will of Sir Arthur Charteris. It is clear from the evidence just presented that the core issue is the legal status of the named beneficiary, Lieutenant Alexander Charteris of the East India Company Army. The plaintiff's claim is that Lieutenant Charteris cannot inherit under the terms of his father's will because he is, *de jure*, a slave, a chattel of the estate, with no rights as a free Englishman.

"My Lords, with the greatest respect, I aver that the validity of Sir Arthur's will cannot be settled by the Court of Chancery until the underlying, and therefore preliminary, matter of Lieutenant Charteris' legal status can be determined. Such a determination is not within the jurisdiction of this court. I therefore request that this case be removed to the King's Bench so that judgement can be rendered on the named beneficiary's status under the law, after which it may be returned to this august body."

Now the judges were wide awake. They whispered amongst themselves while a buzz of conversation rippled through the spectators in the gallery.

"You were right," Hargrave said *sotto voce* to Sharp. "The Chancery judges would rather wash their hands of this business considering how controversial the slavery issue has become, especially with growing support in Parliament for Wilberforce's abolition bill."

"Curious that Pennyman didn't challenge you."

Hargrave made a scoffing noise.

"Not curious. Pennyman has known all along that the sticking point would be the slavery claim. His client, Sir Pemberton, is an idiot. Pennyman warned him that Chancery was the wrong venue, but he insisted."

"God has willed this," Sharp said reverently. "That poor dear young man is His instrument."

The head judge signalled to the bailiff, who called for silence in a stentorian roar.

"It is the decision of this court," the judge intoned, "that the matter before us should indeed be removed to the Court of King's Bench to resolve the legal status of the named beneficiary before any further action before this court, now adjourned."

***

The King's Bench did not automatically hear cases removed to it by lower courts. During the months that passed while the legal action moved glacially from one clerk's desk to another, Chart increasingly felt that he had exchanged one type of imprisonment for another, albeit gilded, one in Lady Augusta's spacious townhouse.

He passed his 18th birthday alone except for the dozen unobtrusive servants. Out of the Season, Augusta spent most of her time at one of her family's several castles and manors, or at the estates of her circle of aristocratic friends. Chart chafed at the inactivity, longing to ride or at the very least to escape for a brisk jaunt through Hyde Park. But his legal status was dangerously unsettled, and he had been warned that the house was under surveillance. Sharp and Hargrave's legal team told him that Pemb and certain powerful people would use any means to prevent his case from being heard by the Lord Chief Justice.

Chart's boredom led to growing despondency. There were only so many books to read to pass the time. After his solitary suppers in the dining room, he would occasionally go to the top of the back staircase leading down to the servants quarters, listening to their chatter and laughter, wishing that he could join them. He often thought about Arabella Sherrard and came close to writing to her. But he reminded himself that he had never heard from her after their parting and he had nothing to offer, not even friendship. She was just one more bittersweet memory of Leicestershire that needed to be amputated like the gangrenous limbs of wounded soldiers.

Other young men of his age and class were rarely forced to ponder their future, but Chart brooded on his. Two years earlier he had sought exile in India, and now he was convinced that with his father gone England held nothing for him except perpetual exclusion and unhappiness. He yearned to return to military service in India, where he had found fulfilment as an officer. On the battlefield one's ethnicity did not matter when faced by waves of howling Mysorean warriors.

When Augusta was in London on one of her rare visits before the Season she would invite him to her bed. Chart yearned for her company, as much for the physical and emotional release of their lovemaking as for the contact with another human being who genuinely cared for him. He missed her greatly when she was away. When sunk in melancholy for several days, he had by chance found a book in her library titled *David Simple*, written by a woman named Sarah Fielding. Chart had been greatly affected by the story of a young man's quest for a "real friend" in a society characterised by avarice and injustice. He realised that Augusta's façade of aristocratic haughtiness concealed a kind heart and a keen mind. She was his only friend and confidant in a hostile world.

As the rainy English summer metamorphosised into a wetter and chillier autumn, Chart decided that he had spent enough time in the purgatory of waiting to learn whether the King's Bench would hear his case. Lying in Augusta's perfumed bed, while she slowly ran a manicured finger down the crisply whorled black hairs of his chest to the moist tangle at his groin, he told her he needed to return to his regiment in India and asked for her help. He had more than eighty guineas left from the funds advanced from Mr. Cave, enough to pay for his passage to Calcutta, the nearest port to his regiment's cantonment at Barrackpore. Escaping from London would require cunning and contacts which he lacked.

The Countess was torn as she looked at his eager face. She believed that without a legal resolution to his status, Chart would be forever considered an outlaw anywhere in the British Empire.

"Please wait awhile longer, my dear," she murmured. "I have heard that Parliament and the courts will be back in session next month, and Mr. Hargrave thinks there's a good chance that the King's Bench will hear your case."

"No," he said sullenly. "I have waited long enough. If you won't help me I will take matters in my own hands."

He rolled out of the bed, threw on a silk dressing gown and stalked to the door, tall and lithe. Augusta was not affronted; her heart was filled with pity for him, knowing the anguish gripping his soul.

At breakfast late the next morning he apologised to her, which she excused with a smile, but it froze when he told her that he had earlier written to Sir William Bensley at India House asking to be reinstated in the First Bengal Native Infantry. She couldn't bring herself to tell him that the previous week she had read an article in the new Sunday newspaper called *The Observer* quoting Lord Cornwallis, Governor-General of India, commenting on his new civil and criminal code:

"Men of mixed race on account of their colour and extraction are considered as inferior to Europeans, I am of opinion that those of them who possess the best abilities could not command that authority and respect which is necessary in the due discharge of the duty of an officer".

She was away three weeks later when he received a curt letter written by a junior clerk, informing him on behalf of Sir William that due to new rules promulgated by the Governor-General, Chart's services would no longer be needed.

Seeking surcease from the fierce grip of depression, in the middle of the night Chart found the key to the wine cellar. He pulled a bottle of claret from a rack and uncorked it, taking long draughts from the neck. He carried it to the gun room next door and selected a large dragoon pistol. After loading and priming the pistol, he carried it and the bottle upstairs to the drawing room.

He was found there by a terrified maid in the morning, gently snoring with the empty bottle on the floor. The butler pried the pistol from his right hand, and directed the footmen to carry him up to his room. No one said a word to the Countess when she returned that evening.

The following day Granville Sharp excitedly rang the door bell and bustled in with the news that the King's Bench had agreed to add Chart's case to its docket.

Chapter 11

"There is no evidence that Chart or his mother were ever manumitted by Sir Arthur," said Hargrave. "On the contrary, it is indisputable that Chart's mother, Weju, was purchased by Sir Arthur."

"Perhaps Pemb destroyed the manumission papers, or they were left in Grenada?" Chart asked.

The lawyer sighed.

"Sir Pemberton's counsel allowed us access to all your father's papers, including his diaries. They obviously felt confidant about their standing. We found no indication of tampering. Your father was meticulous in keeping up his diaries until his death. The only reference to manumission of a slave was to a woman named Phibbah on the 24th of December 1779."

"That was my doing," Granville Sharp said sorrowfully. "It still grieves me."

Lady Augusta looked at the men seated around her library table.

"So what does this mean for Chart's case?"

"It means," replied Sharp, eyes glowing zealously, "that this is our opportunity to drive a stake through the heart of slavery."

"Indeed!" said Hargrave. "The law is unsettled regarding slavery. A definitive decision by the highest court of the land will give the greatest impetus to Abolition!"

He looked at Chart.

"My dear boy, you will be the instrument of God's wrath against the slavers and planters!"

"We will mobilise our forces to make your case the *cause célèbre* of the century!" exclaimed Sharp.

***

"I feel like I am a mere pawn," Chart said to Augusta after the others left. "I don't want to be a *cause célèbre*!"

"What *do* you want?" the Countess asked gently.

Chart was silent for several minutes, eyes moist and mouth working as he struggled with his emotions.

"I want …." He cleared his throat. "I want the world to see me as who I am under this skin, an Englishman like everyone else!"

Chart's anguish made Augusta tearful as well.

"That *is* how your friends see you. But I'm sorry to say that the struggle is only beginning for the rest of society to accept you as a person, as well as others who are of mixed race or African. You must not see yourself as a pawn, but as a man who was fated to be a leader in the struggle against slavery."

"I was a good soldier," he said huskily.

"You are *still* a soldier. Slavery is your enemy and the abolitionists are your army."

***

Westminster Hall, London

24 May 1793

Lord Cransfield, the chief justice, and three colleagues in ermine-trimmed scarlet robes were arrayed on a large, stage-like dais, curtained on both sides, with a multi-tiered shelf of legal tomes exposed on the right. Each judge took his place behind an individual lectern like a schoolboy's desk. A vast mural of the royal arms flanked by the scales of justice and a fasces symbol provided a backdrop to the legal play that was about to enter its final act. Adding to the illusion of a stage performance, opposing lawyers sat behind a semi-circular bench like an orchestra pit in front of the judges.

A sprinkling of black faces, some hopeful, some apprehensive, could be seen among hundreds of spectators packing Westminster Hall, a massive building over six hundred years old. Well-dressed men and women lined the wall beneath the judges' bench, competing with reporters from every major newspaper in the British Isles and the *Virginia Gazette* in the infant United States. Pickpockets plied their trade, as did apple-cheeked women hawking pies filled with meat of dubious origin and pot boys fetching jugs of ale from the Three Tuns on Little Sanctuary Street.

Wearing a sombre suit, Chart sat in an elevated box overlooking the dais with Lady Ursula, Sharp and half a dozen celebrated abolitionists including the politician William

Wilberforce and a sprightly bluestocking named Hannah More. In a box opposite them, Pemb was surrounded by a host of dissipated-looking young men and hard-faced women with painted faces.

During five days of hearings in the case of Charteris against Charteris, Hargrave and his three co-counsels made every possible argument against the legality of slavery in England and their abhorrence for slavery and the slave trade generally. They declared their goal of outlawing slavery both in England and the colonies. Nonetheless, Chart had been mortified to be referred to throughout the hearing, even by the barristers representing him, as "Alexander Charteris, the Mulatto", the common term for a person of mixed African and white ethnicity.

"The question," Hargrave had thundered in his opening statement, "is not whether slavery is lawful in the colonies, where a concurrence of unhappy circumstances has caused it to be established as necessary, but whether in England?"

Slavery, he argued, was contrary to natural law and there was no right of permanent enslavement. It was inconsistent with Christianity and with inherent rights to contract. There were no statutes that permitted or endorsed slavery in England based on race, and no reported case that unequivocally endorsed heritable, perpetual chattel slavery based on race or status.

Pemb's lead counsel rose to proclaim that it was incontestable that Charteris the Mulatto had been born of an enslaved mother in the Colony of Grenada who was purchased by the late Sir Arthur Pemberton, Baronet, and therefore the heritable, perpetual property of his only legal heir Sir Pemberton Charteris, an upstanding member of the highest society. As such, he said, pausing to look smugly around the vast courtroom, "the mulatto to be seen in the box to their Lordship's left is as much a chattel as a commode … or a mule, to which his ancestry bears a resemblance." His remark was greeted with cackles from Pemb's box and more than a few smiles from the spectators.

The barrister cited a decision by the Solicitor General which stated that "Negroes" ought to be "esteemed goods and commodities within the Trade and Navigation Acts." Such a ruling, he said, permitted slave owners to use property law with regard to their slaves "to recover goods wrongfully detained, lost or damaged" as they would any other property. Therefore, the wronged complainant, Sir Pemberton, had every right to recover his chattel, the said mulatto.

English law, he continued, authorised contemporary slavery in England because villeinage, its equivalent, was still legally permissible. Therefore, English statutes allowed slavery in England as well as the colonies. In the alternative, slaves who came to England could be treated as servants, but their return to the colonies was compellable. In a gesture towards benevolence, he acknowledged that while English law recognised the right to hold persons in involuntary lifetime service, this was subject to limits on "cruel usage". Once the said mulatto Charteris was returned to his lawful master, he would be well-treated.

Summing up, the barrister urged the court to consider seriously that a decision emancipating slaves brought to England would endanger colonial slavery, which was of vital economic importance, contributing the astonishing sum of over six millions of pounds per annum to the British economy.

After listening to closing arguments, Lord Chief Justice Cransfield had announced that because he wished his brothers on the bench to be unanimous in their decision, the case required consultation with the other judges. They had thereupon retired for a week. Now, the great hall reverberated to its hammer beam roof from the susurration of conversation as the crowd waited for the decision.

"He *must* rule in our favour," said Sharp fervently. "God is on our side, our cause is righteous! We have reason to believe that Lord Cransfield is a secret abolitionist. He has a mulatto stepdaughter whom he loves deeply."

"What about my father's will?" asked Chart. "It was never mentioned during the proceedings."

"This is only the first step," Sharp replied confidently. "Once you are declared a free man we shall return to the Chancery Court."

Chart glanced at Augusta, heart clenching as he saw her

worried face.

The presiding judge rose, causing cries of "hush" throughout the hall. He waited until quiet prevailed before delivering his oral decision.

"The state of slavery is of such a nature, that it is incapable of being introduced on any reasons, moral or political, but only by positive law. It is so odious, that nothing can be suffered to support it, but positive law. Whatever inconveniences, therefore, may follow from the decision, I cannot say this case is allowed or approved by the law of England.

"Therefore, while English law may not allow the emancipation of Charteris the Mulatto, he may nonetheless not be returned to his master in involuntary servitude whilst in this Kingdom. It is not within my purview to rule on the law in the colonies."

As the Chief Justice exited stage right, followed by the other judges, there was momentary puzzled silence before a great clamour swept the hall.

"What does this mean?" asked Chart. He caught his breath as he saw the shocked pale faces around him.

"It means," answered Sharp in a bitter, choked voice, "that you are a slave."

***

"It is not the end," said Sharp later at Lady Augusta's house. "We must fight on. And now you are free to join us in the fight because you can not be held against your will."

Chart shook his head angrily, black curls flopping.

"I am *not* free!"

The Countess's eyes were reddened from crying. She longed to take Chart into her arms to comfort him.

"Cransfield was in a very difficult position," Sharp continued. "The West Indian planters have great influence. On reflection, I believe that the decision was a minor victory for us, another albeit small step towards abolition! And now that you, dear boy, have become famous throughout the land, we'll plan a series of meetings and lectures for you, possibly in concert with our friend Olaudah Equiano."

But Chart had other plans.

***

Pemb's lawyers assured him that soon the Chancery Court would reconvene and overturn his uncle's will, awarding the entire estate to him. To celebrate, he held a grand debauch at the Chesterfield Street townhouse that lasted for a week. He was overjoyed to discover that he had so many new friends, hundreds in fact, who arrived at all hours of the day and night to drink, gamble and roger the strumpets and rent boys plying their trades in the bedrooms on the second floor. A covey of dukes, marquesses and other persons of quality arrived from Brooks's, rubbing shoulders with highwaymen, footpads, duffers, nappers and assorted queer coves who frequented his grandfather's tavern in Shadwell.

To add to the entertainment, a young belted earl had the clever idea of inviting the entire "parliament of monsters" from Bartholomew Fair, paying a shilling each to the albinos, painted Indians, apes, dwarfs, giants, the man that swallowed fire, and the invisible girl, although afterward no one remembered seeing her. The learned pig and the dog that could tell all its letters were also rented from their owner for five guineas. Sadly, the pig was stolen and roasted by a trio of gypsies who were among the uninvited guests, and the dog ran away after biting off the index finger of a drunken lord who was determined to make the animal sing *The Roast Beef of Old England*.

Sir Pemberton was finally left on his own after the wine cellar was drunk dry and the last of the sodden aristocrats staggered out the door and collapsed in the cobbled street. His two remaining servants spent days cleaning up pools of vomit and disposing of smashed furniture and broken glassware, although they had to call the watch to capture a gibbon that refused to come down from a chandelier in the dining room.

Pemb's newfound friends quickly smoothed the way for membership in Brooks's and Boodle's, and he soon became a regular in the dining and gambling rooms. Although the estate had yet to be settled, allowing him access to its revenues, the clubs and their gentlemen habitués were pleased to extend credit. Although his credit had reached its limit at the better tailors on Cork Street, he persuaded Mr. Hawkes on Piccadilly to run up half a dozen suits with special padding to conceal his uneven shoulders. Pemb was gleeful to take his rightful place in the upper reaches of society after too many years of humiliation.

As the new owner of a sugar plantation in Grenada, Pemb was also invited to join the London Society of West India Planters and Merchants, which represented the interests of the British West Indian plantocracy as well as sugar merchants and colonial agents. The Society wielded immense political power as at least 74 Members of Parliament and a third of those who sat in the Lords were absentee planters or had connections with the Caribbean slave colonies. Its primary mission was the defeat of the growing Abolition movement, which sought the end of the African slave trade and eventual emancipation of the tens of thousands of black people who laboured on West Indian plantations.

Three weeks after the conclusion of the High Court case, Pemb was invited by Lord Liskeard, a leader of the Society, to dinner in a private room at Brooks's. Wearing one of his new suits, he was secretly awed by the eleven other gentlemen at the table, most of whom were recognisable as the country's leading peers, politicians and merchants, including the notorious Colonel Tarleton who had massacred surrendering Yankee Doodles during the American War.

Towards midnight, surfeit with a rich ragout of snails, larded quail and a river of claret and hock, the port appeared and a round of toasts was drunk, including "His Majesty, King George" and "Death to the Abolitionists". Liskeard rose, tapped his glass for silence, and offered a toast to the Society's newest member, Sir Pemberton Charteris. After plopping back into his chair, the lord leaned across the table towards Pemb.

"I say, old boy," Liskeard said loudly for the benefit of table, "What do you intend to do about this mulatto slave of yours?"

"Do?" Pemb replied, trying to shake off his befuddlement.

"Indeed," added a prominent City banker, "Rumour has it those blasted blackamoor lovers plan to take him on the road to speak against slavery throughout the country, star attraction in their circus with other monkeys."

"The blighter could do us some real damage," growled

Tarleton. "I've heard that he speaks rather well, Westminster School, y'know."

"And handy with his fists," added the parliamentary member for Bristol, eliciting a sweep of smirks around the table which Pemb was too inebriated to notice.

"Well, I …" Pemb cleared his throat loudly. "As I've been told that I can't have him arrested and returned to my service, I suppose I could arrange for him to have an accident."

"Good heavens, man," said an elderly judge, "we'll hear no more of such murderous talk! We're civilised men, after all. Lord Cransfield unequivocally stated that the law of England does not apply to that of our West Indian colonies. Best course is to endeavour to send your Darky back where he came from, where you can do as you like with him."

"It would be a waste to kill him," Tarleton drawled. "Prime young buck like him should be worth at least a hundred guineas in any halfway decent slave market."

Chapter 12

Chart began plotting his escape, never hinting of half-formed plans to Lady Augusta or any of the steady stream of anti-slavery evangelists who sought his company. He insisted on leaving the Portman Square house for walks, even though the Countess and her friends believed that his life was in danger. Chart reluctantly agreed to be accompanied by a cloaked footman armed with a pocket pistol and an oak truncheon. In his deep unhappiness, he saw the minder not as a protector but as a gaoler. He scoffed at Augusta's and Sharp's concerns about his vulnerability, reasoning that with Pemb having succeeded in inheriting and prohibited from seizing and enslaving him, his cousin would have lost interest in his "Mulatto":

Over the course of several weeks, he developed a routine of stopping at a small bookshop on Bond Street which sold newspapers, where he would buy copies of *The Gentlemen's Magazine, The Times* and *Lloyd's List*, the latter of which detailed ship movements, wrecks, and prices of stocks and commodities such as cochineal. Chart had spent enough time at sea to understand the basic workings of a ship, and had decided that life as an ordinary seaman on a privateer or merchant vessel was preferable to the tormented limbo of existing in London on the charity of others.

War had broken out between Britain and Revolutionary France, and another option was volunteering as a mercenary with any foreign army that would take him. He had read that numerous black and mixed-race men were serving in the French military forces, some as senior officers. If the opportunity presented itself, he would jump ship and enlist, although he knew that the British Royal Navy was blockading French ports. He had no real plan on how to achieve his freedom, but in his growing desperation he convinced himself that he must seize any opportunity.

In mid July, Chart read in *Lloyd's* that the *Centurian*, privateer, had taken a French prize from Senegal having on board skins, ivory and chests of dollars, and brought it into Bludworth Docks in Wapping. He knew from experience that some members of the crew would be unconscious in a whore's crib or dead in a filth-laden alley after spending their prize money. The captain would be eager to return to sea to capture more rich prizes and keen to sign on replacement crewmen.

The Countess was away in the country, and half the staff of the townhouse, including the footmen, had been given leave to visit the Vauxhall Pleasure Gardens that evening. Dressed in his darkest coat, waistcoat and breeches, with a black stock at his neck, Chart waited until the remaining staff retired downstairs. He considered leaving a note for Augusta, but worried that if he had to abort his mission and return, a servant could find it before it could be retrieved. He would write to her from wherever he ended up to express his gratitude and affection.

As the longcase clock in the entry hall chimed eleven times, he eased open the front door, stepped into the street with cocked hat tipped low over his face and set off on foot. The distance to Wapping was five miles, mainly along dark and dangerous streets, but he was confident that he could defend himself if accosted.

Chart failed to see the trio of ragged urchins lurking in the garden square across from Augusta's townhouse. They watched until he passed under a streetlight.

"That's 'im," the eldest boy said. "That's the black bastard. We'll follow 'im. Per'aps this'll be our night to earn the shilling each they promised us!"

An hour past midnight Chart arrived at the wooden gates of Bludworth Docks, which were guarded by a watchman to deter pilferers. He saw steps leading down to the river beside it, but Chart doubted that he would be able to access the privateer if it was still tied up at the quay, with even less chance if was moored in the river amidst scores of other square-rigged ships.

Just up Wapping Street was a tavern called the *Three Welch Men*. Light spilled from its open door and windows, and the din of roistering sailors reverberated in the otherwise deserted street. Chart decided that his best chance of getting a berth was to befriend some of *Centurian's* crewmen with a few rounds of ale. He was paid no attention as he edged into the crowded pub. The laughing, singing, cursing, boasting men and women were of a dozen different nationalities and every race and mixture. He ordered an earthenware tankard of ale, bought a round for his neighbours at the bar and began asking about the privateer.

No one was sober enough to tell Chart that *Centurian* had weighed anchor on the ebb tide after reboarding her prize crew and was halfway to Gravesend.

Half an hour later a man in seaman's garb with three-days growth of beard approached him.

"Yer askin' about the *Centurian*, I hears. Lookin´ for a berth?"

Chart nodded and the sailor smiled.

"Yer in luck. Cap'n needs crew. Come with me." He turned and shoved through the throng, followed by Chart as he stepped outside.

Out of the corner of his eye, Chart saw three hulking shadows emerge from a narrow alley beside the tavern. Before he could react, the sailor spun and doubled him over with a fist to the stomach. Chart's arms were wrenched behind his back and bound at the wrists as a hood shrouded his face. He was bludgeoned into quiescence.

"Good job, lads," the sailor said, handing the three watching urchins a silver shilling each.

***

Pemb's first thought was to torture Chart to death, slowly.

On second thought, degradation was a much more fitting punishment. What better way to break the arrogant blackamoor who had humiliated *him* than enslaving him in the cane fields on the newly inherited sugar plantation in Grenada. It had certainly been providential that the black bastard had fallen into his hands so easily, demonstrating the superiority of Pemb's cunning compared to the half-caste's stupidity. A good example of the foolishness of those Abolitionists who claimed that negroes were the intellectual equals of the white race! He looked forward to regaling his new friends with the story during the next meeting of the Society of West India Planters and Merchants

Pemb held a scented handkerchief to his nose as he entered

the kennels behind his grandfather's seedy tavern near the Shadwell docks. The bully ruffians who kidnapped Chart had been Pemb's associates since he was sent down from Westminster, using the ale house as their headquarters with the blessing of the old man, himself a former pirate. After lugging Chart the short distance to the tavern kennels an iron ring was clamped around his neck and secured to the brick wall with a rusty chain just long enough to let him sit upright but not lie down. Mastiffs in cages around him barked and growled as Pemb's cloaked figure was exposed by a lantern held by one of his minions.

When Chart saw Pemb his eyes blazed blue defiance above the gag crammed into his mouth.

"Black bastard wouldn't shut up his filthy curses," explained the sailor who had lured Chart from the *Three Welch Men* the previous night. "He's nice and comfy in there, must be a foot of dog shit to sit on as them kennels ain't never been cleaned."

Chart strained against his restraints, making incoherent noises.

"He's tryin' to talk monkey," one of the thugs said, chortling at his wit along with his chums.

Pemb didn't join in the hilarity. He stared at Chart for several long minutes, each man's eyes reflecting intense loathing.

"Subdue him," he growled. "Use your truncheons but I want him awake enough to hear. Then bring him to me."

The ruffians who entered the kennel were experts with clubs made from ships' belaying pins. The sailor adroitly struck Chart's skull with just enough force to stun him. Unchained, he was dragged through the stinking ordure to the cage door. The men grabbed handfuls of his hair and twisted his head towards Pemb, who leaned close to his ear and whispered a few words that made Chart writhe despite his dazed state:

"My lads slit the gullet of your blackamoor-loving father on my orders. Served him right for polluting our family's blood."

***

Chart sank into a stupor, unable to think about the past or the present, and especially the future. He was oblivious to the kennel smell but the constant barking made actual sleep impossible. His hands were unbound and the gag removed to permit drinking stinking water and eating thin gruel from bowls identical to those the dogs fed from. But he refused to eat, which seemed to bother his captors, whom he now knew were his father's murderers.

"His Nibs says we gotta keep ye alive," the sailor told him. "I brung ye some proper vittles', too good for a darky if ye ask me." He kicked aside dog turds and set down a tin plate with bread, cheese and gammon. Another piratical looking bravo reluctantly parted with an earthenware jug of watery ale after quaffing from it.

"If ye don't eat, we'll bloody well force it down yer gullet," the sailor threatened.

Despite his lack of appetite, Chart forced himself to consume the food, not because of the threats but to sustain his strength. Energised by rage, he emerged from torpor. Apparently, Pemb and his gang did not intend to kill him. He was well past being concerned about death, but the prospect of living gave meaning to whatever remained of his life. He reminded himself that he was young and reasonably healthy, and vowed that while he still drew breath he would pursue a consuming goal.

Vengeance.

They came for him after eight days, gagging and trussing him from shoulders to ankles before rolling him into an old jib sail. He felt himself lifted and carried outside to be placed in a handcart that rumbled over cobbles. He smelled the Thames stench as he was bundled into a boat and heard the squeak of oarlocks and grunts of rowers. The boat thumped against the side of a bigger vessel. "Easy lads, don't drop him or there'll be hell to pay," a rough voice said as he felt himself dragged up the ship's tumblehome and dumped onto the deck. Like a piece of cargo he was lowered into a space that stank of bilgewater and dead rats.

He was hauled deeper into the bowels of the ship, hearing his handlers grunting with exertion and cursing as he was tossed onto the deck. The sail was unwrapped and he saw by the light of an oil lamp that he was in a small, clammy compartment. His iron collar was connected to a chain attached to the bulkhead, and the gag and bindings were carelessly cut away with knives that nicked him.

"Where am I you bastards!" he snarled at the seamen as they stooped to leave the space. A hatch was closed, and he was left in unbroken darkness that matched the blackness in his heart.

**

Pemb watched from the *Bristol Trader's* quarterdeck until the group of sailors emerged from a companionway and knuckled their foreheads as a signal to the captain of the barque.

"Very well," he said, "Shall we go to your quarters?"

He followed the captain to his cabin and handed him a letter affixed with a red wax seal of the Charteris arms, followed by a purse that clinked with gold guineas.

"Remember," he ordered in a supercilious tone to demonstrate his presumed authority as a member of the Society. "He must be delivered alive to the man this letter is addressed to."

After Pemb was rowed ashore he took a sedan chair back to Chesterfield Street where he breakfasted on devilled kidneys prepared to his satisfaction by the new cook. Finding their imagined insolence unbearable, he had sacked the entire staff who had served his uncle and hired new servants recommended by his club friends. He never questioned the written references, most of which were forged, and his primary criterion for chambermaids was their sauciness and availability for an afternoon tumble.

The new valet, Hanrahan, was a scarred former dragoon in Tarleton's Green Devils who had been rescued from the gallows by his commander after being convicted of raping and murdering a widow in South Carolina. He discreetly reminded his master of an appointment with a physician on Pont Street who was attempting to cure Pemb's irritating case of the French Pox. The good doctor, whose patients included many members of Brooks's and Boodle's and a goodly percentage of both houses of Parliament, examined the chancres on Pemb's penis, nodded gravely, and prescribed mercury pills and an ointment concocted from mercury, laudanum and goose fat.

After a light lunch, Sir Pemberton retired to his bedroom and summoned a fourteen-year-old parlour maid who was a refugee from Revolutionary France. He paid no attention to the oozing sores around the girl's mouth and afterward felt gratified enough to tip her a half crown. When she returned to the basement, he lay abed trying to decide which club to visit that night. He hadn't been to the Cocoa Tree for a week or so, and he craved some variety.

Thinning hair ruffled, he donned a dressing gown and sauntered down the marble stairs to the morning room to find a small pile of envelopes on a silver tray. Topmost was a letter from the family lawyer, Mr. Cave, informing him that the Chancery Court had formally declared him the beneficiary of the entire Charteris estate. This was welcome news as Pemb's numerous creditors were demanding payment, and now he could borrow against the value of his holdings. He had lost count of the number of notes he had hastily scribbled for his gambling debts, much less for his tailors and bootmakers. Not that it mattered for he was now confirmed as a wealthy man.

Sir Pemberton Charteris, Bt. Leading light of the *beau monde*.

***

Pemb hated the countryside and everything associated with it except for grand balls and dinner parties. However, now that he was the master of Knossington Hall he decided that he must endure a few days in Leicestershire to survey his domain and arrange things to his liking.

As it was not fitting for a gentleman of Sir Pemberton's rank to use a stage coach for travel, he sent a message to Knossington summoning the family coach to London. After it arrived, a day was spent provisioning it from Fortnum and Mason with his favourite delicacies such as their popular "scotched eggs", game pie and jellied eels in aspic. A case of hock was provided plus half a case of Madeira to help him endure the long journey along the dusty summer turnpikes. Hanrahan was allowed to accompany him inside the coach. The valet, whose face was marked by a diagonal white sabre scare, was barely five-and-half feet tall. Pemb felt intimidated by taller men, and chose male servants of a certain stature who fed his ego with obsequiousness.

He arrived at Knossington to find it nearly deserted, the

furniture and pictures covered with sheets. The housekeeper, Mrs. Titchmarsh, had left to live with a daughter when she learned that Pemb had inherited. Barnicle, the butler remained only because he was unable to find suitable employment. He greeted his new master with icy politeness. Pemb remembered him as one of the many who had conspired in his humiliation and he determined to sack the man without a reference or back pay. Molly, the chambermaid he had raped, was long gone, having married a farmer near Melton.

Pemb didn't plan to stay long enough to hire new servants, so he ordered Barnicle to engage women in the village to cook and clean. Dustcovers were removed, exposing an oil portrait of his late uncle Sir Arthur by some inferior limner named Romney. He had Hanrahan set up the painting under an oak tree, and the pair spent a pleasant afternoon using it as a target for the collection of pistols and long arms from the Hall's gun room. When the portrait was shredded, he ordered its remnants burned along with the gilt frame. He had hoped to similarly destroy Sir Arthur's collection of diaries, but was told by Barnicle that these had been removed by his lawyers prior to the court cases.

It took two days for Pemb to search each of Knossington's twenty-seven rooms for cash and small *objets d'art* that could be sold in London. When he came to Chart's old room, he ransacked it, piling all his clothing, books and papers onto a fine Aubusson carpet to be hauled away and burned. In a bedside cabinet he found an envelope addressed to Alexander Charteris, Esq. He nearly ripped it up, but out of idle curiosity he tore it open and read the contents which took up four pages, front and back, in precise feminine handwriting. As he read the writer's outpouring of love, reminiscences of romantic interludes, and promises of undying devotion, his fury and disgust mounted.

"Filthy whore," he muttered. "She should be ashamed of herself!"

The *billet-doux* was signed "Arabella". He looked at the first page engraved with a viscount's coronet and the name of an ancient Rutland manor house. Perverse curiosity drove him down to the library, where he found several copies of a work titled *The New Peerage*, published by J. Debrett. In the most recent edition of 1790, he found the viscount who owned the manor, and the list of his eleven children, including Arabella.

Pemb sat looking at the name on the page for a long time, thinking as the shadows lengthened. Closing the book with a clap, he summoned Hanrahan.

"I have a scouting mission for you."

Chapter 13

Chart was kept in the tiny compartment until Dover was off the starboard bow and the *Bristol Trader* was making five knots on a south-westerly heading with all sails set. The captain was mindful that a hue and cry had been raised for his clandestine passenger by the Abolitionists, which accounted for Sir Pemberton's admonition to conceal him. But he had also been ordered to keep the man alive. As a veteran slaver, the captain knew how quickly disease could erupt and death ensue from unsanitary conditions.

The bosun and a pair of crewmen unshackled Chart from the bulkhead and dragged him up to the main deck, cursing at the stench from his unwashed body and clothes encrusted with his own and canine ordure. They clipped his chain to a backstay so he couldn't jump overboard as the crew had seen captive Africans do all too often. A canvas hose was turned on him from the deck pump before his soiled clothing was cut from him and tossed over the side, then the cold saltwater jet hosed him again while he stood naked and swaying on the deck, weak from hunger but determined to stay upright.

The captain believed that exercising his human cargo reduced the mortality rate. "Run round the deck, ye sod," the bosun snapped, lashing Chart's buttocks with his starter – a whale-bone baton weighted with lead.

"Where are you taking me? Where is the ship bound?" he asked, answered by the bosun with a double lash across his shoulders.

The deckhands ignored him as he jogged past them, staggering now as his strength ebbed. The bosun called time at the captain's shout, and Chart stood panting, beyond caring about humiliation, grateful for the small blessing of the warm sunlight and fresh salt-tinged sea breeze.

He was prodded below decks to his cubbyhole prison, finding it damp from a cleaning in his absence. On the deck were a folded blanket, a jug of water and a tin plate with ship's biscuits, salt pork and pease porridge. As the bosun refastened the chain to the bulkhead he pointed at a wooden bucket in the corner.

"Next time on deck ye'll bring yer slops with ye, or by thunder I'll make ye eat it!"

Chart was left in his stygian hole for twenty-three hours each day. He lost track of time. Aside from his daily visits to the deck for exercise and to slop out his bucket, the only light was in his mind. Sometimes he saw his father and grandmother, their faces so clear and real that he could study them in detail. Yet they never spoke to him. At other times it seemed like a grey fog bank such as he had seen on previous voyages blotted out reality and filled his head with bloody visions of mayhem. He would concentrate on small things; the constant creaking of the ship's wooden hull, distant shouts, the skuttle of unseen rats.

When the ship rolled and plunged in heavy seas he would grip the slops bucket to keep it from spilling, mindful of the brutal bosun's threats. He remembered a word from his school days – "metaphor". Yes, he thought, that shit bucket is a metaphor for my life.

***

Hanrahan returned from Rutland to stand hat in hand before Pemb, who was sitting on the Hall's terrace on the fine summer afternoon sampling a bottle of madeira from the cellar that had been carefully stocked by previous baronets.

"Well?"

"Had a good natter with some lads in their village pub. The viscount's poor as a church mouse – selling off the silver in London and can barely put food on the table. The young lady is still unmarried, and likely to remain so, according to the locals."

Pemb, sipped the wine, rolled it sensuously on his tongue, and nodded.

"We'll be staying here longer than planned," he said.

***

Arabella's youngest sister Penelope brought her the calling card, the last butler having departed two years earlier after His Lordship confessed that he was unable to pay the man's wages, which were in arrears by nigh on eight months.

Sir Pemberton Charteris, Bt.

114

The Charteris name revived bittersweet memories. Chart had never been far from her thoughts over the past three years. She was aware from second-hand newspapers and county gossips of his battles in the courts and their sad outcome, although his whereabouts afterwards were a mystery. She also knew that this Sir Pemberton was the new squire of Knossington and that some sort of unmentionable dark cloud hung over him. She was intrigued; visitors to the Manor were rare, especially young men.

"I'll receive him in the Brown Parlour," she told her sister. "No wait – the ceiling is falling in there. Ask him to wait in the morning room. I'll make tea. And yes," she said in answer to the sister's expectant look, "you can join us."

As she started for the kitchen, she halted.

"What's he like?"

Penelope made a face and rolled her eyes.

***

Pemb didn't like dogs. He warily eyed the two old mastiffs that had sniffed his crotch after he sat on a stained settee that had been fashioned when Good Queen Bess was on the throne. The dogs settled onto the worn carpet and began snoring. He would never understand why English aristocrats such as his unlamented uncle Arthur were so mad about dogs and horses. Dangerous, filthy animals.

He had feigned politeness while Penelope prattled on nervously about some silly novel called *The Castle of Wolfenbach*. He figured the bitch was around sixteen, not bad-looking, and could be ripe for the plucking. But that wasn't why he was here.

Another young woman in a plain, somewhat shabby frock entered the room carrying a wooden tray laden with a porcelain tea service. *No silver,* he thought, *Hanrahan's source must have been right. Was this a servant?*

"Sir Pemberton," said Penelope, "may I present my sister Arabella?"

He rose and bowed, studying her as she bustled about setting the tray on a side table and pouring. She was in her late teens, taller than him, rather plain, largish nose, mousy hair drawn back into a chignon. Breasts small from what he could make out. Definitely not his type. Looking at her, imagining that blackamoor Chart between her legs, made his blood boil, yet also excited him. He felt an incipient erection.

After serving, Arabella took her cup and saucer and sat primly on an armchair, making small talk while similarly scrutinising Pemb. Recalling her sister's grimace, she smiled inwardly. His expensive cutaway tailcoat failed to conceal the fact that one shoulder was higher than the other, giving a hunchbacked appearance. The sallow face was pitted, the nose pug-like above petulant lips, and his eyes seemed heated as if reflecting a fiery distemper in his soul. Pemb's greasy hair was already retreating from his forehead, pulled back into a queue and tied with a black ribbon which, despite her isolation from polite society, even Arabella knew was passé for young men.

After half an hour of desultory conversation it was obvious to Arabella that she and Sir Pemberton had absolutely nothing in common. He didn't know the difference between an Arabian field hunter and a Shetland pony, probably thought a whipper-in was a service to be found in a London brothel, and wouldn't recognise a foxhound if it bit him on his skinny arse. Pemb attempted to awe the young ladies by boasting about the lords, ladies and politicians he knew in London, but it was hard to impress people such as the Sherrard sisters who descended from William the Conqueror.

A crashing bore, as Arabella's late mother would have remarked. She fought hard to stifle yawns and didn't offer him another cup of tea. Gritting her teeth in a forced smile, she stood, followed by Penelope. Pemb arrogantly lingered for a few moments before planting his short legs on the floor and standing.

"I say," he said, looking at Arabella, "would you … and, er, your sister, be so good as to visit me at Knossington? The old pile needs to be brought up to date, and I would be grateful for your advice. Money will be no object!"

The girls were speechless.

"Good", he said before they could think of a polite excuse, "I'll send the coach to collect you tomorrow at eleven."

***

Chart's mind swarmed with myriad memories. He tried to resurrect pleasant ones to stave off madness, but they were usually too poignant to bear. The brief interlude with Arabella and lovemaking with Augusta failed to arouse his abused mind and body. He spent days trying to recall the concerts he had attended until he could hear the music of Mozart, Haydn and Clementi and visualise the performances. He recalled plays, especially comedies such as *The School for Scandal* and, ironically, *The West Indian*. Childhood rambles through London with his father seemed to have happened in another world; at times he wondered if his entire life was imaginary and the *Bristol Trader's* black hole had always been his existence.

The bad memories could not be suppressed. He remembered the humiliation and deep resentment after his first encounter with racial hatred as a naïve thirteen-year-old at Westminster School. Following his sheltered, idyllic childhood, the sadism, especially that of Pemb and his cronies, had been profoundly shocking. His gentle father had tried his best to shield him and instil pride rather than shame, but Chart's reaction had been to reject his heritage and blame his parents for the misery. Some part of him had always hoped that things would get better, that he would awake one day and be the Anglo-Saxon he felt inside rather than the dark-skinned person that was taunted and ostracised.

It was impossible to avoid remembrance of conversations with Abolitionists who had supported him so earnestly, the autobiography and lecture of Olaudah Equiano, and other tracts describing the horrors of the slave trade. Yet he persisted in trying to differentiate his current condition with the experiences of hundreds of thousands of enslaved Africans, packed naked like sardines into the dark holds of ships like this. *I am _not_ one of them!* his mind screamed. *I am _not_ a slave. This is all a dreadful mistake!*

At age nineteen, Chart's store of memories was limited. Slowly, inexorably, during the endless hours he began to accept who he was, and what had brought him to this literal dark place which matched black despair in his soul. He recalled his father's misty-eyed stories of his mother, Weju, and how he had saved her from the slavers' auction. He remembered tales about his heroic grandfather Chatoyer, the Garifuna chief - a man to be admired and emulated, a warrior of mixed race like himself, the offspring of a native Carib man and a Fulani priestess from West Africa who had escaped from a wrecked slave ship.

One day (or night, he was not sure which), after what he estimated was his fourth week at sea, he had a dream. A young brown-skinned woman with luminous eyes and long black hair held him in her arms, gazing at him adoringly as she touched different parts of his body. In a heavily accented voice, she whispered, *"you will have much pain and sorrow, my nisanimy* [son], *but you will overcome all and be a great chief and warrior."* He saw his father beyond, face aglow with devotion. *"You have nothing to be ashamed of,"* Arthur said. *"You can be proud to be both an Englishman and a Garifuna."* His parents dissolved into a light like the core of the sun, so bright that he had to turn away, awakening as he did so with rapidly pulsating heart.

He lay gazing into the utter gloom as his heartbeat returned to normal. Like his father, Chart scoffed at organised religion, but now he remembered a sermon heard but largely ignored when his grandmother was alive and he had reluctantly accompanied her to the church in Knossington village. The vicar had preached about Paul the Apostle's conversion on the road to Damascus after being blinded by a heavenly light of intense brightness. When Paul accepted his mission in life, his sight was restored.

Chart knew that he also had a mission.

I will not remain a slave, he vowed, and neither should any other man, woman or child.

***

"No!" Arabella shouted.

"Yes!" her father the viscount retorted, his mottled face under the ratty grey wig nearly matching his purple velvet coat. "For God's sake, girl, he's from a fine old family, owns two thousand acres, and has an income of over three thousand a year! What more could a girl like you want?"

"Girl like me!" she snapped, shaking with rage.

"Yes," His Lordship said, narrowing his eyes, "A girl like you, an old maid with no prospects. I told Sir Pemberton that I regretted not being able to pay a marriage portion. He was most gracious, said it was of no consequence."

Arabella's father neglected to tell her that not only had Pemb not demanded a dowry for his daughter's heretofore worthless hand, the young baronet had offered to pay him £500, which should allow him at least one more season of riding to hounds before he was forced to sell his last two horses.

"He's a vile little humpback! Why, I've only known him for three weeks and ... and I don't love him!"

The viscount looked genuinely puzzled.

"Love? By Jove, when has love ever mattered in a marriage? Count yourself damn lucky that he even wants you, my girl. It's beyond *my* fathoming!"

***

On the *Bristol Trader*'s forty-fifth day at sea, Chart was allowed on deck as usual for hosing and exercise. The crew seemed excited, pointing to a flight of birds that circled the ship before winging westwards. The next day he caught a glimpse of tall green mountains surmounted by a crown of clouds on the horizon.

"What land is that?" he asked a crewman in a low voice.

"Dominica," the man answered.

"Is that where we're bound?"

"Nay," he answered, shaking his head as the bosun approached, followed by a one-eyed man holding a straight razor and large scissors.

Chart was made to squat on the deck while the crewman with the eye-patch sheared him to the skull with the blunt scissors, then cut his thick black beard and used the equally blunt razor to scrape off the remaining bristles on his face. When he was hustled back to his cell, the bosun pointed at the full jug of water and meagre food on the plate.

"That'll be the last vittles you're getting while aboard," he growled. "So don't eat it all at once, like I know you greedy darkies do."

That night, which turned out to be his last on the ship, he buried his pain and shame in an emotional abyss. If he was to survive, not just physically but mentally, to achieve his avowed mission, he had resolved to develop an emotional carapace thicker than the star tortoises he had seen in India.

He wondered if his sense of humanity could ever be resurrected.

Chapter 14

Colony of Grenada
September 1793

Chart awoke from a doze as he felt the familiar motion of the ship stop and heard the rattle of the anchor chain reverberate through the hull. The hatch opened and crewmen entered with a lantern. He was led by his chain into the orlop deck and made to kneel with his neck against an anvil. The iron collar he had worn for over two months was struck off, leaving weals from constant chafing. He was ordered to quickly dress in an osnaburg smock and loose breeches before being prodded up the companionway.

He squeezed his eyes shut against dazzling light as he emerged onto the main deck. Blinking as he opened them, he was struck by the scene that seemed familiar - a small harbour surrounded by neat brick buildings with tiled roofs, presided over by a white-washed fortress on a promontory. The town was ringed by hills, each crowned by other forts, while beyond rose mountains lushly forested with every variegation of green. Colourfully painted schooners were careened on mudflats around the harbour, swarmed over by black men in loincloths scraping their hulls. He heard the haunting notes of a conch horn in the distance ….

And memory flooded back as he was again a five-year-old child in his father's arms, gazing at his homeland as he left it behind for what Arthur had told him would be forever.

Manacles were clamped on his wrists, a rope looped under his arm pits, and he was lowered into a lighter packed with boxes, bales and trunks rowed by eight black men. Waiting on the quay was a surly middle-aged white man wearing a cockaded tricorne and cross belt on a stained white linen coat held together by a brass belt plate incised *Grenada Militia*. He pointed a musket at Chart and spat a gob of saliva onto the hot cobbles.

"That way," he pointed with the musket barrel. "An' don't get no ideas 'bout runnin' 'cause I'm loaded with buckshot and me finger's right twitchy today."

After weeks at sea, Chart was assailed by a profusion of odours as he set off into the heart of the town. The scents of cocoa, coffee, nutmeg, mace, cloves, and cinnamon wafted from warehouses he passed, competing with animal shit, rotting fish and human waste in the open gutters. Mangy, skeletal dogs fought over stinking heaps of rubbish in alleys. It was late morning and few people were about in the sweltering tropical day. Black women in bandanas and voluminous muslin dresses with wooden trays of fruit on their laps sat in shaded doorways, languidly fanning themselves. A few looked up curiously as Chart passed, unused to seeing a striking young man of indeterminate race as a militiaman's prisoner, especially one who carried himself so proudly.

The long musket barrel jabbed him towards a weathered clapboard building with small barred windows. On the walls were a dozen posters, most faded from sun and rain. As he waited for the militia gaoler to unlock the door, Chart read the most legible placard:

Balthazar Estate 21 August 1793.

RUN AWAY from the Subscriber, a negro man of the Pawpaw country, with his country marks on his breast, and marked J.F. on one of his shoulders. Whoever brings the above fellow to me, or lodges him in any one of the island's gaols shall have £5 reward and all reasonable charges. Jon. Fraser.

The militiaman removed the fetters, swung the door open and took three steps back, nervously covering the aperture with his weapon.

"In ye go," he ordered.

Another prison, Chart silently groaned as the lock clicked behind him. He struggled to overcome his dejection.

Two other people squatted in the dim interior, a black man and woman in rags that barely covered their nakedness. When the man moved through the light cast by one of the windows to use the latrine pit in a corner, Chart saw barely healed scourge stripes on his back. In limited English they managed to tell him that they were Fantis, not long on the island, who had run from

122

a plantation. Starving after hiding in the bush for days, they were betrayed by a slave woman on another estate when they begged food from her. She received a chicken for what her master termed her loyalty.

The couple were removed that evening, chained to each other's wrists then bound together by a double wooden yoke on their necks, the woman wailing, the man trembling with stifled anger.

***

Goff had been born Simon Gough in the American colony of Georgia, one of three surviving children out of nine born to Gaelic-speaking Scottish indentured servants who served their time on an indigo plantation and thereafter lived a hardscrabble existence on the banks of Alligator Creek. Goff's father brutalised his wife and children whenever he was drunk, which was more or less a daily occurrence. His mother had all her front teeth knocked out and a pair of cauliflower ears, both sisters were raped from an early age and then pimped to Low Country hunters and smugglers at the nearest tavern for the price of a bottle of rum. Goff bore livid scars on his shoulders and back from years of beatings.

In 1777, aged sixteen, he murdered his father, threw the corpse into the creek to be eaten by alligators, and joined a British Loyalist regiment called the Royal Highland Emigrants. His kilted and bonneted comrades were rough men, but Goff was respected, and feared, by them for his propensity for violence and atrocities against American Revolutionaries and their families.

After the British defeat in 1783, the regiment was disbanded. Goff made his way to Jamaica, his physique plus military background helping him to quickly find well-paid work as a plantation overseer. After less than two years he had to flee after killing a valuable field hand who had the temerity to demand water after hours working under a boiling sun. The estate's owner demanded £100 in compensation, as was his legal right for any prime piece of livestock such as a blooded horse or a male slave. To escape imprisonment for debt to the slave's master rather than murder, Goff had to leave on the first available ship. At Port Royal he found a barque that was ready to sail on the morning tide to Grenada with supplies for the military garrison, paying five pounds for his passage with no questions asked.

After disembarking in St. George's, by a stroke of luck Goff met a plantation overseer named Munro in a tipple house. Munro was pleased to meet a fellow Scot, even a first-generation American one, and after sharing jokes and anecdotes in Gaelic over a couple bottles of rum, he hired Goff as a driver for the La Sagesse estate. The older man was impressed by Goff's imposing height and strength, as well as for his experience in managing negroes.

Munro was ailing, and he gradually gave Goff more authority. Before he died of a bloody flux in late 1791, he wrote to the absentee owner, Sir Arthur Charteris, recommending that Goff should succeed him. Sir Arthur never responded, which was expected as he took little interest in the Grenada estate. After old Munro's burial, Goff moved into the Great House, allowing the estate bookkeeper Paisley, the only other white at La Sagesse, to occupy the overseer's primitive cabin.

By day, Goff ruled La Sagesse with an iron hand, making it one of the island's most productive sugar plantations, from which he skimmed twenty percent of the profits. At night, he was serviced by a harem of slave women who were given the choice of indulging his sado-masochism or labouring in the cane fields from dawn to dusk. Fearful of being thrown out when they became pregnant, they patronised Molia, the Obeah woman who lived on the edge of the slave quarters and did a thriving business in contraceptive and abortive potions and spells, paid for with stolen silverware which Goff never seemed to miss.

Goff didn't receive the letter from the estate's new owner for nearly a week after the *Bristol Trader* arrived at St. George's. A neighbouring planter delivered it to him with some new flints, powder and shot for his firearms. Goff was illiterate, so he asked Paisley to read Pemb's letter, repeating it several times. The content confused him. He had been told by Munro that a "Lord Charteris" owned La Sagesse. He assumed that the "Sir

Pemberton Charteris, Bt" (which Paisley explained was a noble title) was the same owner, and that he had a good reason for sending the mulatto called "Chart" to him with the letter.

"Alive," he mused, holding the paper addressed to the deceased Munro after Paisley left, "he wants the black bastard worked like the meanest slave, but kept alive no matter what and not sold."

***

A burly form filled the doorway, silhouetted against the exterior radiance. As his eyes adjusted, Chart discerned a white man in a broad-brimmed straw hat cradling a blunderbuss, with a pair of pistols stuck in a wide leather belt along with a whip coiled like a serpent around a long wooden handle.

"Out!" Goff ordered.

He cuffed Chart's arms behind his back, dropped a noose attached to a long rope over his head, and climbed onto a swayback horse. Fortunately for Chart the old horse could barely maintain a walk, so he was able to follow for the twelve-mile journey without stumbling or having to run to keep from being dragged – a blessing as he had been weakened by a diet of cassava bread, boiled fish heads and greenish water during his ten days in the gaol. Twice, Goff halted at streams bedside the rutted dirt road to let the horse drink and he did not stop Chart from falling to his knees and gulping water like the animal. His bare feet were soon cut and blistered.

At dusk they came to a side avenue lined by majestic Royal Palm trees which, unbeknownst to Chart, had been planted by his father a quarter century earlier. At the entrance was an upright flat stone barely visible in the undergrowth inscribed *La Sagesse*.

Wisdom, Chart thought, recalling his French. He realised that he had returned to his father's former plantation.

His birthplace. Which now belonged to Pemb.

It was difficult for him to reconcile the uncertain memories of a five-year-old child with the present reality of a man whose innocence had long since been lost. They passed the Great House on a knoll where he had once gambolled with his friends in the ornamental gardens, which had been replanted with maize and other provisions crops. The white-painted walls of the house had peeled and faded to grey. He noticed a group of black and mixed-race women on the veranda as Goff led him past the house.

They stopped at a row of thatched wooden and bamboo huts raised from the ground on tree stumps. Several dozen black people emerged from the cabins and watched from a distance as Goff dismounted. A boy took the horse's reins as the overseer delved into a pocket and handed a key to a skinny white man who hurried up from a nearby cottage.

"Uncuff him and put him with some of the other young bucks," Goff said brusquely.

Chart was assigned to a hut that was unfurnished except for rolled sleeping mats and a collection of half calabashes and chipped earthenware bowls. He was to share with four other men aged between fifteen and twenty-five. They were wary of him because of his unusual appearance, especially his blue eyes. They whispered and made what he assumed was a sign to ward off the evil eye.

The men picked up their eating utensils and trooped out. Chart was hungry and guessed that they were going to their evening meal. He grabbed a calabash bowl and followed them to an open-sided cookhouse, a "boucan", where a large copper kettle was tended by some women. The food was simple but plentiful, consisting of yams, plantains, and a cornmeal and okra dish which the black people called coo-coo. He approached his new housemates who were sitting on a log and asked if he could join them. They grudgingly accepted, ignoring him as they conversed in the island patois, while a pair occasionally slipped into an African tongue. To his surprise, Chart found that he could understand some of their conversation as a door opened in the recesses of his mind and he remembered Phibbah's rich voice telling him stories in the island dialect.

He had noticed a grey-haired woman peering at him from the moment he approached the cookhouse. Now she left a group of older women and men who had been watching him and slowly approached. The young men fell silent.

"I know you," she said. "You Weju's child. I remember the

126

eyes."

A man with a heavily wrinkled face came up.

"Weju cure me when I almost die," he told Chart. "And your father. He a good master. Not like this," he jerked his chin towards the Great House. "But why he send you back here?"

"He didn't," Chart replied, blinking as tears stung his eyes.

It was a strange homecoming. Within an hour every one of the ninety-seven enslaved persons on the estate knew that the son of the legendary healer Weju and the former master had returned as a slave like them. Throughout the slave hierarchy, from the concubines in the Great House, the black and mulatto drivers, the household staff, the carpenters, drovers and down to the lowliest field hands, word spread and speculation mounted about the tall and handsome young man. Gossip was secondary to sex as a favourite pastime in the insular slave community, and Chart's arrival was the most dramatic event in years.

The gossip reached the ears of Goff that night when he lolled in bed between a pair of his mistresses. He was confused about Chart's background and status. Sir Pemberton's letter had not elaborated. The new slave was to receive the same treatment as the other negroes … except that he was to be kept alive, thereby depriving Goff of the ability to punish him with death, as he routinely did with runaways or blacks that were simply too uppity. Well, he had acquired a prime new fieldhand without having to pay anything, and if the buck was foolish enough to show the spirit that Goff suspected lurked beneath that proud face and form, he had many ways to crush it out of him.

After the communal supper three of Chart's new housemates slipped away to the bush to meet what they called "wenches". The fourth, a man around Chart's age who introduced himself as Titus, accompanied him back to the cabin. He explained that he and one other were "Creoles", born on the island, while the other two were "New Negroes", Ibos brought from Africa a few years earlier. "They trouble," he whispered in the dark as each of them laid on his bedroll. "Talkin' about runnin'. They won't get far, so don't get no ideas you'self. Tomorrow you see what I mean."

Titus said that if he kept his head down, worked hard, and didn't sass Goff or the drivers, he could get by without the worst of punishments, although sometimes slaves were randomly beaten "jus' so we knows who's boss." La Sagesse was better than many of the other plantations, where slaves were fed starvation rations and worked to death then replaced by fresh stock from Africa. Goff had learned that well-fed slaves worked harder and produced more to add to the hoard of guineas, dollars, pistoles and doubloons buried in a chest beneath the flagstones of the Great House cellar, which everyone knew about. "Twice a week we gets goat meat or fish," said Titus, "an' on Christmas we don't gotta work and we get pig meat and grog. It ain't so bad."

Chart was already awake when a bell rang at dawn. A pair of mulatto drivers in cast-off finery and straw tricornes mustered around fifty men and women and ordered them to pick up hoes from a cart before herding them to the cane fields stretching to the Atlantic in a green and brown patchwork. They passed a stone windmill with vanes turning in the steady windward sea breeze, and went down a path bordered by various stone buildings from which he heard clanking and loud voices and smelled the heady aroma of burnt sugar cane and molasses. The drivers cracked their long whips to hurry the gang along.

At the edge of the fields Chart saw a bamboo pole driven into the ground with a human head stuck on the top. The eye sockets were empty but the scalp still had a matt of frizzy hair and patches of dark skin that the birds had yet to be peck away.

"You see what I mean," Titus hissed, "That's Congo Sam. He run three times before they hang him, cut off his head, and burn his body."

Chart's gang had to "trench" the land with hoes in order to plant a new crop of sugar cane. The driver told him that he must dig sixty holes per day or he would not be fed. The work was unremittingly arduous and boring. Each hole was like an inverted pyramid, five inches deep, fifteen inches wide at the bottom and two-and-a-half feet at the top. The cane stalks were planted into the holes, continually weeded, pruned and enriched with manure.

The field hands were allowed half an hour at noon to sit in the shade, scoop scummy water from a barrel, and select unripe plantains from baskets before being driven back to work with cracking whips. Chart saw half a dozen men and women lashed, and a woman who fainted was kicked repeatedly by a driver until restrained by the other one. She lay where she fell until they heard the distant ringing of the bell to signal the work day was over. A pair of fieldhands were ordered to carry the woman to the "hothouse" – the slave infirmary.

They had laboured for ten hours. Since leaving India, Chart had had little exercise and he had never experienced the toil that his companions endured nearly every day of their lives. His muscles quivered and joints ached as he hobbled up the hill to the slave quarters. Although he was exhausted, he was also ravenous, quickly consuming his rations before collapsing on his thin pallet.

More of the same tomorrow, he thought numbly. *And the next day, and the next, ad infinitum.* But he couldn't allow himself to slip into the midnight pit of hopelessness. Running like the decapitated Congo Sam was not an option.

Endure! he told himself. *Stay alive and strong.*

My time will come.

Chapter 15

The wedding was not quite the grand affair that Pemb had hoped for.

He waited for the Season to be fully underway so that the nobility and aristocracy would be ensconced in London. Engraved invitations were sent to everyone even remotely related to the Charteris and Sherrard families, plus other luminaries such as the Prince of Wales and the Princess Royal, but only a handful of responses were received as Pemb was unaware that it was considered frightfully *déclassé* to invite guests with paper rather than by word of mouth.

Pemb worried that some of his more unsavoury cronies from the past would show up uninvited, but less than half the pews of St. James's, Piccadilly, were filled on a frigid Saturday in late November, when the aged viscount in full periwig and silver-braided court suit escorted his eighth daughter up the aisle to meet her smirking fiancé.

The Sherrards had lost their grand townhouse to debtors during the reign of Queen Ann over eighty years previously, so the wedding feast was held at Pemb's Chesterfield Street house. After a second bottle of hock the viscount fell asleep with his flies undone next to an overturned chamber pot, but no one but Arabella noticed. She couldn't budge her snoring father, nor could she abide Pemb and his roistering friends, so she took herself upstairs to a cold bed.

Goaded by his chums, Pemb staggered up the staircase an hour before dawn, collecting a riding crop that he had hidden in a niche behind a statue of Diana. Arabella had been lying awake, dreading the consummation of her marriage.

Pemb locked the door behind him and lurched towards the bed. She could smell the alcohol fumes as he came near. He reached for her pale arm in the dim light and pulled her towards him.

"Whore!" he screamed, lashing her with the crop, "filthy blackamoor fucking whore!"

She was too shocked to fight back. He beat her into insensibility, threw away the bloody crop, then raped her, screeching obscenities. When he finished, he rolled off, panting.

"Now you'll get the punishment you deserve, bitch, every day for the rest of your miserable life!"

***

Chart quickly learned that survival depended on subservience. Goff relied on severe punishment and minor rewards to control the enslaved people and extract maximum production from them. He demonstrated his power through random acts of violence and swift retribution for the merest infractions. The terror regime was intended to humiliate and destroy even the thought of resistance. Like other overseers and slave masters throughout the Americas, Goff believed that only fierce, arbitrary and instantaneous violence could ensure domination of the negroes, whom he considered little more than beasts.

Goff tested Chart's servility. At the end of a work day soon after his arrival at the plantation, the overseer was waiting by a fallow cane field where Chart had been trenching. As Chart trooped off with the weary gang, Goff confronted him, whip in one hand, the other on the butt of a horse pistol in his belt. The slaves gave them a wide berth as they filed past with downcast eyes.

"You only dug fifty holes today." he growled. "What ye got to say for yerself, boy?"

Exhausted, Chart nearly let his caution slip, knowing the accusation was untrue. Resentment flared before he hung his head so the overseer couldn't see his hatred.

"Nothing," he mumbled.

He clouted Chart on the shoulder with the long whip handle and Goff studied him for nearly a minute, searching for rebelliousness. Satisfied, he nodded.

"Double quota tomorrow. And no supper tonight."

Resistance usually was a death sentence, yet a few slaves reached their limit of abuse. On Christmas Day 1793 the La Sagesse slaves were allowed to celebrate with goat stew accompanied by Creolian and African music and dancing. An Asante man called Neptune, imported from the Gold Coast the previous year, became drunk from an illicitly tapped barrel of rum. Brandishing a broad-bladed cane knife called a cutlass, he harangued the crowd of revellers in his native language, Twi, calling on them to rise up, kill their oppressors, seize a ship and return to Africa. The crowd fell silent and backed away from him as they observed Goff hurrying down the hill.

"Spoil my Christmas will ye!" he screamed.

The overseer halted at twelve paces, snugged a musket into his shoulder and shot Neptune in the stomach. The load of half a dozen soft lead buckshot spewed his guts in a steaming mess out of a large hole in his lower back. As the Asante rolled on the ground in agony, Goff retrieved the dropped cutlass and hacked at him until he was dismembered like the Christmas goat. Contorted face a crimson mask of dripping gore, Goff picked up Neptune's head and hurled it into the copper cauldron containing the steaming stew followed by the arms and legs.

"You'll eat it all or damned well starve!" he snarled. "Fucking cannibals anyway, ye goddamn black savages!"

Goff turned his back on them and stalked back to his concubines and suckling pig dinner, knowing that nothing would lighten his foul mood. He had paid £75 for Neptune and would now have to replace him from the St. George's slave market. Plus, his white linen shirt and trousers were ruined. *Damn the black bastard for wrecking his Christmas!*

Enslaved people continued to run, unknowing, or not caring, that their chances of eluding capture on a 120-square-mile island were virtually nil. As Titus predicted, the two Ibos who shared the cabin with him and Chart fled a fortnight after Christmas. Goff alerted the local militia, whose members were whites and free men of colour, and the runaways were caught while trying to steal a black fisherman's canoe. They were marched back to La Sagesse where each received 30 lashes from the mulatto drivers then put in the stocks - called bilboes – outside the boiling house. They were gagged, rubbed with molasses and exposed naked to the flies during daytime and the mosquitoes at night for twenty-four hours. While they were in the bilboes each had an ear sliced off and their cheeks and shoulders branded "LS" to show they were the property of the

La Sagesse estate. After their release they were immediately sent back to work without recuperation.

Chart soon realised that the miserly Goff stopped short of incapacitating workers unless they were deemed incorrigible or, as in the case of Neptune, threatened to incite a rebellion. Compared to planters who thought nothing of working their slaves to death, Goff's seemingly lenient treatment was not the result of benevolence – which he had not a shred of – but was the basic business principle of extracting maximum profit for the least expense as he had learned in Jamaica. At any given time only about half of the plantation's slaves were available to produce sugar, rum and coffee; the remainder were employed as house servants and tradesmen such as carpenters and blacksmiths, or were too old, ill or young to work. Robust slaves were hard to replace and therefore expensive. Infant mortality among the enslaved was always too high for natural replacement and planters had to rely on a steady stream of "New Negroes" from Africa. A slave ship carrying a full cargo hadn't made port at Grenada for five months and most of the surviving black people aboard the vessel were debilitated from virulent dysentery that killed twenty percent of them on the Atlantic Passage. Nearly a third of slaves from Africa who were sold in the St. George's marketplace died before they were "seasoned" into complacent workers, a process that took two to three years.

Goff preferred to squeeze economic value from the enslaved. Surly, recalcitrant negroes who stopped short of rebellion could be sold to other island planters or shipped to Spanish colonies and the southern United States where they were usually worked to death. Children as young as six were put to work at odd jobs – an elderly woman called Kuku had found a role for herself as the estate's driveress of children.

Kuku was one of the lucky ones. Slaves who were too feeble to work were denied the basic rations provided by the estate, and their friends and relatives were forbidden from sharing food with them, even if it came from their own gardens or fish and game they were allowed to catch. Most soon died of starvation or committed suicide. Some were executed.

Soon after Goff took over as overseer he was irritated by an ancient African woman suffering from dementia who would loudly revile him to the secret amusement of her fellows. One day he ordered the mulatto drivers to give her 300 lashes, which he knew would kill her. He was outraged when they sullenly refused, telling him that she was an Obeah woman and would put a death spell on them. Goff dragged the old lady to the bilboes by the scruff of her neck and beat her to death, but not before she cursed him in Mandinka with a powerful incantation that made the watching black men and women tremble and fall to their knees.

"What did she say?" Chart asked Titus after he told him the story.

"She say Ogun, god of war, will kill him same way as Jesus."

In February, the cane was harvested. Swinging a cutlass, Chart moved in a line with the field gang cutting the stalks near the root. It was hauled to the wind-driven sugar mill in large, stave-sided donkey carts where it was fed into a series of three vertical rollers that crushed it for boiling. Labouring in the sugar works was the most dangerous work on the plantation as every year slaves' limbs were accidently crushed in the rollers or they were burned by the massive iron cauldrons heated by stalks that boiled the cane into a glutinous brown mass. This cooled and crystalised into semi-refined sugar which was shovelled into hogsheads and shipped to Britain for refining into sugar for sweetening the tea of matrons in London, Edinburgh and Liverpool. The sugar residue was collected and taken to the estate's distillery to be made into a treacly dark rum.

Chart had adapted to the daily and seasonal rhythm of the enslaved's existence. Not yet twenty years old, he stood six feet and three inches in his bare feet, which had grown a thick hide, hard as a leatherback sea turtle, so he could walk unflinchingly over stones and thorns. His upper torso rippled with muscle from heavy labour, abdomen ribbed like a hardwood washboard and thighs as hard as the great mahogany trees in the jungle on the mountain slopes above La Sagesse. Daily exposure to the tropical sun had darkened his skin to the deep bronze of ancient Greek statues he had seen in the cabinet of curiosities at Montague House in London. His hair was sheared short by the plantation barber, exposing the scars from his near scalping by Pemb as a schoolboy.

He didn't lack for food. The older Creoles who were permitted to keep provision gardens augmented his rations with gungo peas, calaloo stew and pone. Wannica, the grey-haired woman who had recognised him as Weju's child, made him tamarind balls, a sweetmeat remembered from his childhood. He had extra meat from manicous and tatous - which the Europeans called opossums and armadillos - caught in snares by men who had been hunters in Africa. A few trustworthy slaves were given "tickets" - passes – allowing them to fish. Although obligated to give half their catch to Goff, in reality they traded or sold a portion of it to slaves on other plantations.

Chart was generally well-liked, partially because of his kinship with the legendary Weju but also because he was always willing to lend a strong shoulder to help a weaker slave load a hogshead or visit those who were ailing in the hothouse. He was tolerated by Goff and the drivers for his pretended humility as much as for his strength and willingness to undertake the most backbreaking work.

Several of the women made it clear that they fancied him. In the prime of his life despite the gruelling labour, his sexual urges were strong. Yet he swore that he would not risk begetting children who would be born as slaves like himself. Fortunately for him and his partners he had learned various things from Lady Augusta that proved mutually satisfying without risking pregnancies.

His ability to communicate in the island patois had been restored to fluency. As it did, other memories of his childhood drifted to the surface of his mind like bubbles from the hot springs in the island's mountainous interior. As he began work each day, he looked towards the giant poinciana on a ridge above the cane fields. The memory of his last day at La Sagesse nearly fifteen years earlier became as deeply etched on his mind as the inscription on the gravestone beneath the tree which he had traced with his small fingers. When at night he awoke in panic from dreams of the dead and the living hell of slavery, he sometimes thought he heard his father's voice in the wind-driven rain that shook the thatch.

"I hope you can remember this place."

Slaves were rewarded for good behaviour with free time on Saturday afternoons to tend their gardens or "lime" – fraternise – with friends. By June 1794, Chart had won a place in this privileged group, and he felt compelled to visit Weju's grave. Knowing he was always under observation by Goff or the drivers, he first visited a woman in the hothouse whose right hand had been crushed in the sugar cane mill. There was not much Chart or anyone else could do for her; cow dung poultices had failed to cure her, the hand was swollen with gangrene and she was in great physical pain as well as mental anguish knowing that she was now useless as a worker.

He walked unhesitatingly down the slope towards the poinciana, now in full flamboyant bloom of scarlet and tangerine. The grave was as he remembered it, the headstone clean and the plot groomed. A handblown jeroboam held wild orchids, and calabashes contained offerings of food and an amulet carved from shell. Chart yearned to sit on the bench as he had often seen his father do, but instinct told him that Goff would consider this as taking a punishable liberty. Instead, he crouched on the grass and read the inscription on his mother's gravestone.

Mon Coeur est á Toi. My heart is yours.

He had no doubt that Arthur had given his heart to the teenage Garifuna woman, his slave. He had truly loved her. For the hundredth time he wondered why his father had never freed her. Was it oversight, simple negligence by a generally good-hearted but sometimes absent-minded man …or something else? Perhaps, unwittingly, Arthur had needed to keep the woman he had described as a free-spirited, noble savage in bondage, so he would not lose her?

Regardless of the reason for his father's inaction, he was suffering the consequences. Death had freed Weju, but he was determined to gain his freedom and fulfil his vow of fighting against slavery. He would bide his time as there was no point in throwing away his life as he had seen others do. A number of people such as Titus seemed to have docilely accepted enslavement, which was the objective of Goff and his fellow planters. But Chart held to the conviction that *his* servitude was temporary.

He had heard murmurings from others who would rise up if there was even a remote chance of a rebellion succeeding. Despite limited contact with the outside world, everyone knew of Tacky's revolt in Jamaica a generation ago, as well as the revolution in Saint-Domingue which had forced the French to abolish slavery in the colony. There was talk about shadowy figures, French emissaries from Guadeloupe, who came at night like wandering spirits to preach the gospel of revolution throughout the island.

Something had been troubling Chart since his return to Grenada. He remembered almost word for word Thomas Paine's diatribe against his father, when he had called him, and other "enlightened" plantation owners and merchants who profited from slavery, hypocrites. Arthur Charteris had argued that his negroes on the Grenada plantation were better treated than the lower orders in Britain. Could that have once been true?

That evening he sought out Wannica, who worked as the La Sagesse seamstress. He asked her if the people had been better treated when his father was master of the plantation. The old woman gazed thoughtfully into the distance before replying.

"Your Papa never beat or kill us. Not hisself. But old Munro and the drivers whip us sometimes, sell people they don't like. Maybe the Master know about it, maybe he didn't, maybe he don't want to know."

She sighed and looked directly into his eyes, her own reflecting decades of suffering.

"Don't really matter whether he a good or bad master," she said softly. "We still his slaves. Nobody *wants* to be a slave."

Chapter 16

The overseer of a nearby estate stopped at La Sagesse on his way back from St. George's to relay news and gossip over a glass of rum. He told Goff that a slave ship had made port the previous day and that its cargo would be auctioned on the next market day.

Goff was pleased by the news. He had lost five fieldhands over the past two months and urgently needed replacements. The woman whose hand had been crushed had died, another female hung herself, and a prime buck had become so enfeebled from Yaws that he had to be put down by a pistol shot to the head, in the same way Goff would do for an old hound or a donkey that could no longer pull a cart.

The two young Ibos who shared a hut with Chart had run again. When they were recaptured, Goff sold the brawnier one to a Dutch slaver who made a good living cruising the Windward and Leeward islands buying problematical negroes cheaply and selling them in Cuba. The captain wouldn't take the second Ibo because of his emaciated state, so Goff was forced to hang him alive in chains from the plantation gibbet for three days then taken down and burned over a slow fire. At first, it was hard to tell if the runaway was already dead or just unconscious, but he revived and called out weakly as the flames licked him. Chart and the other slaves, including children and the house concubines, were made to watch until the body was reduced to ashes. His stony face masked rage as inflamed as the pyre.

Goff rode to St. George's two days later with one of his drivers and spent the morning inspecting the stock of eighty-seven men, women and children who had been washed and oiled to render them more appealing to buyers. He was disappointed that the slaver had stopped at Barbados en route from the Bight of Benin and sold more than half its cargo. But Goff considered himself a good judge of black flesh and he noted several specimens that could replenish his stock.

One of these was by far the largest man Goff had ever seen, black or white. Goff himself was a big man, well over six feet, but the heavily fettered negro towered over him by a full head where he stood with his eyes raised to the cloudless blue sky. His shaven head, face and chest were marked by tribal scarification. Prospective bidders pushed open his mouth, revealing teeth filed into sharklike points, before inspecting his genitals and armpits for signs of disease.

"Hung like a stallion," one man drawled, "He could sire a passel of suckers off half a hundred wenches."

"Pity most of them pickaninnies die before they're weaned," said another.

Goff picked up a couple of young Yoruba women and a muscular teenage Fon male, but was disgruntled at having to pay more than he thought a fair price due to Grenada's labour shortage. When the giant shuffled onto the auction block bidding began briskly, but most prospective buyers dropped out when the bids reached £100. He recognised the only opposing bidder as a free mulatto named Julien Fédon, one of a number of mixed-race planters who owned estates in the northern part of the island descended from Frenchmen who had colonised Grenada before it was ceded to Britain thirty years previously. Fédon was in his forties and had a sallow complexion, tightly curled hair, and features resembling his African mother more than his French father. He was a substantial planter owning some 400 acres and over ninety slaves. As Fédon raised the bid to £105 he glared at Goff, who returned the look with equal malevolence.

Goff figured that he could afford the equivalent price for the giant that he would have paid for two strong male slaves, reasoning he could get the same amount of labour from him. He countered Fédon's bid by £5 and continued to do so until the Frenchman dropped out at £150 and the hammer fell in Goff's favour.

As Goff was counting out payment, Fédon spoke to him.

"You *Anglais* don't know how to make *les nègres* really work," he sneered. "*Le géant* will be nothing but trouble. When you are ready, I may be willing to take him off your hands."

The big man was yoked in a coffle with the other three purchases and herded to La Sagesse where the two new males were assigned to the empty spaces in Chart's hut.

"Boy," Goff told Chart, "I'm naming this dumb ox Samson. You better quickly teach him how to trench and cut cane or I'll have the hide off you too."

As soon as the overseer left, the man he had named Samson turned to Chart.

"My name is Sori," he said in good but heavily accented English. "I refuse to be known by the slave master's name."

In a proud bass voice Sori told him that he was a Fulani prince of the Kingdom of Fouta Djallon in the highlands of Guinea. He had learned English from European traders in his father's capital city of Timbo, and had been trained as a warrior from childhood. While on a slave-raiding expedition he and his comrades had been ambushed by Hausa warriors and traded to a Fanti slaver for outmoded muskets and casks of rum, who in turn marched them hundreds of miles to the coast where they were imprisoned in barracoons to await the slave ship that transported them to the West Indies.

"I will never be another man's slave!" he declared.

Chart sighed, trying to decide what to say that could dissuade Sori from defiance that could only result in torture, mutilation and death. He gazed upwards at the fierce-looking African, realising that they were near in age, and that his bluster masked fear. As his glowing blue eyes met Sori's dark brown ones, he felt an uncanny kinship with him, despite backgrounds which were literally worlds apart – the public school-educated son of an English aristocrat, and the huge African warrior adorned with tribal cicatrices and fang-like teeth. Chart suddenly remembered that his father had told him about the Fulani seer and medicine woman who had been Weju's grandmother. Was blood calling to blood in some mystical way?

"Only *you* own your heart and soul," he said quietly. "You must believe that this captivity is temporary. But the overseer has the power of life and death over us, as I'm sure the king did in your own country. Bend the knee now and work hard so that you will be free one day. If you don't, you will die in chains, and what a waste that would be."

Sori made a scoffing noise, and went out.

The next day the big Fulani began his campaign of passive resistance. Wearing only a loin cloth while oversized work clothes were being sewn for him by Wannica, he strode at the head of the column to the cane fields. Despite Chart's exhortations and warnings, Sori merely scraped at the ground with a hoe.

Soon one of the drivers lashed him with his whip while shouting at him to work harder. Sori ignored him, and simply hunched his shoulders while both drivers scourged him until raw red ribbons appeared on his broad black shoulders. The drivers retired to the shade of a mango tree to confer. Chart went to Sori and furiously trenched beside him.

"You're making a terrible mistake, man," he hissed. "Put some effort into it or there will be hell to pay!"

Hell was paid at midday when Goff arrived with the third driver, an Ibo, leading a donkey. As the drivers attempted to shackle his wrists and ankles, Sori struggled, calling the Ibo his "dog and eater of dirt". Goff slammed the brass butt of his musket into the giant's head until he collapsed. The American overseer watched as the unconscious man was hitched to the donkey and dragged by the heels up the slope to the estate buildings, before turning furiously on Chart.

"Not up to it, are you? Too fuckin' soft to make him work! And here I was thinkin' you might make a good driver 'cause you're half white. Well, you've some lessons to learn as well."

When Chart returned to the slave quarters at the end of the work day, famished and parched, Goff ordered the drivers to lock him in the bilboes next to Sori, whose back was now a bloody mess of criss-crossed stripes.

"Gave this baboon fifty lashes myself and had bird pepper rubbed on. He'll get a hundred tomorrow if he don't shape up, and you'll spend another night with him here."

As darkness fell, other slaves gathered around the stocks, watched by one of the drivers. They weren't allowed to give the prisoners water or food, but they talked to Chart in low voices.

"Sori don't feel no pain!" exclaimed Wannica wondrously. "Never a squeak when he was lashed!"

"Like a stone man!" added Titus.

Grenada was in the midst of the rainy season, and a pelting shower drove the spectators into shelter. Chart twisted his head where it was secured by a locked board, trying to let a trickle of water run down his face into his parched mouth. He saw Sori doing the same.

When the rain stopped, he snarled at Sori in the parade ground voice he had used to command his sepoys in India.

"You're a damn fool, man! They'll break you and then kill you!"

"I'm a warrior!" the African growled.

"So am I! A soldier. A wise warrior chooses his fights when the enemy is vulnerable. Do you want to die?"

"I prefer death to slavery."

"Not the kind of death I've seen here!"

Sori was silent.

"*I* will beat them!" Chart hissed. "*We* can beat them. But we must be cunning, like a hunter, and await our chance for revenge."

Sori grunted and did not speak again for the rest of the night. But Chart heard him whimper and cry out in his native language as he slept with his head, arms and legs thrust through the bilboes.

Drenched by torrential downpours which washed the fiery pepper from Sori's lacerated back, they were released at dawn and allowed to gulp from a water trough and stuff cassava bread into their mouths before joining the march to the fields. Grateful that he had not been flogged like Sori, Chart wondered if Goff's tyranny was slowly subjugating him to passivity like Titus and many of the other enslaved people.

That day, Sori worked hard at trenching the muddy fallow field, seemingly ignoring the flies feasting on his open wounds from the scourging. Chart hoped that he had heeded his lecture. At day's end, the Fulani giant ate heartily, sullenly keeping to himself. When the sleeping mats were unfurled, he chose a space near the door and appeared to fall asleep quickly on his stomach, the only sign that he favoured his raw back.

In the morning, he was gone.

Goff's wrath was volcanic. He lined up Chart and the other

men who shared the hut and whipped them, but managed to restrain himself from inflicting serious injury that would prevent them from working. When it was discovered that the runaway had taken food from the cookhouse, the overseer locked the two elderly cooks in the bilboes after beating them with his fists. He broke the jaw of one, who died a few days later.

Sori held out longer than most escapees. After two weeks on the run, he was spotted by a slave in the island's northern parish of St. Patrick while stealing yams from the man's provision garden. The island's chief slave hunter, Jean-Pierre Fédon – brother of the planter who had bid against Goff for Sori - tracked him with hounds, one of which the Fulani strangled before being brought down by the rest of the pack. The slave catcher received the substantial reward of £5.

Unconscious from beatings, Sori was encased in chains and hauled back to La Sagesse in a donkey cart. In the yard outside the cook house, Chart and his hut mates were ordered to dig a pit deep enough to hold the Fulani in a squatting position with only his head exposed after the earth was replaced around him. His left ear was cropped and his nostrils slit. All the other slaves, including the women and children, were ordered to urinate on him until he revived. Then his mouth was wrenched open and a woman forced to defecate into it before a gag was applied to keep his jaws closed.

Goff knew that having to eat a woman's shit was a profound insult to a proud African warrior.

The overseer was now in a quandary. Ordinarily he would have had Sori gibbeted like previous runways before having his head cut off and the body burned or given to dogs. But he hated to suffer a loss of £150 so soon after buying the big African, and he was angry with himself for making such a poor business decision. As a man who prided himself on knowing how to manage negroes, he should have guessed that there was a good reason why such an apparently prime hand had not been snapped up on the auction block in Barbados before arriving in Grenada.

Remembering his conversation with Julien Fédon, Goff rode

his spavined horse across the mountains to the French mulatto's Belvedere estate in the centre of the island where he cultivated coffee and cocoa. In his arrogance, Goff was oblivious to the aura of menace surrounding the large decaying house in a valley at the foot of a high mountain known by its ancient Carib name of Mount Qua-Qua. The summit was hidden by a forbidding rain cloud which overhung the plantation and grew darker as his nervous horse negotiated the deeply rutted and puddled road. Furtive figures watched from sheds and huts. As he approached the house where Fédon waited on the veranda smoking a cigar, Goff thought he glimpsed white faces at the windows. *Ridiculous*, he thought, *no white men here, just French half-breeds and black slaves.*

Fédon wasted no time as Goff dismounted; news travelled quickly on a small island, and he was aware that the "new African" slave called Samson had been recaptured after running from La Sagesse.

"So, *le géant* was a disappointment to you?"

Goff stepped onto the veranda, removed his sweat-stained hat and mopped his face with a large handkerchief.

"You know why I'm here. You said you can make nigras really work. You should know," he sneered, "being one yourself, and a French one at that."

Fédon's amber face darkened with anger, but he was used to such racist insults from British planters, even on his own property.

"And what is his condition?" he asked brusquely.

"Punished, but he'll recover soon. Better than he deserved. Still strong as an ox and about as smart as one."

"How much?"

"Seventy-five. I paid double that for him."

Fédon coolly removed his cigar, hawked and spat over the railing.

"You must take me for as big a fool as you are! I will give you twenty pounds, and that is generous."

"I'd take a couple of bucks or wenches in trade."

"No. And what will you do if I don't buy him?"

Goff shrugged.

"Auction him at the St. George's market."

"You would have already done so if you thought he could be sold there."

"Gibbet and burning, then," the overseer snapped.

The Frenchman shook his head.

"You have wasted your time coming all this way, *Monsieur américain*. Now leave my property."

Goff hated to be bested by someone he considered a racial inferior.

"Twenty-five," he growled. "I already paid five as a bounty."

Fédon narrowed his eyes.

"*D'accord*. But you get paid when you deliver him to me here, and you get nothing if he is not fit to work."

***

It was a minor act of defiance, but Chart was at the point where he felt he needed to redeem his troubled soul. An hour after Goff left La Sagesse, he filled an empty wine bottle with water and went to where Sori's deeply scarred black head protruded from the ground. He knelt, tore off the gag, gently opened the Fulani's jaw and rinsed out his mouth. Sori's swollen, bloodshot eyes rolled in his head. People left their huts and gathered in a semi-circle, speaking in low voices to one another.

"What you doin'?" one of the mulatto drivers shouted, brandishing his whip.

Chart didn't look up as Sori suckled from the bottle.

"He was dying," he replied, trembling with rage. "If Goff wanted him dead he would have killed him. He'd be worth nothing then, and you would be blamed."

The driver's eyes darted uneasily around the assembled slaves as their muttering grew in volume. The other drivers were nowhere to be seen.

"You next when master return!" he yelled before retreating to his hut.

When the bottle was empty, Chart put his lips close to Sori's remaining ear.

"Do whatever it takes to stay alive until you're free again."

Chapter 17

When the bailiffs arrived, Arabella plumbed the depths of humiliation.

In her naïveté as a girl from the bucolic heart of England, she could never have imagined the horrors her husband would subject her to in the days and weeks after her marriage. Pemb broke three riding crops beating her, the severity of which varied by his state of inebriation. During the first month, the abuse stoked his sexual drive and he would violently rape her. When he was too drunk to raise an erection, or had lost at the gaming tables as he invariably did, he would take out his frustration by trying to violate her with the crop. She was usually able to fight him off by biting and scratching, which he seemed to enjoy, although on a few occasions he left her torn and bleeding.

Arabella had no one to turn to, and even if she had it would have been futile. A wife, especially one of her social class, was expected to submit to her husband regardless of how appalling the situation. She contemplated writing to her father, begging to be allowed to return home, but knew he would not reply. With nothing of her own, she was a mere chattel to be used wilfully by the monster she had been forced to marry, a slave to his perverse whims.

The abuse subsided when Pemb began dividing his time between the St. James's clubs and "Disorderly Houses" around Covent Garden and the Strand. This changed when he abruptly returned to Chesterfield Street early one morning roaring drunk and pummelled her about the head so severely that her nose was broken and she feared she had lost vision in an eye. As she lay recovering, she overheard servants gossiping in the hallway that "himself" – their term for Sir Pemberton – had been blackballed from Brook's for cheating at cards after incurring enormous debts for his losses.

Banned from his other clubs, Pemb turned the townhouse into a private gambling establishment and brothel. A trio of rather long-in-the-tooth trulls was recruited from alleys and doorways off Fleet Street and installed in guest chambers while games tables were positioned in the drawing room. He was chagrined when his aristocratic cronies failed to accept his invitations, but soon found clientele of the rougher sort from merchant sailors, privateers' crewmen and soldiers from the new barracks in Knightsbridge.

Brawls erupted, furniture, bottles and windows were smashed, and a light dragoon's back was broken after an Amazonian whore tossed him down the staircase. One day, the maid who usually brought Arabella's breakfast failed to show, prompting her to venture downstairs past bedrooms occupied by harlots and their clients. A raddled woman wearing only a petticoat appeared at a doorway cradling a chamber pot. She looked blearily at Arabella before closing the door.

Arabella stepped into the drawing room, warily negotiating broken glass and crockery, discarded playing cards, and puddles of vomit and urine. There was no sign of Pemb, who she surmised was with one of the bawds. An unknown bald man was sprawled in a corner with his wig clutched in a beringed hand. She couldn't tell if he was alive or dead, and didn't care. Gold guineas and silver shillings were scattered on the stained and torn Axminster carpet. She felt no guilt collecting all that she could find.

Arabella descended the back stairs to the basement service area, which was deserted except for the coachman, Beamish, a middle-aged man from Melton Mowbray with a face like rare roast beef. He rose from the kitchen table and knuckled his forelock. She asked him the whereabouts of the other servants.

"All gone, m'lady," he replied in his broad Leicestershire accent. "Said they weren't paid for ages and didn't expect to ever be, considering the master's plight. 'fraid some of the silver went with 'em."

"Master's plight?"

Beamish looked compassionately at her battered face and shook his head.

"Rumour is he lost all his money gambling. Beggin' your pardon, m'lady, but 'tis a blessing that he's still got this house, and Knossington of course."

"Knossington," Arabella said under her breath, as an idea began forming. "And why haven't you gone as well?"

Beamish drew a long sigh.

"Nary a farthing in me pocket to get home, m'lady. And it's not as if I can just use the coach."

"We still have the coach and horses?"

"Aye, safe and sound in the mews. Reckon them debt collectors will come for 'em sooner rather than later."

Arabella made a quick decision.

"Pack your things immediately and make ready the coach," she ordered in a brisk tone befitting a viscount's daughter. "Let *no one* stop you, especially my husband. Take the coach to the corner of Curzon Street and wait for me there."

She hurried upstairs, dreading the possibility of encountering Pemb, but the house was quiet except for the ticking of a longcase clock and loud snores from one of the bedrooms. It only took minutes to throw a few things into a portmanteau. She sat at her little marquetry writing desk and took out a sheet of creamy paper embossed with the Charteris arms. Opening the silver cover of a glass inkwell, she dipped a quill and wrote:

22 October 1794

Sir P. Charteris, Bt

Sir

If you have the temerity to pursue me to Knossington I shall take great pleasure in putting the dogs on you before I shoot you.

> *Arabella, Lady Charteris.*

***

Knossington was deserted except for three ancient retainers – a cook, a seamstress and a former footman – who lived downstairs because they had no other home. Fortunately, the estate farms were still producing and the manor was self-sufficient in food and fodder for the livestock.

Six weeks passed without any sign of Pemb, but Arabella kept a double-barrelled fowling piece and a pocket pistol by her bedside. A mixed pack of hounds kept her company when she resumed riding the three remaining hunters. She rode as far as the long drive to her family home in Rutland, but pride and fear of rejection kept her from approaching the manor house. She sent Beamish with a note for her sisters, but did not receive a response.

Arabella visited the ruined medieval chapel in the depopulated village where she had Chart had made love during a golden summer that seemed to have existed in the distant past. As she sat on the fallen baptismal font, she wondered what had happened to him. She could imagine his bitter disappointment at the outcome of the High Court trial. She hoped he had gone abroad to start a new life where his mixed ethnicity could not be held against him.

If that were possible anywhere within Britain's growing empire.

Her contusions slowly healed but her heart and mind seemed permanently scarred. She was bothered by a small, painless sore in her vagina which she attributed to Pemb's torture, but it persisted. Glands in her groin and armpits also seemed unusually tender, but she chose to ignore them and focus on preparing for the winter by collecting firewood and fodder for the horses with the help of the coachman and the elderly household staff.

At the beginning of December, a blotchy red rash appeared on her palms and she came down with what she thought was the flu due to excessive fatigue, joint pain and lingering fever. She tried to brush this off as well, but some mornings she could barely force her aching legs onto the cold carpet beside her bed. She felt so ill that she had to abandon her cherished riding.

On the second Monday in December the first snowfall threatened, the clouds so low and dark that the hours between dawn and dusk struggled into cold twilight. Arabella was in the kitchen with the aged, myopic cook, the sleeves of her patched gown rolled and flour up to her elbows. The arthritic footman slumbered by the hearth. When the bell to the front door rang, she sent the grumbling old man to answer it. He clumped back down the stone stairs ten minutes later.

"'tis a Mr. Cave, says he's your family lawyer," he wheezed, "wishing to speak with you, m'lady. And a pair of other gentlemen. I put 'em in the green parlour."

Arabella was past caring about her appearance, but her duty as an aristocratic hostess was ingrained.

"Oh dear, and no fire laid there. What will they think!"

She hurriedly wiped her hands and arms, rolled down the sleeves, and donned a heavy woollen shawl.

Three men stood respectfully and bowed when she entered the parlour. The room was so cold that their breaths misted like ancestral ghosts. Arabella vaguely recognised a lugubrious, well-tailored fellow in a grey wig and heavy cloak. The other two wore ill-fitting broadcloth and had the dour, flinty-eyed look of hangmen. All three held old-fashioned tricornes. She guessed that the gentleman was the solicitor, which was proven correct when he introduced himself and remarked meeting her at Chart's birthday party four years earlier.

"Would you care to sit, m'lady?" asked Cave. When Arabella hesitated, he added, "I'm afraid I have some rather bad news for you."

Oh, she thought, *is it too much to hope that Pemb has died?*

She sat on a Jacobean armchair, followed by Cave. The other men remained standing. The lawyer cleared his throat loudly, seemingly at a loss for words.

"Lady Charteris," he intoned, "I am very sorry to inform you that you must leave."

"Leave?"

The solicitor vented a deep sigh.

"You must vacate this house, and the entire estate."

Arabella was momentarily speechless, too shocked to comprehend as Cave droned on.

"What?" she snapped, interrupting him. "I cannot leave. What is the meaning of this?"

The lawyer's expression looked genuinely sorrowful.

"Your husband, Sir Pemberton, lost Knossington Hall and the entire estate in a game of quadrille. He had already incurred excessive debts, but the income from the manor was able to service those minimally. The new owner has agreed to meet the debt obligations against the manor but wants possession from the first day of the new year."

"But how!" she cried. "I thought estates always belonged to the family, through the generations!"

"Not in this case. Knossington was not entailed, deliberately so by the late Sir Arthur Charteris, who intended to leave everything to his natural son. But, as you must know, his will was ruled to be invalid and your husband inherited, unfortunately without the protection of a fee tail."

Already stricken with her strange illness, Arabella buried her face in her hands, trying to ward off waves of faintness. Minutes passed during which she heard clicks as Cave impatiently checked his watch. When she raised her head, her eyes swam with tears.

"What about the London house?" she asked hoarsely.

"I'm afraid he also lost that," Cave answered peevishly. "The only asset left is the sugar plantation in the West Indies."

The solicitor explained that the two men with him were bailiffs empowered to occupy the estate to prevent the removal and sale of valuables, including timber, crops and livestock. He offered to arrange transportation for Arabella to a place of her choice, warning that the new owner would have her forcibly removed if she remained on the premises after the first day of January, 1795.

"I deeply regret that it has come to this, m'lady," he said as he took his leave.

"Wait," she said, then described the plight of the elderly servants.

"It is out of my hands," Cave answered, snapping open the cover of his gold pocket watch again to check the time. "Perhaps the workhouse in Leicester will take them in, although I understand that it is quite crowded already and the pestilence is rife there."

After the men left, Arabella sat in the frigid parlour for nearly an hour, too numbed by despair to think coherently. She wouldn't allow herself to slip into self-pity, even though she saw no way out of her predicament. She began shivering uncontrollably.

She slowly climbed the stairs to her bedroom where the wood

fire smouldering in the grate failed to dispel the chill in her body and spirit. She removed the pocket pistol from the bedside cabinet, tightened the flint, and opened the pan to check the priming. Then she slowly went down the staircase, sliding her clammy hand on the oak railing to steady herself.

The horses were still in the paddock beyond the stables. She leaned on the stone wall around it clutching the little pistol. The first snowflakes began to fall, swirling into intensity, erasing the rolling landscape, reducing the horses to vague shapes and her place in the world into a bleak column of obscurity.

Death must be like this, she thought vaguely.

Clenching her teeth, she cocked the pistol and raised it to her chin with both trembling hands. At that moment she heard a whinny and first one, then the other horses, appeared in the gloom, seeking the carrots she usually brought them.

What will happen to them? And the servants?

Arabella lowered the pistol and uncocked it. She rousted Beamish out of his room over the stables and together they brought the horses into their loose boxes, rubbed the melting snow off their coats, and stocked the low racks with hay and the mangers with oats. As she worked, she remembered a letter received two days earlier from her cousin, Georgiana, Duchess of Devonshire.

Through her unappareled social network, the Duchess was aware of the circumstances of Arabella's profoundly unhappy marriage and her self-exile at Knossington. She had written to invite Arabella to the Devonshire's palatial home, Chatsworth House, for the Christmas holidays, pointedly noting "we would enjoy your presence alone."

"Make ready the coach for departure at dawn tomorrow," she ordered the coachman. "And make ready your blunderbuss too."

Positive activity lifted Arabella's sprits. She packed her scant belongings, including her only marginally fashionable gown which she thought even Chatsworth's servants would turn up their noses at. She found the three old retainers in their habitual places in the kitchen, the only really warm place in the house. She told them they were going on a picnic and ordered the cook to pack a large hamper of roasted ham, capon, cheese and bread with stoneware bottles of small beer. She supervised the packing of their meagre possessions, which no one questioned, and commanded them all to sleep in the kitchen that night as they would leave at the crack of dawn the next day.

She worried that the bailiffs would become suspicious, but fortunately they had chosen to stay in the disused servants' quarters on the Hall's upper floor where they could keep watch over the estate from the windows. They had apparently been ordered to be unobtrusive; that afternoon after the snow stopped falling Arabella noticed one of them tramping across the white blanket covering the park to the village, from which he returned an hour later with a basket which she surmised was food and drink from the public house. This gave her an idea. Not trusting the dotty servants, that night she personally took the bailiffs a large pork pie and two bottles of rum, for which they thanked her profusely. She hoped that all would be consumed by the early hours, rendering them into deep slumber.

She barely slept that night, uncomfortable from pains and chills and apprehensive about her decision. She was dressed long before dawn and carried her portmanteau and fowling piece to the servants' quarters, rousing the trio from their pallets on the warm stone floor. Slipping out the back door, she crunched through the new snow to the stables, gratified to find Beamish standing beside the coach in the courtyard with its four matched bay Yorkshires harnessed and saturating the air with steaming breaths. The coachman lifted a brass-barrelled blunderbuss with a conspiratorial grin.

"I seen them two lads upstairs," he said.

"No matter what, they mustn't be hurt if they try to stop us. Just … frighten them away if necessary."

The servants were shepherded to the courtyard and helped aboard the coach. None had been aboard such a vehicle before, much less *the baronet's*, and they chattered like excited children on an outing despite Arabella's attempts to shush them. She could never have left these simple country people behind to face the degrading misery of the workhouse. It was perfectly acceptable for servants to travel with their mistress to country house visits, although the Duchess would probably be surprised by the decrepitude of Arabella's entourage.

Beamish cracked his whip, jiggled the reins and said "off me lovelies" in the lowest voice he could muster. The coach rattled under the courtyard archway, rounded the Hall and picked up speed on the pristine snow-covered drive as a tepid sun rose behind them. Arabella heard a shout from an attic window but her mind was elsewhere.

Always running, she told herself ruefully. *Where will it end?*

***

Despite her kinship with the Duchess, Arabella had never been to the magnificent Derbyshire estate called Chatsworth sixty miles from Knossington, which made her own ancestral home seem like a peasant's smallholding. Arabella waited nervously on the entry hall's marble checkerboard floor beneath its enormous tapestries and frescoed ceiling, eyed by the supercilious butler and a pair of liveried and be-wigged footmen.

The Duchess swept in fifteen minutes later, aflutter in a muslin gown *a la grecque* and carrying a large swansdown muff. She kissed Arabella on both cheeks.

"Nearly in time for tea," she said, candidly eyeing her cousin from head to toes. "But I think we should find you something more suitable to wear first, don't you think?"

She ushered her up the red-carpeted staircase, chattering animatedly, trailed by a hierarchy of servants led by her personal maid. Arabella was shown her room and the Duchess left her while she bathed her face and hands in a large ceramic bowl filled with warm water from a series of silver pitchers. When she finished, a young woman in a black gown and mob cap curtsied, announced that she was her maid, and showed her a collection of Georgiana's gowns, undergarments and shoes to choose from. During tea and supper, she was treated like an honoured guest rather than a penniless relation, seated close to the head of the table and effusively introduced to all and sundry.

The next morning, Georgiana asked Arabella to breakfast with her alone in the parlour of her private suite. She coaxed Arabella's story from her, causing her to break down into anguished sobs. The kind-hearted Duchess embraced her, stroking her hair as she would one of her own children.

The well of Arabella's tears ran dry. Georgiana kissed her forehead, then held her at arm's length, frowning.

"My dear, you are burning up! Are you ill?"

After Arabella described her symptoms, the Duchess rang a bell for the butler, ordering him to summon the doctor from the nearby village of Baslow. The physician, an elderly man in curled peruke and frock coat, examined Arabella in the Duchess's suite with Georgiana seated nearby. When he finished, he cleared his throat twice.

"My Lady, I'm afraid that you are afflicted with the French Disease."

"What?" asked Arabella, having never heard the term before.

"Syphilis," the Duchess said dryly. "Never mind, many of the best people have it, including a royal or two I could name. I'm sure that the doctor can cure you."

The physician frowned. He was unimpressed by nobility, and after seeing decades of pain and suffering in his long life he always told his patients the truth.

"There is no known cure, Your Grace. However, I shall prepare a supply of mercury pills which may arrest the disease."

Whether it was the mercury treatment, unburdening of her soul to the Duchess, or sharing in the Christmas festivities, Arabella soon felt much better. She understood that other guests were aware of her husband's disgrace, but no mention was ever made in the polite, albeit insipid, conversations during endless dinners, balls, card games, music evenings and rides across the frosted landscape of the beautiful Peak District surrounding Chatsworth. Scandal was as much a part of the aristocratic milieu as taking the waters at Bath – no one minded that Georgiana's lover, Charles Grey, by whom she had an illegitimate daughter, was among the Chatsworth guests, and the Duke of Devonshire treated him cordially. Arabella, daughter of a viscount, was one of their own, despite the fact that her husband was an outcast from Society.

On Boxing Day, the Duchess asked Arabella to walk with her around the lake, both women bundled in greatcoats and newly fashionable brimmed beaver hats. The gravel pathways were newly swept of snow that had fallen overnight and they squinted from the sun shining in a rare blue sky shot with cloudy tendrils.

"As you are aware," Georgiana said, "we have powerful friends who are always ready to help with certain 'arrangements'. Your coach was returned to Knossington with no questions asked, and the coachman will be kept on by the new owner. As for your servants" – the Duchess smiled – "they will stay here for the rest of their lives, sharing an almshouse built by the third Duke with our own estate pensioners. We Devonshires take care of our own, y'know."

Georgiana halted and took her cousin's gloved hands. She gazed pensively into Arabella's eyes before continuing.

"As for you, my dear … that odious creature you are married to has been persuaded to never lay a finger or any other bodily part on you again. He will be paid a small monthly allowance as long as he complies – and as long as you live - but has been left in no doubt that if he relapses he will meet a well-deserved and painful end. He was destined for a debtor's prison early in the new year; however, passage was booked for him on a ship bound for Grenada, where his sole remaining property, a sugar plantation, is beyond the reach of his creditors."

"So, I will never see him again," Arabella said hopefully.

The Duchess closed her eyes and contorted her face as if in pain before replying.

"No, my dear. You will go with him."

Arabella's knees buckled, and Georgina's hands moved to her biceps to hold her up.

"We women at the pinnacle of Society think we are free," she told her, "but even I, Duchess of Devonshire, exist at the whim of my husband, William. I wish that I could keep you here as my companion, but sadly one of the conditions of the 'arrangement' was that you must return to your husband. I'm afraid that every scandal has it limits," she added sadly.

Arabella was shaking her head in bitter disbelief.

"You can make a new life for yourself as chatelaine of a plantation," the Duchess continued. "I've heard that the West Indies are a tropical paradise, a peaceful Garden of Eden with happy slaves at your beck and call! And perhaps Pemberton has changed for the better."

"He'll *never* change," Arabella said acidly.

Chapter 18

Colony of Grenada
February 1795

As Chart wearily returned from the cane fields to the quarters he sensed a current of excited curiosity among the enslaved.

"New master an' mistress come," someone told him as he waited in the supper line.

"Goff not happy," added another with evident glee, "he gotta move out of Great House."

Chart suspected who the "new master" was even though he had assumed that Pemb would remain an absentee plantation owner. He doubted that the new "mistress", whoever she was, would last long. The few white women who were foolish enough to take up residence in the West Indian islands usually died within a year.

Late the next morning, the proprietor of La Sagesse appeared at the edge of the cane field accompanied by Goff, who towered over the small man with a hunched back dressed in a dark frock coat and cocked hat more suitable for London than the Caribbean. Chart was bent low, chopping at the stalks, at the far end of the line of harvesters. His rancour at seeing Pemb clawed at him like a tiger he had once seen mauling a sepoy.

Carrying a silver-headed walking stick, Pemb seemed to be myopically looking for something, or someone, and Chart had no doubt who it was. His face was shadowed by a palm frond hat and he kept his head down to avoid recognition. Bare from the waist up, burnt by the sun over many months, his skin was now nearly as dark as other slaves. He watched from the corner of his eye as Pemb loosened his neck stock and removed his hat to impatiently fan himself. Chart saw that his cousin's hair, worn short in the *Brutus* style, was in full retreat from his sweat-sodden forehead and crown.

After less than an hour Pemb apparently could not abide the torrid heat. He lectured Goff, tapping him on the chest with his cane, as he issued orders. Even from a distance, it was clear that the overseer was remonstrating with him. Both men left together.

When the field hands took their midday break under the shade trees, Goff was waiting to confront Chart with one hand on the pistol in his belt and the other holding a whip. "Hands out," he snapped, "and no trouble." One of the drivers snapped a rusty set of manacles on his wrists. As he preceded the overseer up the hill towards the Great House, he heard Goff muttering "Fuckin' wee hunchback bastard! Don't care that we can't spare a prime hand during harvest!"

A stake had been driven into the ground twenty paces from the veranda. From it snaked an open iron collar at the end of a ten-foot chain. Chart halted as he saw it, but Goff cracked his whip and he stood in mute resignation as the driver closed the collar around his neck. He squared his shoulders and stood straight as if on parade, gazing towards the poinciana tree on the lower ridge rather than at the veranda, where a deformed figure was standing.

"Look at me, you black bastard!" shouted Pemb. "Look at your master!"

Chart calmly ignored him.

"You!" Pemb shrieked at Goff and the driver. "Beat the shit out of him until he obeys!"

As the overseer and driver uncoiled their whips, there was a loud gasp from the veranda and a feminine voice exclaimed "My God!"

Chart turned towards the house.

***

Arabella lost no time after her arrival the previous day in ousting Goff and his three slovenly concubines from the Great House, although she doubted that the women would be away for long as she saw Pemb leering at the comeliest of the trio. She made a quick tour of the house, choosing an airy bedroom with a locking door for herself. Disgusted by the filthy state, she briskly ordered the sullen domestic servants to begin a thorough cleaning, beginning with changing the bed linens in her room. That night she lay awake with the pocket pistol to hand, listening to strange tropical night noises -- piping tree frogs, chirping crickets, bird calls and peculiar rustlings which reminded her of the haunted house she had grown up in.

She slept late until roused by the sun slanting through the jalousies, awakening fatigued and aching from disease. She had brought a three-months supply of mercury pills and hoped that there was a chemist shop in St. George's for replenishment, even though the medicine seemed to have little effect as the pox waxed and waned.

Slipping on a dressing gown over the lightest frock in her meagre trousseau, Arabella went down the mahogany staircase to the centre hall. She heard Pemb shouting and followed the sound to the veranda where he stood against the railing, yelling at three men in the unkempt garden. As her eyes adjusted to the sunlight, she saw that one of the men was chained by his neck to a pole, like old engravings of bear-baiting. He had his hawklike profile towards her as he looked towards a distant tree aflame with reddish-orange blossoms. The prominent nose and proud bearing struck a chord in her memory. She cried out ... and knew for certain when he turned towards her, blue eyes wide in his dark face.

***

"Chart! Oh my God!"

Chart's stoicism cracked as he focused on the woman who called his name. It took a moment to recognise her. She had aged badly in the four years since they had parted, her face pale and lined, looking more like a woman of middle years than a girl who had not yet had her twentieth birthday.

"Arabella!" he cried, too shocked to realise why she was here.

Goff and the driver paused as Pemb turned towards Arabella.

"So!" he yelled, "welcome to the happy reunion with your blackamoor lover!"

Bristling with anger, he advanced on her with his walking stick raised until Arabella pulled the little pistol from a pocket, cocked it and aimed with trembling hands. Pemb halted, mouth working, then turned back towards the group in the garden.

"Did you hear me!" he screamed. "I command you to whip that black turd until he kneels and calls me 'master'!"

They lost count of the number of strokes after the first dozen. Goff and the driver worked alternately, laying on the lashes until their arms grew tired and their shirts were sodden with sweat and spattered with Chart's blood. Arabella wept and stamped her foot in frustration, but she had no authority to stop the scourging. She came close to shooting Pemb but had the presence of mind to know she would be convicted of murder, and she had no authority over the overseer and his minions. After several minutes she fled to her room and threw herself on the bed, pressing palms to her ears to stop the slapping noise as Chart's back was shredded.

Chart clenched his jaw until he thought his teeth would crack, but after half a hundred lashes he could not restrain agonised cries. He grew light-headed from the pain and slipped to his knees, struggling to stay upright, but after another score of strokes he fainted and collapsed face down. Only then did Pemb step off the veranda.

He studied Chart's back with smirking satisfaction. The flesh was so deeply torn that the white bone of his spine and shoulder blades was visible amidst the bloodied mass of torn flesh and muscles. Pemb dragged one of his feet through the dirt and ground it into the raw mass of flayed meat.

"Turn him over," he snapped.

His cousin lay facing the azure Caribbean sky dappled with wispy clouds, eyes closed, breathing stertorously, while his unconscious body twitched.

"Who's the big man, now?" he hissed, then lifted his walking stick and beat Chart's head and chest with such fury that the silver ferule broke off.

Pemb sent Goff and the driver back to work, leaving Chart lying unconscious in the broiling sun while huge blue bottle flies buzzed and feasted on his wounds. During the afternoon Pemb would occasionally step onto the veranda to gloat over the chained man lying in the garden. Goff returned after the evening bell rang.

"Will he die?" asked Pemb.

The overseer nodded.

"Aye, unless he's physicked."

"I'm not *yet* ready for him to die. He hasn't called me 'master'. Do what you must to fix him up."

Goff summoned four young men. After Chart was unchained, he was lifted onto thick bamboo poles and carried to the hot house, where he was left in the care of Molia, the plantation's Obeah woman and healer. Wannica and other women helped to clean his wounds with snake plant water after dousing them with high proof white rum. Using silk thread stolen from the Great House, Wannica stitched lacerated muscle, flesh and skin together before Molia applied soursop poultices to his back and face. Chart's nose was broken, bent to the side, and clogged with blood. Molia cleaned out the blood and mucous with a straw then firmly grasped the nose, reshaped it, and applied a bamboo splint.

"Handsome boy like him need his nose back," she cackled, to nods of the other women.

Arabella entered the infirmary as they were finishing the treatment. The women stood respectfully – the entire plantation was aware of the inexplicable dynamics between the white woman, their new master and Chart, but the animosity between husband and wife was obvious.

"Tell me what to do," she said to the black women.

She spent nearly every daylight hour with Chart, nursing him under the gentle instruction of Molia, who taught her the use of natural medicines such as gumbo limbo and aloe to stave off infection and accelerate healing. Pemb looked in once but quickly withdrew from the almost physical atmosphere of hatred towards him.

"Doesn't look like he'll be in any shape to fuck you again soon," he sneered to Arabella.

On the third day Chart regained consciousness and half-opened the eye that wasn't swollen shut. He looked at Arabella for several minutes, seemingly struggling to comprehend.

"You're really h-here," he gasped hoarsely. "H-how?"

She recounted her life over the past four years while she changed his dressings and made him drink jackass bitters through a reed to reduce pain. She was too embarrassed to confess that Pemb had infected her with syphilis. As Chart grew stronger, he was able to tell her in turn about his misadventures, omitting the atrocities he had witnessed as a slave. She was shocked when he venomously described Pemb's revelation about the murder of his father.

"The magistrates in London should be told!"

"It's too late. And who would believe the hearsay of a slave against that of a baronet, even a disgraced one."

"Perhaps they would believe me," she said fiercely. "And you have some powerful friends in London. Even Wilberforce mentioned you in one of his parliamentary speeches about emancipation."

He shook his head. Arabella's pensiveness changed to a worried look.

"Pemb won't let you live, will he?"

Chart did not respond.

***

To Arabella's amazement, by the end of two weeks Chart had largely recovered. His back was still tender, his nose was slightly askew and his face had bruises darker than the skin, but he was nearly fit for labour, which Goff ordered him to resume the following day.

"You've worked wonders!" Arabella told Molia, much to the Obeah woman's baffled embarrassment. "You should set up a surgery in Harley Street. Chart never would have made it if he had been left in the hands of those quacks who bleed patients and give them tobacco smoke enemas!"

Pemb had been absent in St. George's for the past few days, riding a decrepit old mule that he could just about manage. It was not the dignified mount of an important plantation owner and baronet, but he was afraid of horses, even the ancient spavined mare that was the only horse left on the estate.

Every white and free coloured man between sixteen and sixty was required by law to serve in the island's militia, and one's rank was generally based on wealth or social status. Pemb had decided he would be a captain, and was being fitted by a tailor for a heavily braided scarlet uniform and a sabre that had belonged to a Royal Artillery officer who perished from the Yellow Jack. He had a room at the Antilles Inn, but found time between fittings to spend lazy afternoons at a brothel on Lagoon Road featuring a stable of delectable quadroon and mulatto strumpets. Fortunately, as he was penniless, both the tailor and the madame took notes drawn on the plantation in exchange for services rendered.

When he returned to La Sagesse, he stepped onto the veranda with a tumbler of rum and lime sweetened with cane juice. His eye caught a figure in white muslin beneath the great Royal Poinciana overlooking the fields. Squinting, he discerned Arabella stooping over something on the ground.

Pemb slipped inside the house so she would not see him as she returned and headed for the infirmary. Curious, he retraced her route to the tree, seeing for the first time the neatly tended grave with the French inscription on the headstone.

Weju.

He recalled the name from his uncle's calf-bound diaries in the library at Knossington. Sir Arthur had written of his great love for the slave girl, Chart's mother. The diaries had served as evidence in the High Court to invalidate the prior baronet's will.

Mon Coeur est á Toi. My heart is yours.

He rubbed the pox rash on his neck and smiled.

***

Next morning, Goff appeared in the hot house and ordered Chart outside where a driver waited with a shovel, sledge hammer and a burlap bag. Manacles were clamped on his wrists and ankles.

"I'm in no condition to run away," he said.

"Not my orders," the overseer muttered.

An ominous feeling gripped Chart as they walked down the path leading to the poinciana. Pemb was lolling on the iron bench beneath the tree holding a cocked pistol. He nodded at Goff, who had also extracted a pistol from his belt.

"Give him the hammer," he said to the driver, who held it out to Chart.

Chart knew what was expected. He clenched his jaw, blue eyes drilling into Pemb's shifty brown ones.

"Take it!" ordered Goff.

Chart considered accepting the sledge hammer and attacking

Pemb, but knew he would be shot before a blow could be struck. And it wouldn't be a clean shot to the head or heart that would kill him quickly, but one to the gut that would cause a lingering, agonised death.

"No," he said, never taking his eyes off his cousin.

Pemb seemed to have anticipated this. He nodded to Goff, who in turn looked at the driver.

"Do it."

Weju's headstone was swiftly smashed into rubble while Chart stood quivering with suppressed wrath. Pemb watched him intently, savouring his reaction.

"Now the shovel," ordered Pemb with a smirk.

Again Chart refused.

"Chain him to the tree," he ordered. "He can watch."

As Chart was manhandled to the poinciana and chained to its bole, Arabella ran up.

"What are you doing?" she demanded breathlessly.

"Removing a blight on my lawful property," he replied. "You can stay and watch too, but I fear you'll need a strong stomach."

Arabella looked at Chart's stricken face before turning away, weeping bitterly as she trudged back to the Great House.

Chart kept his eyes closed, features twisted into a grimace, white hot fury coursing through his arteries and exploding in his mind while the driver excavated the grave. He caught a whiff of putrefaction when the sounds of grunting and digging stopped and the slave driver said, "Here the bones, master."

"Hmm," said Pemb. "Not enough even for the dogs to gnaw on. Put 'em in the sack and toss 'em in the cesspit."

There was a long silence.

"What's keeping you, dammit!" Pemb exclaimed.

"Bad magic, can't do, master. I be cursed if I do that. Weju's jumby already vexed!"

"I'll do it," Goff said resignedly. "The dead woman was like a goddess to these ignorant savages. The negroes are more afraid of ghosts and curses than they are of punishment."

When he knew they had finished and left, Chart opened his eyes and looked at the open grave surrounded by chunks of white marble. Witnessed by no one but the spirits of his parents, he sagged against the chains, letting himself succumb to uncontrollable grief. Body racked by sobs, scalding tears cascaded down his stubbled cheeks to saturate the blood red soil at his bare feet.

***

Late that afternoon Pemb called Goff to the Great House.

"This evening, I'll be going into St. George's again. Militia muster, y'know. When I return, I want you to hang that bastard Chart from the tree he's chained to. Keep him there until then, but make sure he stays alive as I want to watch his black soul choked out of him."

Arabella had eavesdropped on the conversation. She caught up with the overseer as he left the house.

"Release him!"

Goff hated being given orders by a woman, and he knew that Arabella's command carried no weight anyway.

"Can't do. Master wants him kept there."

He hurried away towards the primitive overseer's cabin, which he despised after living in the relative luxury of the plantation house. The cabin had been empty since the bookkeeper, Paisley, died of the black vomit. Goff's concubines had not followed him, and he suspected that it would not be long before they moved back into the Great House with the little humpback.

I've had enough, he told himself, *time to set myself up with my own cotton plantation in the Alabama territory. Got enough cash under the floor to buy a dozen or so negroes up there to get started. I'll tell the English dwarf tomorrow and make sure he pays me what I'm due.*

Arabella went to the kitchen and ordered the cook to ladle goat stew into a copper pot along with a bowl of dasheen. She drew water from the ceramic cistern into two empty rum bottles and put them all into a basket with a spoon. She brushed past Pemb, who was sitting on the veranda with one of Goff's former concubines sitting on his lap and giggling.

"Supper *a deux* with your black lover?" he called, and chortled while fondling the slave woman's exposed breast.

Arabella stayed with Chart long past nightfall, cajoling him into eating despite his lack of appetite.

"Don't lose hope," she begged, and he grinned ironically recalling how he had once said the same to Sori, who he guessed had also probably joined the ranks of the dead.

The full moon rose in a clear sky, lighting the landscape and casting shadows which seemed to shift shape like wraiths. The open grave was a bottomless pit of blackness in which Arabella imagined she saw movement. Shivering, she lifted her head towards the mountains, where drums beat, conch horns reverberated and torchlights bobbed through the jungle. Despite his heavy heart, Chart sensed an electric tension in the air.

"You'd best go."

"I have my pistol." She rose on her toes and kissed the dry tears on his cheek.

Arabella was dozing fitfully when she heard tapping at her locked bedroom door. She cocked her pistol and cautiously turned the key to see Wannica in the doorway with a troubled expression on her face.

"Ma'am," she whispered. "Something happening!"

Chapter 19

Illuminated by the full moon, they struck the little coastal town of Grenville just after midnight. A hundred men, some in French uniforms with revolutionary cockades on their hats, combed the town for their prey, united by hatred of the British who had supplanted them on their native island,

Most were *gens de couleur* – free people of colour, descendants of the French men who had first colonised Grenada a century and a half earlier. They came from various walks of life; some were wealthy planters and slave owners, others were tailors, silversmiths and sailors. A few whites and free blacks were among their number. All were in a fervour driven by the lofty ideals of the French Revolution, indoctrinated by revolutionary agents who had infiltrated Grenada from the island of Guadeloupe, where chattel slavery had been abolished.

Their attack was carefully planned. Divided into small groups, the revolutionaries dispersed to the houses of British merchants, tradesmen and artisans. Some victims were butchered in their beds with cutlasses and bayonets, others were dragged into the streets, made to kneel and shot while begging for their lives. The captains of two ships in the harbour were surprised in a shanty bordello. One was beheaded with an axe but the other drew his sword and managed to fight his way to the beach. Badly wounded, he evaded the sharks and swam to his ship, raising the alarm.

A mulatto youth was cut down trying to defend his white father. Half a dozen other mixed-race men of English and Scottish descent were rounded up and summarily tried in the street by what one of the uniformed white Frenchmen called a "Peoples Tribunal". Each was asked to foreswear allegiance to King George III and join the Revolution. When the first two were slow in answering out of confusion or unwillingness, they were shot in the head. The last four terrified men readily pledged their support for the cause and were drafted into the insurgents' ranks together with a score of black men.

Within an hour, every white Briton in Grenville lay dead. The attackers called to the enslaved people, fearfully cowering in their masters' houses, proclaiming that they were free.

"Everything now is yours!" the revolutionaries shouted encouraging others to follow their example of looting the dead men's homes and shops. "*Vive la revolution!*"

Elsewhere on the island, coordinated attacks were taking place against other towns and the plantations owned or managed by British colonists.

***

"You must hurry, Ma'am!" Wannica pleaded. "No time to dress!"

As Arabella followed the slave woman to the back door, she heard yells and conch horns. Torch flames lit the wavy glass in the windows, and one was suddenly shattered by a thrown stone, followed by others. Gunshots rang out from the overseer's house.

"What is happening?" she asked in a terrified voice.

The front of the house resonated with crashes and loud voices. Arabella paused at the door in bewilderment. Wannica turned and impatiently grabbed her arm, pulling her outside where the estate's blacksmith held the sway-backed horse by its reins.

"No saddle, Ma'am. You go now or you die! Ride to St. George's town!"

"Wait! What about Chart?"

"I set him free, Missy," promised the smith. "Now you go!"

The two black people boosted her in her white nightgown onto the horse's back. At that moment a group of slaves came around the side of the house. Thinking quickly, Wannica called out, "It Weju jumby, she come back," and was echoed by the smith, who slapped the horse's croup, making it bolt toward the crowd. "Weju, Weju!" they called as Arabella charged towards them with her nightgown flapping like an pale apparition freed from the grave. The slaves fell back in terror as the horse charged past as fast as its old legs would carry it.

The dark track was clear of insurgents. Arabella got control of the horse and cantered out of the estate's entrance and onto the road to St. George's. Behind her, from the plantation, she heard screaming that lasted until she was out of earshot.

"Saved by Weju," she thought wonderingly. She breathed a prayer to the dead Garufina woman to help her son survive.

***

Goff prided himself on his instinct for danger which had served him well during the American war and in Jamaica. But his lack of awareness, numbed by two flagons of grog to alleviate anger and frustration, proved fatal.

He should have noticed the signs during the previous week. Newly enslaved men had shaved their heads, a traditional African preparation for battle. Both male and female field hands, their hatred unmasked, were surly to the point of insolence, resulting in more than twice the number of daily beatings meted out by Goff and his drivers. The Ibo driver, who had been jumpy for days, ran away the night before the full moon.

Goff slept with his door barred and louvered shutters closed. He came quickly awake when he heard loud voices in patois and African dialects while sledgehammers smashed against his door. He always kept a pair of horse pistols by his bed and fired both through the thin door panels, but they broke in before he could reload.

The slaves swarmed over him. He fought hard, punching, kicking and cursing, but they subdued him and clamped iron shackles on his arms behind his back. He was dragged outside and up the path to the plantation house, spat upon and showered with calabashes of shit and piss. As he passed the rum distillery, he saw the heads of the two remaining drivers impaled on poles.

Several young men waited on the roof overhanging the Great House's veranda. Quaffing rum from a pewter chamber pot, they whooped joyously as they saw the overseer. They dangled a rope with a noose to the ground, where it was caught by their comrades. Goff was clubbed into muzziness with a hoe handle while the rope was tightened around his neck. The men on the roof hauled him up until his toes touched the ground. A ladder was placed next to him and one of the field hands raced up it with a hammer and nails. Goff was hoisted until he was just

170

below the level of the roof where the joists met a wooden pillar. Gasping and choking, his flailing arms tried to loosen the noose, but the man on the ladder grasped each hand and nailed it to the crosspiece while the overseer's urine-stained breeches were pulled off by those below.

Goff screamed as he was emasculated with a dull knife. He hung by his hands, slowly strangling, body twisting in agony. The slaves dragged furniture from the house, smashed it into kindling, and piled it below the convulsing body. A bonfire was lit, and both Goff and the wooden veranda burned while the freed people ransacked the house and cavorted with looted clothing and bottles of rum.

Afraid of angry ghosts, the blacksmith waited until full daylight before going with his tools to the poinciana tree accompanied by Wannica and Titus. When Chart's chains were struck off, he slumped against the tree trunk and gulped water from a silver tankard taken from the Great House, from which a column of smoke curled. Wannica replied to his first question.

"Madame got away. We help her," she told him proudly.

"And Pemb? The master?"

"He go last evening. Maybe they catch him on the road."

When he asked what was happening on the plantation, all three black people seemed bewildered as if unable to grasp the enormity of the events.

"They say now we free," said Titus. "It's the Revolution."

"*Who* says?"

Titus looked uncertain.

"Frenchman. Say France take over now, kill English and free all slaves."

Chart stood shakily, rolling his stiff shoulders and grimacing from the pain of his barely healed back. Casting his eyes aside as he skirted his mother's grave, he went to the Great House, closely trailed by Wannica and Titus. Rain had doused the fire before it engulfed the entire house. A smell like roast pork, which he recognised from the cremation ghats of India, wafted from a shrivelled, blackened corpse lying among the embers of the veranda, its crucified arms still nailed to a charred crosspiece.

"You see," Titus remarked in awe. "Goff die like Jesus, just like Obeah woman said."

In the midst of the milling La Sagesse workers, Chart saw a white man wearing a nankeen uniform with gilt epaulettes and a large brass helmet inscribed *La Mort ou la Liberté!*. He was armed with a brace of pistols and a sabre. His face was pinched and pasty, with days-old beard growth.

French officer, Chart guessed, *so this is probably not a slave revolt.* He allowed a flicker of hope to strengthen. *Perhaps the French have invaded to free us!*

The officer stood with two burly black men in stocking-like Liberty Caps carrying muskets with fixed bayonets. The uniformed man stepped out, raised his arms and, in a heavy French accent, tried to get the attention of the people.

"Citizens!" he yelled. "Listen to me!" All but a few ignored him and some began drifting away towards their quarters.

"Fire the muskets into the air."

The Frenchman spun on his heel to where Chart stood near him. It took him a moment to realise that Chart had addressed him in French.

"That will get their attention," said Chart.

The pair of black men looked questioningly at their officer. When he nodded, they raised their muskets and fired upwards, freezing the exodus.

"Come back, friends!" Chart bellowed in his best parade ground voice. "This man has something important to say to you."

"*Merci, citoyen,*" the officer breathed, then began a lengthy harangue, much of which was incomprehensible to the puzzled workers. He proclaimed that they were now free citizens of the French Republic and that the Revolution, public avenger of the rights of man, had broken their chains. The English were being driven from Grenada so it could be reclaimed by France and her children. Now, though, they must gather all the plantation's livestock and provisions and go with him to the camp of the great revolutionary general, Julien Fédon.

The Frenchman whipped out his sword with a flourish and shouted "*Vive la République! Vive la Revolution!*", echoed by the pair of black soldiers who had reloaded their muskets. When there was no response from the crowd, the officer looked angrily at Chart, who loudly repeated the slogans. There was half-hearted clapping and a few mangled attempts to mimic him from the bemused estate workers, who continued dispersing.

"They will learn," the officer said vehemently. "We will make sure of that!"

He introduced himself as Captain Noguet, sent from Guadeloupe by Victor Hugues, the Revolutionary governor, to assist General Fédon in exterminating the British colonists.

"You speak good French, citizen," he asked suspiciously, "but your voice is that of an English gentleman?"

"I was a soldier," Chart said brusquely, without further explanation.

"And a slave here?"

Chart wordlessly turned, raised his tattered shirt and exposed his cicatrised back. When he faced Noguet again, the Frenchman loftily pronounced that he was now a free citizen soldier of the Republic. He explained that they needed to restore order and bring able-bodied workers and provisions to the revolutionary base camp at Fédon's Belvedere plantation in the island's northern mountains. Chart was ordered to recruit a cadre of men from the estate workers, arm them with cutlasses, and collect animals, food, arms, ammunition and gun flints.

A few of the young men, native Africans, accepted eagerly, their warrior tradition making them eager for revenge against the slave masters. Most of the other people could not grasp the concept of freedom; some formed a line outside the cookhouse, waiting to be fed and given their tasks for the day even though they knew that the overseer and his henchmen were dead. Others broke into the warehouse and broached a barrel of rum. In the yard outside the slave quarters, they celebrated the demise of Goff and the drivers, dancing and laughing to the beat of a tom-tom and a twanging gourd banjo. Someone suggested roasting a pig, and Titus volunteered to take one from the pigsty behind the distillery. Face glowing with jubilation fuelled by rum, he brushed past Chart with a struggling sow in his arms.

"Come join us!" he called happily, hurrying towards the pit

173

being dug to receive the barbecue.

Sharing in Titus' joy, Chart didn't have the heart to stop him. He was sure that the French officer wouldn't mind well-deserved revelry on such a momentous occasion. With his African recruits trailing, he continued towards the storehouse where cloth, leather and other dry goods were kept.

A musket shot sounded behind him. He turned and crouched, watched by frightened black faces, expecting the hum of musket balls. There were no further shots, but the music and laughter had stopped. He ran back towards the yard.

Titus was sprawled on the ground in a pool of blood with his head twisted to the side. One of the revolutionary soldiers stood near him, casually ramming a fresh charge down his musket barrel. Wannica, Molia and a dozen other celebrants stood frozen as if in a tableau.

Chart knelt by Titus and gently turned his head, revealing that the entire right side of his skull had been blasted away. He sprang to his feet in rage, to be met by the point of the bayonet hovering a foot from his chest.

"Death to those who steal from the people!" the insurgent yelled in patois.

"He *was* the people!" Chart replied. "The pig belongs to all these poor people!"

The soldier shrugged. Ignoring him, he ordered the African men, who appeared equally shocked, to throw the corpse into the barbeque pit and catch the pig.

Chart angrily trotted up the path to the plantation house to confront the French officer about the murder. He found Noguet in the yard where the estate's mule carts were being loaded with looted barrels, bags and kitchenware. He was arguing with the trio of women who had been Goff's concubines.

"It's our money," said a mixed-race woman with hazel eyes and long brown hair who was holding a chipped porcelain chamber pot filled with coins.

"We dig it up from where Goff bury it," said another, a pretty black teenager.

"Money belong to us now," declared the third, a girl with high cheekbones and obsidian eyes revealing Carib ancestry.

"No," growled Noguet. "General Fédon decreed that all money and personal possessions belong to the Revolution."

He looked at Chart, rolled his eyes and shook his head, as if he would naturally agree with him, man-to-man.

"Who has time for these foolish *putes*," he said in French.

Without another word, he pulled a pistol from his belt, cocked it and fired into the heart of the mixed-race woman. The chamber pot dropped from her nerveless hands and shattered on the ground, scattering the coins.

"Pick up every one and give them to me," Noguet ordered the horrified survivors. "If I find you kept any you will die too."

As the two women fell to their knees and began scrabbling for the coins, he addressed Chart again, hand on the pommel of his sword, dark eyes challenging.

"What is it, citizen? Did you carry out your orders?"

Chart shook his head and turned away.

Chapter 20

They trekked north from La Sagesse on roads that were little more than tracks and pathways like tunnels beneath the dense green canopy of the virgin mahogany forest. Chart was one of forty-eight former slaves who carried provisions, herded livestock and helped to push carts drawn by recalcitrant mules. The rest of the plantation workers were either too old or too young to be of value as labourers for the liberators and were left behind. A few had run to hide in the cane fields or jungle after witnessing the murder of Titus and the young woman, who now lay mouldering in the barbeque pit that was to have been the centrepiece of the liberation celebration.

Frightened of the unknown and subdued by the killing of their fellows, the freed Las Sagesse workers were shepherded by Captain Noguet and his men. Chart and the half dozen young Africans he had recruited were allowed to carry lighter loads than the others, but were watched as carefully by the revolutionaries. They were joined by hundreds of other black people emerging from plantations marked by smoke columns. Women balanced bundles of loot and plantain bunches on their heads, while their men wielded cutlasses and long wooden pikes with fire-hardened tips. They sang as they marched, African voices combining in martial paens while creoles harmonised with lighter songs such as *Ante Nanny* and *Big Bamboo*.

In the early evening they reached Fédon's Belvedere plantation, which had been transformed into a base called *Camp La Liberté* teeming with thousands of freed slaves. Flimsy shelters made from bamboo roofed with plantain and banana leaves filled every open space amidst the estate house and buildings. Chart's eyes watered from the smoke of open cooking fires which failed to mask the stench of human and animal faeces. Bleating goats and snorting pigs were chased by gleeful children and yapping dogs, adding to the chaos. The few sentries seemed more interested in drinking rum and seducing women. The mood of jubilation was infectious, and most of the

La Sagesse people who had arrived with Chart soon wandered off to join the carousing.

Captain Noguet disappeared after telling Chart to wait on the steps of Fédon's plantation house. The Frenchman returned an hour later.

"The General wants to meet you. I told him about you."

He led the way up the steep mountain dominating the Belvedere Valley, the meandering path so slippery that they had to pull themselves up by roots and branches. Halfway up the slope was an uneven plateau of a few acres with scattered ramshackle wooden buildings. A crudely lettered sign identified it as *Camp L'Egalite*. A battery of two cannon was manned by lounging white soldiers in French artillery uniforms, while several dozen other soldiers of various races and mixtures guarded the camp's perimeter. Chart's dormant military training resurfaced, noting the soldiers' slovenly appearance and the numberous bottles of wine and rum in their hands and discarded near them.

Noguet took him to the largest building and ordered him to wait outside.

"The General will receive you now," he said from the doorway a few minutes later.

Fédon was seated behind a battered dining table which, from its carving in the style of Mr. Chippendale, appeared to have been looted from a plantation. Despite the heat, he wore a double-breasted blue uniform coat with elaborate gilt braiding and large golden epaulets. Two other *gens de couleur* in full Republican fig with red, white and blue cockades on their hats sat at the table, busily writing and shuffling papers. With a cigar in his mouth, the revolutionary general studied Chart through narrowed eyes. Chart had the presence of mind to stand to attention and salute, wryly thinking that he must present a ludicrous sight in his ragged shirt and breeches with mud plastering his bare feet and calves.

"The Captain tells me that you are a strange one," Fédon said. "What is your story?"

In fluent French, he quickly recited his history, from his birth at La Sagesse, his life and education in England, military service in India, kidnapping and enslavement. When he finished, one of the mixed-race officers leaned over and whispered in his ear.

"Lieutenant Ventour has recently joined us from Paris. He read of your legal case in *L'Ami du people*. Welcome Citizen Charteris. You must join me for dinner after you have refreshed yourself."

The general summoned an orderly, instructing him to find quarters and a uniform for Chart. He was shown to a hammock in the barracks then taken to a supply hut where he chose a blue uniform turned up with red facings and brass buttons. Digging through a pile of civilian clothing that he surmised had been looted, he pulled out clean linen and a pair of buff breeches. He ignored a heap of footwear in a corner, being accustomed to going barefoot, which was considerably more practical given the ankle-deep mud of the camps. The orderly insisted that he take a felt bicorne hat but Chart chose a simple red liberty cap with a Republican cockade.

Left alone to bathe in a spring, Chart dried himself with his rags and cast them aside before dressing in the linen and French uniform. After nearly two years as a slave he felt strangely empowered by the uniform, as if he had donned a new skin. But he was wary of the revolutionaries, hoping that Noguet's murderous cruelty was an anomaly. He had known British officers in India who were equally savage, with no regard for human life.

During his salon days in London, the main conversation topic of London's upper classes was the French Revolution of 1789 and the execution of King Louis XVI and other nobles after France was declared a republic. Out of boredom on the long voyage to India in 1790 he had read *The Declaration of the Rights of Man and of the Citizen* and other Revolutionary literature provided by his father. But since his kidnapping and enslavement he had been cut off from news of world events, which until now were irrelevant to the brutal existence of human chattel.

As he was returning to the barracks he passed a low structure which he thought was a dog kennel because of its bamboo bars and crude door secured with a thin chain looped through the jamb. He abruptly halted, gripped by a chill, as he heard a deep bass voice singing the lullaby *Kaa Fo* that Phibbah crooned to him as a child. Now it was sung as a lament expressing suffering and hopelessness. Bending down, Chart saw a person on hands and knees in a cramped space. He recoiled as a scarified black face with filed teeth thrust against the bars.

"Sori!"

A bloodshot eye peered at him.

"Chart! You one of them now?"

"I thought you were dead."

Sori vented a bitter laugh.

"I will be soon."

The Fulani giant explained that after Goff sold him to Fédon he had been comparatively well-treated. The French insurgent had told him and the other enslaved people on the Belvedere estate that the revolution was coming and soon they would all be free if they behaved themselves and worked hard in the meantime.

That morning, the plantation owner – now *General* Fédon – had gathered them in front of his house and proclaimed that the English slave masters had been defeated and they were all now free by order of the French government. Taking him at his word, Sori had simply turned his back and begun walking towards the island's western coast, hoping that he would find a ship that would return him to Africa. On the General's command, Sori was pursued and captured by a squad of soldiers, including some fellow Fulanis. He was beaten and dragged before Fédon, who told him that he was a free man but he must still work for the Revolution. After Sori refused, cursing in his native language, the general said that he would be hanged the next morning as an example to others who made the mistake of thinking they were free to leave.

Chart thrust his right hand through the bamboo bars. After a moment's seeming hesitation, Sori clasped it strongly until Chart gently disengaged.

"Remember what I told you at La Sagesse," he said. "You *will* be free!"

"Yes," Sori rumbled, "Death will truly free me."

Thinking furiously, Chart went to Fédon's headquarters. He was on treacherous ground, knowing that it was imperative not to offend the revolutionaries if he was to have any chance of saving Sori. The bored guard had his musket slung over a shoulder and didn't bother to challenge him. As he stepped inside, Chart saluted smartly and stamped his right foot on the wooden floor, which evidently flattered the general.

"You are late, Citizen Charteris," said Fédon jovially. "Come, we have kept a place for you here across from me so we can talk."

A dozen officers, white, mixed-race and two blacks, ringed the dining table which was set with fine silver and delicate wine glasses. Three female *personnes de couleur* sat at one end; a frowning middle-aged woman who Fédon introduced as his wife, Marie Rose, and two daughters. Chart only caught the name of the younger, a pretty girl with green eyes in her teens called Céleste.

It appeared that the revolutionaries had been discussing him. Fédon poured Chart a glass of Madeira and toasted him.

"To our new comrade, Citizen Charteris, *notre propre célébrité. Vive la République, vive la Révolution!*"

The other diners enthusiastically recited the slogans and recharged their glasses. Madame Fédon rang a silver bell and two black women servants entered the room and began ladling soup.

Are they also "freed" slaves? Chart wondered.

Sipping at his wine to avoid refills, he bided his time, carrying on desultory conversation while listening closely to the boasts and gossip as the officers steadily grew inebriated. He was relieved to hear that St. George's had not fallen to the insurgents, hopeful that Arabella was safe.

"The English cannot hold out much longer," said Noguet. "Our spies report that half their garrison of regular troops has the yellow jack, and as everyone knows their militia is worthless. And now that we have their governor we can force them to surrender."

"And when that happens we will set up the guillotine on the slave auction block in the market square and cut off the heads

180

of every last one of them!" Fédon added, calling for another round of revolutionary toasts.

When the plates were cleared and decanters of cognac called for, Chart addressed Fédon.

"*Mon general*, I saw a man I knew from La Sagesse locked in a kennel. What is his crime?"

Fédon, well into his cups, looked puzzled until an officer sitting to his right whispered.

"Ah yes, the giant. He tried to run away."

Chart nodded.

"Yes, he was a troublemaker at La Sagesse. Did you not buy him?"

"Yes, and I set him free."

"If he was free, why is he now being punished for running?"

The few officers still sober enough to pay attention to the conversation fell silent. Noguet glowered at Chart, who failed to notice that the general's daughter Céleste was listening carefully at the end of the table.

"It is no business of yours," Noguet growled.

Fédon airily waved a hand.

"It is alright, Captain. Citizen Charteris must learn the precepts of our glorious revolution, about the benefits of the *Declaration of The Rights of Man and of the Citizen*, which I'm sure he is unfamiliar with."

Chart's frustration made his caution slip.

"The Declaration states that human beings are born and remain free and equal in rights, including liberty."

"Enough" shouted Nouget, who stood with his hand on the pommel of his sword. "How dare you dispute the General!"

"Sit down, Captain," ordered Fédon, dark eyes glittering, "We see that the citizen is an educated man, familiar with the *Declaration*. *Chapeau, Citoyen* Charteris."

He drank deeply from his wine glass and sighed appreciatively before continuing.

"You must remember that the Declaration also says that the exercise of the natural rights of each man has only those borders which can be determined by the law. *Citoyen* Hugues in Guadeloupe was appointed governor by the National

Convention in Paris, which makes the law for the French West Indies, of which we are now again part. The governor freed the slaves and abolished punishment by the cart whip, but he legally maintained the *corvée* - a system of unpaid obligatory work. Any negroes that refuse or neglect their work can be condemned to be chained by the middle or ankle for five or ten years, and the more refractory are to be shot.

"*Le géant* broke the law by refusing to give his labour to the Revolution. So he will be executed in the morning *pour encourager les autres* - as an example to other *nègres* who make the mistake of thinking they are free to leave."

The general's benign mood disappeared as his patience seemed to have reached its limit.

"Now, you, *citoyen*, must take care not to question the law further. *Le géant* is a simple brute, little more than an animal, unworthy of the concern of an obviously enlightened gentleman like yourself."

Chart glanced at the two black officers in Republican uniforms. To his surprise, they were emphatically nodding at the general's remarks. He thanked Fédon for his wise explanation, hanging his head contritely.

"Come to me first thing in the morning," the general snapped. "I have an important duty for you." He rose from the table to show that the dinner had ended.

"'The Revolution devours its children,'" Chart muttered too softly for anyone to hear, as he remembered the quote from an Enlightenment philosopher admired by his father.

He left with the other officers, noticing that Noguet stayed behind. At the barracks shared with fifty or so other men, Chart settled into his hammock, listening to snores and farts around him. The structure was open-walled and he was close to the exterior. After a couple of hours he quietly rolled from the hammock and stepped outside, straining his eyes and ears for sentries. Fortunately, the full moon was obscured by clouds. If challenged, he planned to say that he was using the trench privy near the kennel holding Sori.

Earlier he had noticed a rusty but serviceable bayonet carelessly thrust into a stump. He wriggled it out, went to the kennel, and whispered Sori's name. The African's face was a darker mass against the bamboo bars, teeth gleaming whitely.

"You can break the chain with this," Chart told him, handing the bayonet through the bars.

Then he was gone, flitting from shadow to shadow as he crept back to the barracks. He was unaware that he was being watched.

***

After retiring to the bed shared with her sister, Céleste Fédon had been unable to sleep. She thought of the tall young man with startling blue eyes who had the temerity to challenge her father about the execution order for the African in the kennel. *Foolish*, she thought, *he does not yet realise the savagery of the revolutionaries, nor is he aware of the reign of terror that is still convulsing France.* She admired his courage, having agreed with everything he said, and hoped that he would survive.

Now aged sixteen, Céleste and her elder sister had returned to Grenada from France two years earlier. They had been sent to Bordeaux, birthplace of their white grandfather, to attend a convent school. The Revolution's dechristianisation campaign took longer to reach provincial cities from the ferment of Paris, and in the early days many of the younger nuns who taught at the convent were enthusiastic supporters of the new regime, yet scornful that the *Declaration of the Rights of Man and of the Citizen* did not extend to women, as only men could be citizens of the Republic. Although only thirteen years old, Céleste eagerly read the *Declaration of the Rights of Woman and of the Female Citizen* when it was published in September 1791.

Her disillusionment was profound when the author of the *Women's Declaration*, the activist and playwright Olympe de Gouges, was guillotined a few months later for sedition. Then they came for the nuns. Céleste and her sister found refuge in the home of their elderly great aunt, but she never forgot the screams from the nearby convent as nuns of all ages were raped, tortured and butchered before the ancient building was torched.

She slipped out of bed and went into the compound for fresh air, unafraid of spirits or brutal men who would suffer instant death if they touched the General's daughter. Movement caught her eyes. Screened by bushes, she followed a figure towards the kennel. The clouds parted briefly, and she recognised the man known as *Citoyen* Charteris. Moments later, he made his way back to the barracks. She crouched in a deep shadow as she heard grunting and the crack of metal breaking. Then the African giant emerged from the kennel with a bayonet in his hand and disappeared into the jungle.

Chapter 21

Chart tried to conceal his nervousness as he again stood at attention in front of Fédon, wondering if he would be hostile after their heated discussion the previous evening. But the insurgent general seemed preoccupied with other matters, chewing an unlit cigar while issuing orders to a stream of officers who came and went. When he finally turned his attention to Chart, he studied him appraisingly before giving a Gallic shrug.

"*Le géant* escaped again last night. It is of no consequence - he is a mere flea and he will be shot on sight either by us or the English if he is caught. We have more important things to deal with."

Fédon explained that the island's governor, Ninian Home, and fifty other Britons had been captured and were being held as prisoners on the peak of the mountain above them, which he called *Camp de la Mort* – the Camp of Death. Chart was ordered to serve as one of their guards during the day and eavesdrop on their conversations, which he would report to the general each evening. He was to pretend that he spoke only French and not converse with the prisoners.

As Fédon was talking, Céleste entered with a silver coffee pot and porcelain cups on a tray. The general seemed annoyed by the interruption but said nothing. While she was pouring coffee for her father over his shoulder, she caught Chart's eye, smiled and winked, which baffled him.

Under other circumstances I would be eager, he thought, assuming she was flirting, *but not now.*

***

The fifty-one prisoners were all males, ranging in age from a boy of twelve to a gout-stricken old man in his late seventies. They were packed into a fetid bamboo *boucan* with flimsy sides and a leaking roof. Half of them, including Home, the Scottish governor, were in stocks ranged around a wooden platform. All were in poor condition, filthy and poorly clothed, many suffering from dysentery. They were allowed to go out singly to relieve themselves, but the guards tired of opening the door and only occasionally let them out, which contributed to the stench and misery. Escape from the hastily built prison was feasible for the able-bodied, but Fédon had warned that if any escaped all the other prisoners would be executed.

Carrying a Charleville musket with rust patches on its barrel, Chart stood shifts with three sullen black guards who squatted on logs swatting flies, sharing pots of rum and dozing outside the prison when there was a lull in the rain. He regularly patrolled around the building, pausing to lean against the wall to shelter under the roof overhang, during which he listened to conversations, praying, moans and weeping. Each evening he dutifully reported the results of his eavesdropping, most of which was innocuous. He omitted telling Fédon about a particularly disturbing piece of intelligence.

There was considerable discussion about what the prisoners called the *Terror* that was sweeping over France and its colonies like a red tide. 17,000 people had been beheaded and more than 10,000 had died in prison or without trial. Hundreds of thousands were arrested, many to disappear into mass graves. Shortly before Grenada's rebellion, Guadeloupe was recaptured from British rule in an invasion led by Victor Hugues. A guillotine accompanied the French Republican forces. Over the past two months hundreds of people per week were decapitated or shot for the crimes of being aristocrats, having taken an oath of allegiance to King George or wearing a black cockade in their hats rather the Revolutionary rosette. The same was expected for Grenada when Fédon's insurgency triumphed.

On the fourth day a young white man in a green uniform and felt bicorne joined the guard detail. He spoke perfect English as well as French. When they were off duty, he introduced himself as Pierre de Suze. Chart struck up a conversation with him, learning that he was well-educated, having attended university in Caen, Normandy, until it was closed in the third year of the Revolution. Pierre admitted that his father was a French chevalier and one of the largest planters on Grenada, owning more than 200 enslaved people. Chart was wary, wondering if his commitment to the Revolution was being tested. He told Pierre that he was grateful to have been liberated and asked if his father's slaves had been emancipated.

"No," he answered flatly, "some of the men have been allowed to join our forces; the rest are required to work the plantation. General Fédon gave us an exemption, like other planters here and in Guadeloupe. One day *les nègres* will all be freed, but they are not ready to fend for themselves."

"Then why are you here? What are you fighting for?"

"Because under English rule I am a third-class citizen in my own land. I am fighting to return Grenada to France. *Liberté, Egalité, Fraternité* be damned!"

"Third-class?"

Pierre snorted.

"Because I am both French and a *gens de couleur*, an octoroon, despite appearing white with my fair skin and blue eyes. Aren't you, as a man of colour yourself, aware of the 'one drop rule'? In America and the British colonies one is considered negro if you have an African in your family tree."

***

Arabella arrived in St. George's naked except for her nightgown, her only other possessions being the faithful old mare that had saved her life and the small gold heraldic ring worn on her left hand. The town was thronged with panicked refugees from every part of the island – planters and merchants with their families, mixed-race offspring of British colonists, and both free and enslaved black people who did not wish to join the insurgency.

She was at a loss as to where to go until she noticed the Anglican church on a hill above the harbour and coaxed the tottery horse up the cobbled streets. She presented herself at the parsonage door, which was opened by a servant who stood in open-mouthed shock at the dishevelled woman in a thin night dress.

"Lady Charteris," she said in the haughtiest voice she could muster, making the maid repeat her name twice.

Within minutes a harried looking white woman of middle years appeared, introduced herself as the parson's wife, and ushered her into a parlour while she ordered a pair of servants to fetch a dressing gown and tea. As a skeleton clock chimed on a side table, Arabella realised that it was just nine in the morning. It seemed impossible that her escape from La Sagesse had happened only a few hours earlier.

When one's family has been interwoven into the tapestry of British society for over seven hundred years connections exist everywhere in the Empire, and Grenada was no exception. It turned out that the parson's wife knew an elderly lady a few streets away, widow of a plantation owner, who was a second cousin once removed of Arabella's father, the viscount. A note was dispatched, and an hour later a sedan chair carried by two black men, perspiring heavily in full livery and wigs amidst the torrid heat, appeared at the parsonage. By lunchtime, Arabella, was ensconced in the relative's large townhouse, bathed, clothed and trying to keep the horrors of the past few days from overwhelming her thoughts.

When her hostess asked if she should inquire for her husband, Arabella said no so vehemently that she frightened the old lady. After she apologised, the matter was dropped. During the following week, other gentlewomen arrived to find refuge, filling the house with dread and bouts of weeping.

Terror gripped the whole town when the beat of a military drum was heard approaching along the northern coastal road. A mounted militiaman raced in on a lathered horse, breathlessly calling that the French army was approaching. Crowds jammed the harbour, frantically offering life savings and keys to shops and houses to ship's captains for passage anywhere away from Grenada. Arabella's companions alternately swooned and prayed as the drumming grew louder.

"It's Fedon's Brigands," wailed a matron whose husband was a captive of the insurgents, "We're all doomed!"

"Aye, we'll all suffer a fate worse than death," a doughty old Scotswoman said, peering out an upstairs window a bit hopefully, Arabella thought.

The French force turned out to be a pair of young white Creoles in Republican uniforms accompanied by the drummer and a fifer carrying a white flag. They brought a letter to the governing Colonial Council demanding the immediate surrender of St. George's and warning that if the British attacked Fédon's base, "on that instant every one of the prisoners shall be put to death".

"Hmph," the acting Governor told the council, "How *dare* those bloody crapaud Brigands! We'll have 'em sorted instanter!"

An order was issued to mobilise the militia and the small number of regular garrison soldiers to attack the insurgents.

***

Pemb tried to bribe his way aboard one of the ships in the harbour, but the captain wouldn't accept his note supposedly secured by a hogshead of sugar, knowing that most of the British owned plantations and their products had been reduced to ashes. Having no other change of clothes, Pemb had to wear his gorgeous scarlet uniform in the attempt to flee. As he fearfully returned ashore, he was jeered by the crowd as a coward and pelted with rotten mangos and a handful of mule turds.

He reluctantly walked up the steep, winding road leading to the blockhouse on Hospital Hill, one of a series of forts ringing St. George's. He had been quartered there with other militia officers who had escaped from outlying parishes, all of whom complained about the poor food and absence of servants. As he approached, he heard British bugle calls and drumbeats, which he surmised were a call to arms. He groaned in despair realising that, between the martial law imposed by the colony and the enemy, he had no place to hide.

***

Once Chart began to know the prisoners as individual human beings, it was increasingly hard for him to accept them as the enemy. The governor, Ninian Home, was an ineffectual Scot in his early sixties, unfailingly polite and uncomplaining despite chronic diarrhoea. Home owned over 400 slaves on two plantations, for which Chart knew he should revile him, but found this difficult the more he observed the man. One afternoon, a liberated woman who had been a domestic servant on Home's main estate brought him a basket of food and clean linen. Chart asked her if the governor had been a cruel master.

"He a good master," she replied, shaking her head, "even field hands like him. We all know he treat us better than other places do."

"Are you glad to be free now?"

She looked around furtively.

"Don't know," she muttered.

After she left, Chart thought about his father, wondering about the incongruity of being both a slave owner and a good man. Sir Arthur's tepid defence of slavery had been similar to Pierre de Suze's: "they are not ready to fend for themselves."

Chart had expected the other prisoners to be monsters like Goff and Pemb, but they also seemed ordinary men. Many were Scots, although he overheard one saying he was a Leicestershire native. He longed to speak with him, wondering if he had ridden across the rolling fields near Tilton-on-the-Hill or lifted a pint of ale at the Ashby Arms in Hungarton. He gathered that only a handful were large plantation owners or overseers, others were clerks, shopkeepers and artificers. A doctor and a Presbyterian minister seemed to have friendships with Fédon, who showed them special favour that the others did not seem to resent.

Chart overheard a spirited discussion about the morality of slavery between a religious Welshman and one of the English planters. He was surprised to hear a number of the others agree that chattel slavery was wrong.

"Aye," one of the Scottish voices said, "but slavery is like holding a wolf by the ear, we can neither hold him, nor safely let him go."

Listening to the British voices, from singsong Welsh to Scottish burr, aroused unexpected nostalgia. *They are my enemy*, Chart fiercely chided himself, remembering the humiliating racism during his years in England and the hellish existence on the plantation.

Or were they all?

He had to admit that he had known more British men and women who had shown him kindness and affection than those who had mistreated him. In his youthful bitterness, he had come to believe that he would forever be an alien, never to be fully accepted in Britain or its empire. But given the time to think while listening to the prisoners' conversations, he realised that he had been accepted as an equal by people who mattered far more than those who would forever despise him for his ethnicity.

Chart concluded that he was a man caught between two worlds, empathising with but unable to truly relate to the enslaved people with whom he had lived and laboured, while feeling in his heart and soul closer to the prisoners than to the French revolutionary fanatics with their parroted slogans and cruel hypocrisy. Who was more worthy of his loyalty – friends such as Lady Augusta, Granville Sharp and others committed to the growing Abolition movement – or the vicious Republicans whose Liberty, Equality and Fraternity was a sham?

The mountain top camp was high enough above Belvedere estate to reduce the hubbub of thousands of people there to a murmur. Now, after days of rain, the weather had cleared and the sun gathered strength as it approached its zenith. The prisoners were quiet except for coughing, groans and prayers.

A rattle of musketry broke the stillness, followed by bells ringing in all three insurgent camps. Artillerymen rushed to the batteries while the barracks erupted with men pulling on uniform coats and grabbing muskets from racks. From where Chart stood he could see a distant line of redcoats led by three horsemen moving up the road to Belvedere.

Fédon ran from his quarters to the edge of the precipice followed by his wife and daughters.

"The *Anglais* are attacking!" he raved, face twisted in fury. "They defied me and now they will pay for it!"

Chapter 22

The British expeditionary force was a shambles from the beginning. A week passed while the militia officers, most of whom had no military experience, found excuses for delaying. Top-heavy with officers, they argued over who should be in command. Rank was based on the number of acres and slaves owned, as well as who could afford the most ostentatious uniform and accoutrements.

In the meantime, the small garrison of 190 infantrymen of the 9th and 58th Regiments of Foot, commanded by a young captain named Gurdon who was the senior surviving British officer, was steadily decimated by disease. By the time the attacking force was ready to embark, only forty regulars were fit to march along with ninety militiamen, a third of whom were squabbling officers. The militia colonels and majors resented being under the nominal command of the 28-year-old army captain, despite the fact that he had served His Majesty for a dozen years in a variety of conflicts.

Pemb, who had decided to promote himself to major considering that more superior officers from his parish had been murdered or captured, was offered a hot-blooded Arabian to ride as befitted his rank. Unwilling to admit his fear of horses, he graciously volunteered to serve as commissary officer and was therefore able to ride on one of the mule-drawn supply wagons.

Setting out when the tropic sun was at its zenith, they marched north along the coastal road to the town of Gouyave, losing a dozen militiamen along the way who returned to St. George's after pleading heatstroke and other maladies. The insurgents withdrew from Gouyave as the British force approached, which the militia officers declared a victory, worthy of a few bottles of madeira to celebrate and refresh themselves. Against his better judgement, Captain Gurdon agreed to occupy the town for the night and attack Fedon's base a few miles away at first light.

It was a grave tactical error.

His men, most of whom took the King's shilling to escape dire poverty and who knew there was high probability that their miserable lives would be cut short by disease and combat, discovered a treasure trove of rum, wine and port in abandoned warehouses. Later, Gurdon's after action report dryly stated that his men "incapacitated themselves for doing good service, by having taken too much strong drink during the night." In reality, the Captain could not contain his fury at the drunken infantrymen staggering through the town and prostrated in the streets.

Although reinforced by a party of sailors and Royal Marines from a British frigate, Gurdon decided to wait another day to allow his force to recover from their inebriation. The next day, however, on assembling the various British forces, it was discovered that the sailors and marines had also raided the liquor stores and drunk themselves senseless. The attack was again postponed. Gurdon marched his staggering command to an estate closer to the revolutionaries' camps, which he hoped would allow the men to dry out.

Fédon was wise to the vices of ordinary British soldiers and sailors and cleverly launched a new tactic. Gurdon reported that "contrary to my expectations, I found that the negroes brought rum to the men from every house or hut that I passed". When he paraded his force the following morning prior to attacking, only 28 of the 50 Royal Marines and a third of the regular infantrymen and militia were fit to march.

Predictably, the assault was repulsed. Under fire from cannon firing round shot and grape, the first wave of redcoats quickly broke, throwing away their muskets as they ran. Waiting behind the lines with his wagons, Pemb ordered the drivers to return to St. George's as soon as he saw the first British soldiers retreating in panic along the Belvedere road. Captain Gurdon was badly wounded, barely fighting free of the insurgents' counter-attack. Two dozen of his men were left behind to be butchered.

But they weren't the only casualties.

***

"The prisoners are to be shot."

Captain Noguet ordered Chart and the other guards to line up facing the prison door. The men around Chart, freed slaves like himself, appeared greatly agitated, trembling with impatience. Pierre de Suze was nowhere to be seen. The guards checked their priming and began cocking muskets.

From within the prison a few prisoners called out "Mercy!" Some were on their knees praying, frightened eyes gazing piteously through the bamboo interstices. A pair of soldiers appeared with mallets. The door was opened and they entered to release the men held in stocks. When one of the prisoners clutched a guard's sleeve beseechingly, Chart saw him shatter the man's arm with his hammer. When they finished, the prisoners were ordered outside, one-by-one.

Chart went cold as he knew what was about to happen. He ran to Fédon as the general left the edge of the mountain peak and stalked towards the prison, sword in hand. A musket went off behind him. He turned to see one of the prisoners take two steps forward and fall to the ground.

"Back in line!" the general screamed at him. "*You* will shoot the next one!"

"Have mercy on them!" Chart shouted, eyes wide in horror as he dropped his musket. "They are innocent!"

Fédon strode past him, surrounded by his personal guards and followed by his family. Céleste was trembling.

"The prisoners are valuable hostages, General! If you kill them the British will never rest until they avenge them!"

Fédon paused.

"They are just the beginning," he hissed, "*We* will never rest until we exterminate every *Anglais* on this island. Their blood will fertilise the Tree of Liberty!"

He turned to his guards, pointing his sword at Chart.

"Put him back in the line with a musket in his hands or he dies too!"

Chart was seized and dragged to the execution squad, squirming and snarling. "No!" he pleaded as the twelve-year-old boy came out the door and stood with a desperate look on his tear-streaked face.

"My turn," an executioner said like a child fighting over a toy. "No," argued another, "I get this one!"

"It's *Citoyen* Charteris' turn," snarled Fédon. "Take the weapon and do your duty!"

"Never!" he pushed the proffered musket away. "No civilised man kills innocent children!"

Fédon signalled to his bodyguards, tapping his head. One clubbed Chart with his musket butt. Stunned, he fell onto his knees, shaking his head muzzily. Noguet stepped up and pointed his cocked pistol at Chart's skull, but the general shook his head.

"*Non.* Tie him up. I want him to watch what happens to enemies of the Revolution."

Fédon gave the order "*Tirez*" to every man who emerged, sparing only the doctor, the minister and a planter married to Pierre de Suze's sister. As Chart's senses cleared he watched in impotent rage, struggling against his bonds, hearing pleas and screams as the prisoners were led out to be shot. The general's family stood to one side, the wife and elder daughter watching stone-faced with crossed arms, while Céleste was curled on the ground near a puddle of her own vomit, weeping uncontrollably.

One man attempted to run and was shot fifty yards from the prison. Fedon counted each prisoner as he was shot. When the prison was empty, he calmly lit his cigar from a tinder box while contemplating the bodies piled in front of the prison door, some of which were still writhing. Chart saw that the general had a look of smug satisfaction.

Noguet approached him, saluted, and asked what should be done with the wounded prisoners. Fedon contemplatively puffed on his cigar, its smoke mixing with that from the discharged muskets.

"I'd like to let them wallow like swine in their blood and shit," he answered, "but we need to get this place cleaned up. Don't waste ammunition. Dispatch them with cutlasses and bayonets and then remove this *saluperie*.[1]"

"And what about him?" Noguet asked, jerking his chin towards where Chart lay, glaring red-eyed.

"Put him in the prison. Keep him bound. Tomorrow we will gather all our people in *Camp de la Liberté* to watch him being hung, drawn and quartered, like the English did to their own traitors."

Savouring his cigar, Fédon strolled back to the precipice, where he walked back and forth with indifference watching the battle in the valley below.

Chart was dragged to the prison over the heap of bodies as the guards set to work with cutlasses and bayonets giving the *coup de grâce* with whoops of joy as they competed to kill the greatest number. One hacked off the governor's head and held it up by the hair in triumph, only to have it slip from his grasp as he discovered he was clutching a wig. He and his comrades howled in laughter.

***

Through gaps in the bamboo bars, Chart saw the mutilated pale bodies, stripped of clothes, dragged to a ravine and tumbled into it. A few hours later the dogs and pigs arrived, snuffling, growling and fighting over their feast.

I couldn't live with myself if I hadn't tried to stop it, Chart thought. *And tomorrow there will no longer be a self to live with.*

He was too numbed to dwell upon his pending execution, resigned to the impossibility of escape. Exhausted, emotionally and physically, he was disinterested in attempting to dredge up memories and regrets.

The insurgents spent the remainder of the day celebrating victory over *Les Anglais*. Fédon descended to his great house at *Camp de la Liberté* like a conquering emperor, greeted by massive cheers and *feux de joie* that resonated through the surrounding mountains and valleys. *Camp de la Mort* was deserted with the exception of two disgruntled guards who had

---

[1]Filth.

been detailed to stand watch over the sole, well-trussed prisoner. They compensated for being left out of the revelry by broaching a cask of rum.

Chart lapsed into an uneasy slumber. He awoke well after midnight to the sound of rain lashing the flimsy thatch and water dripping onto his face. He heard rustling at the rear of the hut, but thought it was scavengers feeding on the dead. There was a crack as of wood breaking and he sensed a presence scuttling across the filth-covered floor. During his time living among the enslaved people he had come to share their belief in the supernatural, and now he recoiled in fright as he imagined vengeful ghosts invading the prison.

"*C'est moi*, Celeste," a soft voice said from the darkness.

He was at a momentary loss, then remembered the brief glimpse of Fédon's apparently distraught younger daughter during the massacre.

"Roll over so I can cut loose your hands," she whispered shakily "We haven't much time. The guards outside are dead drunk, but their relief may come soon."

Chart turned onto his belly. He felt her hands feeling for the ropes binding his arms, then felt a sharp blade sawing at them. He flinched as it nicked his flesh. When his hands were free he flipped onto his haunches.

"Give me the blade."

He felt for the wooden handle of a cutlass, quickly cut through the remaining ropes, and sprang to his feet. Céleste took his arm and led him to hole in the bamboo wall. She crawled through first.

"No one is about. Hurry!" she urged as he followed her.

They stood under the dripping boughs of a tree.

"*Merci*," he said. "But why?"

"Because you are a good man. I saw how you rescued the Giant. And because their Revolution is evil. No more talk, we must go."

They warily circumvented the comatose guards. Celeste preceded him down the steep, slippery path to *Camp L'Egalite*.

"Now I must leave you. *Bon chance.*" She disappeared towards her father's quarters.

Chart pulled his liberty cap low over his head and crept down to the massive encampment around the Belvedere plantation house. People were stirring, stoking campfires and complaining about aching heads as the sky beyond the rain clouds lightened with false dawn. He picked his way through the throng, hoping that his French uniform would allow him to pass even if challenged.

He knew that the road to the east led to Gouyave from which the British attack had come. He had no real plan except to evade the Brigands, but he equally wanted to avoid falling into British hands. Amidst the chaos sweeping the island, his best option would be to find a haven until he could devise a plan to escape from Grenada.

Chart made it to the rutted road, keeping inside the bush along the verge. He passed a dozen trees hung with the naked white bodies of what he assumed were British soldiers. He met no one else, living or dead.

After a mile, the day had brightened to full visibility and he began looking for a side path into the jungle where he could shelter. The road curved, and suddenly a dog barked and charged towards him growling. He stopped, lifting the cutlass, then two black men in ragged smocks appeared, one with a bayonet-tipped musket and the other with a pike.

Picquet guards!, he inwardly cursed, *put here to stop deserters or warn of another British attack. I should have known!*

"Call your dog off," Chart said in French, repeating in patois.

The men relaxed when they saw Chart's uniform and heard his words. They asked his business, and he told them General Fédon had sent him to report on the British force. The soldiers grumbled about missing the victory fête before standing aside to let him pass.

"Wait," said one as Chart came level with them, "Where your gun?"

At that moment bells began clanging at the rebel camps. Chart had no doubt that it was a general alert after the prisoner was found to have escaped.

He swung the cutlass powerfully at the pikeman's neck, nearly

198

severing his head. Blood sprayed from the jugular onto the second man's face, blinding him as he raised his musket. Chart chopped down on his right shoulder to prevent him from firing to alert the camp and other picquets nearby. The guard screamed, dropping the weapon as the cutlass whirled back and swung again doubled-handed. Chart put all the energy of his fury into the blow, cleaving the man's skull to the base of his spine.

It was over in twenty seconds.

He looked around for the dog to silence it but it had slunk into the bushes whining. Chart removed the musketeer's cross belt with its cartridge case and bayonet scabbard, then dragged the corpses into the jungle. He slung the cross belt over his shoulder and tossed the pike towards the dead men before melting into the jungle.

Behind him the clanging bells became frantic, accompanied by the hooting of dozens of conch shells. The danger was acute, but Chart was strangely elated, feeling for the first time in years that he was actually free and had struck back against one form of tyranny.

Chapter 23

He was undone by a chicken.

By the third day on the run Chart was starving. Keeping to the jungle, he avoided roving bands of insurgents and freed slaves. Food crops had been harvested or destroyed and he found only a few unripe plantains and bananas. He dared not venture near the coast, having observed canoes with armed men patrolling offshore.

From a hill a mile or so outside of St. George's he could see the whitewashed walls of Fort George with the Union Jack still flying over it. He was glad that Arabella was probably still safe, but thought that if he gave himself up to the British he would be re-enslaved by Pemb.

Desperation made him careless. In a valley below the hill were the blackened ruins of a plantation. He crept down the hillside, hoping to find a provision garden that had not been pillaged. As he got closer, he saw a few chickens pecking in the yard outside the ruined slave quarters.

He managed to corner a hen in a ruined hut and spear it with his bayonet. As he emerged into the yard with the impaled bird he was met by a semi-circle of horsemen in blue coatees pointing musketoons and pistols at him.

"Thank you for lunch," one of the riders said in French. "Now drop it."

Chart's heart sank as he let the musket fall, thinking that he had been captured by the insurgents. His fear was heightened as he saw that the cavalrymen appeared to be coloured, with one black man among them. Then he noticed that several of the men wore leather helmets and brass belt plates with the GR cypher of King George III. They were all festooned with weapons like pirates earlier in the century, carrying sabres, lances and daggers in addition to a variety of firearms.

British military, Chart thought in surprise. *But French speaking ... and coloured and black men in His Majesty's armed forces?*

"I've just come from Fédon's camp," he said in English. "I have important information."

"You speak good English," a horseman with silver epaulets said, "For a Frenchman."

"I *am* English!"

The rider shook his head mockingly.

"And I suppose that's a Grenadier Guards uniform you're wearing, and the liberty cap is a bearskin?"

"Shoot him and be done with it, lieutenant," the black cavalryman said. "I'm hungry."

"Let's wait for the captain, he can decide."

A few minutes later a cavalry troop rode into the clearing, led by a vigorous mulatto man in his early sixties in a silver-frogged uniform with red cuffs and high collar. Chart was surprised to see that the soldiers with him were also predominantly *gens de couleur*, with the remainder divided between full-blooded black men and those who appeared to be Europeans. The leader listened while his lieutenant reported.

"I am Captain Louis la Grenade, commander of the St. George's Light Dragoons," he said to Chart in English. "Who are you?"

Chart quickly sketched his background, noting the murderous looks of the other horsemen who were growing impatient under the hot sun.

"Brigands are nearby, Captain," urged the lieutenant, "Whoever he is, remember that the Council decreed that any rebel captured under arms is to be executed."

As Chart saw la Grenade nod and begin to tug his horse's reins, he said, "I saw the massacre of Governor Home and the other prisoners. And I know the disposition of Fédon's forces and the layout of his camps."

Captain la Grenade turned back as angry muttering broke out among his men.

"We heard rumours of the massacre. Perhaps it's worth keeping you alive for now."

They gagged him with a stick across his mouth, cuffed him with fetters from a saddlebag and herded him like an ox with the flat blades of the troopers' sabres. Spirits at low ebb from exhaustion and hunger, Chart berated himself for not discarding the blue French uniform, having kept it to be less conspicuous than in his white linen shirtsleeves.

Not that things would have been different either way, he thought despairingly.

Entering St. George's, the troop passed the market square where a raw new wooden gibbet with a dozen nooses had been erected. They took him to Fort George, the military headquarters, and handed him over to a provost guard of regular Army invalids. With his fetters and gag removed, he was prodded with bayonets into a crowded dungeon in the bowels of the fort. No one seemed interested in hearing his intelligence report. A feverish corporal told him that he would be in the batch of Brigands who would be hung the following day.

The dungeon had a single narrow slit window which failed to dispel the deep gloom. It held around a score of men, mainly blacks. A sole young white man sat against a wall, fingering a rosary, his prayers interspersed with sobs. He told Chart that he was a former seminarian and had been en route to St. Dominique aboard a ship taken by a British frigate. He had been denounced as a Republican agent by another man aboard and sentenced to death that morning by a drumhead tribunal. Chart gathered that most of the black men were field workers who had no connection with the Revolution but had been captured with cutlasses in their hands while roaming the countryside and therefore condemned to die without a hearing. Apparently, the vengeful British militia units had a daily quota of captives.

Chart ruefully thought that the Poultry prison in London was like the Royal Clarence Hotel in comparison. The prisoners were given no food or water, and the latrine was a shallow cesspit in a corner that had reached its capacity and overflowed decades earlier.

"What does it matter to them whether we're fed?" the seminarian said. "We will all be dead in a few hours."

Late the next morning the cell's rusty gate swung open and the same redcoats, tottering from rum and sickness, ordered them out. "Rotten fruit for the hangman's tree," cackled the sweating corporal. Chart was chained towards the end of a coffle with the other condemned men and marched out to the parade ground in front of the fort, where they were halted to wait for an officer's arrival to read the death sentences.

Shoulders hunched, near delirious from hunger and thirst, Chart noticed a tall British officer wearing a gilt gorget drilling black soldiers nearby. There was something familiar about the man. He shook his head and tried to focus his bleary eyes. Then the officer called an order in an authoritative voice that brought a surge of memories, and Chart pulled himself erect.

Lord Hugh Drummond.

The Captain of Westminster School. The older boy who had helped him to learn to defend himself against racist abuse.

His friend.

He tried to call out, but only a croak emerged from his dry throat. He tried again, then more loudly as the corporal of the guard hurried from the front of the coffle, cursing. Summoning the last vestiges of his strength, Chart shouted "Drummond! Lord Hugh Drummond!" as the guard struck him.

"Shut yer filthy black gob!"

Hugh's head turned, eyes squinting.

***

Major Lord Hugh Drummond, on secondment from His Majesty's 5th Regiment of Foot, wasn't sure if he had heard his name called or the squawk of a seagull. He looked towards the coffle of condemned men at the edge of the parade ground, forcing back his pity at the daily ritual of marching to eternity. Then he heard it again, undoubtedly his name being called by a dirty, bearded man in a ragged French uniform, who was about to be hit by the brass butt of a musket.

***

"You heard me, ye poxy blackamoor!" the corporal screamed, drawing back his musket for another blow.

"Stop! Quit that man!"

"Sah!" The guard grounded his musket and stood to attention.

"What the devil?" Drummond whispered. The man who had called out was scarcely recognisable. Except for the eyes. Those unforgettable sapphire eyes gleaming from the dark face.

"My God!"

***

Lord Hugh had Chart released. Seeing that he could barely stand, he ordered two of the black soldiers he was drilling to drape his arms over their shoulders and half-carry him to the major's own quarters, where he told his batman to get the surgeon post-haste.

Amidst the chatter of speculation amongst the black soldiers watching, no one noticed the enormous black man in a red coat whose scarred face split into a smile that revealed sharklike teeth.

***

Hugh shook his head in wonder after Chart, bathed and shorn of his beard by Drummond's servant, related his adventures as he wolfed down a breakfast of bacon, eggs and tea.

"Of course, I read about your High Court trial, I was in Ireland at the time so couldn't be there. I wrote to you, and when I was in London I tried to track you down but you had disappeared. Now I know why."

"Do you know if Pemb and Arabella made it here?" Chart asked.

"I understand that the murdering little swine is a militia officer and one of those who survived the assault on the Brigand's camp you told me about. I've a mind to challenge him to a duel as a way to put him down. I don't know about the lady, but will make inquiries."

"You saved my life, Hugh," said Chart. "I'll be forever in your debt. It's a miracle that you're here. But if Pemb finds me he will enslave me again."

"No he won't," Drummond said emphatically. "Not if you volunteer for the Loyal Black Rangers, which I have the honour to command."

"Loyal Black Rangers?"

Hugh explained that he had been given the task of forming a corps of slaves from British plantations who would be trained as light infantry "bush fighters" and given their freedom after proving their loyalty in combat against the French and Fédon's forces. White soldiers were dying like flies from disease and alcoholism at such an alarming rate that Army Headquarters in

London – Horse Guards – had been willing to try radical alternatives despite the fierce opposition of West Indian planters such as Pemb who feared arming the slaves they abused.

"We – that is, soldiers like Colonel John Moore and influential abolitionists such as Wilberforce and your friend Lady Augusta – argued that black soldiers were better suited to fighting in the tropics, especially young Africans who had lived in warrior societies. The Rangers would be men adapted to the climate and terrain, able to rapidly scale precipitous slopes, march long distances without support from a slow supply train, and to track and lay ambushes in the mountain rain forests.

"I volunteered to raise and train the corps, but only on the condition that the Black Rangers would be paid and fed the same as white regulars – eight pence a day. I wanted the legal right to free them at will for meritorious service, but Horse Guards balked at this, insisting that they could only be manumitted after five years or upon becoming invalids. I also lost my attempt to formally promote black men as officers and non-commissioned-officers; one's influence only reaches so far, even when you're the nephew of a duke! I'm sorry – I know that you were an exemplary officer in India, but you would be doing me a great favour to join us as a private. Frankly, most of the white officers and NCOs they've given me are useless, dregs of the Army. Having you to help with the training would be a godsend."

Remembering Sori's ostensible liberation, which was no more than brutal re-enslavement by government rather than an individual, Chart drew a deep breath.

"But the fact remains that we are still slaves."

Hugh vented an exasperated breath.

"Damn it, Chart," he said heatedly, "if it were in my power to free every slave at the drop of a hat, I would do so. But I've come to realise, sadly, that emancipation will be a long process like a military campaign, starting with minor victories such as abolishing the slave trade, before we win the war. The men under my command will be given the opportunity to fight for their freedom. They will also be treated equally with white soldiers. Most importantly, I hope that wearing the red coat and trusting them with arms will give them pride and dignity."

Chart sipped tea as he collected his thoughts.

"Those men who captured me, they had coloured officers," he said.

"Captain la Grenade's light dragoons. French Royalists but now loyal to King George, proving that not all the French on this island went over to Fédon. And they represent one of the few things the colonial government allows that I agree with. Mixed-race men like yourself can serve as militia officers, and free blacks can be NCOs. Perhaps soon the British Army will officially change too. What do you say, old man? Will you join us?"

Chart grasped Hugh's hand and pumped it with his first real smile in many months.

Drummond unrolled a large map of Grenada and asked Chart to point out the location of Fédon's three camps, then gave him sheets of paper to sketch the enemy positions in detail.

"This is the most useful intelligence we've had," he said. "I'm meeting with the Colonial Council and Army commanders this afternoon, and I will present this. They are consumed with fury over the massacre of the governor and those other poor wretches and want to attack again immediately, but I will advise waiting until our forces, especially the Rangers, are ready."

Before returning to his command, Major Drummond instructed his orderly to take Chart to the quartermaster where he was issued with a new Rangers uniform consisting of a short red jacket with yellow collars and cuffs, two shirts, blue cotton duck trousers, and a round hat with a small black plume. He was not given shoes; like the Black Rangers he had observed on the parade ground, his feet were hardened after nearly two years of going barefoot. From the armoury, he received a new .75 calibre Brown Bess musket and accoutrements. The supply sergeant was surprised that he could sign his name on the weapon's receipt rather than the usual "x".

Hugh had told him to take the rest of the day to recuperate. Nearly overwhelmed by fatigue, he found his way to the Rangers' barracks below the fort, racked his musket and sank into deep sleep in the nearest bunk.

He was awakened by a massive hand shaking his shoulder, awakening disoriented to see a cicatrised black face with one ear grinning at him.

"You in my bed, brother," Sori growled, then forgot about his princely dignity to pull Chart to his feet and envelop him in a hug worthy of a bear's embrace.

***

After Sori's escape from the Brigands he wisely discarded the bayonet with which he had freed himself, having heard from other freed slaves along the way to St. George's that the British were executing anyone caught bearing arms. He had no plan except fleeing from Fédon's insurgents; his only choice was certain death with them or dubious refuge among the British.

He had found himself among hundreds of other escaped slaves on the cobbled streets of St. George's begging for scraps of food. Whilst scavenging through a rubbish tip of fish heads and plantain skins along the Carenage a few days after his arrival, a tall British officer had ridden past on a horse accompanied by a black drummer and three scarlet-coated soldiers. Sori was surprised to hear the black soldiers announcing in English and various African languages, including his native Fula, that warriors were being recruited to serve in the British Army.

"Do you give free food?" Sori shouted.

"*Eey*, Yes," answered the Fulani redcoat. "Plenty good food."

Sori drew himself to his impressive height and addressed himself to the bemused-looking officer, saluting like he had seen the French soldiers do.

"I am ready, Mister General," he roared in English.

Chapter 24

Word spread among thousands of refugee slaves sleeping rough outside St. George's that the Black Rangers were recruiting with the promise of food, pay and eventual freedom. Lord Hugh was able to select the most able-bodied and eager young men to fill the ranks of five companies of one hundred men each, including several former La Sagesse fieldhands who were assigned to the same company as Chart. The corps was moved to a plateaued hill across from the harbour where they were housed in tents. Chart shared a mess with Sori and three of his Fulani countrymen, all large, powerfully muscled men. The encampment overlooked a field where the Rangers were drilled.

Each company had a white captain, six junior officers, an equal number of sergeants and corporals, and a drummer and bugler per company. Chart soon understood why Hugh had called many of the officers and NCOs "dregs of the Army". All had been seconded from line infantry regiments whose colonels were delighted to be rid of them. Half of the officers were alcoholics and others were mere schoolboys commissioned as ensigns with no military training. Hugh was aware that a captain and two lieutenants were homosexuals who had been caught *in flagrante delicto* and shipped off to the West Indies to spare their regiments and families embarrassment. Considering that three out of every five British soldiers serving in the Caribbean died within a year, it was unlikely that the misfits would return home.

Only a handful of non-commissioned-officers were what Hugh considered professionals. He was angered to discover that several sergeants and corporals had actually been released from a penal battalion in St. Dominque where they had been sentenced after committing atrocities against the local black and mixed-raced populations.

Although Major Drummond rode out daily from Ft. George to inspect the corps, he could spare little time from rancorous meetings with the Colonial Council and senior military officers who constantly argued with the civilian government over strategy and tactics to defeat the Brigands. There were never enough hours in the day to deal with the endless paperwork and cajoling to ensure that his men received rations, pay and ammunition. His temper was at a boiling point when he discovered that paymasters and quartermasters placed the black soldiers at the bottom of their lists.

Their contempt was shared by most of the white officers and NCOs, who considered secondment to the Black Rangers punishment duty and made only a perfunctory effort to train the men except when their commanding officer was present. The NCOs drew lots daily, the losers having to serve as drillmasters while the others lounged in the shade of silk cotton trees drinking the men's grog ration. The officers were generally to be found sleeping off their nightly debauches until mid-afternoon, when they would rouse to visit brothels in St. George's before the tipple houses reopened. Chart was astonished that the officers seemed unconcerned about the camp's vulnerability to an enemy attack, as it was on the outskirts of the town and the Brigands occupied the entire island except St. George's. This soon changed after Hugh was apprised of the situation and guard posts established.

The men grew resentful. "Why we need to march back and forth every day?" Sori grumbled to Chart, to the emphatic nods of their messmates. "We want to fight! And we never even fire our guns!"

When Hugh visited the parade ground the next day, Chart approached, saluted and asked to speak with him. Watched with resentful eyes by the white NCOs and few officers present, the Commanding Officer nodded and motioned to walk with him to the edge of the field. He scowled as Chart relayed the men's complaints.

"We will begin to have real disciplinary problems soon," Chart said. "Already a fair number sneak out of camp at night to visit wenches and forage for extra food. We've had one desertion with more to follow, I fear. And four muskets are missing from the armoury, stolen or sold. They haven't had live firing exercises, so it's useless trying to teach the manual of arms. These men are warriors, sir. If we can't set them against the Brigands they could end up turning their guns on us, considering how they are being treated."

"The bloody Council *want* us to fail!" Hugh fumed. "Last week they sent a letter to London stating that rather than defending the island, the Black Rangers will actually be more dangerous to the future of slavery and British rule. They are concerned about the influence that the Rangers might have on the slaves on the island once we triumph over the Brigands. They point out that black soldiers will have a higher social standing than slaves and that this might cause discontent amongst the slaves."

"I think we can agree on the latter point," Chart said quietly. "Things here will never be the same *if* we win. These are good men and if properly trained and rewarded, they can be the foundation of a new society here."

"Right," Hugh said decisively. "Live firing will begin next week. I'll have a load of worn-out uniforms sent over so the Rangers can make straw men as targets. I want you to ensure that the men in your platoon master the manual of arms after which you will train the entire company. I shall post a written order to that effect so it will not be challenged."

Hugh looked approvingly at Chart: closely shaven, uniform impeccable, pewter buttons and brass belt-plate polished. *Quite a contrast to the Army's slovenly rejects*, he thought. *Sets a good example to the Rangers.*

"And you can spread the word through the ranks that also starting next week no more close order drill for awhile. These men were recruited to be bush fighters, and by God that's what they're going to be!"

***

That evening Chart signed out five muskets from the armoury. He spent an hour demonstrating the manual of arms to Sori and his other messmates.

"Poise your firelocks! Cock your firelocks! Present! Fire!"

With the flint removed from the doghead clamp, he thumbed back the musket's hammer to full-cock and dry-fired it.

"Handle cartridge! Prime! Shut pans! Charge with cartridge! Draw rammer! Ram down cartridge! Shoulder your firelocks!"

He had Sori and the others attempt the sequence, drilling them relentlessly until they became adept. Other men from their company had gathered to watch, and once Chart was satisfied with his messmate's performance he suggested that they call for volunteers and train others.

The next day a mule wagon arrived at the camp laden with bundles of old clothing, copper-lined barrels of paper cartridges, and lumber with tools. Laughing and joking, the Rangers chopped reeds from the nearby lagoon and fabricated scarecrow-like figures from outdated blue and red uniforms. Under Chart's direction, other men built gallows on the parade ground.

"What are you doing," a bleary-eyed company commander asked suspiciously.

"Getting ready to hang you," one of the Ashantis said in Twi, to the chortles of those who understood him. Although Chart did not understand, he caught the hostile meaning and quickly intervened.

"They are for bayonet practice, Sir!"

After the officer left, Chart rounded on the men, with Sori at his back glaring at them.

"No more insubordination!" he snapped in English, which most of the men now understood. "You are soldiers in the British Army and you must show respect to officers no matter what. Otherwise, you will be flogged and if anyone disobeys orders he will be hanged!"

"You did the right thing," Sori told him later. "These are hard men, they won't respect you unless you are harder than them."

Live firing and bayonet practice began the following week, watched from horseback by Hugh, who wanted his gelding to become accustomed to the sound of musketry. Half the officers and NCOs had made the effort to be present, the others were "Absent – Sick" in their tents or at the military hospital on Richmond Hill, while a dozen were officially listed on the rolls as "Discharged – Dead" having perished from Yellow Fever. Major Drummond took note of the few British soldiers who seemed to take an interest in their duties. To his surprise, among these were the homosexual captain and lieutenant, the former of whom had attended Westminster School a few years before Hugh and Chart. The other lieutenant had died from malaria the previous week.

I'll never call them madges or molly boys again, he thought, watching them confidently issue commands.

The NCOs instructing the men ignored Chart as he strode behind the firing lines, quietly ordering a soldier to adjust his stance or accelerate loading by keeping the ramrod in the left hand. At first, the men had a tendency to close their eyes and pull the trigger hard when firing, missing the target by a wide margin. Sori told Chart that they thought the harder they pulled the farther the musket ball would fly.

It was Hugh's idea to make loading and firing a contest, awarding an extra pint of grog to each man in a company that got off the most aimed rounds in a minute, which the commanding officer timed on his gold pocket watch. By the end of the week, the strawman targets were shredded and Chart's victorious company roistered into the early hours of the morning.

The Rangers had begun following Chart's example of being smartly turned out and Major Drummond rarely found a pewter button dangling or rusty musket barrel during his inspections. They took pride in their red tunics - which they called "The King's Uniform" - and used them to great advantage among the women in shanties along Lagoon Road near the camp who were keen to deprive them of their weekly pay of 4 shillings, 8 pence.

Although the men grumbled about drilling and inaction, Sori told Chart that they were well contented in comparison to their existence as enslaved field hands labouring for ten hours each day on a paltry diet, which rarely included meat or fish. The Rangers received ten or twelve ounces of meat every day, sometimes fresh, and most had never seen a silver shilling, much less been paid for the fun of shooting muskets and bayoneting dummies.

One day they were mustered for a special parade. With drums beating and bugles blaring, Major Drummond formally presented the corps with their own colours, a yellow silk flag displaying a pair of black soldiers flanking a crowned royal cartouche embroidered with "Loyal Black Rangers", which had been sewn by free black and coloured ladies in St. George's. A tasselled Union Jack accompanied it.

The men still occasionally lapsed into "drunk and disorderly" fighting, theft and being Absent Without Leave. Many of the fights were between men from different African tribes. Even Sori had lapsed into verbal insults of traditional Fulani enemies such as Ibos and Yorubas. When Chart took Sori aside to discuss the disciplinary problems the big man was initially defensive. He reluctantly agreed to accept hand-picked Ashanti, Yoruba and Mandingo men into the mess, but baulked at Ibos who he continued to describe as "dogs". Their Fulani messmates took the new men's places in other messes. In return, Sori had a suggestion for improving discipline, after which Chart had a quiet word with Hugh.

"Discipline has greatly improved," he said, "but the misdeeds are still flogging offenses if we go by the book. Most of these men bear flogging scars on their backs like mine. They're starting to forget that they are still legally enslaved. Feeling the lash again could undo all that we've accomplished so far to give them pride in being *Loyal* Black Rangers."

"What would you propose?"

"Actually, it's Sori's idea. Let us sort it out within the ranks, unofficially. If that doesn't work, we can go by the book.

Sori and his new messmates began having their own version of "a quiet word" with miscreants in a grove behind the latrines. The number of offenses declined dramatically, although more than the usual number of men ended up in the infirmary with contusions and bad headaches.

"Doing much better," Sori told Chart, "but it won't last if we don't get action soon. The young men are hot-blooded, need to fight."

"They're not ready to take the field," Hugh answered when Chart relayed the warning. "They're not yet a cohesive unit. They still need to put African tribalism behind them and become soldiers of the King. And they must be trained in light infantry tactics – the bush-fighting which will be their forte. Their instructor arrived last evening from St. Dominique. He will be here tomorrow."

They were paraded by companies just after dawn when the air was still fresh. Drumming was heard on the St. George's road. A small group of horsemen neared, riding slowly behind the drummer. The Rangers recognised their commanding officer at the front riding with a man in full British colonel's uniform with a large bicorn shading his face. A wave of astonished muttering swept through the ranks as they saw that the middle-aged man in the colonel's scarlet uniform was black, as were a captain and two other soldiers riding behind, one of whom carried a Union Jack with the inscription *La Loi Britannique* (British law).

"Silence in the ranks!" screamed the sergeants. "What the hell!" a company commander exclaimed in a shocked voice. "A negro colonel?"

"Rangers!" roared Hugh, "I have the honour of introducing Colonel Jean Kina and his son Captain Zamor Kina. Colonel Kina is the finest bush fighter in the world and under his tutelage the Brigands will soon be in mortal fear of you!"

Drummond turned and saluted Kina, ignoring the disgusted "Bloody 'ell" from one of the NCOs. The black colonel nudged his horse to the front ranks.

"The Republicans," he said in a heavy French Haitian accent, "want only our destruction and your ruin. Their minion, the so-called 'General' Fédon, has blinded a great many of our black brethren by turning them against our benevolent King George with the poison of their Republican fanaticism, their lies about Liberty, Equality and Brotherhood."

Kina paused, intelligent brown eyes alight with passion.

"I know you are looking at me, wondering how can a black man, born a slave, truly be a colonel in the English army? It is because, like you, I chose to serve the king who freed me, who rewarded me as his warrior with rank, honours and money. I showed the English how to fight in a new way, the way of African warriors, and we are going to teach you to fight like this too!"

Chart was watching for Hugh's signal to him.

"Three cheers for Colonel Kina!"

All five hundred Black Rangers lustily roared huzzahs for a full five minutes while their officers and NCOs stood at attention in stony-faced silence.

"I thought that black and coloured men could not serve in the British Army," Chart asked Hugh later that day.

"*Officially* not. But there are exceptions to every rule, and every successful commander knows that expediency and flexibility win battles, not foolish adherence to rules and regulations. Kina holds a commission signed by the principal undersecretary at the Ministry for War in London. He did heroic service for us in St. Dominque and Martinque. An inspiring leader and true force of nature."

Colonel Kina and his son, accompanied by his aide-de-camp and orderly, were waiting on the parade ground next morning at dawn. The Rangers were disconcerted to see that the Haitian officers had exchanged their scarlet tunics for osnaburgh frocks and breeches dyed green and were now barefooted like them.

"We don't have to give up our King's uniforms, do we, man?" a soldier near Chart asked worriedly.

The soldiers relaxed when word spread that the Kinas had changed for their own comfort, although the colonel confided to Hugh that if he had his way all "bush fighters" would wear green lightweight uniforms that blended into jungle foliage.

The Rangers were trained to work as skirmishers in advance of the main line of British regulars, fighting in pairs so that one soldier could cover the other while loading. Unlike the line regiments which fired in volleys, the black soldiers were told they could fire at will from any cover such as bushes, trees and rocks. Since most of their fighting would be at close range, and the Brown Bess muskets were inaccurate beyond ten yards in jungle and bush, the Rangers would use pellet-shot together with standard ball in their muskets.

The corps' buglers demonstrated a series of six calls to pass orders, an exercise which took weeks for all the men to learn. They were expected to run, disperse and rally to the flag upon hearing the appropriate bugle call. Unlike regular infantrymen, who carried 40-pound packs, the Rangers trained in light equipment, carrying only seventeen-inch bayonets hung in sheaths behind their right hips, thirty paper rounds in leather cartridge boxes, and a light haversack with flasks of water, salt pork, dried peas and hard-baked cassava cakes. Each man was issued with a cutlass worn on their belts, which was returned to the armoury each evening along with their muskets and bayonets to prevent mayhem from persistent intertribal fighting. They were taught to march at a rapid 140 paces per minute, and in the third week they went on route marches to the arid southern part of the island called Pointe Salines where there was little cover beyond cactus and light bush for ambushers. They were screened by light dragoons who, like the Rangers, were eager to fight.

At the end of six weeks, Colonel Kina told Major Drummond that the men were as ready for battle as they could be without combat experience.

"They'll get that very soon," Hugh replied.

Chapter 25

Sundays were a day of rest for the Rangers. An Anglican chaplain from the regular army garrison had ventured out to the camp once but found little interest in Christian services among the black troops, who still largely worshipped African deities. An ancient Obeah man came around regularly to sell charms to ward off musket balls and a host of spirits, both evil and mischievous.

Hugh arrived at the camp on the Sunday morning after Jean Kina completed his training. He was accompanied by four troopers of the St. George's Light Dragoons leading a saddled bay mare with holstered pistols across its withers.

"Care for a jaunt?" he asked Chart, who was shaving outside his tent with a straight razor and handheld mirror. "Thought we'd make a reconnoitre to the south, see if we can flush some Brigands, have a bit of sport, what?"

Chart quickly rediscovered his love of riding, although he joked to Hugh that it was the first time he had ridden barefoot. They cleared an army checkpoint on the road half a mile beyond the camp and cantered warily past patches of bush that could conceal ambushers. But the countryside seemed deserted.

Hugh led them down a path to a magnificent beach bordered by Caribbean waters in every shade of blue from palest turquoise in the shallows to cobalt as the sea deepened. Drummond spurred his horse into a gallop and Chart kept pace, both men laughing like carefree schoolboys savouring the joy of racing along sand as glaringly white as the purest sugar crystals. They traversed the two-mile strand in less than ten minutes, pulling up at a cliff at the far end, where they slid off their horses and led them into shade. Their escort dismounted out of earshot, slinging their musketoons.

They sat on a fallen coconut palm trunk. Hugh removed a wine bottle and sandwiches wrapped in linen from his saddlebag.

"Like riding, I'd almost forgot the pleasure of a decent wine,"

217

Chart sighed after sipping from the glass filled by Drummond.

"Claret, cargo from a merchantman out of Bordeaux taken by one of our frigates. How does it compare with your grog ration?"

"Hah!"

They ate and drank while Drummond relayed titbits of news from London. Wilberforce's motion to abolish the slave trade had been introduced, and defeated, at every session of Parliament, and even though the subject continued to be debated, the outbreak of war with France prevented any serious consideration. However, the Commons had found time to pass the Vagrant Act allowing magistrates to enrol vagrants and smugglers into the Royal Navy as an alternative to judicial punishment.

"*That* will improve the quality of our fighting men," he said dryly.

Chart had suspected that Hugh had something else to tell him. When they finished their picnic, Drummond said, "I have news of a more personal nature."

He told him that he had discovered where Arabella was lodging and had called on her. She was greatly relieved to know that Chart had escaped from the Brigands and was serving under him in the Rangers. She asked him to relay her fond greetings but emphasized that under no circumstances should Chart attempt to contact her. She had left her lodgings and moved into a house with her husband, Pemb.

"My God, poor Arabella!" Chart cried. "But why wouldn't she stay in her lodgings after Pemb's unspeakable cruelty to her."

"Because she is penniless, and Pemb is now a man of consequence. The useless Colonial Council is more concerned about social status and the size of one's estate than it is about ability. Pemb is a baronet, and a major in the militia, so he was invited by those middle-class mediocrities to take a seat on the council. He has been appointed quartermaster general and provided with a townhouse formerly belonging to one of the merchants murdered by Fédon. He insisted that Arabella join him to keep up appearances as the only real member of the nobility on the island. Believe it or not, those civilian imbeciles still have receptions and dinner parties even though St. George's is besieged and thousands of people are starving around them!"

Hugh didn't tell him that Arabella was visibly sickly, pale and feverish, her perspiring face drawn, hair covered by a turban from which a few strands had escaped, a blotchy red rash visible on her neck and hands. Although she had not mentioned her disease, he was familiar with the ravages of syphilis from men under his command whom he had visited in various garrison infirmaries.

Now he reached out and shook Chart's shoulder to rouse him from obvious melancholy.

"The good news is that we'll see action soon. Tomorrow the Rangers will march north with the regulars to assault an enemy post!"

***

It was a pleasant little brick townhouse on a quiet side street. Arabella spent most of her time listless in an upstairs bedroom with windows shaded by wooden jalousies that did little to dissipate the oppressive heat. Blessedly, Pemb left her alone and three servants, slaves of the late owner, looked after her at the tug of a bell pull. She had been grateful to know that Chart was safe, but worried about his service as a soldier, which she knew he craved. She felt lost, bereft of any hope, keenly aware that the disease would eventually consume her.

Her room was above the small parlour, and sometimes late in her sleepless nights she would hear Pemb's voice below in conversation with various men. Whatever their business, it was no concern of hers. Like an alley cat, Pemb seemed to have again landed on his feet, and the only thing that mattered was that he no longer molested her.

***

Drums thumping and regimental flags streaming, fifteen hundred infantrymen and cavalry of the expeditionary force marched along the island's windward coast road north towards the town of Grenville where the insurrection had begun with the first massacre. As they passed the overgrown entrance to La Sagesse estate, Chart's stomach knotted into an icy ball as he recalled the desecration of his mother's remains. *You monster*, he thought, visualising Pemb's sneering, pimpled face, *I'll never rest until I make you pay.*

In the column's vanguard rode a brigadier general named Moffet who had arrived on the island a month earlier with reinforcements, nearly all scrawny youngsters from the bleak rookeries of London, Manchester and Liverpool. A quarter of them were now either dead or dying from the Bulam Fever engulfing the barracks in St. George's.

General Moffet, who was fond of biblical quotes, made it clear to Lord Hugh that black soldiers had no place in the British Army according to the prophet Joshua's biblical curse that none should be freed from being slaves and whose natural role was as hewers of wood and drawers of water. He ordered the Rangers to march at the rear of the column, which soon proved fortuitous as snipers hidden in the bush killed three regulars and wounded five in the leading battalions. Following every attack, the general halted the column and laboriously ordered volleys fired to saturate the jungle with lead balls, to the amusement of Chart and his comrades.

"That Brigand long gone before them boys ready to shoot," said Sori. "And them drums beating ain't no way to surprise the enemies."

"Eyes in every bush and in the cane fields," another man said, "I seen 'em."

What had once been a verdant island cultivated from the Atlantic and Caribbean littorals to the feet of the tallest mountains was now desolated. Nearly every plantation building was destroyed, wooden structures burnt to the ground and stone buildings blackened and roofless with new vegetation starting to encroach. Cane fields had been cleared by fire or their plants methodically chopped down, as were plantain walks, banana groves and cassava gardens. Pot-bellied children with skeletal limbs and enormous eyes huddled by the roadside watching the marching soldiers, too dulled by malnutrition to hide like their mothers or beg for food. They softened even the stoniest hearts among the black and white troops, and when the column halted for brief rests, African Rangers and Yorkshiremen alike delved into haversacks and tossed scraps of biscuit and salt pork to them.

It took the column, with its field artillery and baggage train, two days to march fifteen miles. When they made camp the first night, General Moffet summoned Hugh and, seeking to fulfil Joshua's malediction, ordered him to have his men pitch tents, fetch water and make cooking fires for the white soldiers. Major Drummond politely refused, saluted and returned to his command while the general hurled threats and curses of more modern vintage at his straight back.

"He won't dare arrest me and have me court martialled as threatened," Hugh answered mildly in answer to Chart's worried query. "The Rangers are my independent command, and I hold my appointment directly from the Commander in Chief, the Duke of York."

The general's threats never materialised. On the evening of the second day the column was halted a mile from Grenville and Hugh was sent for along with other battalion commanders to go to the front of the column where senior officers were scanning an eminence called Pilot Hill with their telescopes. Major Drummond unfolded his glass, seeing a huge French tricolour flapping over a redoubt encircled by defensive earthworks. The heads of hundreds of soldiers could be seen above the ramparts, with others scurrying to join them from huts at the base of the hill.

"I make out five cannon," announced a captain serving as the general's aide-de-camp, "six-pounders me'thinks." At that moment one of the guns boomed and a black ball could clearly be seen hurtling towards them. "Steady on!" a major cried, and the officers held their position as the cannon ball ploughed into a cane field fifty feet away. A chorus of cheers erupted in the enemy fortification.

Camp was made and the Black Rangers were ordered to bivouac a hundred paces apart from the regulars. They didn't mind. Sentries were stationed around the perimeter and – with Hugh's permission – foragers slipped into the countryside as night descended, returning with yams, chickens and goat carcasses that their owners had thought hidden. None of the officers questioned by what methods the men acquired the provisions.

The Rangers also brought intelligence.

After supper, a message came from the general ordering Major Drummond to attend a conference. He found the other officers clustered around a folding table outside the general's marquee tent peering at a map under the lights of whale oil lanterns.

"Damndest thing," growled General Moffet. "We had good information just ten days ago that Pilot Hill was held by a small force of Brigands, unfortified and with no guns. Our mission was to take the hill and establish a base there as the first step in our strategy of recapturing the island."

"Well, they knew we were coming as soon as we left St. George's," a lieutenant colonel said.

"Not enough time to prepare," offered the general. "And how would they know *this* was our objective when the Brigands have a dozen or more posts around the island?"

"They began constructing the new defences a week ago," said Lord Hugh.

"How do you know?" Moffet asked brusquely.

"My men talked to a number of locals this evening."

"Can't trust the word of blackies," the colonel sniffed.

Major Drummond shook his head in exasperation.

"They were aware that we were coming," he said. "Someone who knew our plans told them at least a week ago."

***

Pemb began on a small scale. Criminal perhaps, but certainly not treasonous. After all, he was a proud and loyal subject of King George III, a field-grade militia officer, member of the Colonial Council, and a member of the aristocracy. But the truth of the matter was that he was skint, nary two shillings to rub together, and the merchants who had been foolish enough to extend credit had closed their doors to him.

Fortune had smiled on him though, when on the agenda of his first Council meeting was the need for a new quartermaster general for the colony, the previous one, a major in the Royal North British Fusiliers, having joined his comrades in the cemetery on the edge of town providing daily employment for a dozen gravediggers. Pemb had volunteered for the role, citing his service as a commissary during the disastrous assault on the Brigands' camp. He expressed his regret at not being able to serve the colony on active duty on the battlefield, mumbling about an old back injury from a spurious hunting accident, which he hoped fellow councillors would assume was the cause of his hunched back.

He didn't mention his long experience as a fence for stolen goods at his grandfather's Shadwell ale house.

Chartered ships were now delivering considerably more military supplies to Grenada than there were soldiers to use them. A large warehouse on the waterfront bulged with a cornucopia of munitions, uniforms, boots, tents, foodstuff, cavalry equipment, bolts of cloth, timber and barrels of wine. Entrusted with the keys, Pemb spent a week there with a notebook carefully cataloguing the most saleable items. He generously gave the two elderly watchmen a firkin of madeira every other day, and they never questioned the comings and goings of various persons and vehicles even when they awoke from long naps under a Soursop tree.

Pemb didn't even have to put the word out that he was open for business. He was gratified by a host of new friends who sought him out at taverns and whorehouses. Deals for a few barrels of flour, two gross of shoes, or a butt of Staffordshire ale were concluded with a naked trollop on one knee and tankard of rum punch in the other. Business was so good that he engaged a pair of malingering Royal Artillery privates, guttersnipes from London's East End who knew some of his old Shadwell cronies. He didn't mind a bit of pilferage by them as there was more than enough booty to go around.

One day a well-dressed gentleman who claimed he was Dutch treated him to a bottle of fine cognac, flattering Pemb's impeccable taste in his gold-braided uniform (which even Pemb had lately admitted to himself was getting a bit stained and worn). The man said that he was a merchant trading with Curacao. After a couple of glasses each, the Dutchman asked if he and a friend could come by Pemb's newly tenanted house that night to discuss a rather confidential business proposition.

Pemb's eyes widened when the man casually took a handful of gold coins from his pocket, delving among them to find a couple of half crowns to pay for the drinks.

They came at midnight, in hooded cloaks despite the warm night. Pemb led them to the small parlour beneath Arabella's bedroom. They wanted firearms, not for Britain's enemies, perish the thought, but for the defence of other islands again the revolutionary forces sweeping through the Caribbean. Could the honourable baronet help them protect other planters and their women and children against the Republican menace?

They shook hands, leaving Pemb with a deposit of fifty gold Louis d'or. The next day, a mule wagon arrived at the warehouse, was ushered inside the wide doors by Pemb, and trundled out with crates of Tower muskets, Sea Service pistols, casks of powder, flints, musket balls and all the necessary accoutrements. Pemb was too busy gloating over the gold received in full payment to notice which direction the wagon took.

Over the next few weeks, Pemb became desperate to find a hiding place for the hundreds of Portuguese Johannes ("Joes"), guineas, doubloons and Louis d'Or he received, resorting to burying them in an old iron kettle in the garden to the rear of his house. The account book in which he recorded each transaction was kept in the drawer of a writing desk in the parlour. The escritoire's key had presumably vanished with the owner of the house, but it didn't matter as Pemb believed he was above suspicion. Gentlemen didn't disturb another gentleman's personal possessions, especially if he was a baronet.

He was unaware that Arabella watched through the slats in her bedroom window as he excavated the hole and deposited his treasure.

One night the Dutchman and a different man, also with a foreign accent, turned up unexpectedly. Pemb had just arrived from the town's best brothel on Melville Street and was befuddled after a bottle of gin and the draining attentions of two of the doxies. When he stopped to urinate on a street corner he thought he was being followed, but when he turned to look no one was visible.

The visitors came straight to the point. They wanted information from his Council meetings: British forces strength, reinforcements expected, campaigns planned against the Brigands.

Pemb was dry-mouthed, witless. While he sat in a daze the strange man went to the front door, whistled, and two strapping black men in dark clothes followed him back to the parlour.

"They are very good at following without being seen," said the Dutchman quietly. "And very skilled with dagger and garrotte."

He took out a leather bag and jingled it.

"And what a pity you would be unable to enjoy the lovely gold if you are dead."

Chapter 26

General Moffet wanted to make an immediate assault on Pilot Hill. While the battalion commanders and his aide-de-camp refrained from using the word "folly", they argued that such an attack could be disastrous, especially to the general's reputation. So the decision was taken to encamp and wait for reinforcements while planning an attack on a smaller enemy post nearby.

As Moffet considered the Rangers the most expendable of his forces, he ordered Hugh to post them by platoons as picquets in the bush outside the British camp to watch for the enemy. Chart's twenty-man unit, nominally commanded by a stuttering sixteen-year-old ensign and a hard-bitten sergeant who made no secret of his dislike for black men, was deployed in a bamboo-walled boucan in thick jungle on a ridge above the encampment.

Darkness fell early, bringing a sea breeze that rustled the foliage around them. Bamboo boles rubbed against each other with unearthly squeaks. Tree frogs began their peep-peeping. Unseen creatures scurried through the undergrowth, unnerving the men. Half of the platoon had been detailed to take first watch until midnight while their comrades rested, but no one could sleep.

The sergeant took the second watch with Chart, Sori and seven others. A quarter moon gave feeble light until obscured by a cloud. When it re-emerged, the Ranger with the best night vision went rigid.

"Something out there!" he rasped.

All the men were now up, crowding around the entrance. Shadowy figures could be discerned moving through the undergrowth. Guttural voices whispered.

"Don't bunch around the door!" Chart warned

"I give the orders here!" the sergeant snarled.

"They're all around us!" said Sori, terror tightening his usual bass voice.

"Jumbies! Ghosts!" other Rangers muttered.

In the jungle someone ordered, *"Tirez!"*

"Brigands!" shouted Chart. "Get down!"

He crouched, grabbing the big African's arm to drag him down. At that instant the jungle erupted in thunderous explosions and blinding muzzle flashes that momentarily lit the clearing in front of the hut. Men around him screamed and collapsed as soft lead balls tore into them. A few Rangers fired blindly into the bush, illuminating the interior briefly so that Chart glimpsed the dead and dying. At least half a dozen casualties, including the sergeant, the ensign curled foetus-like, blubbering. He saw that the two wounded men were so mangled that they would succumb in minutes.

Chart automatically reverted to the role of combat commander ingrained in him in India. He had seconds before the Brigands reloaded and fired a second volley which would kill or wound an equal number of men. A few might survive to become prisoners.

But not him. He would be a dead man either way. Unless they cut their way out.

"Give up now or you all die!" a French-accented voice yelled outside. "Surrender!"

"Fix bayonets!" Chart ordered. "Sori, take the ensign. We'll fight our way back to the camp."

Sori slung his musket over one shoulder and the frail young white officer over the other. He held a cutlass honed to razor sharpness. Chart heard the enemy's ramrods clattering back into their holders as they prepared to fire again.

"One volley to keep their heads down then we go! Present! Fire! Now!"

Enveloped in smoke from the discharged muskets, he led them at a charge out the door and onto the path. Only a handful of the Brigands blocked them, caught by surprise as Chart bayoneted one and Sori swung his cutlass to split the head of another. Others were shot down as the surviving Rangers swept past them. Another volley roared from behind as they pounded down the path, but in the darkness and confusion none of the King's soldiers was hit.

The camp had been alerted by the gunfire. Bugles called,

drums beat and watch fires blazed. To avoid his men being accidentally shot, Chart ordered them to halt behind bushes and went forward on his own, calling out in an impeccable English public school voice to hold fire. He returned to the Rangers, formed them into neat files, and marched them into the encampment with the snivelling ensign bouncing on Sori's shoulder.

***

"I'm giving you command of the platoon," said Hugh. "I'll draft men in from other companies to replace the ones lost."

"What will the general say?" Chart asked. "And the Rangers' white officers and NCOs?"

"What they say be damned!" Drummond replied heatedly. "We're fighting a war, and we must do so in the most practical way, regardless of their prejudices."

He paused, struggling with his temper.

"Sorry, feeling a bit choleric today. Must be the heat and the malady of indecision infecting headquarters. Anyway, your promotion won't be official, no gazetting in London, I'm afraid. And there's no choice, really. That pathetic lad who was the platoon commander has been sent back to St. George's and we've lost many white officers and NCOs to disease with no one to replace them. You'll need a sergeant and a couple of corporals."

"Sori."

"Good choice … Lieutenant. Yours is the only Ranger platoon which has been in combat so far, so I'll put you in the vanguard when we go into action against the small enemy post whenever the general decides to bestir himself."

Chart's unit ended up with four men in addition to the ones lost. The commanders of the other Ranger companies used his need for replacements as an opportunity to be rid of troublemakers. Most fit in well with the original complement, but one, an Ibo in his mid-twenties who had only recently been transported from Africa, was habitually insubordinate and bullying to the other men. Sori's massive fists only worsened the problem, which was exacerbated by tribal antipathy.

The man slipped out of camp the night after Sori's second

beating, taking his musket and wearing his red coat. Two days later, dawn revealed his naked headless body spreadeagled just out of musket range on the edge of the jungle. His head was impaled on a stake in the middle of the road which the column would take to assault the enemy post.

"Is it just possible that you 'encouraged' him to desert?" Chart asked Sori as the battalions prepared for the attack later that day.

"Could be," Sori nodded, displaying his dagger teeth in a hideous grin. "Good reminder for the others that they must behave."

Lord Hugh wanted his men to be blooded in combat. General Moffet required little persuasion to allow the Rangers to lead the attack with the light companies of the regulars. Moving in skirmish order from bush to tree to rocks, they advanced up the hill with minimal casualties and began a withering covering fire for the regiments behind them. The Brigands fired a few fusillades at the lines of advancing redcoats before abandoning the post and retreating down the opposite slope. As they fled through burnt cane fields, they were pursued and cut down by the British cavalry.

Moffet's force occupied the post as his headquarters and the Rangers joined the other soldiers in building batteries for cannon to be trained towards the main enemy fortification on Pilot Hill. Heavy 12- and 18-pounder guns were unloaded from Royal Navy ships and merchantmen, and the enemy post was bombarded while the Rangers were sent to clear Brigands from the town of Grenville in house-to-house fighting. Hugh led them on foot, relishing the fighting. Most of the enemy fled but a few were killed and three surrendered. He ordered a squad to escort the latter back to the British lines to avoid them being summarily executed, as was the common practice of both the black and white British troops. Not that they wouldn't be hung anyway, but first they must be interrogated.

When the town was liberated, Major Drummond gave his men permission to pillage it. "The Brigands resisted," he explained to Chart and the other company and platoon commanders, "and the place is deserted so it's their right. I trust that the Brigands haven't drunk all the rum. God knows our chaps deserve whatever they can find though I fear the pickings will be slim after months in enemy hands. We'll set a perimeter guard in case there's a counter-attack, and do try to ensure that your men are in condition to fight again tomorrow if need be."

***

Arabella never left the house, yet despite her lethargy and melancholia she yearned for news of Chart. She composed a letter addressed to "Major Lord Hugh Drummond, In the Field," and gave it to her chambermaid to deliver to the military headquarters at Ft. George.

She was unaware that in his role as Quartermaster General, Pemb also served as postmaster, which provided access to private correspondence containing a stream of intelligence for which he was handsomely rewarded. He knew that his Westminster School nemesis Hugh Drummond commanded the Loyal Black Rangers. Arabella's letter was on the desk in his office amidst a sheaf of other correspondence. He recognised her handwriting and immediately slit the envelope.

His perpetually simmering resentment boiled into wrath as he read her sentences. So, his slave Chart was serving with the Rangers, and his raddled wife was still pining for the black bastard. He knew that Fédon was offering a reward of one hundred Joes for the mulatto alive and fifty for his head.

Pemb sat back in his chair, took off his powdered wig, and mopped his sweating shaved pate with a handkerchief. He had taken to wearing wigs again as it gave him more gravitas with older members of the council who still wore theirs in formal meetings. Removing it seemed to cool his brain and free his thoughts.

He knew that slaves conscripted into the Black Rangers could no longer be claimed as chattel by plantation owners. They were now the property of His Majesty George III. In time, he would be able to claim government compensation, but he wasn't interested in that. After all, he was now a wealthy man again, and destined to be even richer the longer that the war against the French and Brigands dragged on.

Remembering how that arrogant nobleman Lord Hugh had engineered his beating in front of the school at the hands of his half-caste cousin filled him with hatred that burned like the final stage of Bulam Fever. Both men had looked down on him since they were students, which was doubly humiliating as one was a blackamoor son of a slave whore.

They had to die in the most excruciating way possible. And from what he heard at the council meetings, the Brigand leader Fédon was a grand master in the art of painful death.

***

To keep the Rangers occupied while the enemy fortification was besieged, Major Drummond allowed them to make forays into the countryside in platoon strength. Aided by Sergeant Sori's knuckles, the men responded well to Chart's harsh discipline as interdependence in combat welded them into professional soldiers. They, and other Black Ranger units, had sporadic firefights with bands of Brigands, most of whom were foraging for food. Fédon's men threatened former slaves hiding in the jungle who were barely surviving on dasheen and cassava, murdering them and burning their huts if they couldn't turn over provisions. Within weeks, the desperate former plantation workers saw the Black redcoats as saviours and protectors.

Chart ordered his men to spread the word that any former slaves who had joined the Brigands by coercion, as he had witnessed, could surrender without fear of being hung or shot. With Hugh's approval, he arranged for a printer in St. George's to produce passes in English and French, signed by Major Drummond, pardoning the bearer. Dozens of emaciated, ragged men surrendered. Each was interrogated before scurrying into the bush clutching their chits. They provided confirmation that the insurgents were running low on ammunition and rations.

After two weeks of bombardment, the large enemy redoubt on Pilot Hill was abandoned in the middle of the night, its guns spiked and tricolour left flying defiantly. General Moffet made his headquarters on the hilltop where sea breezes kept mosquitoes – and the fevers they carried – away. He dithered under his marquee drinking tea with staff officers, napping during the heat of the afternoon, and occasionally rising to peer at maps of the island. Each evening he dined in a dozen officers, who supped well on fresh meat and fish served on regimental china and crested silver. The general was proud of his store of claret and port and enjoyed surrounding himself with aristocratic officers – including Major Lord Hugh Drummond despite his insolence and dangerous beliefs about the equality of blacks. When asked by Hugh about his strategy for the next phase of offensive operations, the general mumbled about "awaiting orders".

The men of his expeditionary force were less fortunate. Their tents were pitched in neat blocks at the base of the hill on marshy ground swarming with mosquitoes. Daily rains saturated the earth, sluicing the contents of latrines into a nearby stream used for drinking. What had begun as a small cemetery held a quarter of the regulars within a fortnight. Their putrefying corpses further polluted the groundwater. Infirmary tents housed half of the remaining force, most of whom would never recover from Bloody Flux, Malaria, Typhoid and Yellow Fever.

The Black Rangers' ranks were decimated as well, although not as badly as the white soldiers. Chart lost two men from his platoon to cholera, but his company commander, a lieutenant, two NCOs and a drummer perished from disease. Hugh promoted one of the surviving subalterns to brevet captaincy of the company, but ordered that Chart would be his second-in-command unofficially, which the officer was grateful for as he was afraid of his black soldiers.

After a month of inactivity, the column was simply unfit to take the field again even if General Moffit had wanted to do so. Without reinforcements, the campaign against the Brigands was at a stalemate. The Ranger's reconnoitring resulted in intelligence that regular French troops were arriving to bolster the Brigand forces, which were steadily depleted by desertions, disease and disillusionment. Lord Hugh and the other British battalion commanders were worried their weakened expeditionary force would be easy prey to fresh, disciplined Republican troops.

Control of the island hung in the balance. It was now up to one side or the other of the two warring European powers to break the impasse.

Chapter 27

Colony of Grenada
May 1796.

Like a great serpent slowly awakening and uncoiling, the British Empire began an overwhelming military response to the insurrection in Grenada. The coils tightened as thousands of reinforcements, many of whom were veterans of counter-insurgency fighting in St. Dominique and other Caribbean islands, were disembarked. Royal Navy warships patrolled the coasts, strangling the revolution by intercepting supplies and French marines and infantry. With the soldiers arrived an elderly yet fiercely energetic commander-in-chief named Ralph Abercromby who didn't give a tinker's damn if the haughty English officers under his command mocked his Scottish burr, myopia and brusque manner. He brought with him a pair of equally spirited young Scottish brigadiers named Hope and Campbell.

Hours after stepping ashore, Abercromby went to Pilot Hill. His ruddy face suffused to a hue matching his coat as he observed the line of crude wooden crosses marking soldiers' graves and heard the groans of men packed into infirmary tents. He upbraided Moffet for his slothfulness, calling him a "sassenach walloper" and relieving him of command. Sitting at the deposed commander's field desk, flanked by the youthful brigadiers, the general called in the surviving battalion commanders individually. When it was Lord Hugh's turn, he slammed his right foot to the ground, hoping that the heel of his rotting boot wouldn't fall off, and saluted.

"Well sir, I've heard good things about your black fellas," growled Abercromby. "You've done well and now we will put their bush-fighting abilities to good use. Oh, and you're a Lieutenant-Colonel from this moment. Dismissed."

Leaving Brigadier Hope in command at Pilot Hill, the indefatigable 62-year-old and his staff, escorted by a troop of the 17th Light Dragoons, rode to St. George's and stormed into a hastily convened meeting of the Colonial Council.

"'tis high time we ended this glaikit nonsense!" he thundered. "This island is now under martial rule by order of the King himself!"

Sitting near the end of the long mahogany council table, Pemb managed to keep his composure upon hearing the general's words.

Time is running out, he thought worriedly, scratching notes with a quill pen as Abercromby laid out his strategic plans for the subjugation of the island. *But there is still time to add to the treasure buried in the garden.* While listening to the general he tried to calculate his asking price for the information. The clandestine sale of weapons and military supplies had ended several weeks earlier as the British security net had tightened. Now, his only source of income was purveying intelligence, but he expected that to halt soon as it appeared that the revolutionaries would be defeated.

Pemb's quill hovered over the inkwell as the commander-in-chief said:

"We'll try to capture this damned *cloutie* Fédon. If we do so, the Brigands will quickly fall apart and we can avoid assaulting his redoubt in the mountains, which is nearly impregnable by all accounts. From our intelligence sources, we know that the 'general' regularly visits his remaining outposts to keep up the Brigands' spirits. We will take him on one of those occasions. I will order Colonel Drummond and his Loyal Black Rangers to undertake the operation as soon as we have credible intelligence of Fédon's whereabouts."

Even better, Pemb told himself happily as his own plan formed, *retribution at last! Killing two birds with one stone, and getting well paid for it, by Jove!*

***

He left a note for the Dutchman at the tavern where they had first met. At a few minutes past three the following morning the man and one of his unnamed accomplices rapped the brass door knocker. Expecting them, Pemb was awake, fully dressed. The additional white man took up watch from a window in a darkened room at the front of the house while the Dutchman followed Pemb to the parlour. Neither had heeded the squeak of floorboards above them since Pemb jokingly told his guest about his mad wife who inhabited the upstairs bed chamber.

***

As they periodically and inexplicably did, the symptoms of Arabella's disease had waned. She dozed during the day and spent nights sleepless in the airless oven of her bedroom. Depending on her level of melancholia, she alternated between not caring about Pemb's nocturnal meetings and curiosity arising from boredom. Knowing of his criminal past, she suspected that the meetings and accumulation of gold coins in the garden were connected to illicitness, but it didn't affect her personally and it would be pointless to intervene even if she had a will to do so.

Arabella had received no reply from her letter to Lord Hugh. In her lucid moments when black depression lightened to grey, she told herself that he was far too important and busy fighting the Brigands to respond. Feeling hopeless and abandoned, lately she had been seriously contemplating ways in which she could take her life.

The voices below her became louder. She thought she heard the name "Drummond". Arabella knelt in her sweat-damp nightgown then lay full-length with her ear to a crack in the floor. She caught her breath as Pemb's high-pitched voice said "Fédon can have both of 'em and wipe out the Black Rangers in the bargain. I know he wants that jumped up mulatto slave named Chart who got away from him."

***

"Two thousand gold Joes!" the Dutchman exclaimed. "That is absurd! Your information is hardly worth so much."

"It's worth far more, but I'm not greedy. Your lot can beat the British with this intelligence."

The Dutchman bristled.

"*Your lot*? What do you mean by that?"

"I know very well who your masters are," Pemb replied, smirking, "that chap Hugues in Guadeloupe, and those bloodthirsty Republicans in Paris. Do you think I'm a fool?"

"No, but you *are* a traitor."

Pemb shrugged.

"Well, all our cards are on the table and I've got the stronger hand."

The Dutchman was silent, but Pemb knew he had him.

"I have only five hundred with me and only your word on the importance of the information. Nothing on paper."

"You will have everything in writing when you return with the information to entrap Drummond and his Black Rangers."

"And how will I know that you will not betray Fédon to the English so he will be the one taken in the snare?"

"What, and kill the very goose that is laying such lovely golden eggs?"

***

Julien Fédon was in a horrendous mood.

His wife and daughters were as terrified of him as his lieutenants and body guards. He raved about conspiracies against him and claimed he was stalked by the ghosts of the Englishmen he had massacred. Summary executions were meted out on whims. He personally shot one of his guards who complained about the half-rations everyone was subsisting on. The elderly cook, a slave who had served him at Belvedere for many years, was hung on suspicion that she planned to poison his callaloo soup. A French major was nearly killed for addressing him as *Citoyen* rather than *General*. Only the intervention of the Brigands' second-in-command saved him from being beheaded with a cutlass, after which the officer left in a rage, taking the other French soldiers with him. Only Captain Noguet remained with the Brigands, shouting at his departing Republican comrades that they were bourgeois cowards and Fédon was the only true revolutionary.

Céleste Fédon discovered the reason for her father's anger after her mother confided in her daughters. Victor Hugues, the Republicans' Caribbean governor, had sent Fédon a series of letters, starting with mild chastisement for caring more for his golden epaulets than for spreading the doctrine of *Liberté, Egalité et Fraternité* and steadily increasing in vitriol as the Brigand leader ignored his presumptuous French revolutionary masters. The previous week, a Republican commissioner had landed at Gouyave, the town on the Leeward coast that was the French military base. Proclaiming that the Terror in France had ended and that the more enlightened principles of the Revolution had been restored, he demanded the arrest of Fédon for the atrocities committed by his Brigands. Henceforth, he announced, France's Caribbean military campaign would be humane and conducted with the primary aim of abolishing slavery.

Fédon was effectively outlawed by both his French allies and the British.

The Brigands had less than a thousand fighters left. The rest, along with thousands of women and children who had jubilantly congregated at Belvedere in the early days of the insurgency, had left when the food supplies ran out and it became apparent that the British would not be driven into the Caribbean Sea. Fédon's men were low on powder, shot and flints, as well as every other type of military supplies. His dream of becoming the ruler of Grenada within the French Republican empire was fast becoming a nightmare.

Julien Fédon had long ago ceased believing in the all-powerful God which the Capuchins had delighted in frightening him with as a child. If he had kept his youthful faith he would have prayed for a miracle.

But the miracle arrived anyway in the form of a fashionably-attired Dutchman on a grey mare.

***

The Dutchman – known to his handlers in Paris as Vigneron – had a variety of aliases and numerous allegiances. The only true part of his chameleon-like persona was his nationality as a native Netherlander, which gave great latitude as a secret agent of the French Republic. He had been instrumental in the overthrow of the old Dutch regime and the creation of the revolutionary Batavian Republic with French arms and gold the previous year. Sent to Grenada, he ran other agents in addition to Pemb, also providing information - and disinformation - to the British that contained just enough genuine intelligence for them to believe him to be credible.

Vigneron knew that Pemb's report on General Abercromby's strategic plans was like a treasure map to the lost mines of Ophir, more valuable to his Republican controllers than the foolish little hunchback suspected. With the island blockaded and thousands of British reinforcements pouring in, the situation looked hopeless for the small regular French military contingent, but France's strategic interests could still be served. Four copies of the report with the source identified by name as a member of the Colonial Council were encoded and dispatched by canoe to Victor Hugues. The odds were good that at least one vessel would evade the Royal Navy patrols.

Of course, most of Pemb's intelligence would not be shared with Fédon, only the information about the plan to capture the insurgents' leader using the Loyal Black Rangers, which the Brigands hated and feared more than any other British Army unit. The Rangers had become the most effective counterinsurgency corps on the island; if the Brigands could eliminate them through trickery Fédon could continue to fight on, tying down British forces which would otherwise be sent to invade French-held islands such as St. Lucia and St. Vincent.

The Dutchman knew that he could be entering a lion's den as he rode unarmed up the rutted road from Gouyave, carrying only a staff with a small tricolour at its peak above a white flag. Watched by dark eyes from the bush as soon as he left the French-occupied town, he was halted at a guard post behind a great mahogany tree felled to block the way. There he was made to wait by a squad of undernourished black men wielding muskets and spears until a young mulatto lieutenant arrived on foot to escort him to Fédon's camp.

"Nice horse," the officer said, walking beside him. "We ate all of ours."

He left his mare at the Belvedere great house, hoping it wouldn't be eaten, and followed the lieutenant up the steep and slippery mountain to the headquarters where Fédon in his high-collared uniform sat behind the table serving as his desk, chomping on a cigar. The room was crowded with grim-faced officers.

The Dutchman took care to greet the glowering Brigand

commander as "general".

"I'm here to make amends," he said in French, "and to apologise for the, um, intemperate remarks of the commissioner. He has been reprimanded by Citoyen Hugues."

"I hope he is 'reprimanded' with the guillotine!"

"To restore our cherished alliance," the Dutchman continued smoothly, "I have brought the means of destroying the Black Rangers."

Like a hunting dog scenting its prey, Fédon leaned forward. "How?"

He drummed his fingers on the table top as the Dutchman laid out the plan.

"How do I know it's not a trap?"

"It was meant to be a trap for you, *mon general*, but it will be a trap for the Black Rangers. You can kill or capture their officers, including their commander Colonel Lord Hugh Drummond. He would be a valuable hostage."

Fédon nodded.

"And," said the Dutchman, "you can take or kill that devil called Chart who escaped last year after you condemned him to death. He has become a bold leader, revered by the Rangers, and is a favourite of Colonel Drummond."

"He won't escape again," Fédon said vehemently. "If we capture him alive his dying will take a long time, then we will cut off his head and let the dogs eat his corpse!"

The Dutchman returned to St. George's that afternoon, showing his *laissez-passer* signed by the acting British governor to the army checkpoints. After handing his uneaten horse to a groom and refreshing himself at a tavern, he went to Ft. George to find the Major serving as Abercromby's intelligence chief.

"Fédon will be here," he said, pointing to a point on the large wall map of the island. "A place called Madame Asche's in this valley."

"A week from tomorrow, you say?" asked the major, scribbling details with his quill pen. "Are you sure?"

"Yes."

"Colonel Drummond will be given his orders immediately."

᠁᠁᠁

Two of the canoes carrying Pemb's report made it to Guadeloupe, another was sunk when it tried to outrun a British sloop. The fourth was intercepted by a fast Royal Navy schooner off Bequia. The canvas bag containing Pemb's report was tossed overboard. Insufficiently weighted with grapeshot, it floated just beneath the surface buoyed by an air pocket, where it was sighted by a sharp-eyed midshipman who retrieved it with a boathook.

The document was sealed in a double layer of waxed cloth and undamaged. The young lieutenant commanding the schooner opened the packet and decided it must be important due to the array of meaningless numbers and letters. It took him two days to beat back to St. George's, where he delivered the report to the harried intelligence chief. There it sat on the major's desk for a week before he laboriously set about decoding it.

Chapter 28

Arabella's lethargy had vanished, replaced by desperate frustration.

After Pemb's guests departed and she heard him clump up the staircase to his bedchamber at the front of the house, she lay awake on her damp horsehair mattress, racking her now galvanised brain for a way to warn Chart and Hugh about the ambush. She couldn't go to them directly; even if she had a horse, she had no way of finding them in the island's war-torn countryside, and she knew that she would not survive capture, rape and hideous murder by the Brigands who had eyes and ears everywhere and an almost supernatural ability to quickly communicate over long distances.

Who could she turn to? Pemb was a respected member of the Colonial Council, a militia officer, and quartermaster. She was all too aware that he had led the community to believe that his poor dear wife was a madwoman, and that he was bravely bearing the cross of caring for her while tirelessly devoting himself to serving in the fight against the perfidious French and Brigands.

No one with the authority to intervene would believe her … without evidence.

She rose and crept barefooted down the hallway and stairs, hearing Pemb's snores. Dawn was breaking and there was enough light in the parlour to see the furnishings. There was a half-full square bottle of gin on a side table, empty glasses and a broken clay pipe on the floor. Papers were scattered on a sideboard and an open escritoire. She leafed through them quickly but found nothing to prove treason.

Knowing that the servants would rise soon, she began going through the cubby holes and drawers of the writing desk. She pulled open a drawer to find a small black notebook, inscribed in the flyleaf in Pemb's hand "Sir Pemberton Charteris, Bt." She took it to the window to cast more light on the small writing, catching her breath as her eyes scanned down the neat columns, beginning with "14/09/95, 20 stand arms, rec'd 40 Gold Louis."

It was possibly enough to incriminate Pemb for selling military supplies, but not enough to prove treason, or to save Chart and his comrades.

She had no doubt that Pemb would kill her if he discovered that she had read his account book. And he would soon find out if she was foolish enough to give it to his cronies on the Colonial Council or at the army headquarters. Reluctantly, she replaced it in the drawer.

When she returned to her bedroom a few minutes later she wept tears hotter than the sweat drenching her, feeling powerless to save the man she loved. She had lost her faith in a benevolent God in childhood, but now she did something unusual for her.

She prayed.

***

Leaving a small force to garrison Pilot Hill, the Rangers and surviving British regulars left their pestilential encampment and moved to a new base a mile away at Hooks Bay on the windward coast. Thousands of soldiers from a dozen regiments were landed from a fleet of transports along with tons of military supplies. Chart was amused to see many young soldiers from bucolic British counties watching in slack-mouthed amazement as the Rangers proudly marched past them.

"Most have never seen a black person before," he told Sori, "much less black redcoats."

By order of the Commander in Chief, the Rangers were quartered next to a battalion of German mercenaries called Lowenstein's Jägers commanded by the dashing Count d'Heillimer. Like the Black Rangers, the Jägers were trained as specialised light infantry, adept at fighting in forests and mountains. Their uniforms were grey-green topped by black straw hats with the left brim turned up. Each had a moustache waxed into points. Every man, including officers, was armed with short double-barrelled fusils and sword bayonets worn on a cross belt.

Unlike many of the British troops, the Germans were friendly and curious about the Black Rangers. After the Rangers were assigned tents and fed their standard mid-day dinner of salt pork and peas, the Jägers came into their camp smoking long clay pipes with guns slung over their shoulders. They tried to strike up conversations with the black soldiers, largely relying on gestures as few of the Germans understood English and most of the native Africans spoke the language in heavily accented tones.

Chart approached a man whom he assumed to be an officer from his silver epaulettes and crimson sash. He introduced himself as the German looked at him appraisingly. The officer inclined his head in a brief bow and said he was Captain Louisenthal.

"You are obviously a gentleman, sir. And an officer?"

Chart sighed.

"Unofficially, but yes, I command a platoon of the Loyal Black Rangers."

Louisenthal was too gently bred to probe into Chart's background.

"The reputation of your corps precedes you. We have just come from St. Lucia where I served with Colonel John Moore. He told me that your black troops have many excellent qualities as soldiers, are equal to any European troops, and are invaluable for service in the West Indies. I am honoured to serve with you."

The Jäger captain explained that his regiment would train with the Rangers so that each could learn from the other in preparation for a major offensive against the Brigands. Chart asked about the Germans' unusual uniforms and weapons.

"Our clothing allows us to blend into the forests. The French word for it is *camouflage*. I hope you won't consider this rude, but your red uniforms make excellent targets. I suspect that in time all armies will wear clothing like ours."

"And your firelock? It seems too short to have much range."

Louisenthal smiled.

"It's a rifle. It has superior accuracy to your smoothbore muskets, even though it takes longer to load."

He offered the rifle to Chart, who stroked the carved walnut stock as he had once caressed the thighs of Arabella Sherrard. He sighed with sudden longing for the flesh and blood woman as well as for the weapon.

"Beautiful gun," he said, handing it back.

"Shall we have a competition?" the German asked slyly. "Our orders for the afternoon are target practice with the Rangers."

While both the Black Rangers and the Jägers enjoyed live-firing exercises to break the monotony of camp life, competitions of any type were especially relished. Led by Hugh on horseback, the Rangers marched in formation to a large denuded cane field where canvas targets painted with bullseyes had been erected at ranges of 200 and 300 yards. The Germans followed, breaking out into loose skirmish order on the whistled command of their officers, before reforming behind the Rangers. Their leader, Count d'Heillimer, joined Lord Hugh, who sat on his horse behind the lines.

"My officers and I do not ride on active duty," the German nobleman told him. "We are all equally light infantrymen ... and we have learned that more of our officers survive if they are on foot. If you will excuse me when it is our turn at the targets, I shall rejoin my men."

The Rangers fired by platoons, one round per man. The day was airless and a cloud of acrid black smoke formed over the ranks. The smoke cleared after the Rangers finished and the targets were replaced by fresh ones. The Jägers shot once each from their double-barrels. Their targets were also retrieved and taken to the judges, composed of equal numbers of officers from both battalions, with Chart among them.

The soldiers were paraded and formed into ranks facing each other. A wagon laden with casks was pulled into the centre of the field by a mule team. Lord Hugh and Count d'Heillimer clambered onto its bed, each holding a sheet of paper.

"We have the results," announced Hugh, with his words repeated in German by the Count. "They are no reflection on the ability of the shooters, but rather of the weapons. At a distance of 200 yards, our dear old Brown Bess hit the target forty-five times out of a hundred ...."

He was interrupted by cheers from the Rangers.

"However, the rifles hit the targets double that, ninety times out of a hundred."

There were groans, while the Germans smiled politely under their moustaches.

"I'm afraid that M'lady Bess did rather worse at the 300-yard range. Only eighteen percent of her balls hit, whilst nearly sixty percent of the rifle bullets struck. So, we declare the rifle better than the musket, but every man here is equally a fine soldier. We shall now toast our new comrades in proper style. A pint of rum for every man!"

***

Whether it was the Christian God or an African deity such as Ala the mother goddess or Nyame the creator, Arabella's prayers were answered.

In the early evening her chambermaid tapped on her door.

"Two black women at the front door askin' for you, Ma'am. Say you know them."

"And the master?"

"Gone out."

Arabella knew that meant Pemb was at a tavern or a brothel.

"Should I tell them to go away?"

"No, show them into the back parlour."

She splashed water on her tear-swollen face, slipped into a dressing gown and went downstairs. At first she didn't recognise the pair of older women in bandana turbans standing uncomfortably in the stifling room.

"Heavens!" she said as recognition dawned. "Wannica … and, and Molia. You're alive!" She crossed the room to embrace them in turn. Each stood stiffly for a moment, shocked to be embraced by the wife of their former master, then hugged her in return. Arabella wept as she remembered the terror of her last hours at La Sagesse.

"Thank God you're safe," she sniffled.

"We are well, Ma'am," said Wannica. "Most of the people too. We stay away from La Sagesse, build huts on the beach. No one bothers us, and we catch fish, even have gardens again. Some of the boys who joined the Brigands came back."

"Do you need anything? I-I can get money," Arabella said, thinking of Pemb's horde.

The two black women looked at each other.

"That's not why we're here, Ma'am," said Wannica. "It's Chart. You know, Molia have special powers, like Chart's mother, Weju. She sees things. Bad things."

"Great danger for Chart coming soon, and his friends," Molia told her, aged face creased in concern. "Trap, like what the maroons in the mountains use to catch manicou. Thought you could warn him. We know he alive but not where he is."

Pulse surging, Arabella remembered the conversation she had heard the night before.

"I have no way of contacting him, but I believe he is in an army camp near Grenville. Yes, I also know he and his friends are in great danger!"

She sank heavily into a chair, overcome by sudden fatigue. The two black women looked at each, knowing she was ill, as she massaged her forehead and eyes.

"Is there any way you, or someone you trust, could go to Chart to warn him?"

"We could go," replied Wannica. "But who believe *us*?"

Arabella looked up, headache retreating.

"He would believe *me* if you carried a letter."

***

An hour after the bugles called Last Post, Chart was roused by scratching at the door of his canvas tent. He was awake in an instant, as was Sori, clutching his cutlass. He recognised Hugh's adjutant, a free coloured former militia officer who, like Chart, had been educated in England.

"CO's called an emergency meeting. Sorry," the adjutant said, glancing at Sori, "officers only."

Sori grunted and went back to sleep.

The Commanding Officer's marquee was surrounded by a cordon of Rangers stationed far enough away to prevent eavesdropping. The excitement of the thirty or so officers was palpable as Chart stepped into the amber light of lanterns. Lieutenant-Colonel Lord Hugh Drummond looked up with glittering eyes from a map open on a trestle table.

"We may be able to bag the fox himself! I've just had solid intelligence from Army HQ that Fédon is at a Brigands outpost a few miles from here. General Abercromby chose the Rangers for the honour of taking him. If we sortie within the hour we can be there at dawn and catch the bastard!"

Hugh outlined the plan. A large body of men could alert the enemy so he would personally lead a single company of seventy-seven Rangers who were fit for duty rather than the entire regiment. To ensure operational security, the men would not be told of their destination until they were close to the enemy camp. The senior captain, Brevet Major Bradford, would be acting CO in his absence.

Chart confidently expected his company to be chosen, and was deeply affronted when Hugh selected Company B, which was commanded by the homosexual captain, Launceston.

He remained behind when the other officers were dismissed.

"Why, Hugh, why did you not choose my company? I am the only Ranger who actually knows Fédon, and I have more reason than anyone to be in on his capture!"

Drummond glanced towards the tent's opening to see if they had privacy, then stepped towards Chart and clasped his shoulder.

"I ... we, cannot risk your capture. Not only are you my most valuable officer, but you are already condemned to the worst possible death if captured by the Brigands. If, by mischance, I or other Rangers are taken, we should be treated as legitimate prisoners of war. After all, the Brigands and their Republican allies fight under the tricolour of France, a civilised nation."

"So civilised that they murdered the governor and fifty other innocent civilians in cold blood, not to mention God knows how many of the poor black people they claimed to have liberated!"

Hugh bristled.

"That's enough, Chart. You presume on our friendship and seem to forget that I am your commanding officer."

"What bloody use am I then if I can't fight!" Chart said through clenched teeth, shaking with anger.

"Dismissed, lieutenant!" snapped Drummond. "One more word and I'll have you confined in the guardhouse!"

***

In the end, Wannica and Molia left Arabella's house carrying two letters sealed with wax blobs stamped with her family crest, one addressed to Chart and the other to Lord Hugh. Thinking it would be an unwelcome distraction from warning of the ambush, Arabella had not mentioned Pemb's treachery, only adding the cryptic line that a separate note was enclosed with the small black book which explained its contents. The book and letters were sewn into the cloth covering the bottom of a sturdy basket used by the servants for shopping in the market.

It took the two elderly black women three days to trudge up the Windward coast road past milestones inscribed with the distance from St. George's to Grenville. They were unmolested; the Brigands had largely been driven from the area and they hid in the bush when they heard the clatter of hooves from British cavalry patrols or couriers. Along the way, they met other women – called higglers – en route to the large British camp with fish, meat and provisions from hidden gardens. This gave them the idea of posing as higglers to enter the base, so they filled the basket with foodstuffs bought from other women with pennies and shillings given to them by Arabella. They took turns carrying it on their heads as taught by their African mothers.

Dusk was descending as they approached the camp. They turned off the main road and onto a side road widened by engineers and corduroyed with bamboo. They topped a low ridge from which they could see union jacks flapping in the sea breeze which carried the sound of drums and bugles. At that moment a pack of ragged men sprang from the undergrowth and surrounded them with raised cutlasses, demanding that they hand over the basket. Molia calmly removed the basket from her head and straddled it, then began rolling her eyes, gesticulating and ululating.

"She an Obeah woman," Wannica said in patois, picking up on the act. "She curse you if you touch her or the basket. Make your balls shrivel and your *totee* fall off!"

The would-be robbers fled.

The camp was enclosed by earthworks studded with stakes and embrasures for cannon every 20 yards. The ground outside had been cleared for two hundred yards to make a killing zone for attackers. Guards at the entrance barred higglers, who were directed to a makeshift marketplace in the killing zone where army cooks in stained aprons haggled for provisions.

"Now what we do?" asked Molia.

The two women hunkered down as close to the entrance as possible and sold a somewhat rancid fish and lump of goat meat to a cook from the 25th Regiment's officers mess. He told them he thought the Black Rangers were quartered on the other side of the camp with the Germans.

They bedded on the ground with the basket between them. Molia spread some shell and bone charms around them and chanted to ward off evil spirits, which she said were hovering. Shortly before midnight, a column of barefooted black men in red coats emerged from the camp led by a tall white officer astride a black horse. They both stood and watched until the column disappeared into the darkness.

"Chart not with them," said Wannica. She heard Molia's teeth chattering.

"Feeling the cold breath of Adro, snake god of evil," she whispered. "He waiting for them!"

***

Chart was unable to sleep. With a growing sense of foreboding he paced through the Rangers' lines of tents. As the first glow of the new day tinted the ocean blood red, he went past the sentries guarding the camp's entrance and stood on the roadway gazing toward the mountains in the west. He closed his eyes, straining to hear what sounded like the distant boom of cannon and crackle of musketry. When he opened them he was startled to see a pair of short black women looking up at him. Unlike Arabella, he instantly recognised them.

"We got something for you from the Madame," said Wannica.

Stuffing the letter for Hugh and the account book into his pocket, Chart tore open the message addressed to him, heart clenching and temples throbbing as he read Arabella's warning. He raced back into the encampment, dragged a sleepy drummer boy and bugler from the hut serving as a guardroom and ordered them to awaken the camp with clarion calls to stand to arms and the long drum roll for the alarm. As men tumbled from tents buttoning coats and pulling muskets from racks, Chart ran to the large marquee of General Hope. Two sentries barred his way at the entrance, but the annoyed looking young Brigadier in night shirt and cap told them to stand aside. Chart hastily saluted and handed him his letter, which Hope quickly scanned.

"A trap for Colonel Drummond. Is it to be believed?"

"Indeed, sir," Chart answered, fuming at the delay. "As you see, it is from Lady Arabella Charteris, wife of the council member Sir Pemberton who is also quartermaster general."

"Good heavens, no need to doubt it then."

"General, send the Black Rangers with the German Jägers, we can move more quickly than any other unit."

The brigadier pursed his lips, then nodded.

Chapter 29

The trap was cleverly wrought and adroitly sprung.

The Rangers made good time under the wan light of a crescent moon. A private who had worked as a slave on the Madame Asche plantation served as their guide. Lord Hugh deployed skirmishers ahead and on the flanks of the column as the track gradually climbed into the foothills of the mountains. He halted the company at the entrance to a narrow defile with sides so thickly overgrown that the jungle formed a tunnel. His horse shied at the dark entrance, snorting nervously. A squad went forward to reconnoitrer. They returned to report that the Brigand outpost lay five hundred yards on the other side of the gorge and appeared deserted.

The twisting pass was barely wide enough for two men to walk abreast, so Hugh called the skirmishers in and ordered the column forward. The eastern sky was lightening as they emerged onto a clearing in the bush containing half a dozen open-sided boucans. A perimeter guard was established while the Rangers poked through the huts.

"They were here a few hours ago," reported Captain Launceston. "Embers still warm in the fires."

"Damnation!" Colonel Drummond swore. "Probably tipped off. Bloody spies everywhere."

The men were allowed to breakfast on cassava cakes and water before being paraded and roll call taken. The Rangers were tired and dispirited, their alertness at low ebb. Hugh remounted and sent a two-men vanguard ahead as he led the column back into the narrow pass. When he rounded a bend near its end, he was surprised to see the two redcoats standing stock still with their muskets at port arms.

"What the devil …." He spurred his horse forward so that he could look over the Rangers' heads straight into the muzzle of a small cannon blocking the trail. A black soldier in a French artilleryman's uniform hovered over its breech with a slow match on a linstock.

"Above!" shouted Captain Launceston. "They're above us!"

The sun was now high enough to discern that the heavy undergrowth covering the slopes was filled with scores of men aiming muskets into the tightly packed Rangers' company. Struggling to maintain his composure, Hugh calmly turned his horse in the narrow space and began slowly riding back along the file of frightened soldiers, quietly telling them to stand ready for his order to break out.

The enemy had anticipated his impromptu plan to fight their way back to the outpost.

"Forget it, Colonel Drummond," a French-accented voice yelled. "There's a gun at the far end too. Both loaded with cannister. Surrender now and I give you my word that you will all be treated as prisoners of war."

He knew my name, Hugh thought. *How* ....

"Whose word is that?" he answered, stalling for time.

"I, General Julian Fédon, commander of the French Republic's irregular forces on the island of Grenada!"

Drummond's horse shied, eyes rolling as it picked up the fear of the Rangers who had cleared a space around it. Launceston caught its bridle to calm it.

"*Préparez vos armes!*" Fédon ordered, followed by clicks as the hammers of dozens of muskets were thumbed to full cock.

"If you don't surrender now you will all die. Give me your word and everyone's life will be spared. You know it is the honourable thing to do."

"They've got us," rasped Captain Launceston. "Not much choice is there? There are certainly worse things than surrender. Our duty now is to spare our men's lives."

"*Choisissez vos cibles et préparez-vous à tirer!*" [Pick your target and make ready to fire!]

Hugh clenched his jaw before drawing a deep breath.

"We surrender!"

By Fédon's command, Drummond ordered the Rangers to stack their muskets against the sides of the defile and divest themselves of cross belts holding bayonets, cartridge boxes and cutlasses. Dismounted, Hugh led them back to the outpost. The men were cursing and muttering in fury. "Silence in the ranks!"

bellowed one of the two white sergeants.

The clearing was now surrounded by what Hugh estimated to be over 150 Brigands, mainly black men in ill-fitting blue uniforms and liberty caps. A small bronze cannon embossed with the crest of the Bourbon *ancien régime* was being dragged to one side. Hugh and his officers handed over their sabres and pistols. A white Brigand officer with a drawn sword demanded that Drummond assemble the Rangers in double files on the far side of the clearing beneath a towering mango tree. Hugh ordered Captain Launceston to stand his men at parade rest, then stood at attention in front of the ranks watching his horse being led away.

A few minutes later, another hundred Brigands debouched from the ravine carrying the Rangers' weapons and accoutrements. They were led by a thin mulatto man in a gold-braided uniform wearing a large bicorne with a red, white and blue cockade, who Hugh guessed was Fédon. A twin to the light cannon followed the column, pulled by its gunners.

Both guns were positioned with barrels aimed towards the Rangers, while the Brigand troops formed lines on the other two sides of the clearing.

"Colonel Drummond!" Fédon shouted, "You will attend to me together with all your white officers and non-commissioned-officers."

Hugh beckoned to Launceston and the two lieutenants.

"I don't like this," he said quietly. "Something's amiss."

"Colonel Drummond!"

He would have expected the enemy troops to be jubilant and jeering at their prisoners, but they were eerily silent, standing with fingers poised on their muskets' trigger guards, grimly watching with narrowed eyes. His feeling of dread was not personal fear, he realised, but an awareness of profound wickedness alien to one such as himself who played by the civilised rules of war and naïvely thought that his enemy would do the same. He remembered Chart's reminder about the massacre of the British prisoners and casual murder of his fellow slaves.

I was a fool, he thought bitterly.

He was at the Brigand's mercy, yet hope had not completely vanished that his fears were unfounded.

There were eight white men in the company, three officers, four NCOs, and a bugler. He called them from the ranks and ordered them to accompany him to stand half a dozen paces from Fédon. The Brigand leader ignored Drummond's salute.

"Where is the one called Chart?" he asked, eyes glaring malevolently.

"Not here. He didn't come with us."

Fédon muttered something in French under his breath then used his sabre to motion the white Rangers to one side where they were immediately covered by a squad with bayonet-tipped muskets under an officer armed with a brace of pistols. The Brigand general stepped forward and addressed the seventy-seven black men in red coats, speaking first in French, followed by patois and English.

"Why are you fighting for these white Englishmen who enslaved you? I call upon you to cast aside your red coats, symbols of oppression, and join us who have freed you!"

Fédon waited impatiently, swatting the flat of his bared sword against his leg, while the Rangers talked amongst themselves. He saw heads nodding and bodies tensing. He raised his sabre above his head and walked backwards to stand between the two cannon. Two hundred and fifty Brigands raised muskets to their shoulders and squinted along the barrels.

A tall black redcoat stepped forward as if on parade.

"Fuck you!" he shouted "*Va te faire foutre!*"

As if on cue, the Rangers scattered.

"*Tirez!*" screamed Fédon, slashing his sword down.

At point blank range the two cannons flashed flame and smoke, jumping back on their carriages as they spewed a swarm of lead musket balls at the Rangers. Simultaneously, every musket roared, filling the clearing with choking black smoke.

"No!" screamed Captain Launceston, "You fucking treacherous bastards!" He tried to break through the guards to get to Fédon, but was instantly shot by the Brigand officer. The pistol's .62 calibre soft lead ball drilled through his left eye and blew out the back of his skull, scattering scraps of brain tissue and bone chips on his horrified comrades.

The cannister shot fired like giant shotgun blasts from the cannon and the massed volley killed or severely wounded all but three of the Black Rangers, two of whom were lightly wounded. These three made it into the jungle. Fédon sent fifty men after them while the remainder used their cutlasses to butcher the wounded weltering in the blood-soaked clearing before looting coins and tobacco from the dead. As flies began swarming over the mangled corpses, the Brigands who had pursued the escapees returned, carrying the severed heads of two of them.

Fédon looked at the morning sky to judge the time.

"More *anglais* will be here soon," he told his officers. "What worked once can do so again."

He quickly issued orders, then began the march back to his mountain redoubt with Lord Hugh and the seven surviving white Rangers in the middle of the column, leaving fifty men behind. Fédon slapped the croup of Drummond's horse as it was led up the steep trail.

"We will eat well tonight," he cheerfully told his lieutenants.

***

The sole survivor of Company B was a strapping nineteen-year-old former fieldhand named Abidemi by his Yoruba mother who was now entered on the muster roll of the King's Loyal Black Rangers as Private Toby Gunn. Saved by his quick wits and equally swift reflexes, he had flung himself to the ground a second before the Brigands' barrage tore his comrades to pieces. The dense cloud of smoke shrouding the enemy gave him cover to dash for the bush before they charged out with raised cutlasses to murder the wounded. He ran as fast and as far as he could, but as his pursuers neared he slid into a stream bed, rolled in mud, and wriggled into a shallow cave behind the roots of a tree. He heard shouts and screams as the Brigands caught fellow escapees.

When Toby felt he was safe from pursuit, he cautiously emerged and crawled on hands and knees beneath dense foliage up a hill overlooking the ravine and the Brigand outpost. When he reached a hidden vantage point he shook with impotent fury, tears of rage coursing down his muddy cheeks as he watched the Brigands strip the corpses of his comrades and mutilate them. They did the same with the body of his captain, one of the few white officers aside from Colonel Drummond who the Black Rangers liked and respected. Launceston's cadaver was dragged across the clearing and dumped amongst his men.

His keen eyes saw the enemy general assemble a company of men and direct them back to the slopes above the defile. He used his fingers to count fifty of them. While they redeployed, the main body of Brigands headed west towards the mountains, taking the white prisoners and two field pieces.

Looking east, Toby could see the sun gleaming on the ocean several miles away where the British camp sprawled on the coast. He rose to a crouch and set off towards it as swiftly as possible.

**

General Hope gave command of the relief force to the Jägers commander Count d'Heillimer, who took all 500 men of his battalion and the four remaining Rangers companies. The English captain of Chart's A company was ill with dysentery, so Chart assumed *de facto* command of the unit.

As drums beat *Assembly* on the camp's parade ground, Captain Louisenthal came up to Chart who was pacing in agitation in front of his restive company.

"I have a gift for you," he said, handing him a double-barrelled rifle and shoulder belt with a leather cartridge box. "Leave your poor old Brown Bess behind and make love to your new mistress, this fine German lady will give far more satisfaction!"

Bugles sounded *March* and the battalions moved out at the fast pace set by the Jägers, three steps walking, three running. The Count gave the vanguard to Chart's company, and the men ranged ahead, darting through the bush on either side of the dirt road as the sun rose to burn off the morning coolness. It was fortunate that the Rangers led the column, as the Jägers had a tendency to shoot anyone appearing suddenly out of the jungle; the mud-covered figure in a barely recognisable red uniform that called to them from a banana grove might have fallen to the

German rifles.

"Toby Gunn," said Sori. "Where the rest of you?"

Toby was shaking and babbling incoherently. Chart deployed the company as flankers in a wide circle, where they hid behind tree trunks and flattened themselves under shrubbery. He drew Toby into the shade of a cashew tree, allowed him several deep swigs from a flask of rum, and calmed him enough to hear his story. Chart was struggling to contain his own fury by the time Count d'Heillimer and the column reached them a few minutes later.

"All of them?" the Jäger commander snapped after Chart reported.

"He's the only survivor aside from Colonel Drummond and seven other white Rangers. He said that Fédon gave the men the choice of joining him or dying, and not one accepted. About fifty Brigands are waiting to ambush us in the ravine where B company was trapped. It's about a mile ahead."

The German commander smiled wolfishly, grey eyes murderous.

"*Kinderspiel,*" he muttered, then translated for Chart. "Child's play."

Word of their comrades' massacre quickly spread among the Rangers and they were like lupine hunting dogs straining at their leashes for revenge. Chart went from company to company briefing them on their attack plan, and the white officers did not demur at his assuming command of the operation. The Jägers would leave one company as a rear guard on the road, while the rest of the battalion circled around to prevent the Brigands from retreating into the mountains.

The Rangers divided into two units of 180 men for each side of the slopes above the defile. The Brigands had only posted a single sentry at the top, and his throat was silently cut by Sori's razor-honed cutlass. The redcoats surreptitiously worked their way down the inclines as closely as possible to Fédon's men, who were so unwary that some were dozing.

The signal for attack was the first shot from Chart's new rifle, which killed a red-capped man with a bullet through the head. A volley from nearly four hundred muskets followed instantly and the Rangers slid down the slopes screaming African battle cries as they swung their cutlasses.

It was over in minutes, the enemy getting off only a handful of shots before they were cut down, with Chart in the thick of battle wielding his cutlass with blood lust. Bodies cascaded down the slopes to thump into the narrow ravine. A few Brigands who managed to slide down unscathed tried to escape but were riddled by rifle balls from the equally vengeful Germans positioned at the abandoned outpost.

Chart begged Count d'Heillimer to pursue Fédon and rescue Hugh and his other comrades, but the German shook his head emphatically. While the Rangers were digging a mass grave for their dead amidst lamentations and endless calls for revenge, the Jägers commander ordered Chart join him in the shade of an ancient mahogany tree with a trunk twelve feet in diameter.

"I share your sentiment, sir," said the Count, "but by this time the enemy and their prisoners will already be at their camps, which by your own reports are nearly impregnable. Our small force would achieve nothing by trying to assault them, except the almost certain murder of Lord Hugh and the others, whom I suspect will be held as hostages like the poor souls who were massacred last year."

He tugged at his waxed moustache and looked speculatively at Chart, wondering about the mysterious background of the tall young man with Meissen blue eyes set in a dark face who had the demeanour of an English milord but could fight as savagely as his African warriors. The Count was a good judge of character, and he sensed that there was no guile in the redcoated soldier who carried one of his own unit's rifles. He decided that he could be trusted.

"I will tell you something known only to a small circle of senior officers, and not even shared yet with the Colonial Council, which leaks like an incontinent crone. We are planning a major storming of Fédon's camps very soon, within ten days. There will be a pincer movement, with a British force moving up the leeward coast and ours from the base at Hooks Bay. My Jägers along with your Black Rangers have been chosen for a crucial role in the operation."

Chart expelled a breath of profound frustration.

"But, as you've said, Colonel Drummond and the other prisoners will be murdered during the attack!"

"*Ja*, that is the dilemma."

Chapter 30

Three days passed before Pemb realised that his account book was missing from the escritoire.

He searched frantically for it amidst the alcohol-stained papers, bottles, clay pipes and a discarded wig littering the parlour. He often came home drunk and misplaced things in his foggy state. Soon though, fear-driven paranoia set in and he sought others to blame for the loss.

Arabella hurried downstairs when she heard Pemb screaming at the servants. The two black women and elderly mulatto man named Joseph stood in a row, cringing before his verbal onslaught.

"What is the meaning of this?" she asked.

"They've stolen something of mine! I know one of them did it, dirty thieving blackamoors!"

He was reluctant to answer her question about what was missing, vaguely replying it was a notebook with important government information, no concern of hers. Knowing that the frightened servants could be bullied into revealing the visit of Wannica and Molia, Arabella took the initiative to protect the two La Sagesse women.

"The only people who have been in the house apart from us were a pair of higglers from the market selling food …but wait …" She pretended to be thinking as she fashioned a lie to feed his paranoia. "I found the front door ajar when I came downstairs a few mornings ago, and I thought I heard footsteps at night. Could someone have come in and taken this notebook? But why would they?"

Pemb's normal pallor increased as blood drained from his face and the pupils of his eyes dilated in fear.

"Get out!" he croaked. "All of you, begone."

When Arabella returned to her room she was grateful for Pemb's unremitting contempt, as in his arrogance he had not thought to blame her for the theft.

Not yet.

***

They're on to me, Pemb thought desperately, *someone's going to rat me out! Was it the Dutchman, or those Stepney shites who had been seconded to work for him in the military warehouse? Ungrateful swine!*

He knew that time was running out. From what he overheard at council meetings, it was obvious that the French and Brigands were losing and that it was only a matter of time before the now formidable British forces snuffed out the insurrection. Pemb had always been a gambler, although largely an unsuccessful one, and he had enjoyed a rare winning streak over the past year. That would soon come to an end, and it was time to throw in his hand and move on with his substantial takings. His sugar plantation was derelict and no one in their right mind would buy it. It was a pity that he wouldn't be able to round up and sell the La Sagesse slaves, but their value would have been minor anyway compared to his golden horde buried in the garden, which he estimated to be worth more than £10,000 sterling.

He hated the tropics, and could not return to England and the debtors prison that awaited him there. Neutral American merchant ships occasionally called at St. George's, and the cooler climes of Boston or Philadelphia beckoned. He had heard that Americans loved titled English gentleman, and with his wealth he could move in the highest circles of Yankee society. Their yokel pretences could be endured if it meant a fresh start.

As for Arabella … she no longer served a purpose, even for revenge now that Hugh and Chart would soon be eliminated by General Fédon if his bargain with the Dutchman succeeded. She could rot, and by the looks of her she was well on the way there.

***

"These are serious charges," said Brigadier Hope, "I daresay, positively *bombshell*."

Chart stood at attention in front of the general, his adjutant and aide-de-camp, the latter busily taking notes on foolscap. Beside Chart stood Count d'Heillimer, his temporary commanding officer. The Jägers colonel had been given overall command of the Black Rangers and his own battalion in the absence of Lord Hugh.

"Are you familiar with the contents of the account book and the letter accompanying it?" Hope asked the German nobleman.

"I am, sir. Lieutenant Charteris brought them to me first, exactly according to your own army regulations."

Chart noticed that the adjutant made a face when d'Heillimer referred to him as 'lieutenant'.

"Lady Charteris alleges that her husband is a traitor," continued the brigadier. "How are we to know that she was not misled or, for want of a better word, delusional? And this 'account book' purporting to show that Sir Pemberton was selling military stores could easily have been fabricated to cast him in a bad light. The Frog-eaters are quite diabolical, divide and conquer, y'know."

"Her letter to me proved factual, sir," said Chart, struggling to keep exasperation from his voice. "If it had reached me earlier, we could have prevented the deaths of an entire company of men and the capture of Colonel Drummond and other Rangers."

"While that may be true, Lieut- ... er, Mr. Charteris, her letter to you only warned of the ambush. It did not mention, as she admitted in the second message, that she eavesdropped on her husband providing this and other information to an enemy agent. And she did not reveal what that 'other' information was."

Brigadier Hope sat upright in his chair, sweat trickling down his rubicund face from under the powdered white wig, 90-degree heat and high-collared wool uniform contributing to his tetchiness.

"I have two things to say and then we will put an end to this business. First, it is outrageous for Lady Charteris, a *noblewoman*, to eavesdrop on her husband. I understand that she is in poor health, but even that is no excuse for the gently bred daughter of a viscount.

"Secondly, I am well aware of who you are, Mr. Charteris. Your legal case was the talk of the country and published by every newspaper and broadsheet from *The Times* to the *Caledonian Mercury*. I daresay, I was not without sympathy for your plight, but the fact is that Sir Pemberton is a respected member of this colony's government and you, I'm sorry to say, are legally his chattel, with an axe to grind against him."

As Chart was about to retort he felt d'Heillimer nudge him to keep quiet.

"Now, we shall hear no more of this," Hope said brusquely. "Count d'Heillimer speaks highly of your action against the Brigands. Keep your nose clean and carry on. Dismiss."

Chart stood frozen for a moment, then gave a crisp salute, executed a clockwork about face, and marched out of the marquee with a temper hotter than the Caribbean noon. He went to his tent and dashed off a few lines to Arabella on the back of a frayed receipt for rations.

"*Nil desperandum*",[2] he wrote, not believing his own brave words.

***

Major Ambrose Phelippes, Royal Engineers, espionage chief of His Majesty's forces in the colony of Grenada, loosened his linen neck cloth. took off his steel-framed spectacles and rubbed his reddened eyes. He had no doubt that working by candle light night after night was ruining his vision, but General Abercromby depended on him to correlate the various threads of intelligence and weave them into realistic analyses of the enemy. He ran a number of spies, double and even triple agents. Among them was a charming Dutchman.

Unlike most British officers, Phelippes was a university graduate, a Cambridge man like his ancestor who had served as a skilled decipherer and code breaker for Queen Elizabeth's spymaster, Sir Francis Walsingham. Military intelligence work was far more interesting than the study of higher Arithmetic, Mathematics and Logic, even if it was murderous for one's eyesight.

The report plucked from the sea the previous week was written in a simple monoalphabetic substitution cipher. He could crack it, but the cryptanalysis was tedious using the technique called Letter Frequency Analysis. Assuming that the plain text was in French, he consulted one of his precious notebooks recording the frequency of letters in a typical piece of text in that language. Fortunately, the cipher text was large

---

[2] Never despair.

enough to provide a good statistical sample, allowing the Major to map from plaintext to ciphertext, and then back to French plain text, which he translated into English. He transcribed both versions onto thick paper in copperplate writing.

Serving as a spy master in his own right required a cool demeanour and emotional detachment. But ire coloured Phelippes' pale face that was rarely exposed to the sun as he grew aware of the treachery that had produced the report. The Republican spy identified by the code name Vigneron stated that the document contained the strategic plan of the British expeditionary force given to Grenada's Colonial Council on the 29th of April 1796, noted verbatim by his agent, the council member who also served as quartermaster general named in the secret report.

Sir Pemberton Charteris, Bt.

***

Dressed in a sombre new suit to avoid drawing undue attention, Pemb walked along the St. George's Carenage with a low-crowned hat shielding his eyes. There were a number of ships in the harbour, most riding at anchor rather than tied up at the wharves. None flew the Yankee flag with fifteen stars and stripes, but the harbourmaster told him that a brig out of Baltimore with a cargo of lumber and gunpowder was expected any day.

He was on the verge of seeking shelter from the sun in a waterfront tipple house when he saw the Dutchman stepping ashore from a jolly boat. The spy saw him at the same time. He crossed the cobbled street gesturing for Pemb to follow him into the tavern. In the dingy interior, Pemb saw the man sitting at a table in a dark corner.

"You are compromised," the Dutchman whispered without preamble. "They know about you. You are finished."

Pemb's stomach curdled, followed by a spasm of nausea.

"H-how?" he gasped. "Did you?"

"Of course not! It doesn't matter how I know, I have many contacts."

"Wh-why are you telling me this?"

The Dutchman leaned closer, his usually urbane face

stonelike.

"Call it fate. I was planning to have you killed so you would not talk, but that might create more problems than I care to deal with at this time. No need for that now as I have passage today aboard a packet leaving on the evening tide."

"Take me with you!" Pemb begged, hands trembling so badly that the large gold heraldic ring that had been his murdered uncle's rattled on the table top.

"No. You find your own way."

"How much time do I have?" Pemb wailed as the Dutchman swept past him.

"Not long," he muttered.

***

Pemb had longer than he thought. After Major Phelippes gave the deciphered report to General Abercromby, the Commander-in-Chief decided to execute the strategic plan, hoping to pre-empt action by Republican forces in Guadeloupe who he surmised had received the same document.

"We will deal with this traitor later," he told the spymaster, then began dictating a series of orders to his aide-de-camp.

While Pemb was meeting with the Dutchman, a knock on the front door of his house was answered by a maid. She informed Arabella, who came downstairs to find a fresh-faced young cornet of the 17th Light Dragoons who told her he was a courier from General Hope's base at Hooks Bay. He had a letter for her, to be delivered personally. He had been ordered to wait for any reply.

Her hands shook as she saw the signature was simply "Chart". Sighing plaintively, she dropped into an armchair as she read of the fate of the Rangers' company and Lord Hugh. "I won't rest until he is freed," Chart wrote "and justice dealt to Pemb. Until then, we must try to stop more of his treachery. Never despair," he ended in Latin.

She rose, thanked the uncomfortable looking young cavalryman, and wished him well on his return to the camp.

"Going back later today," he said sadly. "First must attend the burial of my friend, perished two days ago from the Yellow Jack."

"I'm so sorry," said Arabella. She paused as an idea formed. "What was his name?"

After the cornet left, she summoned Joseph, the grey-haired factotum. She explained the task she had for him.

"We will need a wheelbarrow. And we must hurry."

****

As Pemb hurried home he nearly voided his bowels when he turned a corner and confronted a platoon of redcoats marching up the street. He skulked in a doorway, fearful tears pricking his eyes, until he saw them turn off onto another street in the opposite direction from his house.

He went straight to his bedchamber, missing old Joseph by minutes as the slave pushed a wooden wheelbarrow down the alley and returned it to the garden shed. Mind reeling, he was unable to focus on an escape plan, veering from using his official capacity in some pretence to demand being taken aboard a ship, to suicide. He loaded and primed a pair of pistols and contemplated them on a side table while he paced until cockcrow, pausing to drink straight from a bottle of cognac to calm his nerves.

He daren't try to take passage on a British vessel, all of which were required to keep passenger lists and which would almost certainly not be bound for a neutral port. Waiting for the Yankee ship was no longer an option. There were always canoes and small fishing boats along the Carenage and hauled up on the lagoon strand. He decided that his only possibility was to pay one of them to take him to Trinidad or another Spanish colony. Thank God he had the money to do so!

In the lambent tropical dawn Pemb crept out the back door, took a shovel from the shed, and went to a low mound of fresh earth behind the privy that was topped by a withered rose bush in a cracked chamber pot. As he moved it aside he pondered how to carry the weight of two buried army knapsacks filled with hundreds of gold coins which he had transferred from the iron pot when it overflowed. He wondered if he could risk going to the stables below Ft. George and signing out a mule. The first task, though, was to retrieve a few of the coins to flash at a native boatman to arrange passage.

Sinking the shovel into the mound, he began digging to reveal the shallow hole in which he had deposited his treasure, expecting to see the canvas bags ….

… something was wrong.

He dropped to his knees and began tearing into the soil with bare hands like a hungry dog seeking its bone. When he reached the unchurned bottom of the hole he sat back on his haunches and moaned in horror, swiftly replaced by frothing rage.

"Goddamn fucking thieves, filthy devils, I'll kill you, you bastards!"

It must have been that half-caste gardener Joseph! He grabbed the shovel with his dirt encrusted hands and ran towards the servants quarters, where he could see frightened brown faces peering out the window.

"Kill you all, black devils!" he screeched. "Beat your woolly heads in!"

"No you won't."

Arabella stood outside the kitchen door, steadily holding Pemb's fully cocked pistols in each hand.

"Nothing would give me greater pleasure than to blow out your dwarf brains, but I'd rather see you hanged."

He stepped menacingly towards her, reaching into a pocket for the small pistol he always carried.

"Another step and I'll save the hangman the trouble. The Provost guard has been called and will be here soon," she lied, "so you'd better run far and fast."

Face twitching with spasms of anger, Pemb seemed on the verge of charging her when bugles began sounding reveille from the garrisons encircling the town. In his panicked state, he thought the calls were alerting the army to capture him. With an anguished cry, he charged around the side of the house.

When she knew he was truly gone, Arabella dropped the pistols and collapsed in a swoon.

Chapter 31

The British Army prepared to march.

General Abercromby's detailed order of battle was read by brigade commanders, who quickly transmitted relevant sections to each regiment, battalion, company and platoon. The expeditionary force would move in three columns to encircle the enemy, with Brigadier Hope's battalions advancing from the east and north, while the units personally commanded by the canny old Scot attacked from the south and west.

Bugles blared and drums rattled throughout the morning. Invigorated by the prospect of combat, dozens of men in hospitals and infirmary tents dragged themselves from cots and returned to their units. By early afternoon over two thousand infantrymen, gunners and cavalry troopers were assembled on the coastal road leading north from St. George's, accompanied by a dozen field pieces, hundreds of supply wagons, and cheering townspeople who thought that watching a battle would be quite a lark. The troops moved out with colours streaming, fifes shrilling and drums beating. Small black boys marched alongside, merrily imitating the redcoats with bamboo stalks on their shoulders.

A courier escorted by the St. George's Light Cavalry had carried the Commander-in-Chief's orders to Brigadier Hope the previous evening, and the general lost no time in convening his senior officers. An hour later, Count d'Heillimer summoned all the Jägers and Rangers officers to his marquee lit by fat candles to issue marching orders for the next day. No one questioned Chart's inclusion as *de facto* commander of Company A, the King's Loyal Black Rangers.

***

Hugh had never known such hunger, or witnessed such cruelty.

He and the other Rangers survivors were incarcerated in the same large hut at *Camp de la Mort* that had been the final shelter of the planters and merchants who had been slaughtered the previous year. From where he sat with arms and legs gripped by wooden stocks, he could see their pathetic messages scratched onto wooden surfaces: "N. Home, God help us, VII Aprilis 1795; Tell my wife I love her, R. Webster; Valley of Death, I fear ye not, P Fotheringham."

Prodded at bayonet point up the slope to the camp four days earlier, they had passed human bones scattered on the surface of what had been a mass grave. With cold despair he remembered a line from Dante's Inferno he had laboriously translated as a schoolboy, "Abandon all hope, ye who enter here."

There were five other British soldiers in the hut, all sick with dysentery and fever and confined in stocks. The putrefying corpse of a drummer boy was slumped next to Hugh for two days until the stench grew so bad that even the brutal guards could not stand it. They looped a rope around the corpse's neck, dragged it out and tumbled it over the precipice. All five of the previous prisoners died within the first few days of the Rangers' incarceration; four from disease and malnutrition and the fifth beaten to death by a guard who couldn't stand the delirious redcoat's moans and rants.

Everyone, including the guards, was starving. The prisoners were lucky to have half a green plantain and a quick gulp of scummy water every day. Hugh overheard the guards complaining in French about keeping the prisoners alive, but their officer reprimanded them, saying anyone questioning General Fédon's orders would be executed on the guillotine erected in the yard outside the prison.

The threat was not idle. The Brigands were so low on ammunition that those convicted of crimes against the revolutionary order were no longer shot but punished by what Parisians called *the national razor*. One day Hugh watched through gaps in the bamboo walls as eight of Fédon's men were guillotined for eating a mule, a woman had her right hand sliced off for giving milk from one of Fédon's goats to her hungry baby, and three soldiers lost feet for desertion.

From the guards' worried conversations, he knew that the British forces were closing in. As the senior officer, he tried to cheer the other prisoners with this news, briskly telling them to keep up their British pluck as he expected them all to be released when the Republican forces surrendered. He was certain that General Abercromby would offer reasonable terms once the Brigand's camp was besieged.

***

Bereft of supplies due to the Royal Navy blockade, the few hundred French Republican troops occupying their base at the town of Gouyave accepted the inevitable and raised the white flag as the vanguard of Abercromby's column appeared on the road from St. George's. A capitulation agreement was swiftly negotiated, recognising the Republican troops as legitimate prisoners of war to be well treated without reprisal. The French commander explicitly did not include Fédon and his Brigands in the surrender document, stating that as they had violated the rules of civilised war they were no longer recognised as soldiers of the Republic and were therefore outlaws.

Within days, more than six thousand British troops occupied Belvedere Estate and established outposts around the mountain camps to which Fédon and the remaining three hundred of his followers had retreated. The Black Rangers and Jägers patrolled the jungle at the base of the mountain to prevent the Brigands' escape. Both Chart and Captain Louisenthal had to continually prevent the execution of deserters, trying to justify their intervention by explaining that those fleeing the camps were needed for intelligence. But the African and German infantrymen cared more for vengeance than information and no quarter was given.

***

The last pig had been eaten weeks before and every living animal, even lizards and birds, had disappeared from the bush around the two mountain camps. Céleste wept when the sole remaining goat, which she had raised from a kid and tended daily, was slaughtered, but she knew that broth made from its meat was needed for her dangerously ill mother and sister.

Each day she sat with her father on the parapet of the highest battery at *Camp de la Mort* watching neat rows of white tents appear around their old home at the Belvedere Great House. The

British soldiers appeared like thousands of red- and blue-coated ants as they drilled and bustled about the expanding encampment. She became accustomed to the bugle calls and the occasional shot aimed at them which she had learned could not harm them at such extreme range.

"They won't attack us," Julien Fédon said confidently as they breakfasted on coffee – the only abundant foodstuff – and stone-hard cassava cake. "They cannot make it up the mountain without heavy losses. We still have a dozen cannon. I have heard that their General Abercromby hates wasting his men unnecessarily."

Céleste knew that it would be unwise to remind her father that there was only enough gunpowder and shot left for a few rounds for each cannon, and barely enough cartridges for a single fusillade from the muskets.

"You may be right, Papá," she said carefully, "But they will win by starving us. Maman and Marie will die if they do not get food and medical care. We know that the French soldiers surrendered and were unharmed by the English. Could we not do the same?"

She took her father's hand and squeezed it as he gazed out over the valley swarming with his enemies. Studying his profile etched with the grief of lost dreams, she realised that he had aged twenty years in the past few months. He turned to look at her and nodded.

Thanks to the nuns of Bordeaux, Céleste had elegant penmanship. Her father dictated the terms in French, which she also translated and transcribed into English. She made several suggestions to soften his bitter language, which he reluctantly accepted. In return for the surrender of all the forces under his command and the release of his prisoners, he requested safe passage to Guadeloupe for himself, his family and his lieutenants. She suggested that he ask for clemency for the black and mixed-race soldiers who had stood by him from the beginning of the rebellion, but he waved that away with a Gallic gesture learned from his father, saying that would be asking too much from *l'anglais*. "Only blood will slake their thirst for revenge," he growled, "and my black *sans-culottes* must be sacrificed for the Revolution."

One of the surviving officers slid down the mountain waving a white flag and carrying the letter in a leather pouch. He was blindfolded, searched and escorted to Abercromby's headquarters at the great house. Sweat trickled down the back of his odoriferous uniform as he felt the sharp jabs of taunting bayonets and a torrent of curses.

Twenty minutes passed before an aide-de-camp returned and thrust a large folded piece of paper into the Brigand officer's shaking hands.

"Here is General Abercromby's answer," he said brusquely. "Just received from the printers in St. George's. It will be on every wall on the island by nightfall."

At the foot of the mountain the blindfold was removed and the officer unfolded the paper before he began the return climb. He quailed as he read the broadsheet's bold lettering in English proclaiming that General Abercromby "strictly forbade any treating or negotiating whatsoever with Fédon, with a reward of 500 pounds Sterling for that Monster Dead or Alive". Only Fédon's unconditional surrender was acceptable: "The Atrocity of his Character and the Cruelties of which he has been guilty, render it impossible to treat with him upon any other Terms."

Céleste was with her father when the officer, fearful of Fédon's wrath, handed the paper to him at his headquarters in *Camp L'Egalite,* halfway up the mountain. She read it over his shoulder, and was surprised that he showed little emotion except for the tightening of his jaw. He started to shred the broadsheet, but paused and called for a quill pen and pot of ink. On the back of the paper he wrote in broad strokes, signed it with a flourish, sanded the ink, and handed it to one of his hovering officers with his orders in rapid French.

Céleste had read what he wrote and was quietly weeping as her father buckled on his sword and went out.

***

The prison door was violently flung open and Fédon stood silhouetted in the entrance. He stepped inside, holding his nose against the stench, eyes narrowing as they adjusted to the gloom. Hugh was closest to the door, and he looked up defiantly as the Brigand leader stood over him contemplatively.

"Not yet," he heard Fédon mutter, "We shall see what value a colonel milord has to his friends."

Followed by the guards, he moved around the square wooden platform supporting the stocks, peering at the seven other Rangers prisoners. Fédon completed his circuit and went back to Company B's bugler, a teenage Welshman popular with the black troops, several of whom he was training to play his horn. The boy was barely conscious.

"Him," he said, and a guard used a wooden mallet to hammer open the stocks and drag the bugler outside. Hugh's throat was so parched that he could barely croak a protest.

Minutes later he heard clanking as the guillotine's blade was raised, then a rumble and thump as it fell. Laughter and cheering followed.

***

The bronze 15-inch mortar had been taken from a fort in Gouyave and hauled up to *Camp de la Mort* by gangs of disgruntled black men who thought they had been freed from enslavement. The artillery piece had never been used, as only after it was emplaced in a battery did the Brigands discover there was no ammunition for it on the island. Fédon and his artillery officer, a white Catholic priest named Mardel, were pleased that they had finally found a use for the weapon.

The projectile was wrapped in layers of canvas and sewn closed. Father Mardel fussed over the charge, carefully measuring enough gunpowder to plunge the ball into the midst of the British encampment. The crash of the mortar rolled over the valley below, and thousands of redcoats paused to watch the white object arcing towards them. They scattered as it struck less than fifty yards from the Belvedere great house where Abercromby and his staff were standing on the veranda.

"Fetch that here," the general ordered an aide, a kilted Highlander, when the ball failed to explode. The Scottish officer gingerly carried it back to the house and set it on the veranda floor.

"Open it."

Using his *skean dhu*, the aide slit the lumpy canvas object's crude stitching and unwrapped its core to reveal a pale head with surprised blue eyes that were already clouding. A bloodstained packet was tucked beneath it. The officer opened this too and handed the contents to the Commander-in-Chief, who cleared his throat loudly after reading it.

"Fédon's got Colonel Drummond and six more of his lads prisoner. He will execute one each hour unless his terms are met, and if we attack they will all be executed at once. Fédon will save Drummond until the last, and will then have him hung, drawn and quartered, which, he says, should be the fate of every aristocrat."

The general glared up at the mountain where tiny figures could be seen moving behind the earthworks.

"The main force will storm the bastards' redoubts at dawn tomorrow," he snapped. "Inform Count d'Heillimer to make ready for his assault at the same time."

He looked down sadly.

"And give what's left of this poor wee laddie a decent burial."

***

The Jäger commander called Chart to his command post in a derelict boucan on the far side of the enemy-held mountain.

"I am very sorry," he said quietly after reciting Fédon's message to Abercromby. "I know that Lord Hugh is your friend as well as your commander."

Chart looked unseeingly into space, breathing heavily.

"There is nothing to be done, I'm afraid," continued the Count. "The general will not negotiate with the Brigands, and Fédon will murder the prisoners before we take the redoubts. Now we must prepare for our role, which the general says is vital to the success of the assault. The Jägers and your Rangers will climb up the steepest part of the mountain where the Brigands will not expect us and be in position to attack from the rear when the general attack begins. We will surprise them, and your corps will have its vengeance."

"And they will kill Lord Hugh and any other survivors, unless we can rescue them first," Chart said vehemently.

Count d'Heillimer shook his head.

"My orders are firm, lieutenant. Over a thousand of our men

274

will attack, and even if we have complete surprise the Brigands will have time to kill the remaining prisoners. We do not know where the prisoners are held."

"I do," said Chart.

His plan had taken form while they were talking. He outlined it for d'Heillimer, who was sceptical at first.

"If you alert them too early, they will be ready to repel us."

"I am confident that I can succeed, sir, but I need your permission."

The German thoughtfully stroked his moustaches.

"Permission granted." He looked warmly at Chart. "If only every man had a friend like you."

Chapter 32

At the top of every hour during the rest of the steamy day, the mortar thundered, hurling prisoners' heads to splatter like smashed pumpkins amongst the waiting battalions. One landed on the roof of the Belvedere estate house, dribbling gore down the shingles and onto the cocked hat of a sentry, who flung his headgear away in horror. The last shot was at 8:00 pm as rain began falling, by which time seven headless corpses in red coats had been tumbled down the hill to sprawl in the bush.

As midnight passed, the men of Company A huddled in misery, soaked to the skin from driving rain despite banana leaves and canvas groundsheets held over their heads. The dye from their uniform coats ran like blood, dripping onto bare feet.

"Bad juju," said one Ranger.

"Bad for the Brigands, not for us," growled Sori. He turned towards his company commander, addressing him formally. "Ready, sir?"

Chart was ready. Sori had found him a Republican jacket taken from one of the Brigand deserters, rent and blood-stained but still serviceable. Both the enemy garment and his faded red coat were rolled into tight bundles; the blue to be worn if needed to infiltrate *Camp de la Mort*, the scarlet to be donned in the coming melee so he would not be mistaken for an enemy by his comrades. The double-barreled rifle was slung down his bare back upside down, muzzles blocked by bottle corks to keep out water and mud. The flintlock pans were unprimed and protected by an oiled sleeve that could be quickly released. From Chart's cross belt dangled a cutlass honed to hair-splitting sharpness, a sword bayonet, a cartridge box with thirty rounds, and a wooden mallet.

Chart squinted at the sheer incline lost in darkness above him as muddy water cascaded down the slope and blurred his vision. He figured it was an hour past midnight, giving him four hours to climb the precipice and be in position to execute his plan before dawn. Captain Louisenthal, rain dripping off his hat brim, shook his hand.

"We'll set off an hour after you so that we can be in position at first light. *Viel Glück!*"

Bare-chested, he climbed in disorienting blackness, blindly scrabbling for shrubs and rocky outcrops as handholds, using his sword bayonet as a scaling ladder by ramming it into the hillside. Once he nearly lost his grip and tumbled in panic, dangling from his left hand as his right grasped a writhing scaly body. He flung the snake into the void, pausing to still his racing heart while wondering if the serpent was a venomous fer-de-lance such as had killed one of the La Sagesse fieldhands.

The rain tapered off and he could see a lighter area marking the sky as he neared the summit. Uncertain of the time, he worried that dawn was near, and climbed faster, occasionally slipping backwards as handholds pulled loose. He dug fingers and toes into the clayey soil, dragging himself up by brute strength as the slope became nearly vertical. Then his clawed right hand reached into empty space and Chart realised that he was at the top.

Peering above the cliff edge he could see and hear only the sighing of the wind. Like the snake, he slithered over and flattened himself under a bush while he tried to get his bearings, visualising the layout of the camp which occupied less than two acres. The prison hut should be to his left, the guardhouse, barracks and other buildings on the right. Despite the arduous climb and lack of sleep over the previous days, he felt no fatigue; surging adrenaline provided preternatural strength and enhanced night vision.

Chart rose cautiously, slipped off the rifle and cross belt, and put on the Republican uniform. The rain had stopped, so he quickly loaded and charged the rifle, slung it over a shoulder and moved to the left with the mallet in his belt and cutlass in his right hand. The camp was on the island's second highest peak, and he could see the ocean to the east beginning to glow from the rising sun as clouds were wafted by the dawn breeze.

He crouched as the silhouette of the prison hut emerged as a darker mass. All was still except for the piping of tree frogs and water dripping from thatched roofs and the few surviving trees.

The stench of putrefying corpses dumped on the opposite slope permeated the air. Chart hoped that he was not too late.

Dim lights glowed in the windows of barracks on the other side of the clearing. Reports from deserters and camp followers said that Fédon still had several hundred fanatical Brigands under his command, all clustered at *Camp de la Mort* after abandoning his former headquarters at *Camp L'Egalite* lower on the mountain. Chart knew that Hugh and any other surviving prisoners would be secured in stocks fastened by thick wooden pins which could only be removed using a mallet such as he carried. The noise of freeing the prisoners would probably alert the whole camp, which was probably restless in expectation of a British assault.

Timing was crucial. The plan was that a dawn attack would be made by Abercromby's battalions while simultaneously the camp was stormed from the opposite slope by the Black Rangers and the Jägers, creating a diversion during which Chart would liberate the prisoners.

But he was impatient. He had to know if Hugh was alive.

The prison seemed to be unguarded, which Chart hoped was due to a lack of concern about escape by decrepit prisoners secured in stocks rather than the inhabitants being dead. The flimsy prison door was unlocked. He gently opened it and edged inside, grimacing as he inhaled the fetid miasma from ordure and cadavers left to rot. The interior was pitch black. No movement, no groans, no prayers. His heart contracted as he thought he was too late.

"Hugh?" he called in a sibilant whisper, reaching out until he felt the rough wood of the stocks. He groped his way along it until he came to a cloth-covered shoulder and gently moved his hand upwards to a face, which moved at his touch.

"Is it time to die?" croaked the voice of Lord Hugh Drummond.

"No, Hugh," replied Chart. "It's time to live."

***

Julien Fédon had not slept. His entire being was suffused with bitter disappointment that had long since swept away the vestiges of defiance. He had stood by the battery below the

278

guillotine for most of the night after drafting his final manifesto under the brooding eyes of his officers. Just before midnight his daughter Céleste had begged him in choking sobs to go to the side of her dying mother who was asking for him. But he ignored her and sent her back to the family's simple hut under guard.

"Our revolution takes precedence over *all* personal matters," he told his officers fiercely, as if trying to justify his callousness. "A revolution is a struggle between the future and the past. We are still the future, and we will not submit but live to fight another day."

Now he watched hundreds of bivouac fires dotting the dark valley around his former home, seeing how they flickered like fireflies as troops moved past them. Abercromby's army was massing at the foot of the mountain and he knew the redcoats would attack at dawn. The Brigands could delay the infantrymen as they struggled up the slope but would be unable to repel them. He was especially fearful of the Black Rangers and their German comrades in arms, who he expected to be in the vanguard. But the rebel general had an escape plan; it was risky but needed to bolster his men's spirits so they would not feel trapped.

A last act of revolutionary bravado was needed. When Abercromby trained his telescope on *Camp de la Mort* as the sun rose, he would see the quartered pieces of the English milord dangling from the top of the guillotine, and his aristocratic head would be the final missile launched from the mortar.

Fédon turned to the renegade French captain Noguet.

"Fetch the English colonel here. Take two men in case he must be carried."

***

Chart's fingers scrabbled across the side of the rough-hewn stock until he found the crude dowels securing Hugh's arms and legs. Both were hammered too tightly into the holes to extract with his fingers.

"Is anyone else here with you?" he rasped.

"I'm the only living one left," Hugh answered in a barely

perceptible voice. "Couple of bodies in the far corner, I think."

"Are you injured? Can you walk?"

"No and hopefully. Need water."

"Need to get you out of here," said Chart, coming to a decision. He took the mallet from his belt, felt for the bottom of the lowest dowel, and began gently tapping to loosen it. As he finished the upper pin a light appeared outside the doorway accompanied by voices speaking in guttural patois.

Chart leaned close to Hugh's ear.

"Keep still!" he hissed, then moved swiftly to the side of the doorway with a cutlass in one hand and sword bayonet in the other.

**

"You hear that?" the man carrying a rushlight torch said in a tremulous voice. "Coming from inside."

"Lot of jumbies here round this place," another Brigand said. "They make tapping sound like that!"

"Primitive nonsense!" snarled Noguet, who had failed to hear the noise which had now ended. "Ghosts do not exist!"

As the two ragged soldiers with slung muskets hesitated fearfully at the prison entrance, the French captain thrust forward, seized the torch and opened the door.

"Follow me," he ordered, sweeping the torch over Hugh's inert form as the men hesitantly followed.

"You see, no 'jumbies' here," Noguet sneered, "just the milord, although he does look dead."

Chart sprang from the darkness, whirling like the dervishes he had seen in Bengal. He swung the cutlass, nearly scalping Noguet, who screamed and let the torch fly into a heap of rags and dried thatch. Simultaneously, Chart stabbed the bayonet into the chest of one of the soldiers. Pivoting, he hacked and stabbed with an almost superhuman fury at the other man. Both Brigand soldiers were dead in seconds.

"Behind you, Chart!" Hugh gasped.

Chart spun to see Noguet, face twisted in a rictus of agony, fumbling for a pistol in his belt. Despite his blood-curtained face, in the light of the spreading flames Chart recognised him as the French officer who had ordered the killing of his friend

Titus, the murderer of the concubine at La Sagesse and the commander of the firing squad that had massacred the British prisoners. Teeth bared in rage bordering on madness, Chart slashed open the Frenchman's belly spewing his entrails like purplish serpents down his waist. Chart was on the verge of beheading Noguet as he dropped the pistol and doubled over, but halted the cutlass in mid-swing.

"*Non*," he hissed in French, "you die slowly."

Hooking the bloody cutlass to his cross belt, he dragged Noguet to the fire consuming the bamboo walls of the prison and hurled him into the flames, where the Frenchman convulsed and screamed weakly. Panting, he returned to Hugh, pulled out the loosened dowels and flipped open the heavy wood stocks.

"They'll be on to us in minutes," he said, helping Hugh to his feet. "Can you walk?"

Drummond took a few tentative steps and croaked "yes".

"We need to hold out until the assault comes. I remember a spot that's the best defensive position we can hope for."

He gave Hugh the Frenchman's pistol and stooped to retrieve the muskets with cartridge boxes and a canteen from the slaughtered soldiers. Slinging the firearms over his shoulders, he helped Drummond outside as the building erupted in flames behind them. They made their way towards an outcropping of boulders fifty paces from the burning hut, hearing shouts from the direction of the barracks.

The sky was steadily lightening as they knelt behind the rocks. Chart handed the canteen to Hugh, quickly shrugged off his blue uniform and pulled on the scarlet coat.

"Hope that slakes your thirst," he said as he checked the loads and priming of the two muskets.

"Grog," replied Hugh, wiping his whiskered lips with a dirty hand, "Better than mother's milk at the moment."

"They're coming," Chart said, handing a musket and cartridge box to Drummond as he saw figures running through the twilight towards the burning prison. He looked at the sky and frowned.

"The Count will hold back his assault until Abercromby attacks to create a diversion. Where in blazes are they?"

Hugh rested a musket on a boulder and watched the Brigands coming into the circle of light cast by the flames.

"Appears that we're the diversion, old man," he drawled, clicking the flintlock's doghead into full cock.

***

Suspecting such a diversionary ploy, Julien Fédon split his force of roughly 300 men, ordering half to guard the approaches to the redoubt from *Camp L'Egalite* and leading the rest towards the inferno. The heat was so intense that he was forced to halt, sword in hand, fifty feet from the prison. His men bunched around him, in awe of the flames shooting into the air and the thick smoke from the damp thatch spreading like a pall over the Camp of Death.

They made perfect targets.

"Abercromby has ordered that Fédon be taken alive if at all possible," Chart said, momentarily sighting on the insurgent general. "But the rest of them are fair game:"

He sighed in resignation, realigned the rifle' sights on a white officer in a cocked cap standing beside Fédon and fired the right barrel. The man collapsed at Fédon's feet. The general seemed stunned, looking around frantically as a ball from the second rifle barrel killed another man near him. Hugh knocked down two others with musket shots.

The men scattered in panic but Fédon stood his ground and began issuing orders. Muzzle flames had been spotted at the outcropping, and the leader and his surviving officers quickly began bringing the soldiers into order. They retreated beyond the deadly firelight, but not before Chart and Hugh killed or wounded three more men. They reloaded, Hugh finishing both muskets in less than a minute while Chart took longer to ram the charge down the rifle barrels' spiral grooves.

"Will they charge?" asked Hugh as he bit off the end of a paper cartridge.

"They're bush fighters. They'll circle round and creep in close before rushing us."

Chapter 33

The gilded orange ball of the rising sun cast its first rays, sheening the sea before touching the island, crossing pristine beaches and slanting up the vibrant green foliage clothing the mountain slopes to fully light the camp. The Brigands warily crept closer, crawling on their bellies and dashing for sparse cover. Chart fired a couple of rounds at them, then cursed as he saw the glint of a telescope lens which he guessed was held by Fédon.

"They'll know it's just us," he said bitterly. "Where the hell are the Jägers and our fellows!"

***

Shaking with ire, Fédon collapsed his brass telescope with a furious snap.

"It's that ungrateful traitor we freed from slavery and the milord!" he shouted. "I should have executed both immediately. They won't escape this time!"

The Brigand leader rallied his men, waving his sword and screaming orders mixed with oaths.

***

"Any moment now," said Chart. "You've got the pistol. Don't let them take you alive."

"Nonsense. Hundreds of 'em against the pair of us?" replied Hugh dryly. "Good odds in our favour, old man."

"Here they come."

The Brigands broke from cover, red-eyed and howling, led by Fédon in his general's uniform and gold-braided bicorne. Chart and Hugh fired into the horde at point-blank range then reversed their firearms to grip the barrels as clubs. Chart felt no fear, only exultation as he prepared to fight until his last breath.

He was so focused on the enemy scant yards away that he didn't hear the bugles calling behind him. He and Hugh stood half-crouched with their weapons raised in readiness, transfixed in bemusement as a tidal wave of red-coated African men surged like a flood from behind them, screaming war cries and brandishing cutlasses with muskets slung. They plunged into the Brigands, blades flashing as heads were lopped and torsos opened to spill coils of entrails.

The Brigands were driven back, some pausing to get off shots which dropped a few Black Rangers before they were cut down. Chart saw Fédon's personal guard coalesce around him, while a brave black officer tried to form a defensive line, fighting hand-to-hand with bayonets and spears against cutlasses. The Brigand officer died with most of his comrades, but their sacrifice enabled Fédon and his cohort to escape by sliding down a steep slope on the eastern side of the mountain.

Chart heard shots and yells from the direction of the barracks and the path leading up from the valley. He hurriedly reloaded his rifle as he saw Sori coming towards him, showing dagger-like teeth in an enormous smile. He nodded happily at Chart first, then came to attention in front of Hugh, saluted and handed him a sword.

"Fédon's. He dropped it. He smart to run because if I catch him I cut off his head even if general punish me."

"Thank you, sergeant-major," Lieutenant-Colonel Lord Hugh Drummond said brusquely. "Let's join the battle. Find your company and carry on, Captain Charteris."

Sori led Chart away, passing dozens of Rangers viciously chopping at the bodies of Brigands as they cursed in a babel of African tongues. As they neared the prison the structure collapsed. Flames danced over the remnants as Chart again smelled the sickening odour he remembered from the burning ghats along the Ganges.

"Sergeant-major?" Sori said in wonder. "And you Captain? Was the colonel telling truth, man?"

"Yes," answered Chart. "I believe he was. What kept you?"

Sori explained that the Rangers had climbed the incline faster than the Germans, and had been ordered to wait beneath the cliff edge for the Jägers to get into position to storm the camp's barracks and main buildings. Then they had waited for Abercromby's assault. As Hugh had surmised, Count d'Heillimer had thought that the two-man firefight signalled the arrival of the British regulars.

"Typically bloody late as usual," Chart growled. "Officers probably had to wait until the mess served their coffee and their batmen wiped their bums after a morning shit. And they'll take credit for winning the battle."

"They're here now," Sori observed, as a stream of muddy redcoats flowed into the camp up the steep trail leading from the valley.

Although fighting around the barracks was continuing, many of the Rangers and Jägers were busily hunting for rum and loot. Chart managed to assemble a dozen men from his company and quickly led them towards what had been Fédon's family quarters. He frowned as feminine screams came from the building, hoping he was not too late.

With Sori at his side like a human battering ram, he forced his way through a knot of British and German soldiers clustered at the doorway.

"Wait yer turn ye bloody darky!" an English corporal shouted before shrinking away from the murderous look on Chart's face and the blood-crusted cutlass in Sori's huge hand.

It was too late for Fédon's wife and eldest daughter. Both lay dead on the earthen floor, genitals exposed and bloody. But Céleste was backed into a corner, the front of her gown ripped to the waist exposing her breasts, swinging a sabre at a knot of chortling soldiers who were making a contest out of trying to subdue her.

"Clear the room!" Chart bellowed.

"Oh fuck off, blacky!" a cockney snarled.

Anticipating Chart's orders, Sori was forming his men into a line across the room.

"Make ready!" Chart shouted. "Present!"

The Rangers raised their muskets to their shoulders.

"We goin' to shoot them?" asked Sori. "Don't mind, but could get us in bad trouble:"

"Over their heads," he answered, and Sori repeated the order in patois to the Rangers.

The muskets roared deafeningly, filling the room with pungent smoke as the balls punched through the walls inches above the heads of the would-be rapists. They froze, raising their hands in terror.

"Out!" Chart snapped, and the line of Rangers parted to let the half-dozen redcoats and Jägers rush out.

Céleste was so traumatised that she did not recognise Chart as he slowly approached. She continued to wave the sword in both hands while he stood a few feet away and smiled. He watched the dread in her eyes recede as her face relaxed. The sabre dropped from her fingers and she collapsed onto her knees, sobbing. Chart took off his coat, draped it to cover her nakedness, then gently helped her to her feet. She averted her eyes as he took her arm and escorted her past the bodies of her mother and sister.

***

More than a hundred Brigands were killed during the final assault, with no quarter given. Seven Rangers and Jägers were lost and a dozen wounded. Fédon's escape route was searched at the base of the mountain, where a few bodies with broken necks were found, but the insurgent general and most of his surviving men got away. During the following weeks and months they were relentlessly hunted after Abercromby's army, including the Germans, sailed away, leaving only the Black Rangers and a British garrison. Many Brigands were captured and hung, but Fédon had disappeared, rumoured to have drowned while trying to flee to Trinidad in a canoe or to have found refuge in Cuba or Louisiana.

The back of Fédon's Rebellion had been broken but Grenada was utterly ruined economically, with nearly every plantation destroyed. While this was lamented by the surviving planters and their supporters in Parliament, a sense of defiance and independence had been instilled among the island's black population who had tasted temporary freedom.

***

The Loyal Black Rangers were charged with mopping up pockets of resistance and snaring Brigands hiding in the mountains. During the following two months, Chart and his company tracked the refugees, exhausting themselves on missions along hidden jungle trails into the most remote parts of the island. Chart became adept at patiently cajoling frightened runaway slaves to provide information. Sori suggested harsher interrogation methods, but his commanding officer forbade it.

At Chart's request, Hugh persuaded Captain Louis la Grenade, a deeply religious man, to give Céleste Fédon refuge. Proclaimed a hero by the British for fighting on the winning side, the *gens de couleur* officer enjoyed such high esteem among the white merchants and planters that he felt no qualms about taking the rebel leader's daughter - still in a state of shock and deep depression – into his home and family.

Despite his exalted reputation, Captain la Grenade was still considered of a lower social status than even the meanest white soldiers and overseers. He was feted at official functions, but never invited into the homes of the men and women he had fought to defend.

Chart's Company A made its base camp in a fire-gutted stone warehouse on a devastated plantation called Balthazar Estate. The men re-thatched the building, and it was there that Hugh found Chart on an inspection tour of his regiment. Chart was lying on a pallet recovering from a bout of fever, but he unsteadily climbed to his feet and saluted his commanding officer. Hugh lazily returned the salute then clasped his friend's hand with a look of concern.

"You've been ill, and I see you've lost weight. D Company is following me and will relieve you. Take your men to St. George's and for God's sake burn those disgraceful rags you're wearing and draw new uniforms."

Hugh dragged over a charred chair and ordered Chart to sit. He extracted a letter adorned with a wax seal from his tunic and cleared his throat.

"Left for me at HQ with a cover note. Sorry I couldn't get it to you earlier. Now, company inspection time. I'm expecting great things from Company Sergeant Major Sori! I'll leave you to it."

The feminine handwriting was the same as the belated messages warning of the Brigand ambush and relating to Pemb's treason.

St. George's, 3 September 1796

Dearest Chart,

When you read this, I will have left Grenada. My brother inherited and kindly invited me to return to live out what remains of my life at our family home in Rutland.

I am afflicted with an incurable wasting disease. While I mourn for what may have been, I am grateful that we never again met, for I would not wish you to see me so bodily deteriorated.

Pemb has disappeared and is presumed dead. He has been proved a traitor, and my lawyer in St. George's, Mr. Foister, informed me that under English law his property would therefore escheat to the Crown. However, colonial law permits a widow to inherit. When the Grenada court declares him legally deceased, I shall be the owner of what is left of La Sagesse and – distasteful as it may sound – all its enslaved people.

Foister has signed deeds leaving all my property on the island to you. He also has drawn up an inviolable manumission document freeing you. I trust you will follow suit with the good people at La Sagesse, but will leave it to you to effect this.

All is not lost. You must find the grave of Lieutenant Francis Savile, 17th Light Dragoons, in the officers section of the town cemetery. Exhume him and extract what lies beneath from the soil.

I wish that I could have seen you, held you, one last time. We were fated to meet in Grenada and I am glad that we did so despite the dreadful circumstances. Memories of our precious few carefree days together will sustain me for the rest of my days. You are the only man I ever loved, or will love.

Arabella.

Chart knuckled moist eyes after reading, and re-reading, the letter. He regretted many things, but at that moment nothing greater than his failure to reveal his heart to her.

Hugh and his aides had arrived with several spare mounts. He told Chart to take one of the horses for the ride to St. George's. Despite his weakened condition, Chart insisted that he would march barefoot with his company, but the Rangers' commander sternly ordered him to go on horseback.

They took the coastal road, the Rangers singing in their bass voices as they marched in formation behind Chart's gelding. Along the way, hundreds of black people emerged from the bush to cheer them on and ply them with scarce food and still plentiful rum.

Sori, marching beside Chart, beamed.

"They proud to see black men in the King's uniform," he said, "Gives them hope for better things to come."

As they approached the entrance to La Sagesse, terrible memories flooded Chart's mind, piercing his heart like an icy dagger. He saw a handful of people squatting by the stone signpost and reined his horse to a stop as he recognised Wannica and Molia.

"We knew you were coming," said Wannica.

Molia pointed down the darkly overgrown road to the plantation buildings.

"Evil spirit there in the Great House. We don't go near, but *you* have the power to drive the jumby out!"

Chart sat in his saddle for a minute, remembering the words of Arabella's letter. He wanted nothing to do with La Sagesse, but the estate, and the people who had once been enslaved on it, were now a responsibility he could not shirk.

Trailed by Wannica, Molia and other former slaves, the Rangers followed Chart as far as the bush bordering the overgrown yard surrounding the plantation house. They squatted in the shade, silent and apprehensive, necks swivelling towards bird calls and rustlings amidst the jungle. Chart left his horse with them and strode on alone with a pair of pistols in his belt and cutlass in his hand.

He fought against a rising sense of unearthly fear as he approached the Great House. It was still largely intact, glassless windows like dark portals into the underworld. The burnt veranda had collapsed into blackened scraps of wood. Next to it was a charred, partially dismembered skeleton with fetters on its wrists. The skull had been stuck on a pole as a grim warning.

Goff.

Rage erupted with vivid memories of the overseer's cruelty. Knowing that he was being closely watched by the people waiting behind him, he snatched the skull and hurled it into the weeds, breaking the spell of superstition.

Chart circled the house, feeling that he was being watched from its interior. By the kitchen door was a small garden, recently tended. *Jumbies don't do that*, he thought grimly.

He stepped into the shadowy interior, pausing to concentrate all five senses plus the ineffable one that warned of danger.

Someone living was here.

He walked through the dining room and parlour. Broken glass and smashed furniture had been swept aside to clear the floor. A floorboard creaked overhead as he moved to the staircase and climbed to the upper hallway. As he neared the first doorway a figure suddenly emerged holding a pistol and fired.

Chart felt the ball buzz past his ear by a hairsbreadth. He attacked without thinking, charging forward to chop down on the hand holding the pistol. The assailant screamed as the hand and weapon flew away. The slight figure doubled over, clutching the blood spurting stump of its arm. Chart hoisted the cutlass for a killing slash but as he recognised the attacker he used the wooden hilt for a stunning blow to the head.

He reached down and flipped the unconscious man onto his back. Despite the ginger beard and ragged clothes, his identity was unquestionable.

Sir Pemberton Charteris, Bt.

Chart ripped a piece of cloth from Pemb's once fine shirt and wound it round the truncated arm to staunch the bleeding. He picked up the severed hand and pulled his father's gold ring from a finger. Then he dragged his cousin out to the yard and waved to the people waiting for him.

"Here's your evil spirit," he told them as they approached.

They built a fire and while he heated the cutlass blade to cauterise the wound Chart asked his people to find an iron slave collar. After it was affixed to Pemb's neck, Chart unashamedly revived him by urinating in his face, followed by three Rangers who had once suffered as La Sagesse fieldhands. A rope was found in one of the men's knapsacks and fastened to the collar, then tied to Chart's saddle.

During the long march into St. George's, Pemb wept and

cursed as he was jeered and pelted with dung and rotten fruit by the black people lining the road.

Chapter 34

Pemb was tried in a court martial a week later. The evidence presented by the intelligence chief Major Phelippes and by Lt. Colonel Lord Hugh Drummond was irrefutable. He was found guilty of treason and sentenced to death. Along with a dozen captured Brigands, Pemb was hung in St. George's market square watched by hundreds including Chart. The corpses were dumped into the town's garbage scow, taken out to sea and fed to the omnipresent sharks off Point Salines.

Chart was surprised to feel no sense of satisfaction at watching Pemb slowly strangle, kicking and twitching until he finally dangled with piss dripping from his breeches. Years of suffering, the brutality and horrors he had experienced and witnessed, seemed to have hollowed his once loving heart. His thirst for revenge had been quenched, but his other vow to fight against slavery was unfulfilled.

He had once wondered if his sense of humanity could be resurrected. Chart realised that it could be given the right environment in which to fulfil his life and mission.

He sought out Arabella's lawyer, Mr. Foister, who shook his hand solemnly and handed him the deeds and manumission papers, all now valid with Pemb's death. He showed Foister her letter with the cryptic reference to the grave. The lawyer consulted with the colonel commanding the garrison who agreed that the corpse could be disinterred.

He took Sori and a half squad of Rangers to the cemetery dotted with over a thousand humps marking the graves of soldiers, most to be forever unknown. The grave of the young Light Dragoons officer was marked by a small wooden cross carved with his name and death date which was already rotting into oblivion. The grave was shallow and the privates digging in shirtsleeves soon uncovered a decaying wooden coffin. They shifted the box onto a canvas tarpaulin and gently lifted it out, grimacing at the stench of putrefaction.

Chart ordered them out, slid into the pit with a shovel and

began scraping away loose earth at the bottom, revealing the outlines of two bags. He used his hands to expose army knapsacks. He turned each upright, surprised at the weight, hearing clinking as he did so. He opened each in turn, revealing hundreds of gold coins.

Chart suddenly felt vulnerable in the grave. He looked up into the black faces gazing raptly down at him. There was no sign of avarice, no murderous jealousy or greed. Just curiosity.

Later, after the treasure had been deposited in the fort's strong room and he received a detailed receipt from the adjutant, Chart took Sori aside as he watched the Rangers privates leave for their garrison camp.

"There was a moment there when I was worried," he confessed. "Those men have nothing. They could have killed me, taken the gold, covered up the grave with me in it and no one would ever have been the wiser."

Sori pushed his hat back on his shaved head, scratched at his missing ear and made a scoffing noise.

"They good men. They loyal because you are a true warrior and they like and respect you. You make them proud to wear the King's uniform. You their ..." He struggled with the English word "... *hero*. And besides," he said savagely, touching the sergeant's chevrons on his new uniform coat, "I am their chief and they know I kill anyone who threaten you."

Two days before Company A was scheduled to redeploy back into the remote mountains, Chart received a note from Hugh asking him to come to his quarters at Fort George. He drew himself up to his full six feet and three inches and snapped a salute that would have rivalled any Grenadier Guard officer's.

Hugh rose with a warm smile to shake his hand and waved him towards an armchair. A moment later his servant entered with two glasses brimming with red wine on a silver tray and handed one to each officer.

"Your good health, old man," Hugh said, sighing after taking a sip. "Ah, a classic Bourgogne. HMS *Galatea* took a Frenchman laden with the nectar off Statia and her captain kindly sold me a few cases."

"It's been awhile," Chart admitted, savouring the wine. "A

welcome change from grog!"

"Wine fit for a celebration."

"Celebration?"

Hugh set his glass aside.

"I've been gazetted colonel of a new infantry regiment. The 1st West India. One of eight regiments raised specifically to be manned by black Caribbean soldiers, with equal status to all regular British Army units."

Chart raised his glass.

"Congratulations. But what happens to the Black Rangers?"

"Reduced in force and reorganised as a militia unit until their mission of hunting down the last Brigands is completed."

Chart drew a deep breath and sighed.

"Not much future for me, then, is there?"

"Oh, very much to the contrary."

Hugh handed him a rolled parchment bound by a red ribbon. Chart opened it and read the opening lines:

George the Third by the Grace of God of the United Kingdom and Ireland, King, Defender of the Faith, & c., to Our Trusty and Wellbeloved Alexander Meynall Charteris, Greeting: We reposing especial Trust and Confidence in your Loyalty, Courage and Good Conduct do by these Presents constitute and appoint You to be Captain in Our Army.

With his throat too constricted to talk, Chart read the document twice, then emptied the wine glass, careful not to spill a drop on the precious parchment.

"I ..." he coughed to clear the hoarseness in his voice. "I thought that black men couldn't serve as officers in the King's army or navy?"

"As I once told you, Chart, there are exceptions to every rule," Hugh replied, "such as you saw with Colonel Kina. The outstanding service of the Rangers and other black soldiers throughout the Caribbean changed *some* prejudices in London. You are a shining example."

He leaned forward and looked earnestly at his friend.

"This is a King's Commission which allows you to serve in any British Army regiment. But I want you with me as a company commander in the 1st West India."

Epilogue

La Sagesse Estate
Colony of Grenada
June 1797

Chart stood on the ridge beneath the reddish orange leaves of the Royal Poinciana, watching the bustle around the plantation buildings. With the help of Wannica and Molia, he had tracked down sixty-one men, women and children surviving from Chart's sojourn as a fellow slave. Each had been formally freed and, remembering his personal travail, Chart had insisted that even the youngest child be legally manumitted as well.

He and his lawyer Mr. Foister had fought the colonial council for months to subdivide the estate acreage and deed plots to the men and women who had worked the land as slaves. Colonial law forbade ownership of land by free blacks, which Foister circumvented by giving long-term leases for peppercorn rents to families who chose to work their own land. None were interested in working the land communally – "We too independent to work like slaves again," said Wannica – and some of the young men preferred to seek a better life elsewhere as freedmen, helped with generous payments from their former master Pemb's golden hoard. Each family which elected to stay on the estate was given the large sum of £20 to use to build housing and buy tools, seeds and livestock. Another £1,000 was donated to the Society for the Abolition of the Slave Trade in London, with the balance invested in 1.5% government consols.

The great house had been repaired and turned into a school for the plantation's children. Chart smiled as he watched their teacher, Céleste Fédon, attempt to call a boisterous gaggle of a dozen youngsters back to their classroom. Teaching reading and writing to slaves was against the law, but this did not apply to free blacks, much to the consternation of the plantocracy.

A sudden wind shook a cascade of fiery blossoms onto his gold-braided bicorne and the captain's epaulettes of his new scarlet uniform. He closed his eyes, wondering if the breeze moving the branches and shaking the long seed pods manifested the presence of his mother and father. Molia, the Obeah priestess, had told him seriously that his parents returned to this place that they had loved, and if he listened carefully he could hear them. But the wind died and all was silence except for distant happy childish shouts and the braying of a mule ploughing a new garden.

He opened his eyes, allowing tears to flow as he looked at the marble monument he had ordered to replace the one destroyed on Pemb's order. Just their names and *Nos cœurs ne font qu'un* – our hearts are as one.

He hoped they were at peace.

Chart turned and looked out over the ocean where the white topsails of a ship, hull down below the horizon, glowed in the sun descending to the west over the Caribbean. It was a reminder that the troopship would leave on the evening tide. Sori and the other West Indian soldiers would already be aboard.

His eyes swept La Sagesse one more time. No longer a place of hellish misery, he thought. Unlike the first time he had left the island as a child, he promised himself that he would be back.

Historical Note

Ranger is a work of fiction, but many of the characters and events were real. The horrific atrocities committed against enslaved people in the West Indian colonies may seem exaggerated, but were actually much worse. Jamaican planters such as Thomas Thistlewood – a psychopath by the standards of the 18th century as well as today – kept diaries which casually documented decades of murder, torture and rape of the black and mixed-race people under their domination. The sickening practices described in my novel which were designed to terrorise the enslaved into submission are based on works such as Trevor Burnard's *Mastery, Tyranny & Desire*, Christopher Petley's *White Fury*, *Tacky's Revolt* by Vincent Brown, and other sources, many of which remain unpublished in British, Caribbean and North American archives.

Abolitionists such as Granville Sharp, Olaudah Equiano, Francis Hargrave and others were as described in the book, and worked tirelessly to pass *The Abolition of the Slave Trade Act* in 1807, although they did not live to see West Indian, Canadian and South African chattel slavery abolished in 1833. Chart's High Court appearance is based on the famous 1772 case *Somerset v Stewart*, which, although disappointing at the time to Abolitionists, is now considered to have established precedent in a series of legal and parliamentary actions which eventually ended slavery in the British Empire.

Chart is a composite of a number of 18th century mixed-race West Indians, many of whom successfully integrated into British society. Among these was Robert Dalzell (1742-1821), the Westminster College student mentioned in the book, who inherited half of a Jamaican estate and its enslaved people and has many descendants. For further reading on this subject, I recommend Daniel Livesay's *Children of Uncertain Fortune: Mixed-Race Jamaicans in Britain and the Atlantic Family, 1733-1833*, and *Belle: The True Story of Dido Belle*. Dido was the mixed-race grandniece of the First Earl of Mansfield, the Chief Justice who presided over the *Somerset* case, and who raised her as a member of his family. A delightful portrait of her owned by the current Lord Mansfield can be seen at Scone Palace, Perth, Scotland.

Chart's boxing coach Bill Richmond (1763-1829), the former American slave, led the fascinating life sketched in the novel. One of England's leading pugilists and trainers, Richmond was selected to act as an usher at the coronation of King George IV in 1821, earning a letter of thanks from the Home Secretary Lord Sidmouth.

Fédon's Rebellion, the French Republican-inspired revolution in Grenada during 1795 and 1795, was as bloody and devastating as I have detailed. I lived on Grenada for several years and have spent decades researching the island's history, especially relating to the insurrection. I believe that I have accurately portrayed Julien Fédon, the revolutionary leader, who was a major planter and slave-owner. History is nuanced, and Grenada's past exemplifies this. Fédon's brother, Jean-Pierre, was indeed the island's chief slave hunter. Captain Louis la Grenade, the mixed-race commander of the St. George's Light Dragoons, was considered a hero by the British colonists for his role in crushing the rebellion even by many who subsequently considered him a social inferior because of his ethnicity. How fitting that Grenada's current governor-general, Dame Cécile Ellen Fleurette la Grenade, is a direct descendant of the 18th century cavalry commander.

Colonel Jean Kina and his son Captain Zamor Kina were commissioned King's officers considered pioneers in early "bush-fighting" tactics and who subsequently led colourful lives serving in both the British and Napoleonic armies.

Finally, the Loyal Black Rangers was a real British Army unit that performed exemplary service during Fédon's Rebellion, praised by the British and German soldiers they served with such as William Dyott, who commanded the 25th Foot during the insurrection. Lieutenant-Colonel Dyott wrote of the Rangers' courage, discipline and fighting qualities in his diary. Like Chart, many of the Rangers later transferred into the West India regiments, composed of black Caribbean soldiers with equal status to all regular British Army units.

Printed in Great Britain
by Amazon